A SPY
AFFAIR

To JOSEFINA
The Very best!

Bob Davey

A SPY AFFAIR

BOB DAVEY

Pentland Press, Inc.
www.pentlandpressusa.com

PUBLISHED BY PENTLAND PRESS, INC.
5122 Bur Oak Circle, Raleigh, North Carolina 27612
United States of America
919-782-0281

ISBN 1-57197-239-0
Library of Congress Control Number: 00-133641

Printed in the United States of America

To Steven and Michelle for when you are of age.
Sometimes daddy cannot always be there.

A Spy Affair, originally called *The Inspector*, was swapped in title at the last minute to out play an amateur spy operation.

The Characters

Longo's—a place of intrigue
Don Fusaro-Debenadetto—Mafia Don
Carlos Sanchez—drug cartel leader
Marcus Wolfe—former East German Spy Master
Yevgeny Primakov—former head of the Russian KGB
Renee Jadot—undercover cop/double agent
Ariadne/Americain—a multinational corporation
John Custer (Hardy) Harding—CIA spy
Joe Covic—friend and DEA asset
Monique Gaudinier—lover
Pam Wellington—journalist and lover
Julie Lee—the new live-in lover of Joe Covic
Joni Cone—former model, escort and Hardy's lover
Vito Longo—owner of Longo's
Steve Summers—journalist
Leonard Cohen—DNN staff
Dana DiMaggio—Pam Wellington's friend
Zaporah—beautiful ex-Israeli commando
Henry Chatsworth—SIS/MI6 liaison with the FBI
Robert Torres—CIA liaison officer from Langley, Virginia
John Blacke—head of the Atlanta FBI office
Günther Von Müller—legendary old cold warrior
Vera Lopez—journalist
Dave Harding—brother
Colonel Harding—father
Colonel Clay—liaison officer for Caliber Communications
Czechoff—KGB agent
Capt. Credo—officer on General Clark's staff
Yossi Cohen—Israeli agent
Gemel—terrorist
Kevin Slyer—Caliber Communications
Ben Netanyahu—Prime Minister of Israel
Ariel Sharon—Israeli General
Trevor Downing (sometimes known as Trevor Cadwell)—SIS/MI6 agent
Patwijec—KGB agent

Prologue

Some people in this world do not believe spies like Hardy exist. They neither believe in Santa Claus nor of the spies who play *The Great Game*. John Custer Harding, "Hardy" is real. In the spy game different personality types are used for different tasks, each being of their own workhorse. Hardy, born of a U.S. Army Officer in a life of honor and chivalry was covertly trained and spun out of a covert operation to play *The Great Game*.

The Cold War is over, yet the spy game plays on. One Cold War into the next. Eastern Europe falling back eastward with Moscow desperately trying to recover what she had lost, or at least work the game into a stalemate before the next Cold War is born and Moscow is forced to insulate herself through Beijing. There are still great geopolitical prizes left in this world for The West to protect from those who wish to drive us backwards in time, or into the evils of ultra nationalism and fundamental terror.

Men like Hardy exist. His escapades are best told though his many liaisons of romance. There is much romance and intrigue in this novel of pure fiction, hopefully both the ladies and the gentlemen will enjoy it.

But be advised, *A Spy Affair* can be intensely playful and intensely serious at times. This novel is also chillingly real to life. It can also be chillingly deadly.

The romance contained within can crush a man's soul, or leave a lady's heart shattered like broken shards of crystal on the floor. Hardy's nature and his dive into the erotic causing conflict with his lovers and making his affairs of the heart, heated and passionately intense.

CHAPTER
1

He was his best friend. His odd couple partner. The creative one, big on stupidity, or what Hardy would call "balls." Hardy his friend, his caregiver and unwitting accomplice. When the scandal broke, Covic had ended up with one hundred million dollars, disappearing somewhere in the Caribbean. Hardy, his loyal friend being forced further out in the cold by the exploding cataclysm and overzealous press. At least for awhile.

They had done the same to Hardy. An overly endowed and excessive hatchet job on his family, character and single life style. They gave him a handful of psychosis on paper out of several dozens that they set aside for whistle blowers who cause so much trouble for billion dollar corporations who tend to be their own doctors, who in return endure the uncontrollable shaking of their writing hands, a condition brought about over a Mafia contract, to jot down one of the more popular illnesses— "a paranoid something." Though Hardy was lucky, his being a debilitating condition on paper, two or three notches below the psychosis rendered to Covic. Even if Covic was a nut, he was; he was crazy like a fox. Hardy suspected he was borderline something, like the rest of the working class of rural America who fell into one category or another. Covic just over the edge. And so it was, schizophrenia being as contagious as it is between childhood odd couples, that Hardy came down with a severe case of paranoia and a $780 disability pension, the reward for doing what is right in this world when common sense tells you to look the other way.

But amongst the exploding factions of the press, settlement came quickly and Hardy was spotted more than a few times at local cafés pondering his pending investments and 401K. Often with a copy of *Barron's* by his side. At the end of "The Southern Spy Affair," as it had become known by the press, Hardy had been the one to better his financial situation the right way, unlike his fellow conspirator Covic, who was still wanted by the FBI, even if they turned a blind eye to any attempts to procure his capture. Which of course was not so much embarrassment as it was considerations of sensitivity all intelligence agencies have to be concerned with. Covic had gotten himself into matters of national security, as well as concerns of the United Kingdom and handful of other countries. The whole world wanted Covic! Not knowing Covic tended to sleep well these days, often with two whores in his bed. Covic was a pig—a creative pig, but none the less a pig.

Hardy was the Ivy League looking son of a retired U.S. Army Lieutenant Colonel, spending a good many years of his younger life experiencing life in the in the sleepy little Village of Highland Falls and its better-known twin, West Point, New York, where his father was based much of the time. Hardy was six foot two with blond hair and blue eyes. He could have been a ball player or easily a state cop. His attitude and appearance was all phoneman and U.S. Army. In his younger years Hardy's skills with girls were legendary, though he tended to want to be faithful to whatever sweetheart he was dating at the time. Letting the girls call the relationship and letting school-born jealousy take its natural course. He was always the gentleman. The kind of son and daddy's boy to make an officer very proud.

It was now Hardy the hero. Hardy, the officer's son turned CIA spy, honing his craft through on the job training with military culture from the day he was born always guiding the way. Hardy now was the one with the inside information, a good rapport with the press and a steady pool of female reporters and journalists to date—a trade off of mutual affection and of information gathered and exchanged. Hardy landing on their good side, the press now in a feeding frenzy of the likes of which would make a Great White proud, and Covic disappearing to "whoreland" on some far off island. It was now time to have some fun. And it was his playful side the press loved best; Hardy taking turns between playing the devil and the altar boy. Living it up on the town with his large legal settlement, the promise of a job of intrigue and steady flow of warm new friends; trusted, learned and more than willing to help Hardy invest his new found fortune wisely. Forty-one is the age of men, though being single deducts fifteen years off one's sensibilities. Hardy more than welcomed their investment advice.

Atop his settlement, the phone company had agreed to pay his full salary for the rest of his life. Longevity being one of the virtues which surfaced in his family tree along with some silly British blue blood fable unearthed by the KGB in an effort to false flag him or change his sympathies. One great something or another being a Socialist, the other being a Jew, instantly changing forty-one years of Roman Catholicism and many long and difficult years at Sacred Heart. John Custer Harding had secured a very good deal and settlement from Savannah Telephone at the very youthful looking age of forty-one. He had sent the Socialist KGB spy away with a face that needed six hours of plastic surgery at St. Joseph's. By the time the altercation occurred, the entire countryside viewed his kind as somewhat lower on the food chain than the common cockroach. No charges were brought. It was reported, however, sometime later, that the KGB spy had further and severely injured himself at the police station when he fell up a flight of stairs on his way to booking.

The phone company had been a good cover for this CIA covert operation. Hardy was assigned to the hi-tech group known simply or referred to in slang terms as *Specials*. Langley had recruited many over the years in all aspects and walks of life in the great Bell. There were good guys and bad guys, criminals, lawmen and spies. What was truly amazing was that one could see the same structure of cops and robbers, spies, double agents and enemy agents no matter which chain of command he wished to explore; corporate, management, union, or outside independent contractor, for so much of the work in the telecommunication industry is farmed out. The entire massive operation would be akin to having an entire FBI field office go undercover on a slightly bigger scale and different structure. Some of the men buried twenty years before, others modified *sleepers*; they joined the phone company after Korea, the big one or the may conflicts over the years. Once in the Army, always in the Army. Intelligence assets from their first day of boot camp forty years before. They all knew how to play the game, and nobody plays *the game* better than a phoneman.

But the mix of cops and robbers coupled with the spy game did not fare well. The old feud between intelligence and enforcement and which national security issue is more important flared up. Cops and spies do not mix well. Spies play games, cops like to throw handcuffs on people who play games. In the end, the only ones who were not set up were Langley's people. To the embarrassment and terror of some in law-enforcement who suddenly found themselves caught in the middle of a monster spy game, snared between the many warring factions and having to play themselves back. Kill or be killed. They simply became hit men for the U.S. Government—turning their guns on the KGB agents who were trying to handle them, the problem children of Wall Street and organized crime, who really deserved it. Surveillance being what it is these days, some of which with black holes that only a lawman would know, other tracking techniques "classified," if they did a good job—most of them did—they then could play on. Their souls of course, forever owned by the CIA in Langley, Virginia. We have laws in

America, and murder is still against the law, even for lawmen who do so out of service to their country, or because they were left with no other choice.

The KGB and their *illegals*, Americans that were recruited by Russians to run operations against our government had been equally snared between the many warring factions of "The Southern Spy Affair," a nut called Covic who wrote too much and his friend who corrected his papers. Their demise was extremely cruel. Of the many who played the great game, lawman, outlaw and spy, the only words one could hear when the whole house of cards came crashing down was "God Damn Them!" to the chagrin of about two dozen wylely old phone men who were preparing to go back to sleep for another twenty years, or simply retire to some far off land to avoid the witch hunt of a fabled CIA Station Chief who never really existed.

The FBI had listed Covic as a Russian agent, Hardy a double. Both were CIA from the very beginning. Their little game having stuck the cops within the camp of all the bad guys of this world in their obsession to catch two rogue Russian agents. By the time the nice gentleman from Langley had pointed out their politics to the head of the Atlanta FBI field office, it was really too late. He knew this, and sooner or later a blood bath would ensue. He was already looking at options on damage control. People would have to be played back.

It was not so much the FBI that Covic and Hardy had stung, but the people they used for undercover or covert operations. Their undercover wing, made up mostly of various state organized crime task forces and police groups, and as Hardy pointed out over a friendly or not so friendly questioning session, "were obviously politically incorrect in the intelligence community of a Western society." The KGB, or whatever the hell they call themselves these days, had done pretty much what they had done throughout the entire cold war, they had moled into the only niche in the intelligence community that they could. In this case, the FBI undercover wing; sting operations, psychology of. Subcontracted by law-enforcement, psychology by the enemy. Their well-insulated patrons in Moscow, the FSB, same leopard, different spots, still promoting Socialism, still in control of the intelligence community, still in control of their parliament and still hoping for a return to the old days. This even if they had problems at the top. Yelsin being somewhat of a clown and very predictable to the needs of the West.

"Cops! God damn cops!" Special Agent In Charge Blacke could be heard bellowing down the hallway from his office in the ninth floor of the Atlanta FBI field office. The FBI had real problems here. Along with these many police groups stung were a handful of agent liaisons; double agents within the law-enforcement community. Go-betweens between the FBI and various state and local police groups. Insulation meant to keep catastrophe from happening. The psychology had gotten out of control, the KGB were now using the illusion of FBI cover to run covert operations. He wondered silently if he could still trust them. Special Agent Blacke, though absolutely furious, was now in the process written about in great spy affairs and touched on loosely over the years on his visits to Quantico, of just how to go about playing the people he controlled back on the enemy, and how not to leave the Bureau's fingerprints on the drama if things needed to be done. They would. "God damn Hardy! God Damn Covic! God Damn press!" Though Hardy had done most of his job for him playing the KGB back against the Sicilians and falling into grace with Don Fusaro-Debenadetto, the man who controlled the traditional rackets throughout the South and ran Dixie with iron fist to the Mason-Dixon Line. A Mafia Godfather and Man of Honor Special Agent Blacke could not touch. An obvious CIA asset as well, who went back to the old days and knew Joe Bananas personally. Though the age difference and the old Godfather giving young Don Fusaro his introduction into the New York Family and sending him down south to run things.

The Great Game has finally come to the shores of America, were his final thoughts that afternoon as he put down his Parker pen and tossed his outdated file of Socialists/Russian agents in the trash, and readied himself for the long commute home.

Covic had gone out in the cold to do a job, freelancing with a wink and a nod. He had played Parisian on all the shops, cafés and pizza parlors in the Atlanta area. Making the bad guys, the KGB and the phone company he worked for as mad as hornets—not to mention a half dozen Colombian and Mexican groups not as structured as the mob but twice as deadly. It was, however, their lack of structure that allowed Don Fusaro to take apart their organization like a heart surgeon in the heat of battle, realizing the poor gent really did not need all of what God had given him.

The job complete, Covic started writing letters to come back in from the cold and began mailing them off to the press. They struck terror in the hearts of everyone and sent the whole spy affair into motion. Hardy, his unwitting accomplice who majored in English, would correct his penciled writings before Covic would deceptively change things a bit, add a heading, type them up and mail them off to terrorland. Covic was the unkept creative beast who failed high school English and never attempted college. Hardy was the polar opposite. Their unlikely relationship continuing from grade school through the phone company.

Their creative writing project had caught the KGB and an array of scoundrels off guard.

As angry as the boys made him, for *The Kiss Of Death* in those days had become as common as jellybeans on Easter morning, Don Fusaro-Debenadetto had let them both live. Their activities had played right into his hands, the hands of the traditional rackets. While at the same time pulling the rug out from under the drug cartels and the narco-traffickers, further strengthening his iron hand and making him a power that the five families in New York would have to reckon with. The contract, so as not to lose face, would have to stay but he was in debt and to repay this debt, he would let the boys live. "I'll hit you when I can" which meant if they did not fuck up, they could live to a ripe old age. Covic exiled off to "Whore Island," Hardy was fastly becoming his second son.

Covic was now gone and Hardy was left with a new father and Rabbi, who will most likely go down in history as being the first Mafia Don to sting the FBI. This even if he fell short of his mark, or had piggybacked on the escapades of two spies he would have really preferred to have shot. The FBI were extremely hot in temperament over the turn of events, and even if the accused were really not their people, the Bureau's fingerprints were all over the spy affair like a crime scene of passion.

The FBI had their hands full, often spending more time investigating their own people or the "Shithead Division" as they had become known with disdained affection amongst the steady pool of Special Agents Agent Blacke, Special Agent In Charge, had under his command. Cops and one bad apple. In this case, the fruit flies of the spy affair had brought the virus to the doorstep of his field office. The misconception of an undercover cop who has the ill-conceived notion he can do whatever he damn well chooses if he has an FBI umbrella. Psychology being what it was, and the overwhelming desire to have one's enemy murdered, maimed, or tossed in prison for the rest of one's life. The KGB more than willing to help guide the thoughts of a few dirty cops, who were better equipped by the upbringing of their craft to be chasing around drug dealers, than mixing it up with world class spies. Should they not succeed in their fox hunt, the constellation prize being an FBI field office set up and more open to and sensitive of Socialist dogma.

The problem both Special Agent John Blacke and Don Fusaro knew, and perhaps it was the only issue they could agree on, was that the Shithead Division was hitting American assets in the traditional rackets while leaving Russian assets, which tended to be in narcotics, in place for obvious reasons—ideology, more money and political influence.

Special Agent Blacke was well aware of the deck being stacked and played against him.

The spy affair had taken Special Agent Blacke by surprise. It had taken everyone by surprise. Feelings of affection and rage would run wildly through his mind, missing each other by mere seconds. He did not know whether to kiss Hardy like a son before bedtime or shoot him. Covic exiled and the thoughts of Hardy overseas and out of his hair had compelled Blacke to fudge a background check for Kohl Associates, adding an extra star to Hardy's name and hoping Hardy would be happy in the employment of Caliber Communication, Georgetown, Grand Cayman Island and secretly conveyed his wishes to the nice gent from Langley that Hardy should stay in the Middle East for more than a season or two.

Robert Torres was a good looking Hispanic American, developed and Recruited by the CIA after spending many hard years at Georgetown University outside Washington, D.C. He majored in foreign affairs and government and was the leading expert in South American covert operations. Robert Torres also possessed a deep knowledge of Far Eastern affairs and the European Theater of Operations. He had minor, a CIA workshop and think-tank in Middle Eastern diplomacy. Robert Torres was the agent liaison sent by Langley to the Atlanta FBI field office to smooth things a bit and give Special Agent Blacke a hand. He was of course the first link in the chain of command that was to be established to guide agent Blacke in the playing back of the men he controlled, along with the geopolitical ramifications and shifts in ideology that both agencies had to be concerned with. At forty-two, he was a handsome man who possessed a knowledge and gift with words that soothed tensions and made perfect common sense with anything he said. Special Agent In Charge Blacke and Robert Torres would develop a very good relationship, which started that morning when he assured Agent Blacke that Hardy would certainly be spending a few years abroad.

And it was there at the Atlanta field office while Hardy played nearby in his shiny newly leased Chrysler convertible with the ladies of the press that the "Southern Spy Affair" slowly wound down. The trouble with treading on the expertise of another's domain is not knowing the tricks of the trade. It was here, by instruction of his superiors back in Virginia, that Robert Torres showed a pool of Special Agents tricks and shortcuts of the spy craft of playing wayward cops back, and the subtleties of psychology which often guide one's decision;

choosing between death, your family name and reputation. Often to avoid the inequity exploited by the KGB, and now subtlely reminded by the CIA, the subject will do the right thing—face death and possibly survive. "About what the same we did to Noriega's men," he retorted to a group of twenty or so Special Agents in an impromptu seminar he set up one morning. Having fun with the Secret Police or the torture of a spy's soul seemed to be the theme.

Until the arrival of Robert Torres, chaos was abounding coupled with belligerence and obstinence. It wasn't just the Shithead Division or the overly playful antics of a couple of spies who set them up, it was institutional. A culture where denial of failure and embarrassment were to be diluted in reports launched off to the Justice Department or to whatever U.S. Attorney was overseeing their efforts.

There was infighting from top on down. The FBI not being immune to the basic theory of the Peter Principle. This could even be found at Cabinet level in the back rooms of the Clinton White House. There were endless streams of directors and deputy directors for FBI field offices across the South voicing their opinions in arguments so heated that they fell just short of fist-a-cuffs and a call to arms against their colleagues in intelligence. There were U.S. District Attorney investigations being influenced and pressured by the giants who reside on Wall Street. The very ideological direction of the nation was in peril. A victim of Sting operations, psychology of. Which had been severely influenced by Socialist doctrine.

And so it was a steady stream of red-faced stung directors with hair looking like it had endured a session of chemo, were told by Director Freeh who had come over to Mr. Tenet's side, to play themselves back. Especially some out of control cops who needed a modern version of being taken to a Southern woodshed.

But it was the snickers of the DCI and his Deputy Director Of Covert Operations that the misbehaved lawmen remember most to their disdain; the humor one must endure which cuts like a knife in the process of letting you know you must cut your own throat.

There was also an import from British Intelligence that they despised the most. A happy man with a good sense of humor and a deep knowledge of the traditional spy game, which would prove to be the most valuable to the CIA since the landing of the Great Game on American soil. He was a fabled George Smiley kind of fellow, having learned much of the experience of the games he played in Europe many years before, and the expertise Langley and the FBI now needed. When one has been stung and is Irish Catholic it is easy to take one's frustrations out on the new kid on the block, especially if he happens to be Brit. But the stung in the over all picture of things were few and Henry Chatsworth fit right in the intelligence community.

But like every good soldier, Henry Chatsworth had his scouts do a little recon before beginning the mission. Covic had gotten into too many sensitivities and Whitehall wanted on board. His man Trevor had been milling about the Atlanta area for the BBC. The British always love a good spy story. By the amount of Israeli press, along with several guest appearances of Prime Minister Netanyahu, coupled with his ambassador to Washington and several other high ranking Israeli officials including General Sharon on DNN, it was clear the Israelis did too. Leaving half the press, the FBI, and Hardy in various stages of undress, the leather seat laid back and top down on his fun mobile having his way with the girl from *The Athens Post*, wondering just what the hell Covic had gotten himself into. Not yet fully aware that the seeds of riddle of intrigue were already tucked deep within Hardy's soul.

The burning of Atlanta, or at least the burning at the stake of many who deserved it. Langley and Whitehall had come up with a win, an army of bad apples were facing their terror, or about to. At the Justice Department, a review of a dozen or so directors of the FBI were underway. Many would receive more than a well-deserved spanking. Senator Hatch was keeping keenly abreast of the developments.

Towards the end, it was Covic the beast who skipped town, leaving Hardy to tend to a spy affair all to himself. It was Hardy, the poster child of JC Penny sport jacket sales, slipping into the shoes of Satan's twin. Hardy, the good kid of an Officer's son and overall nice guy that law enforcement loved to hate, left to fill the void of an exploding spy affair. In the end it was Hardy, the world class spy developed through on the job training, which in simple terms meant if you live you move on to a higher plain of intrigue, who taught the law-enforcement community the spy game. They had set themselves up. Hardy simply knocked them all down. Sweeping away a sea of misery and undesirables in the process.

CHAPTER
2

The Newsroom had been busy that September morning, as it had been since the beginning of the long Southern summer, which tends to start early in Georgia, when Leonard Cohen dropped the files on Pam Wellington's desk. More chaos, she thought, as it had been since the temperature hit the nineties last April. Hot even for Atlanta—more uncontrollable havoc, even for the newsroom.

"Here's your homework, Pam. Chapter one of your next assignment. Photocopies of old love letters too. It seems your Mr. Harding is quite a guy. Fast learner too, from his friend Covic. Added a few twists of his own to his past activities. Good with the ladies. Not really a jock."

"This guy thinks he's hot? Full of himself? Conceited little spy, ain't he?"

"Seems like a nice guy, tends to get his way with the ladies. Jill from *The Athens Post* was his last conquest," a smile reeled from Leonard's face to the angry smirk of Pam, a lady who never gets set up, tossed or loses a war in romance or a simple skirmish between the sexes.

"Conquest?"

"Yes, a conquest. Corporate said that if you sting the guy, you'll get an extra bonus." With that, Leonard turned to go back for a dip into chaos.

Conquest was the word that played gracefully across Pam's mind like an old Rascals tune being carried gently on the breeze at the seashore while she slowly turned the pages of the dossier Leonard had compiled for her. The summer of '98 had been hot, and reviewing Mr. Harding's legendary escapades made her even hotter.

The lounge at the Crowne Plaza was quiet that Thursday afternoon. A handful full of lounge lizards kept the barmaid, Linda Kolo, with her flowing blond hair, stripper's body, and cocktail dress cut up to her waistline, company. As lizards go, they were well-dressed top shelf lizards—the business crowd on a pre-happy hour assault. Lizards just the same. Pam had chosen a table next to the vacant dance floor and away from a handful of reptiles in business suits, where the distraction of muzak was on its way to being replaced by disco.

She had met the two at a news conference, and although no interview took place, they did have a chance to chat with Special Agent In Charge John Blacke, Robert Torres and John Custer Harding. Who, unbeknownst to Hardy, was under her surveillance from time to time.

She understood the different cut of cloth between the lawman and his counterpart that Langley had sent down. But, what fascinated her most was the difference between Robert Torres and her quarry, John Custer Harding, ("Hardy"). They were both CIA , both spies, both gifted and both extremely bright (on the borderline of brilliance), but they took different roads on the journey in life to rise to the level of where she discovered them. This certainly changed her life and the way she looked at the developments of this world.

Robert Torres was the chess player and all around nice guy. He was a good-looking man who coldly avoided Pam's advances—a lady reporter's ploy to gain an extra tip. Silently, she wondered if he was married and had kids back in D.C.? He looked like the family type.

Was Hardy a womanizer? she wondered. Married once, according to her records, in his early twenties. He was a chess player type who preferred to play checkers—an intellectual street fighter. Buy you flowers, clock some guy in a fight for your honor, tie the creep up in knots of paper work that lawyers are so fond of, and toss you the following week for another girl.

Both men had about the same absorption of knowledge along the trails of life. One was a legal agent of the CIA, recruited from the best schools and the other was an illegal spy, recruited over a lifetime of on the job experience and military upbringing of an Officer's values. Between the two, she could honesty not tell who was brighter or had the bigger IQ. Both men were very attractive and really nice guys. They were both a good match for a lady who attended a few schools along the way herself, and they both really turned her on, *this*, even if she was patiently waiting for the one she had not formerly met. Though his antics with Sara the girl who waited tables at Maria's Brick Oven Bistro had really pissed her off. A passion flare of jealous fury, Pam had been a victim of her own reconnaissance that summer morning.

A certain air filled the room—an air of a man condemned to die many times over and the confidence one receives from cheating ones demise. A confidence, a sense of command which lizards take notice of and overly do their advances to a barmaid more concerned with tips and the air of a stranger cantering across the floor, making would be actors and body builders squirm and the dangerous back off. Hardy did not have the looks for television and had been fortunate to keep his profile off the front page of the morning paper, even if it had made the *Daily News* in New York once. An illusion, an air apparent of a film legend, which drew stars like moths to a torch on the twinkling of a warm romantic summers night. Only for Hardy to upstage the actors who could not decide if they wanted the autograph of a nobody or if they should portray him in a movie, leaving the fashion models weak in the knees desiring that which they could not have. For Hardy had become a covert celebrity in a world that could not decide whether to hug him or shoot him. The press and television journalism had guided his portrait to all the right people. Hollywood liked the story and wanted to tell it even if the bulk was sealed "Classified." Pam Wellington had done her research well, she held her ground at the introduction of Mr. Harding, who needed no fanfare of his own. Hot, though cold in her appearance, Hardy could taste the sexual tension as they shook hands.

"Mr. Harding, let's get down to business. It's getting late and I have a lot on my itinerary tonight. I have to be back at the news desk at six o'clock. I have a few stops to make in between. I want to ask you a few questions. As agreed on the phone we will keep it all off the record."

Hardy was silently furious at the coldness of her demeanor but a slight smile came to his face at his gifted realization of the inner workings of a lady he was obviously going to bed. The deep insight and understanding of a gentleman who has been around the block a few times. Pam's ice queen outwardly appearance told him she was boiling hot inside. Not knowing that Pam herself was a spy and had picked off a date he had secured with Sara in her undercover work a few days earlier. "Please, call me Hardy."

"Mr. Harding..."

"Hardy."

"Okay, Mr. Hardy..."

"Just Hardy."

Pam was furious. This was their first battle and she received a casualty. *Goddamn nickname*, she thought to herself. "Hardy, you stung the FBI?" To the inner thoughts of *you gott'a be kidding?*

"I guess the FBI now know why the whole world hates us. Though I really am only a phoneman who hit it big. I can only use the phrase, I will neither confirm nor deny any ties I may have to the CIA. I have never been to Langley, never been to school for them. No, not really. We stung those who really deserve it—cops. We stung cops. It's Mark Twain really. Isn't it best to let the other guy think he's won? Off the record Pam—it is Don Fusaro-Debenadetto. It would break his heart if he knew he fell short. We did. I did. Best for diplomacy. Respect. The FBI has been nice enough to keep me out of jail. Don Fusaro does not know. He's feared by the others. I cannot take that away from him. Nice guy too, for a gangster. He stung the FBI."

"Cops?" moving her writing hand to her brow, pen still in grip, looking like a pool reporter who just lost an exclusive.

"Move on Miss Wellington."

"Pam."

"Pam, I have to be sensitive about Don Fusaro.... move on."

"I call them the 'Shithead Division.' Please pardon my language. After a brief get-to-know-you session with the FBI, I suspect the name has caught on."

"You have met with the FBI?" Knowing, but playing coy and brushing her flowing brown hair to the side.

"A couple of federal something-or-others, a few times. Our meetings range from rage to a slap on the back, and can you recommend a good French table wine for my wife?"

"What other agencies besides the FBI? French wine?" Pam was now softening up a bit, crossing her legs and hoping to avoid embarrassment. "DEA? Customs?"

"Can't talk about that. Some of the guys there are real nice. Give and take, back and forth. Their wives like wine and candle light, we both don't like the shithead division," to Pam's gentle giggle of the humor of his obscenity, which had gotten the Bureau in so much trouble. Hardy was confident like a rock and now smiling at Pam's mild outburst. The meeting was quickly changing from an interview to a date.

"Candles...?" was now the most humorist question of a lady and journalist on the verge of losing yet another battle in the wars we so often play between desiring lovers.

"Candles. I collect French wine and keep candles in my apartment. Dad was an Officer. I was raised to be an officer and a gentleman." In the foreground a D.J. could be seen setting up shop.

"Oh God, the time," she said, glancing at her watch. "Maybe another half-hour or so. What is Parisian, Hardy? I have heard the term tossed around a few times."

Hardy relished the opportunity to put his knowledge to use. "The term Parisian goes back to occupied France during World War II. During those years, the French Resistance would go from shop to shop making contacts throughout the city of Paris. They also set the Nazis up using this technique. I used this technique here in Atlanta and so did Covic, but I picked it up and really made an art of it."

With Sara fresh in her mind, Pam was suddenly furious. "You mean cafés and pretty waitresses, Hardy?" she blurted out in anger, revealing to Hardy that his beautiful interrogator had done her homework.

"I had a job to do. I liked coffee, good food and beautiful women. I mixed the two." Hardy was now calmly stirring, ambushed, realizing he was in a war of trophy romance and Pam was gunning to take him down a notch or two.

Bastard...he did not break...the coolness of his attitude held. An over sexed, self-assuring lady's man with ice water in his veins. He should have broken. He should have squirmed. Sweat should have been pouring off his brow and down his face. Caught in the act, and you know damn well I caught you, were the blizzard of thoughts before Pam's next barrage of questions, which Hardy stopped short and deflected away.

"Any favorites Hardy?" she demanded, about to cast the dagger into his heart.

"Pam, this is business." And it was. "I agreed to help you out, not go over my failed romances. As it is some little agent of influence from *The Globe* has been tagging me around."

Hardy was furious. Pam could see it in his eyes, yet she could not see the wisdom in backing off. "Failed romances, Hardy, or flavor of the week? Are these girls your agents or theirs?" Pam was hot. Seeing the anger in Hardy's eyes made her even hotter. It was then she realized what Hardy had in the pre-handshake assessment of the one you want to kill before you bed.

"Excuse me, would you two like to order something? It's four thirty and the grill is open." It had been a combination of the gathering of tips from drunken lizards, teaching a handsome gentleman a lesson, and a passion play of which Linda, like most beautiful women, wanted to be a part of in the pretext of coming to the aid of another sister soldier in the heat of battle between the sexes in the war of romance that had first delayed her, then brought her over to a sister at arms. Two sodas, one with lemon, one with lime, and thoughts of *where have I seen them before?* Though in different scenes and different movies.

It must of been the ice. When Linda arrived back at the table, the drinks were mostly ice. Whatever the case, the disposition of both combatants was cooler and somewhat more reconciled. Pam took a sip and continued with her questions.

"Milosevic?"

"Classified."

"The White House?"

"Classified."

"Someone told you this was classified?"

"When someone is a spy, Pam, he need not be told what is classified and what is not. It is understood. From one's position in the spy game, one sees things that others miss or which make perfect common sense. It's ideology really. So many people try to influence your views in such a way that the only thing you really can do is what you feel is best for the country. In the West, you stay to the Right.

This spy affair certainly had influence, and still does in the Balkans, Iraq, and in White House policy. It is highly political, actually. I do not know all of what Joe knows. Covic kept some things to himself. He set me up. He did not confide in me all of what he should have, or shouldn't have. I needed to know some things—others I did not. Still others I did not want to know.

He started dating my ex-wife. I dumped her when I was twenty-four. She had strong ties to Washington politics on the liberal side. She was from New Orleans. French. Her folks, Frogs from Quebec. She had special interest at play here. My dad knew that she was no good. When she lost the baby by way of a clinic, I dumped her. She was playing a game, she was very cruel.

That was seventeen years ago. She grew and her placement in the spy game grew. God knows what she is into these days. Then, 'good old Satan,' my best friend, starts sleeping with her a couple of years back. I was furious but what can you do? I stayed clear, started dating an old flame that 'Satan' was bedding too. I wanted to kill Joe.

But we reconciled. We both were out of work and Joe always had cash. I took his hand-me-downs in subsidies and in women. I would correct his papers for him, at least the ones he let me see before he mailed them off to DNN. But I always, I mean always, stayed clear when he was tapping away at that old electric typewriter. I think he had to use WD40 or CRC on the damn thing every time he wanted to use it. The thing looked like it had been around for ages.

We helped each other out—exchanged information and shot the breeze about girls. I'd correct his papers in return for tips—the low-down of what he was up to. We'd play Parisian, setting up the narcotics trade and KGB, who threw in on that side to try to stop us. He was good, but I was better. The malls were best and the most fun; beautiful women to flirt with and one of us always needed to pick up something from the book store or sporting goods store."

"Influence? How?"

"I'm not sure myself. Blackmail I suspect. There are things Covic knows that I believe the Russian government would blackmail us over. Things are heating up in both the Balkans and Iraq. This Fall, I think...? The Balkans, Kosovo. Just a guess. Whatever it is, it would give

Milosevic the upper hand—the same for Iraq. Politicians, Politicians must do what the polls of the wind tell them to do...and *Special Interest*. The Russians have silently thrown in on both sides and are looking for ways to pressure Washington. Joe, Covic had been spotted on a couple outings milling away around Paradise Island. Dead letter drops I think."

Wylely smiling, Pam asked, "You ever do dead letter drops, Hardy?"

"No comment," he replied to Pam's little outburst of a feminine chuckle.

Hardy was now desperately trying to wipe the smirk off his face, looking like an old WB cartoon.

"Poor *puttycat*, did I catch you off guard?" Pam had just scored a basket in overtime.

"It's getting late. You said you had things to do...?"

The DJ was still playing with wires and Linda had apparently broke some toad's heart and a steady plague of reptiles had moved in to devour the toad and cast their best lines on a damsel in distress.

"It was overtime Hardy, the newsroom can do without me. See if you can catch her eye. Less ice, I'll have my club soda with lime this time."

"She's been ignoring me—a little game of romantic tag. I believe she wants to teach me a lesson before letting me know that she thinks I'm attractive."

"So I've noticed," Pam replied though she was not quite as angry this time as ladies often are when a gentleman talks to one beautiful woman about another. Her response was more than playful, "I'll try."

"I was good in English, Pam. I love history, social studies, government, foreign affairs—I ate the stuff up. In those days I would always spend an hour reading *The New York Times*. After West Point and the move down here to hook up with Savannah Telephone, I would often take a run to the airport to pick up a copy of *The New York Times*. About the only place down here that I can find it.

"Covic? Joe used me for his pipeline of information. Oh, I knew I was being used. What he was into was serious. He's a creative beast, but not good when it comes to geopolitics. I'd give him the tools and let him make his own decisions. If it were serious, I'd step in with a little psychology of my own. Joe was a pig, but he did stay to the right.

"Helping him landed me out in the cold. I was fired and then listed as disabled. Mental illness is like the common cold when conspiracies abound and a lot of money is lost. Everyone comes down with a paranoid something."

Pam was laughing, "Hardy, you have a settlement and a new job as an arms inspector? Sounds pretty heavy for a telephone man."

"The settlement is good Pam, a few friends are helping me out with my investments. Covic? Joe sold out. Joe was more money than CIA. Hit for a hundred million as the rumor goes. Some account in the Grand Caymans. Caymans, it's logical. With Joe gone, I had to pick up the ball and run with it. Damn near been killed a few times over. I guess that is why I am the way I am. I have looked into the eyes of death too many times to be scared anymore.

Arms inspector? No. I do sensors and telecommunications installations. A lot of sensors. I make sure they are up and running and not tampered with. I fix them if they break down. It's about the same as what I had been doing at the phone company. Dangerous, these people do not like Americans or infidels. I have a few months left to have fun. I've been dating a girl from *The Athens Post*."

Pam broke in, "So I've heard. You really should be more careful where you put the top down on your car," she said turning her face away gently laughing, a mild blush starting to show on Hardy's.

"No, not me but I've heard," Pam added scoring three more points in overtime.

"I leave the fifteenth of January. Jill's a sweet kid, a good reporter too, but I have to toss her. Not love, lust. Sweet kid; a lot of fun." Hardy toned it down a bit as not to anger Pam and took another sip of his soda. "The phone company? Iraq? Some of it's classified. Everything goes by telecommunications these days. Fiber has cut down on a lot of enemy eavesdropping. The Russians used to saturate the copper cables around D.C. with microwaves to see what they could pick off. You can't hear anything off of glass, and where you can is 'classified.' It's about the same as the phone company. It's good cover. Play for a few months until I leave. Jill? It's nice to have a lover. I date a few girls and enjoy my covert fifteen minutes of fame. I have to pick up a multi-band radio and gather everything I need over the next few months."

"Why the radio, Hardy?" Pam asked, looking very inquisitively.

"It's the spy game, Pam. You always hear about any big spy game on the radio first. It's the *power of suggestion*, The Tokyo Rose thing; riddles, fun and games. We do it first and then we let the Russians take over and try to control everything. Ideological paranoia is what I call it. You cannot let people have thoughts counter to Socialism," Hardy said to the breakdown of Pam's laugh. "We out play them. The people the KGB imported to Atlanta to try and stop us must have been imported from someplace like Oklahoma City. God, it makes you stop and think. The power of suggestion goes a long way in the spy game. God, I despise these people. Radio Free Europe, VOA, Radio Marti, we set it up and then we set them up. The spy game is more than dead letter drops or Salt II and how many missiles you have.

Socialists Pam, I've seen things that make me sick, things done by psychology and the power of suggestion that turn my stomach. People killed, children killed." Pam could see by his eyes that he was getting emotional and was having a hard time continuing. "I cannot talk about it now, maybe some other time?"

Pam waited for his eyes to clear. "You hate Socialists, so your politics are extreme Right?"

"No. I am a moderate. The right to bear arms, but reasonable gun control. Center-Right. I vote my conscious. I voted both lines in the past and center in my thoughts for the future. I do not like extremes in government. Extreme shifts in politics destabilize governments. The KGB throw in on both sides. They play the far-left against the far-right, like what the mob use to do to labor unions to secure a kickback. In this case, the kickback is chaos. Like the '60s. When a person is a spy you know these things. The object is not so often how many missiles you have, but your leader screwed up." Hardy suddenly found himself lost in the beautiful eyes of a television journalist after his discourse; Pam was equally lost in his.

"Hardy, have you made a lot of enemies?"

"Yeah...after this, Iraq will be a whole lot safer than Georgia. Don Fusaro-Debonadetto can only protect me so much. The FBI are furious. We get along, but playing the KGB back against the Sicilians to their demise...well, you can see the spot the Bureau is in. The 'Shithead Division,' the FBI can take care of playing back their own. I went after the Socialists who came out of the woodwork to try and derail our operation. That's my job! With a wink and a nod, of course." Pam again was mildly laughing. "It reached The White House Pam, these Socialists and special interest narco-traffickers almost toppled the government. Impeachment. Damn lot of wisdom in Senator Hatch. Classified Pam."

"Oh damn it! Look at the time...it's six thirty. Hardy, before I have to go," Hardy listening over the D.J.'s soundcheck, "how did you get your nickname?"

It took a while for Hardy to come around gently laughing to himself as he walked Pam to her car, feeling that perhaps it would be best to have her *inside* (Pam now feeling the same about Hardy on a different line of thought) before he gave his response to an interrogator he now desperately wanted to have a tumble with between the sheets.

"Come on Hardy, you can tell me."

And so he did in a good natured gentlemanly way between whispered laughter to himself. "I was caught making love one night—I have a big cock!"

"You conceited bastard!" Pam laughed as she drove away in her corvette.

It was Monday when they arrived at DNN Public Information, a nerve hub and screening center for the news giant.

"Miss Wellington you have something here from a Mr. Harding. *Cut flowers, a mixed bouquet.* I will send them through."

It was a modest grouping of flowers that had cost Hardy a better part of eighteen dollars to have put together, but a crowd gathered around the newsroom just the same. Pam read the card: *Please excuse the origins of my nickname and accept these flowers out of respect and as an apology for the lack of sensitivity in our departing last Thursday evening. John*

"Look Dana, a stalker," Pam bellowed in her best *scared* pretend school girl voice to the howl of Steve Summers and a handful of others who had gathered around. "What are you doing tomorrow night, Dana?" to the playful smile of another TV journalist turned high school cheerleader for the moment. "I want Hardy, but I want Hardy on my terms not his," she said, this time with a serious smile of school girl turned back into a TV journalist again.

Damn voice mail! Couldn't he have an answering machine? she thought. "Hello John, Pam Wellington from DNN. Like to meet with you again, give me a call back at the station when you can, you have my card. I'll be here all day. I prefer 'Hardy.' Bye!"

Hardy had been out securing a deep French kiss from Sara when Miss Wellington had called. Even if he had fallen short of securing a date or *scoring a quickie*, his big warm hands were on her tight buns next to the pay phone strategically placed across from the ladies room in the darkened hallway of her father's bistro. It had become more than a game of romance tag or flirt kissing. Sara used the ladies room way too many times over for simple peeing. Hardy liked the phone. They both wanted to see how far the other would go. Hardy always looked his best at eleven o'clock brunch after working out all morning with his Malibu tan. Sara always looked her sexy, sultry, seductive best when she came out of the ladies room. The arrangements worked out well. Except for the fact that neither one could tear their clothes off because daddy would not approve and Sara was a good little girl. They also tended to be busy. Still, most of the steadies could testify in the circles of gossips around Atlanta's Little Italy about Sara's mad dash to the ladies room every time Hardy was around, and how Hardy always seemed to need to use the coin phone at about the same time.

"Hardy, Mitchell Johnson. Where you been pal? Wednesday night, Mountainberry's."

"Mr. Harding, Kevin Slyer, Caliber Communications. Would like to meet with you. Buy you dinner, we can chat. My number is..."

"Hardy old boy, Trevor. Going back to London soon, stop by the old watering hole."

Hardy, T. J., where you been, Bud? Give me a call back. Mikey Buckhols, Paul Marrs, George Brent and the guys are all getting together Wednesday night for happy hour at Mountainberry's. See you then."

"Hello John, Pam Wellington..."

Hardy was being stalked that Tuesday afternoon when he strolled into the Crowne Plaza lounge just before happy hour. The Crowne Plaza in Atlanta was the crown jewel of the chain. It was a five star high rise of an upscale hotel, which DNN used frequently for a steady clientele of guests that they regularly reserved rooms for. It was also the place Pam liked best for her lesser impromptu interviews. The truth is not everyone has a face the camera would love. Facts had to clarified, stories had to be checked out, pathological liars had to be shown to the door by hotel security. Linda Kolo, a friend, partner in crime on a party night and failed actress, could more than handle the horde of regular lizards or the needs of a lady journalist in distress. It was there at a corner of the bar where the barmaid met her steady stream of table waitresses that Dana DiMaggio staked out her turf, ready to pounce into battle and etch another notch into her lipstick case and turn over an over sexed spy into a lump of apologetic putty.

"Hardy, I liked the flowers. They are sitting on my desk at work. Our last interview worked better when I didn't ask any questions. Tell the story. Tell anything. Better yet, tell me about your friend Covic. Don't hold back."

"I've had a love-hate relationship with Joe my entire life. The guy is so much my opposite that we have everything in common. For a while we shared everything, especially women. Any girl that I had, he had to have. It's a wonder that we haven't killed ourselves.

He's a lunatic, a nut! I guess that's why I love him. He's the big brother who just seemed to take a different course in life. He's a braggart—a white...what's that guys name...? A white Reverend Al

Sharpton. Instead of dazzling you with brilliance, he baffles you with bullshit. He has a gift of gab and a weak heart—he's a victim of consumption. Consumption of everything one should not ingest when he is out partying on a Friday night. He's a hell of a guy, but not the kind you want as a roommate or a friend that you want a steady diet of.

He's a nut, but he is not crazy. The shrinks did a number on him, gave him every psychosis listed on paper. The problem is he is normal, at least when he is not high or tooting coke. When the whole affair fell apart, they paid him off. Then, they came after me. Dad: They tried, but they didn't fuck with me, at least not the way they did with Covic. But the KGB worked him over pretty bad. In the early days he had a break down—something called the Jerusalem Syndrome. He thought he was God or one of the saints, I forgot which one. He went around like a prophet. They had him bad. Constantly fucking with his head. Look, I'm sorry Pam."

"That's what I want, heart-felt feelings. Leave the language in Hardy."

"Then, one day he faked it and spun himself out. He fooled everyone—set up the KGB, set us all up. At the end, just before he disappeared, things got real crazy. The KGB were again trying to get Covic to believe that he was God. Give him another breakdown, really discredit him. Organized crime, the Socialists and some of the executives who were into narcotics money hired psychiatric workers and paid off some in the occult to practice and highlight witchcraft, Voodoo and Satanism to drive him nuts. He even had some Bible Belt Christian sect running around thinking that he was the second coming. Christ, it was off the wall! He'd go from one extreme to the next, cracking them up and making our fellow union brothers..."

"Union?"

"I thought you knew. The CWA. CIA too."

"Anyway, one moment he'd be making fun of one group doing the beast 666 thing. The next moment he was the repented alter boy. The Prodigal Son come back for the feast, only to have the Baptists come back the next day to find three girls in his bed playing part of *Caligula*. He drove everyone nuts and ended up giving the second in command at Corporate a nervous breakdown. That's when the shit finally hit the fan and they paid him off. And the women...you just would not believe the women. They were all top models and expensive escorts. All practicing the black arts trying to program him and make him do what Corporate wants. Christ! The women almost fucked him to death. Kicked me out. The girls started reading and correcting his papers. It was best. I couldn't take it anymore. There always seemed to be an orgy going on. Nice girls, they needed money. Then there was Monique. I walked in one night and he had three women in bed with him—Monique and two of her girls..."

"Dana, this is Mr. Harding. I'm doing a little background on the spy affair." If timing in this life were always timed perfect, it was that evening at five thirty-seven. Dana had broken Pam's concentration in her bout of mutual jealousy and boredom at the bar, leaving Linda with the blues of having to be working while she inadvertently rescued Hardy from revisiting an episode of emotional turmoil in his past.

"Hardy, this is Dana. She's one of my colleagues."

"Oh, I think I've seen you before. Ten o'clock evening news?"

"I'm just going to hang out, guys. I'll just watch, keep an eye on things. I have never met a spy before. I'll be good."

Hardy was now under the gun of two beautiful women—in the crosshairs of one and sitting comfortably with the other that he tamed. Though, you can never tell with women. One minute you are making love to them and the next minute they are tossing your earthly belongings, including expensive stereo equipment and shredded clothes, out the third story window. At the moment, Hardy was having a three-way of his own and God really did know what he was doing when he created us without the ability to read another's mind. Though women at times often prove to be the exception to this rule, especially when the opposite sex is in play, or about to.

Hardy continued, "Back in those days, more than once and a while I would end up with *sloppy seconds* , as Joe would call it. Whores but they were good girls. I look at things differently than most and I have a lot of respect for these ladies. Most of the time I'd get freebies. I guess that's how I got my nickname. Joe walked in when I was with his number one flame. They would change by the week. Anyway, we were very oral and Covic caught us in the act. He was pissed, it lasted about a day. But then he forgot about her—there were so many. Monique and I dated for several months after that. Joe did not know that we knew each other as kids. Then one day they paid him off and I ended up out in the cold for a spell." The name had surfaced twice, Pam was silently boiling away, an emotion that Dana picked up on but Hardy was blind in his discourse. "It was towards the end and I didn't suffer too much. When the scandal broke, I ended up with a good retirement that should last me for life. Not too bad for a kid who just turned forty-one in April."

Pam smiled and her thoughts darted wildly to an array of sexual fantasies, which washed over her mind like some teenager sitting in the front seat of a hot rod convertible at an Atlanta Drive-In on a hot summer's night. Deep inside she was furious, about ready to explode at the betrayal told by her targeted lover. The betrayal one feels when you return home at night to fantasize about the one who kissed you good-bye, in this case enlightened you about his over sized manhood, only to have him betray you in a confession and tale of some tumble between the sheets he had with some over gifted whore, when you know damn well it is you he wants to bed! Hardy was on thin ice. Dana had her lipstick case out, ready to load it into her 30/30. Mature man or not, blue-eyed Robert Redford look-a-like on a toned ball player's body, Hardy was very close to losing about four inches off of what he prized most in this world.

As furious as both ladies were, Hardy still did not seem to realize the mortal danger he was in. He now had two ladies who were torn between thoughts of wanting to bed him, or labeling him a Yankee and handing him over to the KKK to use as some lawn ornament on a Friday night bonfire!

"Dana, the soda, I have to go to the ladies room," Pam said as they both got up and turned to their sanctuary at the same moment, waking Hardy up to the eminent danger he was in.

"That insensitive, over sexed, over sized conceited bastard!" were the words blurted out by Dana amongst the haze of cigarette smoke that filled the room to the consoling of Pam, the betrayed understanding wife of a lover that she hadn't slept with. It was also becoming playfully apparent to Pam that she would have a little competition in the pursuit of the affections of John Custer Harding. Her trust in her soul sister and partner in crime was quickly disappearing.

What transpired in the ladies room that evening would remain a mystery to Hardy. The truth that lies in those torrid tales of romance is that women tend to be worse than men when it comes to sex. Amiss the blue haze and cigarette-butt-lined floor could be seen several triple-x flicks projected across the egg-shell colored walls, and surely if the smoke was too thick to view such entertainment, all one would have to do is gaze into the eyes of Pam Wellington or Dana DiMaggio, who were on the verge of setting the hotel ablaze. Though by the look in their eyes caught by a handful of the walking wounded who wandered in to escape the lizards, perhaps a call to the bomb squad, then pulling down the lever to the firebox would have been more appropriate.

When men are left alone for more than the allotted time in meetings that are quickly turning into a night out of pursuit to fulfill the hunger of desire for lust, a gentleman's thoughts will often drift to where they should not. It was there amongst the amplified inner thoughts of *God I'd love to give her a good, stiff...* that Dana and Pam magically returned from that fabled land where Chippendales hand out hors d' oeuvres to the inconsolable scorned amiss blue cigarette haze.

"So tell me Hardy, this Monique, she's a pretty hot babe!" Pam demanded sarcastically with intent to avenge a tale and confession, which was better off left untold.

"We were in love Pam. I love her."

Pam and Dana now looked like two college girls who just found out that the man of their dreams is married and has ten kids. Hardy continued, "Our whole life, our entire lives, we were either in love, or lovers trying to destroy each others lives. It's just tragedy at its most tragic. I want to do this scene, finish and go to Iraq. I want to forget. Just forget. Jill, Jill helps me forget. I want to leave that part of my life and never return. There are other lovers I can spend my years with. Why be in tragic painful love if one does not have to? I have always had my way with the ladies—sorry Pam, Dana, but you understand? There are others I can build my life with. Why nail myself to a lover's cross? bleed and devour my life in tragedy? Some loves are tragedy. They consume tragedy and make tragedy out of tragedy. Commit emotional suicide for the desire to be with the one who would destroy you? Knowing if she did not burn your flesh she would give her life for a lover she can never really consume or understand? Knowing there have been too many casualties and deaths in this spy affair to ever be able to be one in flesh and spirit. Why put myself through that? Why put her through that? Why destroy each other for the sake of destroying each other, or to fulfill some other's foolish fantasy? The KGB know. They have played us against each other for most of our lives. Flowers. Flowers—if you don't tend to them, they die. This love is dead. At least it is when she is not in my life."

"You really loved her Hardy?" Pam's eyes were watering in emotion for the loss of a love story, and the sudden realization that it was she and Dana who were the insensitive ones by not picking up on the change of direction in Hardy's eyes. They both could now see that Hardy was in severe emotional pain.

From across the table, Dana could see the same. The way Hardy aged ten years in five minutes. He had the look of a man who almost died over love.

"I did. We were damned right from the beginning. Every time...well it just fell apart. Pam...Monique is black. She is of mixed heritage."

Pam could see by his face that he could not go on. She wanted to comfort him, make love to him. In her mind she enticed him, *Make love to a new lover. Make love to me. Let me help you forget about the tragedy of your past. A man who tossed untold many lovers in an endless cycle of failed romances. Tragedy begets tragedy. Love me Hardy. Forget about the lover before; and how would I fair in your life?*

Again, Hardy tried to continue, but a loss of words. They took a break and the talk changed into small talk. An exchange of pleasant conversation broke out between the three of them, like a date, or an evening out. Dana, the loving sister-in-law. Pam picked up on the drafty silly feeling of atmosphere, which surrounded the table. It had gone from emotionally intense to corny, and she remarked, "I guess we are all old friends Hardy, and this must be Pleasantville?"

"Look, I'm sorry ladies but I'm glad you let me go off like that. After I unloaded I needed small talk. I need to hide away from this mess, which has blown up all around me. Monique? I'm sorry. I should not have brought her up, but I'm glad I did. We use to play together like little kids in the old days. She is with Covic now."

Pam glanced at her watch, "Hardy, it's getting late. I have to get Dana back to Olympic Village by eight o'clock."

"Someone can fill in for me, I'll make a call."

"Where to now, Hardy?"

"I fly up to D.C. in a couple of weeks for Senate hearings. Then I'll go to New York, maybe Jersey and play the game. I have a couple of months before I leave.

Pam, I have lived here for many years now and I'm surprised we have never really crossed paths before, well almost," and with that the evening returned to meaningful small talk.

Dana had expected a dumpy little old man with circled spectacles in a wrinkled old gray tweed business suit before the flowers had arrived that Monday morning. Hardy was refreshing, fun and a challenge for any young attractive single woman. Had it not been for his many years at Savannah Telephone, he could have easily made a fortune in show biz. He was a good. After awhile, when the evening wore down and the formal chat was over, they each had a glass of the house Chardonnay while Hardy lightheartedly explained, "One can often, and usually does learn quickly to give an Oscar winning performance when one is on the verge of being shot to death." Many times over they both realized.

So it was there by the grand entrance to the great hotel with cars in different lots that Dana parted company with the two, and Pam slowly turned and gave Hardy a warm gentle kiss while she waited for the valet to bring her white Corvette around, gently tugging on Hardy's right arm. They lived in different worlds most of their lives. Now a phoneman crossed over into her's, changing her views of geopolitics giving them both a chance to play.

Valets...and the long wait for a Corvette parked out in no man's land to avoid nicks and scratches. They watched Dana drive out of sight in her blue Toyota. Valets should never drive Toyotas, she explained to Pam over coffee one outing, different hour.

*The Inspector, not an arms inspector. The Inspector walks me to my car and gives me a kiss goodnight. If anyone messes with me, he'll hit them in the head with a telephone...*but the kiss lasted longer than it should. Hardy watched her disappear out of sight, lingering there even longer, lost in the moment and deep in thought. Hardy wished a final good-night to the valet and slowly cruised out of sight with the warm Atlanta night air wrestling with the golden locks of his hair. The top was almost always down, even when it was raining. Roads seem to be the friendliest at ten o'clock at night in the warm Georgia air. Pam also had the top down, taking her time winding down the highway, gentle music playing to ease her thoughts. Hardy was on her mind: *If I do we will be lovers...if I do he has to toss me...if he does I will be crushed. Neither of us deserves another failed romance. There are other loves out there for both of us. Jill is not bad—a good reporter and a sweet kid. Good looking...All is fair in love and war and Hardy is going to play the game when he arrives overseas. Why not? He is handsome. I would be a fool to wait for his return, which may never happen.*

Yet that night, while she wrestled with the sheets all alone, she knew they would be lovers. She had already decided. She prepared herself and was pissed from the anger that comes with letting the heart make such decisions.

CHAPTER 3

Hardy was the lone wolf every young girl's mother advised them about. Others ran with the pack, Hardy hunted alone. The eternal phoneman; I don't want to hear this BS, get in the truck and drive. First stop, coffee, job orientation and operational maneuvers with the lady of the café. Whichever coffee shop was the designated meeting place for his CWA union brothers. A little coffee, a little bagel, a little waitress tag, and a discussion of all the various new candidates for the Peter Principle. The Peter Principle was legendary at Savannah Telephone, which was told by the handing down of folklore from generation to generation by the elder statesmen of the great Bell, and goes as such: *one will rise through the organization to the highest level of his or her incompetence.* Simply put, if you are talented you stay in the craft. If you are an idiot, then there is a very good chance that some day you will be the one to run the company.

It was there over sessions of morning coffee and waitress tag, that the jobs were planned and executed flawlessly. Though in the heated summer of scandal, when paranoia and flu were in competition for the most victims on paper while spy affairs spun out of control, the opposition did come forth with a list of waitresses that they had found in less than wholesome attire in gentlemanly dens of inequity, and decided to play them back against one John Custer Harding. It was, however, discovered some time later that these girls were excellent dancers, most times in the buff. Though it was still further reported, that on occasion some of these young ladies did wear a G-string.

But Hardy was retired and on his own now. Geopolitics and T1s took a backseat to the future needs of what a handsome wolf would carry with him in the Gulf, where he would mill about from where life as we know it began for a season or two. Leave one phone company, join another—same company, different logo. In those days, before mother Bell had thought to marry off her offspring, the trucks of The Bell System were colored army olive green. One a star, one a bell. Caliber

Communication, like the great Bell, would be good cover. He again would be doing the hi-tech work. Hardy would be a part of their Special Services Division, which meant that he was still in the phone company, or U.S. Army, this, even if he never enlisted.

Planning one's daily job responsibilities was no longer a priority in Hardy's life, waitress tag took a backseat to the errands of a lone wolf in need of provisions. He certainly could have used Sara in the backseat of his car after a stint at the Galleria Mall during one of his legendary evening raids on a hot steamy Atlanta night. By the end of the second week of September, Hardy was sure he would have procured all the provisions he would need for his adventure. It would, however, become painfully apparent by the end of that week that he would need a bigger backseat. Though as much as it was his baby, it was a leased baby and when he went, baby went. Hardy was fortunate leather was as durable and stain resistant as it was.

The crowd was hopping at Mountainberry's at five forty-five Wednesday evening when Hardy pulled in with the top down. Another steamy night. No rain, the top stayed down with his baby in all her glory freshly waxed and decked out for everyone to see. A nice place and reasonable dinners. The CD's locked safely in the trunk. It was now time for Hardy to take a stroll in; taking his time, tasting the sweetness of the evening air along the way. To the left a tall row of hardwoods, halfway down a brick flight of cement stairs leading down to a well groomed mini mall. To the right, a row of ornamental evergreens hiding the highway on the other side. In front of the barnwood sided restaurant two young lovers exchanging affections, though modestly, good kids about to go home and make love.

"Mr. Harding? Kevin Slyer, Caliber Communication. How are you tonight? I've reserved a booth for us overlooking the garden. Its pleasant, it's quiet and we can talk."

"Lead the way, Mr. Slyer."

"John, I'm the divisional Vice President of Human Resources for Caliber Communication. I'm base here in Atlanta and I fly throughout the country looking for talent. Before Caliber, I spent twenty years working for Atlantic Telecom and I had six years In the U.S. Army Signal Corp. In general John, we do not take any dead wood. We are tied too closely to the military and there is no 'Peter Principle' in our organization. I did not know your dad. Your background at Savannah Telephone is quite impressive, we could use you on our team. I knew this when you called, actually before then. Trevor is one of our friends, he uses us for cover from time to time. It's a trade off.

"First up, your first pay checks, it should help with expenses. Next, a list of twenty to thirty topics of telecommunications that we want you to file a report on. If you cannot finish the list, it's no big deal. Do one a week. When you get to the Gulf you will have to file these periodically and it will be good practice. This should be no problem for a man of your experience. We've seen your work, you'll be okay. Last, a laptop," and he suddenly became quiet. "John, we have to be cool about this," he said while he handed Hardy an envelope. "John, this is how you will file your reports and exchange information," only *exchange information* was said in code. "Take a few minutes to read this John."

In general the laptop had a covert satellite link. Anything that he typed would be transmitted back to Langley. It was digital for security and the CIA would be piggybacking onto the Caliber operation.

In addition, there was a code sequence attached to the E-mail section that he was to check everyday, which would not be able to give a print out. Read it and it's gone. The whole set up was very similar to what the guys did for John at Specials when he was trapped and they needed to know what was going on. His word processor, or laptop with training wheels as he called it, was analog. The guys had convinced someone in the GBI to let them couple their surveillance equipment with some neat phone company on the job gizmos. In general, every time you depressed a key on an analog piece of office equipment it emitted a frequency of tone. This tone was intercepted by the surveillance equipment modified by some Savannah Telephone System Technicians and turned back into letters of the alphabet. Towards the end of the spy affair, Hardy even had an interactive thing going with the local cable television station in Athens. It seemed that everyone was undercover in those days.

"No need to talk John, we know about Channel 16 and your laptop with training wheels. The girl who read the news in Athens was cute. This model is somewhat more sophisticated, and as you can tell, it does quite a bit more and it's much more secure."

Hardy handed Kevin Slyer back the envelope. He quickly tucked it away in his briefcase on its way to a secure safe or comfortable shredder to be burned afterwards or flushed down the toilet, or both. It would be shredded and burned later.

"You will both send and receive reports, get your daily work load, instructions and any other useful information over this piece of equipment." Again, the word "other" was said in code, and Hardy thought, *Damn he's good.*

"There's one other thing John. We prefer the term 'Inspector' as opposed to 'Technician.' A little game we are playing with the Army and Scott Ritter's boys. Dick Butler is not too happy over it. Fuck 'em, he ought to go back to the Outback." Hardy was silent, though serious and good natured. "I've been there. It should be fun."

"John, we have a contract on a dozen or so installations throughout the region, including the Mediterranean and *stand-by* on just about the rest of the world. The guys are good, the work is enjoyable, and the game? About the same as what you left at Savannah Telephone." This time the words spoken in code were "the game." Hardy understood immediately what was meant. Kevin Slyer continued, "John, we'll get you over to Riyadh, check in with Colonel Clay, the liaison officer between us and the military, and you'll be on your way. When you get to New York in October, stop by our training center. Try to keep your face out of the press. I spoke to DNN, they have been very understanding and will pass the word along to the others. Keep your chats with Miss Wellington off the record. Now, can I buy you dinner and a beer?"

"Dinner would be fine. I drink club soda with lime."

"God, you can always tell a true professional by what he drinks, or what he does not drink. It's good to have you aboard, John. Do you indulge at all?"

"Only when I'm in bed. Though having a glass of wine, naked, in the company of a young lady can prove to be much more dangerous than mixing drinking and driving." With that could be heard the two in harmony of good hearted laughter while they waited to catch the waitress's eye.

"What do you think, Henry?"

"It would not be a bad idea for you and Robert to have your people keep an eye on Caliber. They are both pros and your people in D.C. will most likely tell you so tomorrow or the next. My job now is on your soil. This spy game...? The whole spy affair has polarized a good swatch of strategically placed people across your country, regardless of how they found their placement in life. They either have to fall out to the West or they go KGB. If they are leaning left, they most likely will go to the left. If it is some Wall Street baron they sunk their teeth into...? and he has a lot of money to lose...? he may very well go to KGB. Tonight...? Best to review the transcripts in the morning. It will be good to see where I will be starting the old game. After dinner? He has friends there. Should be more."

"What do you think, Robert?"

"About the same as Henry. Caliber is ours. Never said but pretty well known. It is common sense. Langley will put it in writing for us. We will tag along on Hardy's adventure. Let Henry do his thing here on the Georgia clay. Oh, by the way Henry, how is your boy Trevor doing?" to the slightest flinch of embarrassment.

"'You weren't suppose to know about Trevor, old boy."

"I know."

"Flying back to London soon. Friendly game of spy. Thought you wouldn't mind. I had to have some people in on the ground before I arrived. Tight with Caliber."

"I know."

"He has friends there tonight that he'll see after dinner. Sara Bolino has a crush on him. I suspect she is on her way. His friends are all there... See what the transcripts say in the morning."

"Pam Wellington? Out of his league?"

"Used to be John, not now. They are playing in the same world now. Hardy can afford to compete. Good in English, no creativity. Too bad. He ought to write a book. Isn't that what you did, Henry, between spy affairs?"

"I'm pretty good at it too, old boy."

"They really like each other, John. My guess is that their hearts will prevail and they'll have a fling. Sara Bolino? the girl from *The Athens Post*? My guess...? Pam Wellington wins the prize. Dumping her would be emotionally difficult, even for Hardy, even if he disappears in the Mideast for a season or two. Hardy knows this. Pam Wellington is not just any girl. Hardy has an ego."

"Jennifer, have Special Agent Tenza and Special Agent Reading come in here. And Jennifer, thanks for staying late."

Hardy had a certain pride in being antisocial, the pride that comes from being a proud tough lone wolf. This, even if the crowd demanded his presents. Such was the case that evening. Mikey Buckhols and the gang were all there but since the departure of Kevin Slyer, Hardy had been deep in thought, tucked away in his own world in the corner of the bar. It was there in the corner when Sara spotted her prey, understanding that complex Mr. Harding was oblivious he was going to get laid that evening. Even more understanding Mr. Harding would need a little help for his mood to run its course. By the look of Hardy's face, it was an important mood—serious mood of a spy caught in the depths of intelligence work. Spy work at play. Spy work and spy thoughts Sara wanted to be a part of. Spy thoughts of a covert legendary hero. Thoughts Sara wanted to know if they had anything to do with her brother Andrew's construction company. Serious thoughts of a spy which always spelled mayhem for whoever surrounded him or tried to be a part of his life at the time. Even when Hardy had playful thoughts playful havoc always followed. The kind of playful havoc people inadvertently get shot over.

Hardy was caught somewhere in the Arctic Circle of spy thoughts, which often lead to the chess game of survival for a world-class agent. His thoughts that evening were of the different degrees of being pushed out in the cold.

Illegals often spend their whole life out in the cold, never seeing the inside of an embassy or consulate. They are never invited to a seminar or homecoming at Langley. They toil their whole life plying their secret craft out in the cold—often spy against spy and enemy against enemy. Set up his network and have his people killed, or have yours fall victim to his, developing your cover as you go along. Some, the best—as was the case with Hardy—were developed as agents through childhood. But there are different degrees of being out in the cold. Hardy knew this well.

At Savannah Telephone they all were out in the cold, even management. Hardy knew this, and as much as the "Peter Principle" was an institution at the great Bell, Hardy knew that most in management and the folks at Corporate were good people. They were also CIA. There are good and bad people in all walks of life, even spies. Every institution has its dead wood, perhaps not Caliber, their screening program being kind of a psychological boot camp. Hardy after having seen so much combat, was already an officer in their eyes. Out in the cold they were, but they were also receiving a good pay check. The phone company was their cover and their livelihood.

Covic went into the deep cold for a while. A lineman turned technician, adjusting a D4 channel unit circuit card with a line hammer. Ma Bell's version of a sledgehammer with a hole in it. Covic never did quite make the transition from construction to a business environment. *Fired!* for filing a labor grievance that infuriated both lawman and outlaw, Mafia and spy, drug cartel and enemy agent. The whole world was in an uproar over a phoneman's payback for a missed half hour of double time. But in this case, Covic was right!

Covic was wily and survived the deep freeze by his wits. He sold minor drugs for pocket money, yet had dirt on the lawmen to hold them at bay. He'd script off a letter and the whole world would shutter before he could walk to the mailbox. He did dirty movies to survive, had something going with the mob, yet he did not take a bullet. When the money started flowing in, the whores did two. Covic tossing his friend some cash and a lady or two from time to time. With guilt by association, Hardy was the next victim of a psychosis. Then one day, it was not so much the noise that Covic made, but that he struck a sensitive nerve with one of his correspondences, professionally polished up by Hardy with a new fancy heading scripted by his laptop with training wheels so the folks back at Ma Bell's wayward son could read what was going on, and off Covic goes with Monique and few of the other ladies to Whore Island. It was cold were Covic was, Hardy knew. It was damn frigid where Hardy landed, but they survived. Survived by different styles and techniques, with the whole world as mad as hornets swirling all around them desperately trying to destroy the odd boyhood couple.

Hardy knew how hard it was to survive in the deep cold. He had been there, almost killed more than a few times before he gained the upper hand playing the KGB's people back against the Sicilians and gaining the affection of Don Fusaro-Debenadetto. Hardy had almost lost that which is more precious than life, the lives of those that he loved. It was cold, damn cold.

It was there, someplace between the Arctic, Caliber and Covic, that Sara jumped into his lap, her hand finding it's way to his cock, giving it an affectionate squeeze through his slacks with a deep soulful *fuck me kiss; I want you tonight*. Stealing him in from the cold and warming him up with her desire. Magically whisking him off to his baby and out to some lovers' lane in the Georgia countryside, leaving her younger, but very gifted fast-learner sister Maria to fend for herself.

It is true that the backseat of a Chrysler Sebring is too small to get laid in. However, when the seats fold down they tend to make a wonderful bed for lovers. And it was there to the howling of a lone wolf to a full moon at the moment of climax, a she-devil nailed her prey while the night owls hovered overhead to watch the flesh of a she-devil and lone wolf melt into one and explode!

Confession as payment secured, Hardy enjoyed an extra treat on the long ride home, the seat tilted back just a bit.

He awoke all alone in terror that evening, having dropped Sara off two hours earlier. The dream was about a man, himself, freezing to death in the hot desert sun while the eagles gathered to make war, lofting in the sky on the thirteenth hour of the thirteenth day. The sheets were soaking wet from a cold sweat that flowed from his pale white body, which was usually shown a bronze Malibu Tan.

He went to the cabinet and poured a glass of twenty-year-old Port. It was there in the dark of the flickering of one lit candle, he sipped his terror away, drifting off to a six-hour nap somewhere between the evil of the darkest hour and the twilight of dawn.

"Good morning Robert, Henry. I'm glad we waited until eleven. Our man Hardy had quite a night. Henry, you were right. Langley called this morning. It seems that both the DCI and Director Freeh want us to tag along on Mr. Harding's pending adventure. Colonel Clay is based in Riyadh, our end of the operation will be run out of the CIA station in our embassy in Kuwait City. Colonel Clay does not need to know everything. It is obvious that Mr. Harding knows the CIA and SIS, Henry are piggybacking on the Caliber operation. And yes Robert, it is very apparent that Caliber is a CIA invention. You both had time to read the transcripts from last night—Good."

"John, this girl, Sara Bolino, had quite a good time with Hardy last night. She is really of no interest to my people back at Langley at this late stage of the game. When Hardy gets over to the Middle East we are going to have our hands full—the Bureau too. Oh, and yes, you do have two FBI agents stationed in Kuwait City now?" asked Robert Torres.

"Yeah, Robert, actually we have up to six when we need them. Pull them over from Riyadh. The human element, like your man Hardy, who you still officially deny running by high-tech influence? Like you, we do most of the important stuff back here in the states, the real big analysis if in D.C."

I've decided to have Special Agent Tenza and Special Agent Reading hand the Bolino file over to the GBI. Let the State of Georgia worry about Sara and her brother's construction company. From what I understand, they are targeting the old man anyway. The restaurant. Cash through the bistro, naturally. We are going to have our hands full. Oh, Henry, you will keep us abreast of your activities? No more surprises on our soil please."

"A trade off actually John, in exchange for the backdoor gossip on Caliber. I get the info which comes through the front from Whitehall."

"Oh gentlemen, DNN has been more than accommodating. Cards close to their chess. A trade off for the inside dope when the story breaks. Didn't push it when the GBI would not give anything up. Oh, and by the way Robert, Hardy was nice enough to play the Socialists back against the Sicilians, I've arranged to have our own *problem children* assigned to give the GBI a hand. Be nice to have a few of the 'Shithead Division' wedged between the Mafia and our people. If they live, they can have their jobs back."

"So our man Hardy got a little present last night, Robert?"

"It's the new laptop by Apple, closer to a notebook. It came with a pocket calculator. Nice package. I am sure it has a little extra something inside. He had a rough night last night after he dropped Miss Bolino off. He called Pam Wellington about ten o'clock this morning. It looks like they are going to spend the day together on Saturday. Should be fun. We delve into the erotic sometimes back in D.C. too. Makes the day fun. Hope they'll have nice weather."

"So what do you have, Henry?"

"Actually old boy, I'd like to trade you Hardy for one of ours. Your man no one admits to owning is pretty damn good. Caliber wants him there. Wants him bad, wants him in place. Some of his union brothers will be in Iraq to tuck him in bed at night. Thank God we don't have a labor union like the CWA in Britain. He's a damn good player. Damn good at the human element in the spy game. Plays the game well."

"Robert?"

"He is good, John. About the best I've seen so far."

"The spy game, Henry? What will you be up to now?"

"I have people I can use. A little of the George *Smiley* thing. Go out, explore. Maybe you toss us an occasional file. I will have one of my men approach the case as a writer. Just out looking for something to write about, tap away at the old typewriter. Good cover. They will freeze up if they hear FBI. They will never suspect a Brit. Pretty much how we do things. SIS then has an in with the book agent, publishing company, a few avenues along the way. You share, I share...Damage been done. This is just clean up. If your little Southern Spy Affair went the other way, we all be getting a spanking and you would be taking orders from your 'Shithead' division."

"Thank God about that."

"I would not worry too much, John. I overheard the DCI say one day that his Deputy of Covert Operations plays too rough. Damn if he didn't snap his fingers before he said, 'Oh well, just too scared to fire him,' before George went snickering down the hallway. Something about covert auto accidents. You know me, why dig into any affair which does not concern you. Actually we like problem children, John. We have a little fun with them before they leave the CIA for better careers. If we really like them, we let them scap a document or two, then play them back as modified doubles before your people grab them and toss them in jail for twenty years. We pretty much let them set up the KGB.

Documents? You have to give something up sometime. I would not worry too much about your 'Shithead Division,' John. Shit happens."

"Henry?"

"The same, John. We eliminate our problem children in the U.K. John, I would not worry. It happens sometimes. The Mafia will do most of your dirty work if you look the other way. These clowns are liabilities now."

"What is the story with the French and Israelis, gentlemen?"

"Hardy's friend Covic really upset these people. Hardy most likely knows why on a subconscious level. In other words, he has not put the riddle or information together yet. I suspect it is not just the technology, John. Covic got into sensitivities, he really stepped on peoples' toes. It's a wonder he is still alive."

"Henry?"

"The same, John. Sometimes it's not that someone absconded with the Queen's jewels but that he caught the Crown Prince sleeping around. Could be he caught onto some cabinet minister doubling for the Russians and doing call girls. The type of information that a president or prime minister does not want exploding under their seat. Sometimes you deal with the minister and play the doubles game instead of facing scandal or the threat of your government failing. Both France and Israel would do the same at times. Israel? Could be the technology. So damn small, she needs every technological advantage she can steal to keep the wolves at bay. It could be technology if it is the Israeli angle."

"The French and the Israelis John are the eternal odd couple in the intelligence world. Though not quite as rocky a friendship as they would have everyone believe. Vichy. They were rough on the Jews, so they feel guilty, the guilts, and toss Jerusalem a bone every once and awhile. The same for Jerusalem. The French have been the Holocaust whipping boys, unfairly at times, so Jerusalem tosses a few issues of importance their way. Their legendary feud over the years makes good cover for their covert friendship. It works out well for both governments. The French are always playing 'good cop/bad cop' for us. The State Department loves them."

"Don't trust the French Robert? No more Tel Aviv?"

"The French are going to play the role that they have always played throughout the Cold War—good cops to the bad guys. They are real good in this role. The Russians know it and they have a love/hate relationship with Paris. The Israelis? About the same. Only their government and the mind of their intelligence community are often at odds. The Mossad will play the traditional role that they have always played. Expect this intrigue when Hardy gets over there. And yes,

Jerusalem. Jerusalem whether or not we like it. Jerusalem. I have a minor in Middle East diplomacy.

"What's next Robert?"

"His date with Pam. It will be fun to tag along. The boys. We should keep a real close eye on the bar crowd at Mountainberry's. Hardy had a lot on his mind before Sara Bolino jumped into his lap but his friends were all there. Surveillance said he woke up in cold sweats last night. Interesting. Drugs? Poisons? Stress? Even more revealing, he called Pam Wellington in the morning instead of Sara Bolino. This is going to be a hot affair. My bet is that Miss Wellington will lay a head trip on Hardy. They both have egos. Hardy never had a TV journalist, Miss Wellington has never bedded a spy. Fireworks are about to happen. At least that is my guess, John."

"Henry?"

"I agree with Robert's assessment. John, the socialists?"

"They were pretty rough on Hardy. Came right out of the woodwork after him—from the arts to the psychiatric community. All because of his politics. Mostly because he was CIA and out in the cold. Circled around him like wolves Henry. I have never seen anything like it. When the spy affair exploded, the Mafia started hitting them instead of Hardy and his friend Covic. Scum. We have our hands full of Wall Street run amuck, but these Socialists are so creepy that not even the liberals like them. I felt bad that we had to target Hardy. His relationship with Don Fusaro-Debanadetto, we had no choice. The same for Savannah Telephone. I felt bad, but what can you do? Good people almost went down with the ship. Damn Socialists. God, I am glad you are on board Henry. It's out of my realm, Henry. Robert?"

"Better to use SIS than run a legal CIA covert operation on American soil. Hardy is one thing. No one can prove Hardy is ours. But if we run covert operations here in Atlanta and it goes wrong, the American public would crucify us. If SIS gets snared, we just have the State Department to send a nasty letter to 10 Downing Street. Two weeks later, Ms. Albright will be breaking biscuits with Robin Cook in London over tea. No big deal. London would be creative in their explanation."

"We have played this role before, John. No big deal if one of your Special Agents does not look the other way when he is suppose to and one of my lads got caught with his hand in the till. We'll explain it at some level or label him a Russian. The people I will use to clean up these Socialists are deep, deep cover. More CIA—the CIA like Hardy than SIS. It's damn hard to trace them or prove that they're mine. Like Hardy, but with a distinct British flavor. These Socialists? They've been Polarized. Toss out a document from the past of this affair and they will attack it like a hungry rabid pit bull. They have to now, or we will have them for dinner. If they don't, we have them for dinner anyway. It should be fun. Robert, let the DCI know how much I appreciate Langley letting my people have all the fun."

"The old: *What is London doing on my turf*, Robert?"

"That is about the extent of it, John. Some thinktank at Langley is most likely already preparing the needed documents and scenarios to send to the State Department should Henry's men fall victim to one of your guys or the GBI. New York State Police too. Hardy will be dancing around Manhattan before he leaves. There could be a problem in New York. We stung their guys a while back, they are looking for pay back. Hardy is pretty much a declared agent even if we still deny that he is ours."

"I will have the New York Director of the FBI put the word out to NYPD and State Police, hands off where Mr. Harding is concerned. I think Schrillo is still there?"

"Trevor could be a problem, John."

"Henry?"

"Do your boys really need to dig into Trevor? Not just SIS, Caliber too. Oh, Caliber is CIA, but we are sharing everything."

"Jennifer, bring me the file on Trevor Caldwell. I will have it sealed gentlemen; *Classified, eyes only.*"

"Socialists, John! I haven't been this excited since Dublin decided to be our satellite against the IRA. There is a price to pay when you ply treachery against one's government. I am only so glad to be able to help your government out. I plan to have fun. Hold these KGB *illegals* over an open flame. Your Smokey Mountains?"

"Both you guys be careful. The Israelis are real hot over this."

"We know the sensitivities at play here, John."

"I know, Robert. This is your domain, but this is my field office. I do not want to get burned over this. Last item, Kevin Slyer?"

"Seems pretty honest, John. More Army than phoneman. Caliber is shadowy because we built their legend that way. They are actually pretty clean for a company we are piggybacking on. Just enough of a legend to tell the bad guys, *if you fuck with us you are going to get hurt!* Most of the people at Caliber I have studied are pretty nice guys. Outlaws with a cause."

"About the same, John. British Telecom has a big presence at Caliber. Robert is right, no need to worry about the personnel at Caliber. If they break a law or bump some poor lad off, do we really want to know?"

"Yes! But not directly. We cannot do anything on Saudi soil. They would not let us anyhow. Henry, Robert, the only problem I have with you guys is every time lawmen and spies play together, covers get compromised. There are real problems here. I do not want any of my people killed. You know about the Israelis, the French are equally furious. I have concerns here. I have big problems from this mess Hardy left me with.

Jennifer, when you get a chance, see that agents Tenza and Reading have this file sent over to the GBI. Okay guys, let's go have lunch. I'll buy."

"Good morning Mr. Harding, Eleanor Knoll, Senate Subcommittee on Investigations. Sorry I did not catch you when you were home. Mr. Harding, you should receive two certified letters in the mail return receipt, in a couple of days. One will be from our subcommittee, the other from the Senate Subcommittee On Intelligence. We would like your presence when our Joint Select Subcommittee hearings get underway in a couple of weeks. If you could, when you get in, give us a call back. Thank you."

Like most lone wolves preparing for a winter's mission, Hardy was out hunting and gathering that morning. Breakfast at The Brick Oven was filling but as much as Sara tried to light the eternal flame of a predator, Hardy went away in spiritual need of a romance left unquenched.

He had talked ever so briefly with Pam that morning, leaving his inside burning like a hot piercing sword had torn away his heart. The emotions had scared him. Sara for all her efforts and talents of the evening before was only transparent in Hardy's desires. Just another waitress who brought him a bowl of fresh fruit and berries for his morning brunch. Had it not been for her need for information, and her obvious understanding she was about to be dumped, Hardy may as well have been a victim of a sharp kitchen utensil from behind the doors of where Sara's father barked out orders.

It was of thoughts of Miss Wellington like a sixth grade boy with a case of puppy love over his tender teacher, knowing any course of action was the wrong road to be on, that carried Hardy off that day to the art district of Atlanta to clear his mind of what he so desperately desired but dare not to admit to. It was more than physical or ego, Pam had teased a nerve, stirred an emotion, that had long since been buried since the time of the pain of Monique, and his crushing defeat of romance at the hands of a beast. Who now ravaged the one he loved on some far off island in the Caribbean. It was there in Atlanta's version of SoHo, amongst the antiques and nudes, Hardy knew in his heart, Iraq or war, he needed to know if Pam were his she-devil or angel of mercy. A heart on fire of man facing a mission of life or demise; a confusion of love on the dawn of lone wolf heading off to the wilderness to make war with a beast, or at least help contain him. *Bury my soul amongst the paintings, let my spirit wander the portrait down the path and disappear by the lake. Make love to me Pam, or release my ghost to go die in the desert.*

"Excuse me Sir, do you like the work? It's called 'Nude Walks A Flowered Path,' by Robert Cancade."

"Very much so. It reminds me of a meadow I know out on Lake Lanier. I go there sometimes to rest the soul, or with a lover. It is very romantic. I have a date on Saturday, I may take her out there. Bring some cheese and a blanket. Crack open a bottle of wine, spend the afternoon talking. It is quiet, peaceful. I think she will like it. Robert Cancade, is he very popular?"

The girl at the gallery was sweet and very attractive. Had it not been for his affection of Pam, Hardy surely would have had another flame to be tossed before his appointed time in the Gulf.

He parked out in the far end of the lot near a grove of hardwoods. A summer's mist had cooled the air and dusk was quickly becoming dark. To his left in the woods could be heard the cooing of a couple of raccoons, their young not far off. Though it was late in the season and Hardy's thoughts drifted back to his journey in.

When he reached two ornamental pines, Junipers, that maintenance had landscaped, he noticed a light on in his studio and felt silently in rage. Hardy always prided himself on his little apartment, which he kept like one of these rooms that could be found at a classy Savannah bed and breakfast. While other men would adorn their quarters with baseball posters, beer cans or the latest firearms, Hardy's was kept spotless and had an array of antiques one could let his mind wander about; still others, adorned with lace of his late mother's crafts. He had seen so much combat in his day, he now needed a soft sanctuary where he could lay out in comfort. The thought of maintenance coming in without him being home or not letting him know ahead of time, made him absolutely furious, on the verge of a personal eruption.

The sweet smell of perfume filled the air when Hardy entered his Bed and Breakfast to find Jill spread out naked amongst the antiques and lace wearing only a thong, beckoning for Hardy to fulfill her needs and let her wash the memories of Sara from his mind. It was not Sara she was in competition with, and it was at that moment Hardy was ever so glad he had voice mail and not an answering machine. Hardy was furious!

"Get your clothes on," he said as Jill's naked form moved to Hardy and unzipped his pants. "No! I do not want you here," he said, moving her hands away from his cock.

"It's been a week Hardy. Why didn't you call? Hardy, Sara is only going to use you. She is setting you up. She's fucking you for information. Hardy, don't think with your cock!" Jill was hot and her naked form was begging to melt into his.

"I know, what of it? It is a trade off! I told you when we started this fling that I would have to toss you;" Jill's hands had his cock out and her lips were meeting his to his angry rejection and his pending predicament, which Hardy now desperately needed to resolve. "Damn you Jill! No! Look, there are others. It is not just Sara. I have to leave. You're a sweet kid and a good reporter, Jill, I'm just out to have a good time," he said as their lips came together now in a torrent of lust-filled exchanges. "Damn you! Stop! It's not fair. Look, I'm breaking up."

Jill was now tugging at his massive namesake, "So tell me Hardy, does she give head as good as I do? Tell me hard-on! Is she as good with her tongue as me? I want you naked hard-on!" she said to a few more jerks of his affection, knowing he was building, knowing she was winning. "You want to break up, Hardy? Okay, let me leave you something to remember me by. Are you having trouble Hardy? Can you hold out hard-on? You want to fuck around on me hard-on? You like me as your lady Hardy? Now I'll be your whore," she said as she slowly kissed her way down his torso.

There was nothing Hardy could do when she took him in her mouth but let his clothes mingle with hers on the floor, watching her while she affectionately worked to his pleasure to wash the sins of Sara Bolin from his soul.

Hardy stood back and enjoyed his stalker's affections, his hands gently playing with her hair as they rested on her shoulders, stopping her once as he neared his point of no return to bring her up to where his lips and hers would meet for a season; a gentleman's thank you for the pleasure he was receiving. Then allowing her to go back down and finish her sabotaging of his love life.

Jill had talent, and it was that talent which brought about his explosion and carried them off to bed.

Jill's form seemed to melt into the white down comforter, while she slowly played with Hardy's affection, gently kissing his neck and resting her head upon his chest.

"I have to leave at one o'clock. Can I tie you up once before I go? It'll be fun in the candle light," Jill said, softly kissing and teasing as she went along.

"No."

"Hardy, tell me about Caliber. Who is Kevin Slyer?"

"Sara's a slut for bedding me to get her brother off the hook, and you want to know about classified matters?"

"That's right," she said, gently tugging at his cock and kissing his neck.

"No, you cannot tie me up to the bed posts, but yeah, we have time to go a few more rounds before I toss you after you get your revenge. And no, you cannot know about Caliber."

"Why not? Sara's a slut and I'm better than her in bed."

"Because. And I want you on top this time."

Donna Guererri was shuffling papers and reading CEO Jeff Dylan's itinerary when the fax came through standing the hair on the back of her neck straight up. Ray Jones of Digital Atlantic Telephone had sent a little love note to CEO Dylan, essentially saying: *I love you, now cut your own throat.* As most women in a panic attack, she did not know what she should do first, run to the ladies room or pop a Prozac. As it was she picked up the phone and called her boyfriend Dennis, knowing that the head of Savannah Telephone would not be back until 4 P.M.. She was deciding how to covertly leave the building to rendezvous with her married lover without having her boss and lynchman of Wall Street shoot her, the messenger. She serendipitously laid the document on his desk while doubling up on Prozac, and went off to screw her lover, who on advice from his wife was about to dump her. Something about two kids, a bed, a pair of shears, and having what he loved best tossed down the kitchen garbage disposal.

"God Damn that man! Who does Ray Jones think he is! I ought to tell him to go write another screenplay and get the hell off of Wall Street politics! At least let him worry about Digital Atlantic Telephone. God damn competitor!"

"You know Jeff, it would not be a bad idea to fly Hardy up to Washington on your Lear. Make it look like you are on his side. If it ever comes out that you were going to put a contract out on him and his loved ones, God, you know what is going to happen. Look, not only that, you were going to use the South Americans and blame Don Fusaro-Debenadetto for the deed. Be reasonable. Befriend Hardy with baited breath, make it look like you are on his side now. It's a silly misunderstanding. What does he know anyway?"

"William, if he ever learns that I was fucking his childhood flame, Monique for five hundred an hour, he'll kill me! God help me too, if one of these select senate subcommittees finds out. Just the flavor in the wind and they'll crucify me! And that goddamn beast of a friend Covic! First he comes in and guts me, then Hardy moves in for the kill. Goddamn those people."

"Look Jeff, I've asked around D.C..The official line from the CIA and the Pentagon is that they never heard of Hardy, as they go walking away chuckling to themselves. What do you want me to do Jeff? It is obvious that Hardy is their man. What can we do? We cannot prove it. Even the CIA do not know the group who are running him, or influencing him. You tell me, what do you want me to do?

You know what I say? Have Oscar fly him up on your jet after he's had a couple of double scotches and hope for the best. Befriend him Jeff. Could be your son-in-law someday. I hear Amy has a crush on him. Play it cool; take him under your wing. Then, someday when times are smooth and issues are resolved, do him in. Amy will have her hands full with your grandkids by than. You can comfort her and play the understanding father—just make sure it is a *carrier* you have no stock in when it crashes."

"I'll think about it William, but I want you to have Donna get off a real sugar coated 'fuck yourself' letter to Ray Jones. You tell that over educated *S.O.B.* to worry about his own phone company. Oh and William, when you get a chance, have one of your boys tell my daughter to stop this Dylan with a "K" nonsense. Thanks."

"I'll take care of it boss. I will have my nephew Ernie take care of it. She likes Ernie, I will have him take your daughter to a movie."

"Good, that over-sexed spy has his plate full these days. I do not need Mr. Harding playing mind games with my little girl. Look, I know my daughter is no angel. I do not need to come home however, and find them naked in bed! I appreciate it William. I will toss you some *options* when the time comes.

But you know what is scary, William? Hardy, he thinks like me."

"I will take care of it boss."

❖ ❖ ❖ ❖ ❖

"Our man Hardy has been having a lot of fun these past few nights. Tomorrow or Sunday he has a date with Miss Wellington," then John Blacke continued. "Henry, it is official, SIS is to have all the fun. DCI agrees Robert, best to let SIS do the clean up. I also received this classified document by secure fax this morning. Both of you take a minute and read this. You both did have a chance to read about yesterday's escapades?"

"That is what I love about our man Hardy. One moment he will put on classical music, the next punch some guy in the nose, then in the afternoon we will find him balling some wise guy's daughter over a bottle of French wine. Likes Rock and Roll , likes the Arts," added Robert.

"The girl from *The Athens Post,* problem here?" asked John Blacke.

"Maybe. She's a reporter and she likes him a lot. She likes the story. The confluence of the news business. There could be a problem. Their sex is hot. I think Hardy is going to dump her," Robert said.

"Christ," as Henry turns, hands the fax to Robert and stares momentarily out the ninth floor window. "This could be a real problem, John. France or Israel. I was leaning Jerusalem, I think Paris is going to be more upset over this. I'm really not sure. You chaps do not think Mr. Harding has put this together yet? His ex-wife? This is very sensitive," added Henry.

"This is problems John. I suspect Hardy's career at Caliber is going to be a lot more dangerous than he knows. These people at Caliber are extremely sharp. Smart like Ph.D.'s, tough like long shoremen. We put these men together. I have studied them, tagged along on some of their adventures back at Langley. There are real problems here. Caliber also has contracts with our military throughout the world. They could send him out for coffee one morning and tell him to pick something up in Somalia on the way back. That is how these guys are."

"Should be quite an adventure gentlemen. We will have to follow it closely. I know Whitehall will instruct me to do the same."

"Last item gentlemen, Eleanor Knoll, senate subcommittees, Intelligence, Investigations...."

CHAPTER
4

It was a small house, what one might refer to as a ranch, big picture windows lining to front, as it rested on a hill overlooking this very affluent part rural Georgia just north of Atlanta. Beneath a pine atop a wrought iron post sat a lantern illuminating the drive when Hardy pulled in. A cat scurried past, dodging his front high beams. In the backyard played a skunk under a grove of oaks where a rope swing hung. Hardy wondered to himself if Pam was married once and had a couple of kids? Past the skunk, a big empty doghouse and row of wild roses.

Pam was wearing a black silk wrap top, modestly cut and a black leather skirt with black stockings when she came to the door. Her long black hair combed, her hand tilting it to one side. Not ready for a cocktail party, but she was not on her way out camping either. The inside of her home was decorated modern, though comfortable. Everything had it's place. If not for the pines and fine trimmed lawn outside, one might get the feeling he was walking in to a penthouse suite in Trump Towers in New York, or some fully refurbished loft in Greenwich Village. On the coffee table sat a copy of the latest edition of a Victoria's Secret catalogue. Beside it, a book on eroticism, mature sexual fantasy and romance; a coffee table book. The cover was black and white, and of Victorian age with a couple of nudes dancing about. Oddly it fit in well with the rest of her surroundings. Her place was modern but well lived in, and very comfortable. It was quite elegant.

"Did you have any trouble finding the place?"
"No, good directions."
"Come on in. Anything to drink? Wine?"
"OK, one. Some ice water on the side."
Pam poured a glass of white while Hardy had a seat on the black leather couch and pondered which coffee table book he should thumb through while he waited. But covers, and good common sense, he let the books lie.

Pam came over, handed Hardy his wine and water and sat down in the matching chair next to Hardy at the far end of the coffee table.

"Pam, I feel really bad. I already have two girlfriends too many. It is not very fair. Twice the heartache soon when I leave. This weekend? Maybe it would be best to call it off? I have my hands full lately, you are already not a meaningless relationship, or we would be. You know what I am trying to say?"

"I know Hardy. I have my spies too. Mountainberry's, and Jill likes to talk. We swap a lot with the *Post*."

"Jill is using me, Sara for a different reason. And it is fun for a gentleman to have his way with a few different ladies when he is leaving and ground rules have been set; Sex, lies and secrets. Or at least whatever they glean from my soul by theft or trickery. Both girls are talented and a lot of fun to be with. But we would not be sleeping together if it were not for this crazy situation. We all would have lovers and loved ones to hold at night had this spy affair never surfaced. We are all only whores consuming each others flesh for gain. The girls and I, we are the same. Only I have a cock.

Pam, I have already developed feelings deeper than lust for you. Monique. After we talk the other night. Have a roll in the hay? a fling? when I have to leave soon? You know what I am saying, and I already need a bigger backseat."

"I hear the buckets fold down Hardy," taking a sip of wine and gently laughing to herself.

"Pam, it would not be right. It is not lust and you do not play fair. If you need background for your show, or a story you are covering, we can talk on the phone."

"Love..?"

"Not yet, but I am sure it would be. Now? Deep feelings a gentleman should not have for a lady he has only met? Dated...? Kind of...? The other girls tie me up to the bed posts and torture me awhile till I toss them some tid bit of value or two. It works both ways. But the only emotion we let burn is what we share between our thighs. Look, the girls would not be doing this nonsense if not for this spy affair."

"How do you know I don't like fun, bed posts and silk neckties Hardy? Could use the inside scoop on this story as well," Pam said with one of these smiles a lady has when she knows she has just bedded and married her lover if she dare chooses so.

"Burn a lady's flesh? OK. Burn her heart? I am not into cutting a cross into a lady's soul just for sport Pam. Though it is nice to get to know your lover a little before you sleep with her. If we do this weekend, it would be for sport. We could come back in love. I have to leave, and I have had enough tragic love in my short life time.

Pam my entire life has been an endless cycle of tragic love. Starting with Monique, my ex, and few other tried relationships; lovers from hell. You and I would not be just a fling. I'm here, you can interview me. Professional and friendly?"

"What if I don't want professional and friendly Hardy? What if I am willing to take the chance? Friends. We can handle friends."

"OK, friends. Do you always leave a handbook on Victorian eroticism laying around for friends to see?" Pam was smiling wylely and took another sip of her wine. "Friends. But you don't play fair. I can handle friends, and we both know we are playing a dangerous game.

Picnic Sunday? The weather is suppose to be nice. We'll spend the day, talk. I know a nice place for dinner afterwards. Sound good?"

"Ok, Sunday. You bring the wine, I'll pack the lunch. You eat light? I have to: TV."

"Sure."

"Now, I have these documents, which came into my possession from corporate..."

The kiss at the door had lasted longer and had been sweeter than it should have been. Landing somewhere between bed me tonight and flirtatious friends, who leave and go back to their respective lovers. It had played on Hardy's mind the long drive home that evening and a better part of Saturday, when he tried to focus on a game of one on one with one of the local kids of his complex in the courts by the pool that afternoon. It was now Sunday morning, the church bells of the Bible Belt rang out as he took a slow drive over to her place; Pam still delicately etched across his mind like a ballerina and her lover dancing magically atop a music box, his mother's music box; Friday's midnight kiss cutting his soul to shreds.

Women make such natural and good double agents were the thoughts playing on his mind, and how he did not want to use Pam like the others; throw-away lovers for tricks, sex and a trade-off of information, which usually lead to hot sex before self-destruction of their respective lives. Fuck me, bed me, now let me try to kill you. It was the games he was tired of, and now scared of, of which he now wanted so desperately to avoid with Pam. Knowing he had cast his dagger in one too many hearts already, and knowing his had either been by now surgically removed, wounded fatally, or now bleed inside him black. *How many times should a man die in romance?* were his thoughts, as he made the final turn in to her cul-de-sac.

It was eleven-o-three by his watch when he pulled in to the drive. The finely kept yard missing a cat and an evening skunk asleep for the day. Pam still readying herself motioned through one of the picture windows for Hardy to come right in.

It was elegance and the upbringing of a lady not quite ready for her date with a lover of destiny; a lady journalists caught in the pains of an afternoon date, not quite sure in which style to dress, falling somewhere between farmers daughter, the great ball and glass slippers, or, Pam, you're on in three minutes, which drove her to a frenzy in the bath and captivated Hardy's thoughts while he thumbed through Victorian eroticism.

When Pam finally emerged from her sanctuary she had taken Hardy by surprise and he took a step back in personality. She had caught him off guard, and her beauty had made him a little insecure. Sara was beautiful, so was Jill, but nothing like this. Monique. Monique had come back to torture his soul and was now taking on the image of TV journalists to burn his flesh.

Pam was a lady of ladies. He knew she learned her poise from a life of not only culture but of naughty pursuits as well. Daddy's little girl is such a lady, daddy's little girl would never do that. When you know damn well she has. Hardy wondered to himself as he tried to regain his composure, of what kind of naughty endeavors Pam was party to when she was in school those many years before? Though he was sure he could guess.

"Are you OK?"

"Yeah, I just seemed to have gotten my hand stuck in eroticism between pages sixty-seven and sixty-eight," Hardy was just smiling and trying his best not to give a school boy blush.

"Good thing you did not reach sixty-nine. Ready?"

"Sure," though Hardy was not quite sure by the way Pam was dressed if the picnic was still on. Pam was wearing a white peasant top with a floral print earth skirt with mauve inlay. Still she looked a bit over dressed for a picnic in the woods.

"They're old clothes Hardy, lets go," she said as she handed him the basket and held on to a half gallon blue water cooler with her left hand.

It was a sleepy Autumn day that morning when they pulled out in Hardy's fun mobile, the gentle breeze making love to Pam's hair. Seducing her and highlighting her would-be lover behind the wheel. On the radio played the latest pop. It was sunny and warm but a bit cool, to top out around seventy-nine according to the DJ in his rudeness between songs. A good day for a romp in the woods, or a blanket in the meadow. It was fun, sleepy warm romantic fun on a nice cool warm sunny day. The haziness between seasons when the weather seems to seduce young lovers; the Spring fever, which reappears in the dawn of Autumn.

"Where to Hardy?"

"Lake Lanier. You like picnics?" knowing she had and eyeing the canvas bag she had with her.

"I have a bottle of Chardonnay and a bottle of of Médoc. You have a couple of wine glasses in that bag with the rest of the goodies?...Just checking. I have a couple of backups in the trunk just in case," with that, Hardy just let the morning air weave its magic.

The drive was sweet in the Georgia air, washing away time and years from their soul. Hardy found a place to park near a small deserted private beach. Oddly enough it had been the same lovers lane Pam had danced at with various lovers from her younger past. It was a sleepy little park with a couple of Weeping Willows guarding the waters edge. In front to the left a bit, leading out between the trees and the car, a small trail opened up past the willows skirting the shoreline and a handful of rocks the fishermen would stand on to cast for bass. Beyond the rocks the trail turned up a bit to a grove of hardwoods and a meadow just beyond. A certain déjà vu and security filled the soul of both Hardy and Pam; the enlightened knowledge of sexual desire of deniability. Knowing they had both played here in their young adulthood, not knowing how far they should go.

The winding of the trail seemed to weave a seduction through the soul of both Hardy and Pam. Suspending Hardy effortlessly between love and beauty while Pam's form stopped to toss some bread to a handful of ducks and a couple of Trumpet Swans; the breeze playfully tugging at her top, the swans demanding their dinner al fresco. Not far off they reached the clearing.

Little purple flowers lined and filled the meadow giving it a lavender tint; a lovers soft purple haze soothing their souls and hoping to witness the seduction its fairies were weaving on two reckless lovers, who had not the common sense to avoid the enchantment of this lovers paradise contained within a fabled woodland meadow. Two grown adults entering into a world where only teenagers should tread with no defense against an army of Autumn enchantment. They both knew they were damned when they reached the clearing and the purple glow.

Pam tossed about the blanket, then readied the lunch of fresh fruit, cheese and crackers. Hardy played with the cork screw, pulling open the Médoc first. Then they both settled down, playfully finger sampling with the grapes, strawberries and delicate cheeses. Hardy looking like the groom about to receive his first piece of cake; then quiet. Sipping wine and quietly gazing into each others eyes. Hardy knew, Hardy had made a living of survival by reading other peoples faces. "Monique...?"

"Tell me about Monique, Hardy. I want to know. It would be good for your soul. Let me help exercise your demons. Tell me about her. I know you are in pain. I saw it back at my place. I remind you of her a little?"

"A little," and Hardy took a sip of wine. "Monique...Monique and I grew up together for a short time in Highland Falls. As Army brats we were pretty lucky. Dad for much of his career was stationed at West Point. Oh, I don't know, seven years? We spent a good deal of our lives in the Hudson Highlands of New York. Monique was the little girl next door until one day you step out your front door and you realize the tomboy you use to wipe the snot off of is now the beautiful young lady you desire. I was four years older. Monique was sixteen that morning, I was a young buck of twenty on my way to work. I too use to turn heads and break a lot of hearts in those days."

"She knew?"

"Yeah, she knew. I tried to avoid her, she would just come down to the gas station, the Sunoco where I worked. We would get a lot of tourists back in those days going to the Point, or to the Wine Cellar, a popular restaurant. Any way, she would ride her bike down in one of those skimpy halter tops and just hang out, hang out all over me. I was twenty, she was too young, kind of. You get the idea. She had me bad. She was a fast learner at a young age, she could see my condition and would drive me nuts. It was a very hot summer that year.

The summer of seventy-seven, Dad was sent overseas for a while, Europe, I think? Dave was down South and I was holding the place down pretty much on my own. Mom had died two years earlier. Dave had gone back to Georgia, and my little sister Debbie had just graduated from high school. Debbie was Monique's best friend.

Like I said, it was a long hot summer and than one night in August, just after her seventeenth birthday, Monique limped her way into the station. Her bike had a flat. It was dusk, my shift was ending, and Monique needed a ride home. I finished up and she hopped on the back of my Harley, a hand-me-down from Dave, and off we went. It was love at first feel. She knew, as soon as she wrapped her arms around me she knew she had me.

We cruised a bit. First down by the Wine Cellar and across the freight tracks, hung out at the river for a short time. Talking. Then back up to 9w and a side road turn off, which took us to the Point. We ended up on a bluff over looking Constitution Island where Gen. Washington had his men stretch a great chain to keep the British from coming up the river during his war.

So there we were, surrounded by old canon and history with Monique flirting and dancing all around in her skimpy halter top. The two of us playing like little kids. She grab my backside and ran down the path, down like a knoll. When I caught up to her down the hill her halter top was showing more than it should and she was sitting seductively straddling a small canon, the end of the barrel between her legs while she stretched forward like a stripper and kissed the mouth like, well you know. Good clean seductive fun. We kissed, she pushed me away and ran up the hill. I caught up to her at the mouth of a small tunnel, which links up to the parade ground, *Beat Navy* was painted boldly on the walls. We tumbled to the ground, a short time later we were making love behind some bushes just above the left side of the opening of the tunnel on a slight hill. It was all we could do from keeping ourselves from sliding down in the movements of our passions. Our love making echoed through the tunnel.

Our climax was intense. Intense for both of us. Oh, I don't know? we stayed there naked for a while. Than an MP came by. He thought we were cadets. He recognized me and sent us home. Debbie was out and Monique spent the night. She told her mom she was with Debbie. The next morning Debbie covered for her, covered for both of us.

We tried to keep it a secret, our age and race. But soon the whole village knew. Dave had some contacts and if I could finish up at Rockland by next summer, he could get me in the door at Savannah Telephone. The *craft*, it paid better than any job I could land with a degree."

Pam stuffed a cracker and some cheese in his mouth, "shut up, you need a break," and kissed him.

The cheese melted in his mouth, shortly after so did Pam, as they busily exchanged kisses and the warmth of each others bodies. Hardy with his hand sliding up and finding it's mark. Pam countering with a barrage of affection upon his lips while her blouse slowly slipped off revealing two very beautiful unclad breasts, which Hardy's mouth encircled, making love to each nipple one at a time.

As it was, it was best Pam's panties came off first and her skirt stayed on while Hardy passionately continued to make love to her breasts, exploring each other further in romance. Daring each other to go a little further like two high school virgins in the woods. When out from the hardwoods crashing through the meadow came a trio of would be Cub Scouts breaking up their passion strategically around four, though it could have only been two o'clock when the twelve year olds came across two lovers just before they were about to lose all their clothes.

Pam had thought to pack one of these red checkered table cloths, which Hardy made good use of covering up her naked flesh, as not to educate the boys before their time. He kiss her once and pulled up his jeans. "I remember that age once too," Hardy said, as the boys yelled, "wow, neat," and ran off into the woods to Pam's embarrassment.

"I didn't bring one Pam, I did not really expect to go this far. Sorry."

"It is the man's place to carry such items Hardy, I refuse to carry them. At least on the first date. Doesn't make sense... I can always say no, or lay a head trip on the guy. I'm late. I am careful with who I go out with and sleep with. Some times it's fun to play the head trip."

"You would do that to me..?" taking a strawberry and placing it in her mouth, than licking the juice off her naked breast again. I think you better put your top back on. Where there is three scouts there is more. Bass must be biting, the fishermen will not run off into the woods, and I did not bring any beer. It is only two thirty, we can talk for awhile," and he poured her glass of the Chardonnay to see which she preferred.

The table cloth to the side gently resting on her thigh, the strawberries rather ripe and the sweetness of Hardy's tongue on her nipple while the nectar squirted forth from each piece of passion fruit felt kind of pleasant, even if it threw Pam off her line of thought and seductive interrogation? Hardy, now a new born babe enjoying the bonding of a lover. But it was when he had come up for air that a revenge of an over ripe strawberry bursting in his mouth; the juices exploding all around like a teenage boy's first time, or a bride's revenge on her wedding day when the slice of cake should have fit but exploded all over a black tie instead, Pam found her payback and regained her line of thought.

And so it was with one hand on Hardy's cock, shielded by his jeans, and strawberry juice dripping down his chin that Pam resumed her questioning. Though Hardy's condition uncomfortable, and Pam could surely see his situation was obvious, and it felt kind of nice to have the great spy so compromised.

"So what is next Hardy?" and she gave his manhood a playful little squeeze.

"You do not have one so I guess we can't."

"That is not what I mean. Though the day is long and you may get lucky later."

"After Iraq? Someday I would love to play the George Smiley role. Do the traditional spy game. Maybe write. I am good in English, I have no creativity. After Iraq I have to continue to build my cover. They call it *real cover*. For instance, I am a phoneman, so my cover is telecommunications. If I become a writer, then my cover is 'writer' or 'novelist'. If I teach; 'teacher'. It is a little different than someone someplace in law-enforcement who goes undercover and pretends to be someone he is not."

"So if I work for the CIA, journalist would be my cover? I would just live a double life."

"Right. Some agents, what we call *illegals* are developed on the job, or through childhood. If an agent was developed through childhood he is called a *sleeper*, though there are different kinds of sleepers. Some just come over to America and forget their past for twenty years. Then one day everybody wakes up and plays a game, the great game.

"Illegals on the other hand, even more so if the are CIA, stay in place after the spy affair is over. Especially if their cover is not compromised. Others go back to sleep. How do you prove we are spies? CIA? Dead letter drops are far and few with the games we play. We tend not to want to get involved unless our instincts tell us so."

"Instincts?" giving Hardy another warm sensitive squeeze.

"Instincts. A higher form of psychology we use. Our psychology tends to be completely different from what most in law-enforcement use, or that which is practiced by the enemy and their *illegals*. Very different. Very high-tech at times as well. It is the damnedest thing, sometimes you just know.

The problem we had with some in law-enforcement was that some of the psychologists they were using for sting operations were themselves controlled by the KGB. Their field being a hotbed and bastion of liberalism. It is where the enemy recruits in this country. The professional community. Most times the doctor, or for that matter, his patient, thinks he is helping out the FBI. They call it *false flagging*. Sometimes law-enforcement will play a game with these people, and why not? Where they merge is social issues like street crime, drugs and gun control. Pretty much a friendly game of spy and the only ones who usually lose are the mob. But both groups tend to know the reality of the situation, even if these people still believe they are working for the FBI. The Feds watch, the KGB try to set us up. Like what happened here in Atlanta. These people may help out with street crime but they are real problems for us in the intelligence community. Socialists tend not to like NATO and have their own political agenda, which tends to be more friendly to Russia and other last bastions of Socialism and Communism."

"Communism?"

"You should know that Pam. The Communists still control the government and intelligence communities in Russia. One cold war rolls over into another. The Chinese are pretty damn sharp too."

"So you are now playing the KGB's people back against the Sicilians? That does not seem too fair Hardy. These people and their families may be killed;" moving her hand away and becoming journalist serious of a disapproving lover, or one about to suggest that this is not the best way to get lucky later.

"There is a price to be paid Pam when one adheres to a doctrine, which runs counter to United States national security. They get what they deserve. If the Sicilians now have a problem with these people, I will not interfere."

"'You bastard! You set these people up!" Pam said, with an angry but playful voice. "Ok, they're Socialists, why do you hate them so? You despise them! Why?"

"When I was forced out in to cold, almost to point of being homeless, this after Covic took off, the only friends I had were Joe and Carol. The Socialist were furious with Joe and Carol for looking out for me. They had two kids, a little girl by to name of Michelle, Michelle was nine. They also had a cute little boy by the name of Steven. He was a very funny and friendly kid. Kind of like a six year old Robbin Williams. Anyway, Joe was off one afternoon and I went over to hang out and have a beer. I settled for coffee. Down on the carousel, about one hundred and fifty yards away the children would play.

Well that afternoon Steven was playing with his friend Vincent. Vincent's mother was one of these social worker types, the cops would use undercover as *handlers*. Set the background and psychodrama of whatever sting they were working on. She was a Socialist. Well the kids are playing for a half hour and one of her friends stops by, another Socialist.

Joe and I are having a beer or coffee and shooting the breeze, and then we notice. Every time Steven moves to the right, one of these Socialist would confuse the boy, psychobabable. Steven moves to the left, they reward him. Praise. Then there was something with a large key chain one of the ladies was holding. Well, Joe and I both realized something was going on. We called Steven in. It was close to dinner time anyway.

The next day at the school bus stop the children's school bus pulled up but delayed putting his flashing red lights on. The children were busy playing, running every which way. There was about twenty kids at that stop. From out of no where comes a car speeding, doing about sixty. The speed limit in that complex was ten miles per-hour. Joe screamed at the kids. Instead of moving to the right, Steven moved to the left. His subconscious was looking for a reward. The car struck him and kept on going. Blood, bright red blood flowed from his mouth, ears, and nose. On the sides of his head were chunks of gray and liver colored matter, squeezed out through his ears by the impact. There was nothing we could do. To this day I cannot talk about it. I try not to think about it.

That's why. Children in the spy game are like the big store front windows the Mafia will break to secure protection money. The KGB just point out to their intended targets that they love their children very much, and if you should choose not to help us, your kid could be next. This is why I despise these people so."

"You were there?" tears welling in Miss Wellington's eyes.

"Yes, Joe had work for me that morning. I was there... It's getting late," but as soon as Hardy finished his sentence he found himself kissing Pam like a wife kisses a husband when he needs the pain of a lost loved one washed away.

It took awhile but the exchange of flesh filled desire had subdued Hardy's grief and he soon was holding Pam's naked flesh firmly enmeshed in his own. Sometimes, most times, women are the best at easing the pain us gentlemen suffer, who for the most part keep to ourselves. The kissing, the warmness of her body. The need to be held when the whole world falls apart around you. The emotions, which separate flings, women you toss, and those you wish to build a life with. The anguish one feels when he knows he is already damned in his future and abut to be exiled off to another world. Maybe even to his death. Much was traveling across Hardy's mind, as the breeze played with the hardwoods and the purple lovers glow of the meadow dimmed in the failing light of the late afternoon sun.

It was not the sex or the need to explode in climax, for surely their day was quickly coming to a close, but the need just to lie naked in her arms for awhile till the bleeding inside him had stopped. Steven had been his Godson.

They took a slow ride back, winding their way to peace around the sleepy curves of to lake. Pam resting her head on his shoulders. Hardy quiet but warm in thought. Pam had taken a steel rod from his heart at the end of the day. Here Hardy sat driving with a wife he just met a week ago. For surely Pam had given him comfort not even his ex of many years ago could come close to in compassion. Monique? Monique in his thoughts only brought forth tragedy and out of control emotional turmoil.

It was about seven when they pulled into Longo's. Vito Longo had met them at the door and seated them himself in a quiet little spot in the corner. The table just big enough, the candle light playing with the warm features of Pam's face, highlighting her soft affection.

"Hardy, how is'a that crazy friend of yours Covic? Tell 'em to stay in the Caribbean, Will you? You stay a'right here, I be a'right back."

"The wine, Don Fusaro-Debenadetto. He said dinner, on him."

"Let Don Fusaro know I will come over for cappuccino and espresso after dinner."

"He would like that Hardy. Now, you eat."

"So how did you learn to be a spy Hardy?"

"Dad was a Lt. Colonel, I was kind of born into it. When your dad is an Officer, you grow up army. It is in your blood; your family. You really cannot escape it. There was always some kind of game going on. I guess you can say I was a modified sleeper. The games started very young. In those years you think army, not spies. You learn fast."

"Talking in code?"

"Yeah, the usual stuff sons and daughters of Officers grow up with. You never really know who is listening. The enemy? You always used double meanings."

"Good, next newscast I will talk to you in code," and with that Pam playfully kissed Hardy over the reflection of the candle light.

"Excuse me sir, the wine is from Don Fusaro-Debenadetto. He would like a word with you before you leave. He knows you are with a lady. He has business, he will be here late."

"Yes. I have already spoken with Vito. I will join Don Fusaro after dinner. Let him know I will stop by after desert."

Longo's is not just any restaurant. It is a step up from a family establishment. The atmosphere most times is lit by gentle candle light, the dinners reasonable and the portions are big. If ever one were to visit Atlanta's Little Italy, Longo would be the place to go. Those of importance in the Atlanta's Italian American community are always in regular attendance during the weekends at Longo's Restaurant. One could easily fall in love in such a place, or one could sign a contract, construction or otherwise.

Hardy had ordered the veal parm, Pam the chicken marsala. The wine was of course the house best. A Sicilian deep red.

They talked romance, they talked about Covic, they lost each other in each others eyes. They avoided Monique. Pam was captivated about the tales of his dad. After dinner they tumbled their thoughts and desires over the last of Don Fusaro's wine, coffee and Grand Marnier. The food was good, just enough, and neither one could fit desert.

"I'll be back in a little while," Hardy said.

It was a short time after Hardy left that Pam found herself lost in thought wondering how he got this way? So confident so self-assured. Comfortable in sex and romance. As relaxed with a lover, as he is with the guys watching the game. How? Though knowing more about romance than a gentleman should, *Monique and his ex* she thought to herself.

Sex? She knew more. More than she was letting on to. Though with Hardy, what is the difference? He saw right through it that morning thumbing through Victorian eroticism. Beautiful women have beautiful problems, Pam knew she was no exception. She had her fair share of worthless trysts and lovers from hell, as beautiful women often do. But Hardy, Hardy knew more about romance than any man should, much more than any man she had ever been with, or shared a platonic friendship with. Too much for his own damn good, and it really turned her on. Again, she wondered, how?

And was it the wine playing on her spirits? she thought. She was warmly numb of both romance and desire. Not sure if it were the wine or Hardy playing gently on her soul, as it numb her emotions and further stirred her desires of a lover she now desperately wants to bed. Before her thoughts turned to how she would spin her plan into motion, pondering the lovers web she would weave to ease the emotional pain of a choreographed seduction; a lovers decision of how to secure her greatest, or at least at this moment, her favorite mistake, she played with the last of the flavored cognac, tumbling the glass between her fingers, which now once again longed for a return of a lovers ring.

"You're in love with him. I would be careful about Hardy."

Joni Cone was the hostess at Longo's three nights or four nights a week. Beauty had been her cross in life bear. She tried modeling a few times. Made it to the catwalks a handful of times completing her brush with fame, though falling short of Paris, and landing somewhere between France and Seventh Avenue.

But most of her modeling was done with her clothes off, like the many who brush fame's brow and fall back into the flesh abyss, missing that one little something which makes a supermodel, or tosses the lady back to break bread with the whores. Most of her modeling now was on her back, or with a few fill in dates with an escort service on her nights away from Longo's. Still again, her beauty was her asset as well as her wooden cross, her dates commanded a three hundred and fifty dollar an hour fee. Of which this callgirl would give her escort service their cut.

She had dated Hardy once. They were lovers for a time; Hardy getting freebies and willing to put up with the scene for a while. But it was her attitude and fondness for coke, Hardy tossed her, and tossed her hard. He had ended up in a B&B that very same weekend with Monique in Savannah. Joni had taken it hard. Though it was so damn tough trying to smear any misdeed on the legend, John Custer Harding. The truth be known, Joni was in love with him. Deeply in love with him. And when Hardy dumped her, she never really quite got over it.

"Your in love with him, aren't you? He'll be with the Don Fusaro-Debenadetto for a while—we need to talk. Your wine is just about gone, save the cognac for Hardy. He still loves his Grand Marnier. Let me get you some coffee."

As she waited for Joni to return' Pam glanced around the room, she had always prided herself of being a voyeur of people. She check the crowd, the place was full but not overly so and winding down. But it was her lover, or her soon to be lover, her eyes would always find their way over to. The place where Don Fusaro and Hardy talk quietly amongst the honored of Atlanta's Mulberry Street. Don Fusaro had three of his body guards keeping watch by the door not far off–A strange security Pam had never felt. But is was the freaky young German couple in the corner adjacent to Hardy and Don Fusaro, which caught her eye most.

"They're creepy," mentioned Joni, as she slid a fresh cup of coffee in front of Pam. "They have been here a few times before. Sometimes when Don Fusaro is here, sometimes when he is not. Tourists, they act more like stalkers. They are German, some kind of Green Party nuts. They seem a little extreme to me. I have no idea why they stop here, or why they are hanging around Atlanta. Olympic Park? I do not know. They scare me. Don Fusaro does not seem to pay them any mind, they scare me just the same. Than again, anyone with half a mind does not mess with Don Fusaro. Especially after Covic, and this damn spy affair that has spread across the South over the past few years. You did hear about the massacre?"

"Yes, I covered it. I guess the South Americans will not be messing with the Mafia again any time soon?"

Both women now laughed in low tones as best friends often do when sharing a juicy secret. The Godfather had dealt severely with the South Americans and his own who broke the code; sins, omerta, and you do not blame the traditional mob for your treachery. He was well aware when people spoke about him, even if he could not hear their whispered voices. The Mafia tend to have their own spies, it would be rude for the women to break a friendly omerta. In good common sense and respect, they kept their voices low.

The time went by, new friends became good friends, old friends by the time they explored the feats of an over sexed spy who was fortunate he had not been shot. They talked about men, they talked about sex, flings, naughty pursuits and X-rated endeavors. Both women were beautiful, both had their share of meaningless sex and love affairs from hell. Both had their tales of the darkside of beauty, of how gentlemen will give a leg up on a career. The mill of gentlemen's clubs, which so many get caught up in; trouble and trying to better ones self. A haven for quick money when a lady is down on her luck and is trying to dig herself out of misfortune. Pam had made it, misfortune was Joni. Joni had the better resumé should she need to return to the theater of the triple-x. Both women were stronger from their respective experiences. By the time Hardy returned, both women were not just old friends, but good friends and soul mates on the way to being best friends. By the obvious lurid tales spun by Joni, had it not been for the deep affection of his new found lover who she had been unable to bed yet, Hardy would have been in deep shit.

It was September and the night air had turned cool by the time they worked their way out of the restaurant and found their way to the car.

"I believe these are yours?" Hardy said, taking Pam's silk panties out of the pocket of his sport jacket he had worn for dinner. Pam smiled, moved close and kissed him while Hardy opened the car door for her. He had left the top down and Pam sat and waited patiently a few moments until it was raised back up and locked into place.

"Longo's, no one would bother it here. She looks pretty good all waxed up and decked out with the top down. I like to show her off Pam."

As they drove off Pam tugged gently at his arm and did her best to rest her head upon his shoulders, the bucket seats like a child demanding to cuddle between his parents spoiling the needed affection on a long ride home. But Pam was able to over come this obstacle with minimal discomfort and gently kissed his neck and ran her hand under his shirt and across his chest. She was now the wife gently pulling forth barroom dirt on the boys, or the sexy mistress of a double agent set out to stop his treachery, in this case his pending adventure to the Gulf. She wanted information and slowly devoured his neck like an ear of sweet corn. By the second attack of her affection Hardy gave in.

"We talked about Covic—this damn spy affair. We talk about my move to Iraq, and what my needs would be. He said, 'Covic was lucky he had let him live.' He said, 'the price Covic would have to pay, would be to come to my needs if I get into a jam.' Covic having skipped off to the Caribbean with way too much money for any man to enjoy, and my lover. Don Fusaro-Debenadetto said, 'Covic was to look out for me.'"

"Why?" and she again kissed his neck and kneaded one of his nipples with her long fingers.

"Stop;" Hardy took her hand and placed it by her side. "Covic was a beast but he was an honest beast. He wrote letters, he wrote some in code to the press. The whole world was reading Covic letters. He got pretty good, he became real good. He clocked all his enemies, highlighted this spy affair for the press. Everybody who was somebody was following his little exercise in creative writing. Then one day he wrote a letter, wrote the whole damn thing in code; double meanings. It was written to connect to someone, and it did. It connected to Don Fusaro-Debonadetto. Which advised him to keep his granddaughter home from school on a certain date.

Covic was good, he was damn good, and he was on to the KGB. The KGB were all over him. Covic apparently found out the creeps had surrounded some poor confused little shit, I think the kid was fourteen; just been dumped by his high school sweetheart, just lost his virginity, doing a lot of drugs, mother was religious, he went the other way; Marilyn Manson—devil worship. It was a combination of everything, drugs, just getting laid for the first time. The creeps surrounded the kid in one of these traveling psycho-therapy sessions/circus's the KGB are known for. They wound him up, gave him access to an assault rifle and pointed him in the right direction by way of psychology. He shot eighteen school mates in Don Fusaro-Debenadetto's granddaughters class. Maria had stayed home that morning, and was alive. 'No one disagrees or goes against Poppy,' she said when asked afterwards. I had delivered the letter personally to Don Fusaro the week before after I corrected his mistakes. It saved Maria's life. I later found out the cops after the shooting had done a drug test on the kid and found traces of prozac in the boys system. The KGB, the people they had used to handle the boy were no where to be found. Apparently once they programmed the boy with psychology they all pulled back and just let it happen. The kid was what we call an unconscious agent, or a programmed robot assassin. Very scary stuff. So often the KGB will let some poor confuse teenage boy or deranged nut do their dirty work. Maria and her friends were of course the intended targets. The Socialists did not like the way Don Fusaro-Debenadetto was falling out in this spy affair. It was more than a message, the KGB wanted to hurt Don Fusaro really bad. Don Fusaro-Debonadetto was falling out CIA.

Two weeks later six were found shot to death at Nicholson Psychiatric and Counseling Group. The seventh, a doctor was found beaten to death with a baseball bat. The KGB got the message! It was also just what U.S. Intelligence wanted. These doctors, who were eliminated were all key players in this spy drama. The KGB could not function without them, it crippled them bad. Real bad. A short time later their networks started to collapse. Don Fusaro-Debenadetto after the killings not only became the most feared godfather in the East, he also became a CIA asset. The FBI could not touch him.

The cops? They couldn't prove the psychology. They could not prove the Mafia had put out a hit on the doctors either. Though in both cases it was obvious. The FBI, however, tore the whole set of events apart but to no avail. Still this time their heart was with Don Fusaro-Debenadetto. They realized, they owed him one. Most doctors are *ours*, but still. They got what they deserved.

It had started to become a little foggy, a fine mist was filling the air and the windshield was steaming up a bit. Hardy now had to concentrate on the road. Pam was concerned more with Hardy. His discourse had made him very tense, emotion had flowed from his veins when he had been telling the story. Hardy now showed signs of stress and Pam desperately wanted to ease his suffering. She gently stroked his hair and then moved to unbutton his shirt another notch or two and ran her hand across his chest, resting her head upon his shoulders one more time.

It was still early and she let it be known she had some nice wine and cognac back at the house. She did not tell him about the ripe strawberries dipped in chocolate keeping cool in her fridge. Though perhaps they had had enough to drink, but Pam had a plan had the day gone well, and it did, and now was the time to secure her spy for a place in her life. Not even twelve-year-old Cub Scouts, or the anger of their timing when they happened by in the meadow would cheat her of Hardy's flesh. And perhaps it was best, she thought to herself, that she had taken Hardy to the edge and ended up in the arms of a naked lover confessing tragedy he would have had just a soon had erased from his life. Bringing her naked body closer to his and allowing her to run off with a part of his soul while denying him the sexual release, which would have freed him from her bondage.

"Damn twelve-year-olds," she said softly to Hardy and kissed his neck again while pondering to herself, *brats, and the tables are turned. No excuses, I have one. The first few times for safety, but you know damn well I know you play it safe. I will take you when you are really in need, and be with you on your adventure in Iraq, make the guilt pour from your soul should you tumble a whore. Or keep you here in Dixie to be mine only. We will see just how good you are Mr. Hardy. I have what you want, and you need it bad. I denied you your climax, or the brats did, and too much in emotion. But that is what you need more than an orgasm, to be held tight in my warm naked flesh and let me stroke the back of your neck like a mother with a little boy. You need love Hardy, and you toss for sex. You drive here besides me and you know you are dying, dying of need of love. I need love, I need your love. I want you Hardy. I have a four post canopy bed of fine linens. Do you want to fuck like a man and a whore, or do you want a lover to devour your soul? The psychodrama is mine Hardy, you take me any way you want. My bed, my room, my things, my life. After tonight I will leave my imprint on your soul. Take me spy! Have me anyway you desire! I know what you need and it is not sex. But our sex will make it more intense. Tonight I will have you spy! It will be on my terms now with no children picking purple flowers. Though I am sure our seduction will be mutual.*

They were now nearing her village and it would not be long till they turned off into her neighborhood. Pam quietly sensing Hardy's thoughts and not wanting the mood to drift away ran her hand across his bare chest between the folds of his shirt, and then resumed kissing what she so desperately desired. His neck was sweet and both her lips and fingers made love to it, her teeth nibbling away like baby ears of sweet corn. Hardy pulled into her drive and she gently kissed him one more time to relieve the stress.

"You damn near had me today in the meadow. Any man who gets his hands under my blouse, or where they should not be, usually has his way with me. And you, you held me naked in your arms." Hardy smirked, and Pam's only discourse was: "Damn kids."

The car stayed motionless in the drive, the lights on but timed to go out while a Madonna song, "Get Into the Groove," played on the radio. Pam again was making love to his neck, her right hand finding his cock, as she lead on with a series of kisses that seemed to last forever.

She glanced at the dash board clock, "It is still early, why don't you come in? I have some wine. Don Fusaro has made you tense...Not no, not yes, we can listen to music or something...?" and Hardy smiled.

"OK, something...?" and again he smiled.

And as he opened the car door and escorted her up the path to her front door, it was thoughts of the classic seduction Pam so desired to play on him, *and will he spend the night...?*

CHAPTER

5

Monique, Pam and the plane ride was pleasant, were Hardy's thoughts as he passed through gate 13 at Dulles International Airport. Jeff Dylan had sent Donna Guererri along as a peace offering to brief, and hopefully debrief Hardy on his testimony before the joint subcommittee. Hardy's discourse before half of Washington would not be very favorable to Savannah Telephone. Hopefully Donna could smooth the wrinkles and possibly Hardy's coarseness to some of the staff at Corporate. Donna was extremely attractive and Hardy had a fondness for beautiful women. Dave had taken a day off from his teaching post at Georgetown and it would be good to shoot the breeze with big brother and his wife over dinner.

"Dave! How's Bonnie and the kids? Bet the twins are getting big? And the three other ones?" and with that a pat on the back and a warm embrace of brothers.

"Let me take that from you Hardy. Have you heard from Dad? He's real proud of you Hardy. The company he is with is stationed in Brussels. Wants to retire."

"I have heard that. No, I have not heard from Dad. He hates voice mail. NATO, they have something to do with NATO? He is real busy Dave. Oh, Debbie, Peter and the kids are all doing well. Christmas every year at the LePrey's. Whether I like it or not."

"Hardy, you know I like Peter, it's just he is armed to the teeth. Dad never raised us like that. Look, you and I out hunting birds at the old farm in Mahopac, or deer in Orange County, but we really respected the guns, or Dad took off the old belt. Remember that day? Christ, we were fourteen, you were, I was seventeen."

"Yeah, couldn't sit for a week. Thought he'd kill us. Good thing Beau, that old German Shorthaired Pointer grabbed his arm. Thought we saw the last of that dog that day."

"Oh, I have a great place to hunt ducks this year, the back of the new place. A little river, feeds into the Potomac. Oh Christ! I have to get you out of here. She is trouble. CHANNEL 22 News's best try at a Jennifer Lopez with fangs! Lets go."

"Woe, she has a nice ass. Besides, I like sexy lady vampires...Oh Debbie and Peter are going to look after the apartment when I'm overseas. $450 a month, I can afford that. She wants to use it as a guest house. I said she could, we get along great."

"Hang on, looks like we are going to be ambushed little brother."

"Mr. Harding is it true all the girls you bed are double agents? Dave did you educate your brother? Are you sleeping with journalists for information? Or is this how you are paying for your sex!"

Hardy was absolutely furious! Nice ass or not! The veins, bulging from his neck to the silent simmering of Dave's temper. "No Comment!"

"How about you Dave?"

Dave so angry the words could not come forth, so Hardy answered instead. "My brother has no comment too."

"Is it true CEO Dylan is seething at you? Did you break the law or did he?"

"He is apparently seething as I am right now. No. But perhaps you should ask him! You are not getting on my good side, Miss...?"

"Lopez."

"She is not related Hardy."

"Related to what?"

"It is not important Miss Lopez. Here is my cellphone number, give me a call tonight. We can talk then," with that Hardy and Dave made a sharp right into the crowd and disappeared to baggage. Though along the way Hardy did mention the batteries being dead and no need to recharge his cellphone till he found his way to New York in a week or two. But it was to Hardy's misfortune that Dave quickly brought forth the news; Vera Lopez is based in New York, and it was quite by fate that she was in Washington covering Puerto Rican independence issues when news of the hearings broke with the instant public demand that much of coverage be made open and not concealed behind senate closed doors. CHANNEL 22 by the fifth of September had advised Vera to stay put in D.C.. Friday the eighteenth had started out for Hardy with a bang and the only words spoken to brother Dave once the baggage was plucked from the carousel was the need Miss Lopez had for "a good stiff cock—with affection," as they lumbered out the main foyer to brother Dave's car. They had been both consumed with laughter since ditching Miss Lopez, fangs and all just past gate 13.

"Pam, it's Hardy. I know you are working, Dave has you on in the other room. After D.C. I go to New York. I'm sorry Kiddo, it's over. I have one too many Monique's in my life. You were quickly becoming more than just lust. It was not just a fling or a toss Sunday night. I usually do not stay until four in the morning. If I waited to tell you in person, I would not have been able to break up. I'm sorry I stood you up Thursday evening. Something did come up...but...You know? I'm sorry. I cannot take a broken heart to Iraq. I...I have to go. Bye."

Victoria Fusaro-Debenadetto Corizzi was just leaving Longo's with her husband Dino Corizzi that Friday evening about seven thirty, when a couple on one of those new high-tech rice burners, as the motorcycle boys would call them, pulled up along side their Lexus. Four shots rang out from a European made 9mm, two striking her husband Dino in the head and neck, a third hitting her in the shoulder, the forth shattering the glass to the side of her face. The couple then just drove off calmly into traffic. Neither the shooter, or her boyfriend seem to show any emotion or stress, though the wrap around helmets did tend to hide any clues to their state of mind or identity. She just tucked the gun away and he just drove off. Had it not been for the gun shots muffled by the silencer and the blood, which seemed to gush from the white Lexus like a red waterfall, it would have looked to the crowd like just a couple of young lovers off to McDonalds or Dairy Queen to have a hamburger or a cone on their shiny new motorcycle. It was of course the emotion in Dave's voice, like that of a brother which ushers in a family tragedy, which brought Hardy running into the TV room to see a shaken Pam Wellington give her eight o'clock DNN report to an even more shaken Dave Harding. Hardy had just put the phone down after giving the bad news to his lovers ghost, now only to see his lover of last week so shaken that DNN had to go to a momentary station break, as the local affiliates filled in with the home shopping spots.

"I will give her a call at the station when the show is over. I'll use my cellphone. Dave give Debbie a call. Have her have Peter stop by the restaurant and let Don Fusaro know he is in our thoughts. I will send a get well card to the hospital. I cannot call Don Fusaro direct, the FBI would go berserk and so would Don Fusaro."

"You have time Hardy, she will be on for awhile. I will have Bonnie fix us both a rye & ginger. We both could use it. Have you heard from any of the guys up north?"

"Christ, that is what I love about you. You are so damn mellow for a guy of five feet seven and a half, with a slight case of little man's disease, I'm still shaking Dave."

"Hey...Remember it was me and Uncle Charley who taught you how to box?"

"I have heard from some of the old crowd from around Highland Falls. Was working with a handful of guys from New York Telephone. One of the old timers used to come into the Point in the old days."

"One of Bill Nest's boys?"

"No, I think one of Uncle Charley's men out of Compound in the seventies. You know the Telephone garage out of Peekskill. Said he belonged to CWA Local 1103, Danny Keanan was his President back then."

"Damn fluff on DNN, it drives you nuts and tells you nothing. Good to see Janey Moss likes Rattle Snakes. Didn't think there were any on that side of the Hudson. I'll take a break and have Bonnie call Debbie. Tomorrow I will just have her sit and take notes. She likes DNN, I have to be at Georgetown in the morning. We can do something in the afternoon."

It was a little after nine when Hardy made the call that evening. A messy tearful consoling breakup call shattering two broken hearts. Leaving one in flames in Atlanta, and the other in shards before his acting debut before the joint senate subcommittee. He would be going to Iraq with an overly enlarged broken heart, whose tragic life of tragic love affairs had now done more damage than bullets ever could.

Luck was with Hardy the morning of Monday the twenty first, as he made his way up the white steps of Capital Hill amiss the hazy morning sunshine. There had been a storm in the Caribbean, Vera Lopez had flown off to her hurricane leaving Washington to a more seasoned press corp and Hardy with one less wound to his heart. Though it surely would have been another piece of anatomy Vera would have consumed. Though he was sure if they did cross paths again, his heart surely would have taken a bullet. It was best Vera was where she belonged.

The hearings Hardy found out would be *closed door*, at least most of his testimony. A screen would be erected for the televised portion and so the public could not see the face of now legendary spy. The compromise had come late Sunday evening letting most of The Beltway sleep comfortably the night before. Hardy against the world, at least most of Washington and some irate executives, who were not at all amused U.S. Intelligence had exploited their corporate inequities to trap the KGB.

Hardy sat quietly in the waiting lounge of gate 23 at Dulles that Wednesday September 30th, hoping his brother Dave would return in time with coffee so they could chat a bit before his flight to New York's La Guardia Airport; secretly hoping Dave would take enough time with his ritual errand to give his thoughts time to settle. Dave was intense at times, a polar opposite of Hardy's easy going nature. A by-product of a slight case of little man's disease of ego gone astray. They loved each other but the intensity did show at times.

Pam and Debbie had gone off to the hospital to see Vicky and had become Hardy's personal envoy to Don Fusaro-Debenadetto, attending the funeral of her husband and going back to the house afterwards. Don Fusaro was highly impressed with Pam. He had taken her aside personally when the gathering of his son-in-law's funeral had cooled down in temperament. He saw in Pam's eyes love, a love she would not surrender easily. He too did not wish to lose a hold on such a gifted and valuable man. To Debbie and his trusted lieutenants a wish to find the whereabouts of a one Joe Covic, though it would be a short time after his son-in-law was buried, Covic himself would send a card with a return address.

D.C. had been boiling since the 18th, Hardy was glad to be getting out of Washington while the getting was still good. He had gone from saint to the antichrist of Capital Hill and back to saint within minutes of meeting his well dressed and surgically gifted interrogators of The United States Senate. Falling somewhere between Oliver North and William Casey. In the end the Beltway realized, Hardy had only sent the spy affair into motion. He had only been doing his job. Covic the greedy outlaw for America, with everyone else having a lot of questions to answer. The KGB, narco-terrorists and a few others had been snared. Hearings would flush out the rest, and the scoundrels, who were using the enemy to insulate themselves from what they thought would be an escape from prosecution, would fall to their demise. Hardy had escaped his crucifixion. Had he actually been in the Army, he surely would have been decorated; the Bronze Star or better. Back in Atlanta, situations had gone well. Don Fusaro had liked the idea of Pam Wellington as Hardy's liaison. Her cover was natural; Journalist. Hardy even knew better. He liked the old Godfather but he also know how he thought. Hardy had fallen in love with Pam. Pam knew it, and Hardy knew Don Fusaro-Debenadetto had sent Joni Cone that evening at Longo's on a mission of his own. Hardy knew Don Fusaro knew what he had, and knew Don Fusaro knew Hardy knew it. Breaking up with Pam on the phone over the past two weeks had not been easy. And as much as Hardy liked the old Godfather, he did not want Don Fusaro to have his hooks in him.

After the shooting both the FBI and the mob had sent a legion out. Both finding out about the same; old guard German Communists, the war had been over and lost, their activities had played on. The FBI had suspected something about NATO expansion, the mob knew it to be a bold message. Both the FBI and the mob were looking to the many

Sicilian faction, which operated in Europe for guidance. The FBI to study present day and past Cold War operations and spy affairs, the mob to hook up to old contacts and the Sicilian old guard who know of such things as spy affairs. Both came away with the realization that the games to be played by Langley, Henry Chatsworth's people and the Socialists, would be a European style spy game. 9mms, the Classic intelligence hit and all. Both understood Vicky had been more than a message. It had gone farther than a hostile case of handling, or shots fired over one's bow. This was simply, *if you fuck with us you are going to get hurt.* The war to the European leftists was not over.

Most of the behind the scenes info had gotten back to Hardy, including the last seen whereabouts of two extreme Green Party terrorists at Miami International Airport on their way to Bonn, before they would disappear into the underground of Eastern Europe. Pam was both an asset and a problem. Love always is a problem for a spy. But still he had procured much more from Pam, than in his last roll around his bed and breakfast with Jill. Which the following day had caused him to slit the carpet just outside his apartment door to conceal the two extra keys he would need in case of misfortune. Maintenance had also been made aware that morning of the *persona non grata* of a one Jill Pignizzi of *The Athens Post.* In any case it was now up to his sister Debbie to keep the uninvited from her newly acquired guest house.

Hardy now sat quietly looking over the front page of *The New York Times.* It was Marty Bear's turn on the hot seat. The President of The Communication Workers Of America in Washington had decided out of political pressure and greed that it would be best to look the other way. Inadvertently causing a dozen or so phonemen in Atlanta to lose their jobs or take forced early retirement. Senator Mitch McConnell would be working him over like a prize fighter this afternoon if all of what Hardy read in *The Times* was true and accurate. Thank God these days *The New York Times* seemed to be back to its old self. For awhile Hardy could not decide if it would make better confetti or toilet paper. He settled on using old editions for Windex and cleaning windows.

"Here's your coffee bud. Your Spanish lady vampire is still stuck in the Caribbean. She is a pretty good reporter Hardy. A little pushy, tough, but the word is she is damn good. Your next Barbara Walters in fifteen or twenty years. She is good but hot, and I mean 'hot' in few different ways."

"I know, I actually like her, like her a lot," as Hardy took a sip of coffee. "It is just that the timing was all wrong. Not so much her attitude, you know me, I like these romantic and subtle games we play between the sexes, it was just I had a lot on my mind. You, Bonnie, Debbie, the kids. Too bad really, Vera Lopez would have taken my mind off Pam. You know? I really have to do something about this situation. Col. Clay, Kevin Slyer, I cannot be playing Romeo and Juliet when I get over to Iraq. Damn Don Fusaro. I like him but I know what Don Fusaro-Debenadetto is pulling. I really have no choice but to play his game with Pam after the hit. Damn Joni."

"Where are you staying when you get to New York?"

"The Half Moon Inn. You know? the little bed and breakfast on the corner in Cold Spring by the gazebo on the way to the old Dockside Restaurant. Caliber has set me up there indefinitely until I have to leave on January 15th," Hardy said as the PA blared out, *Flight 1021 leaving for New York's La Guardia Airport is now boarding....*

"This is it little brother."

"Dave let Bonnie and the kids know I will send them a card once and awhile. I will give you a call when I get to Israel every six weeks. I do not know the game yet. Until I find out it is best I only call you and Bonnie when we are allowed. Pass it on to Debbie. Tell her, I said, good-bye.

"She is friends with Pam now."

"I know. I have to go. Bye."

Günther Von Müller showed none of the aches and pains a widower of 73 normally reveals to the world of man about to turn seventy four this November 17th, when he left his apartment at six-thirty in Atlanta's Westledge Retirement Village clutching a copy of the day's *New York Times* in his left hand. His face was carved with the lines of age, his body fitter than most thirty-seven-year-olds. The air had turned cool that morning in Atlanta, the out come of a convergence of a cold front and a tropical storm. Günther was wearing his trade mark black leather coat the one he wore all through Europe from the early fifties to young seventies, when he and his late wife Ohma immigrated to America. The coat was Günther, most times in the Fall Günther would abandon his trade mark by nine-thirty due to the Southern climate. But it was Günther, Günther the old German who claimed to be more Austrian, than by-product of The Fatherland. Günther the old gent, who always brought back something for Joe Caccio from New York, a trip he would make every two weeks. It was difficult to find good Italian food in the South, Günther made his legal contributions. Everyone knew of Günther, though no one knew him. Günther had been one of the madman's youth group during the war, entering the SS at fifteen and rising to Captain just before VE Day, when his children would shoot back against Crazy Eddy, Kilroy and General Bradley's GI's. Hitler had no one left by the end of the war but children to defend the Reich. He had been in the SS, though too young to have sinned. But he did sin, though not of mortal value of which one would develop blisters on his knees in any attempt to do penance. Günther loved his church but was not a religious man. He was an Austrian Catholic and proud of his German roots. Günther had not attended Mass since the death of his wife three years before. History was Günther's curse, the SS would attract the Israelis from time to time. A Captain at twenty Herr Günther..? Tell me about the war Günther Von Müller. They even thought for awhile they had their hooks in him. Out of guilt, Günther even helped them out at times. He knew the game. But sin being less than it was he had to send them on their way one day in sixty four. Only about half a *Hail Mary*, maybe three quarter *Our Father*, he told them. Their people had gotten burnt, Günther Von Müller was an old pro.

And now he slowly made his way out of Westledge up Cannon and down to Flag Street amongst the mist and early morning fog. His long thin gaunt frame adorned by his black leather coat cutting stealthily through the mist like a ghost rising from the grave November 1st after the black Sabbath of fun the night before, falling short of heaven and being damned to eternity to wander the earth for all time. His wire rimmed spectacles and thinning gray hair only added to the sense of doom one feels when confronted with one not of this world. But Günther Von Müller was of this world, very much of this world. He not only had been a victim of history but viewed the less fortuned of history as well. Günther was a part of history, a subject of history. History flowed from Günther, history came looking for Günther, history engulfed Günther. Though few knew of it. Only those whose job it was to know.

Günther the apparition was now closing in on the yellow storefront windows of Joe's Italian Deli, whose dimly lit light shined out upon the sidewalk of Flag Street. In the background could be heard the lonely bark of a stray somewhere far off on the other end of the little street village. In his hand that morning clutched between the folds of *The Times*, was not a sickle or a cide, but a bottle of Beaujolais Nouveau wrapped carefully in a brown paper bag.

"Giovanni, tell your daddy to come sit with me. I have something for him. And who makes the strudel these days? Tell him I have the order but I have more. We need to talk. Tell him more than olive oil."

"I will Mr. Müller."

Joe's was more than just a deli but an attraction as well with fountains and a petting zoo in the back. Aside the deli, a café wedged between a pizza parlor, which he had an interest in. Outside was a small patio overlooking Flag Street for when the weather was nice. It held six tables. Günther took his coffee and apple strudel and claimed his table in the corner. For it was Joe's table, reserved only for Joe or honored guests.

"Joseph, come and sit down, we need to talk."

"Günther, you take my table what's on your mind?"

"A gift for Don Fusaro. A bottle of wine. Give him this copy of *The New York Times*. No one carries it down here, he can have mine. Tell him to read this article here, page eight: Two gunned down on the streets of Paris."

"Is this your gift for Don Fusaro, Günther?"

"The wine is," wiping the mist away from his spectacles, his thinning gray hair damp with dew from his morning ritual walk to Joe's. "Page eight? I know of such things. I can do without *The Times* for a day. Now tell me, who makes the strudel...."

The couple shot to death on a sunny afternoon at a Paris street café were of a marriage of Chinese and East German intent of both politics, love and philosophy. His father had train different cells of the Japanese Red Army Faction and The Black September Group for legendary Spy Master Marcus Wolfe. Her mother was a Taiwanese Communist, who joined the Japanese terrorist cell in the early seventies. Through family friends the couple had come together a few years back, becoming childhood sweethearts shortly after The Berlin Wall fell. They were both Communists, both Green Party and both supported extreme causes covertly in this fastly shrinking Communist world. For the most part it was the indoctrination from their parents of a dying ideology and slow progress of German reunification coupled with decisions by the German Government, which enraged them and pushed them emotionally to the friendship of Marcus Wolfe and the causes he still supported: Covert Communism, covert Socialism, covert terrorism, and a new spy game made up of resistance fighters of Western imperialism and NATO expansion into what was once forbidden ground. The offspring of two terrorist families had found their calling, they had also met for maker on the streets of Paris on a sunny afternoon while their nine month old baby girl was left all alone wailing amongst the gushing blood of the bodies of her two dead parents. It was a pay phone the couple on the motor bike had stopped to use. It was two shots each from a 9mm equipped with a silencer, which had ended their short lived lives. The calling card of one of Hitler's wayward Boy Scouts, who now worked for one of a half a dozen Western intelligence agencies; covertly.

❖   ❖   ❖   ❖   ❖

The assignment was a gift from Mr. Tomilyn to Pam by way of Don Fusaro-Debenadetto, Pam for the eight weeks would be doing a six week expose on Italian-American culture. Her series would air once a week on her TV magazine show, "Spiral," beginning the week before Columbus Day and ending on Veterans Day with a one hour show dedicated to the Italian-American war effort, including contributions to the OSS the Mafia had made during World War II. Pam had her bags packed that very same afternoon. She would land at JFK and be setup at The Hilton on Seventh Avenue a day before Hardy would even enter the loading gates at Dulles. She had a lot of work, she would also have a lot of free time. After she wrapped up after Veterans Day, paid leave until after the first of December, another gift from Mr. Tomilyn.

It was of no coincidence Ted Tomilyn had invested heavily in various United Nations endeavors. He liked foreign policy, thought himself savvy, and constantly strived to keep DNN the best and the mark of excellence in the business. A target the other networks would envy and reach to achieve and fall short of in their own broadcasts. It was for about the same that he had developed loose liaisons with Don Fusaro, which he had always covertly nurtured over the years. Mr. Tomilyn for many reasons was very much on the in with those who run and direct the operations of Caliber Communication of Georgetown, Grand Cayman Island. Hardy was a man, a powerful man, with little money compared to his, but a man of great importance just the same. Like the people behind Caliber, who no one ever mentioned even if they were lucky enough to know their names, Don Fusaro-Debenadetto and Ted Tomilyn both knew the value of Hardy. So did the folks in the intelligence community back in Washington, who actually controlled the people who controlled Caliber. All were in agreement, Hardy was way too important to go off in adventure of reckless romance. Aside from Langley, Mr. Tomilyn seemed to be holding the trump cards of Hardy's future of missions and romance. There would of course always be a story wherever Hardy was to land, Mr. Tomilyn liked this even more; the inside track of whatever John Custer Harding could not talk about, or what the out come of his activities would send into motion. Pam was to spare no expense.

The suite at the Hilton on Seventh Avenue was not presidential but was far more than what a TV journalist would need. It even had its own little kitchen complete with stove, microwave and refrigerator. It was big and aside the bed, a living room set with a coffee table. There was even a small table to dine or do work at. The furniture was oak, the linens, drapes and upholstery were of a mix of subtle greens, reds and creams. Though not really her taste, Pam liked it and setup camp for a month or two. She also kept her rolodex and personal director handy by the bedside, a brochure of The Half Moon Inn protruding from the seams.

Pam's biggest decision for this paid working vacation would be to decide whether to surprise Hardy, let him find out on his own, or let him surprise her. It is very true in the scheming of the ladies, *oh what a tangled web we weave.* Pam was no different than any other beautiful sensitive lady who loved to play games. This time, the game to be played was for keeps, and Pam knew it! Hardy was more than a nice guy off to face danger in a new Cold War of terrorism, rogue nations and a saber rattling China in the quiet halls of the U.N., Hardy was a sensitive gifted lover who she had kept locked in the throws of love making till four in the morning. In his eyes she had seen her family yet to be. She would not if she could help it, let him be used as bait for the beast of Iraq or terrorist chum for an enraged Islamic cell's call to duty against the legions of an imaginary Satan. She was in love! He was in love! And the unfairness of life would not cut them asunder, not against the will of Atlanta's present day Scarlet. Pam was emotional but Pam was strong willed. If Hardy was to leave against the desires of the flesh he was to hold and consume, he would take with him a part of Pam's soul. Or lose that which most men cherish most. But Pam knew Hardy. Hardy could not hide in his eyes that which he felt; the picnic, Longo's, making love till the twilight of the morning when she had to playfully push him out the backdoor of her ranch against the chirping of the morning song birds. Surely it was more Pam than Hardy who guided his way out of her bed with the suggestion, *time to go home lover.* She had Hardy, she knew so on the many calls they shared on the phone; a breakup song never meant for its loving verse to be heard by tender ears of two very much in love lovers. *She had him,* her thoughts as she set up her suite: *Let him sweat.*

The scene was utter chaos at the ninth floor Atlanta FBI field office. John Blacke's Special Agents had woke up and come to work October 1st only to find the whole world exploding all around them. It was now ten-thirty, Special Agent in Charge John Blacke was pacing the corridor outside the ninth floor elevator waiting for Henry and Robert to return from their meeting with the Georgia State GBI. There had been two mob hits overnight, page eight of the mornings *New York Times*, and Günther Von Müller showing up at Caccio's, as he always does but this time with a bottle of Beaujolais Nouveau, coupled with the widening investigation of the shooting of Vicky Corizzi, Caliber, the senate hearings in D.C., the French Government going nuts, the Israelis extremely hot as well,

Langley likewise, and Hardy flying off into another storm, New York State law-enforcement had an obsession, and John knew he would have to deal with it. Most of the intelligence, including a briefing from D.C. had come in a short while ago. The GBI still left in the dark, hopefully; *thank God*, he thought.

He had sent Special Agent Reading to fetch the three. His two chief spies having attended the meeting with cover as the guests of Special Agent Tenza. Robert's cover being Special Investigator for The United States Senate Select Subcommittee On Intelligence and Investigations, Henry's was Special Consul To British Foreign Interests, on loan from The British Embassy in Washington, D.C.. Both were obviously spies to the GBI, who put up with their attendance out of respect to the FBI. Though picking their brains by the lead GBI Inspector proved to be an unforgiving task. They did not give up much and held their secrets of craft and of the Southern Spy Affair close to their chests.

The atmosphere even appeared to become hotter when the five reenter through the bullet proof glass windows and steel door into the main room. Mary the operator and receptionist happy to buzz them in before John could grip his ID card of red, white and blue, which doubled as a key for the electronic lock assigned to the door to keep lunatics out or overly brazen criminals who watch too many movies, not understanding how unhealthy it is to one's career to break into an FBI field office. Once in and few steps down the corridor, agents Reading and Tenza broke away from the three to join their comrades in arms amongst an army of IBM computer tubes and a Merridian phone system in a maze of paper work, telephone headsets and technology. Two computer tubes to a work station; surveillance, data, and intelligence at a push button. Amongst the stacks of paper, tangled wires of newly furnished telephone headsets and stressed out colleagues, agents Tenza and Reading did not know where really to start first.

"What do you have for us John?"

"Here is the file I had Jennifer compile from overnight. I will let Robert read it first, I need to talk with you Henry. First, Günther Von Müller, should be someone from your world. Here is his photo."

"Oh...Yes, I know Günther. I am not as old as Günther but I remember Günther. Günther seems to have had a recurring role during the Cold War, which to us spies never really ended. He burnt the Israelis pretty bad in January of 1964. Former SS, the Mossad thought they had hooked him out of sin. It wasn't much of a sin, Günther Müller sent them packing one afternoon. Does not hate them, even helps them out from time to time. Guilt maybe? Mostly business. From what we know, Günther kind of feels like the SS has reincarnated itself in the Mossad.

Likes them. But not really of Israeli interest his activities. Günther likes to keep it that way. He has work for a handful of Western intelligence agencies, kind of. A little like Hardy, can't prove he is ours but he always seems to move in our favor. Who...? Some in West Germany at the time, the French, played games with the Belgians in Brussels, went around eliminating a KGB spy network in Portsmouth for MI6 before the Dakar sailed in '68. You know we can but we don't in merry old England but can we help it if poor Günther Von Müller has a fondness for black leather gloves, English fog and 9mms with silencers? He is your classic cold warrior, black leather trench coat and all. What his counterparts do with documents, Günther will play the role for bullets. Does documents too. Played the traditional spy game on both sides of the Wall in '63. Strung the Israelis along as they strung him along, all at the same time running a network for us inside East Germany. Quite a man. Quite a spy. As a matter of fact spy writers search him out on occasion. Günther never disappoints them."

"The work in Paris his?" as Robert handed back the file to Special Agent Blacke and sat quietly listening.

"Most likely John. NATO expansion has made a lot of the old guard Communists hot in the East. Marcus Wolfe is still up to his old tricks, this, even if we have taken most of his toys away. Just goes underground. I read a report at our embassy from SIS the other day: Green Party kids, rebellious MTV types with attitudes. 1999 version of flower power. A lot of anger in the East, not just in Germany. Jobs. The kids cannot find jobs. So they turn to Socialism, or worst."

"Robert, Henry, this morning, the French government is off the wall! The Israelis are not much cooler. I need to know what Covic has done, or knows. I want you both to be aware of to two mob hits last night, the first, a woman in her forties at a doctors office. She was a receptionist and health aide. It was the same office Joseph Canizzaro, one of the Don's trusted Capos had his prostate checked at. The second mob hit was an antique dealer in Savannah, Sarabec Treasures Of Old. We believe our man Hardy used to play a little game there. My men suspect KGB, there was an import-export house next door. Robert, I have a real problem with New York. It seems your friends back at Langley stung a New York State Trooper on a job interview back in '91. I'm not sure? I will have Jennifer check the dates. Well it seems the badest asses in law-enforcement feel they had been setup. A scandal followed. They want a rematch. Hardy is who they want the rematch with. I will put word out to Federal Plaza in Manhattan I do not want Hardy fucked with. But I have real problems here, these lawmen in New York are obsessed. The

New York State Organized Crime Task Force was all over Hardy yesterday as soon as he arrived at La Guardia. Robert, any thoughts?"

Robert Torres was gently laughing to himself. "John, I know the people who were behind that job interview. The Justice Department did a real nice job regarding that cop. Imagine, going on a job interview and bragging about committing a felony. Hardy can handle it." All three were now gently snickering.... Robert continues, "from the report here, my people back in D.C. are upset as well. I suspect we know the riddle Covic has put together, or the technology he controls. I could make a call to my supervisor later, I suspect Langley will not even share this secret with her children. I could try. Günther Von Müllen.? I have heard the name. This is more Henry's territory. So Henry, when do you retire?"

"Old spies never retire Robert, we just become *illegals*. You will see. The same for old Günther here, and he is not that old by today's standards. Your Clark Cliffort played on till his nineties. I know...he wasn't a spy. Even spies are not spies in the games Günther plays at his level. If you catch my drift? Your man Hardy will get there someday Robert, if he lives? Maybe not 9mms but he will get there."

"The information about Caliber in this file is interesting Henry, John."

"I suspect gentlemen that my people will have to loosely keep a watch on Mr. Tomilyn. Sensitive, we can cover him through Pam Wellington. Breaking up is hard to do, Pam may not be a bad idea. Don Fusaro likes her but we do not want to place Pam into any situation by any means where she will become a liability to Don Fusaro-Debenadetto. I will have my men send Don Fusaro a little subtle message. Hardy is gone, it is back to cops and robbers."

"John, Robert, one item I want to mention..."

"Yes Henry."

"Günther Von Müller is a lot like your Mr. Harding but he is from the old school. A captain in the SS at twenty, British, French and a half a dozen more after that. He knows how the game is played. Unlike your man Hardy distracted by love, Herr Müller reads *The Times* every morning before he even gets out of bed. He is a reader. He is also quite fond of the new Western high-tech spy game. Even if he is on our side, I believe he is, we have to be careful. He will not care if your men are FBI, John. If they have to go they go. He did the same to some of our people in Portsmouth years ago. *Nothing personal, say hello to St. Peter for me and the Queen.* You have the idea John..? Robert knows what can happen in these big spy games."

"Yeah," Special Agent Blacke lost in thought for the moment. "I see...."

"I have seen it before John. In Panama, just before we invaded and Noriega fell. We lost some good agents. You have to be careful. I will have to mount some kind of minor operation to let Günther understand the chess value of John Custer Harding. He will respond, I cannot afford to lose Hardy."

"Well, OK Robert, this is your domain. Don't break the law. Gentlemen, lets break for lunch!"

The weather in New York was sunny, breezy and pleasant on the first, maybe a bit chilly the morning air for a Southern spy. White caps were nipping at the morning wind, providing ghostly energy for a handful of wind surfers darting to and fro back across the river. The foliage in New York was starting to turn, though about two weeks off its peek, highlighting the face of Storm King Mountain, further fueling Hardy's desire for Pam. Maybe a weekend off somewhere in Vermont with his lover before he would be exiled off to the Gulf, where he could do no more damage than a slip of his tongue could cause in this blossoming scandal of a Southern spy affair. He had been unable to reach her at home that morning. Early he placed a call to DNN, getting past Public Information and chatting with Dana DiMaggio briefly who explained to Hardy she was on assignment, though playfully leaving off where: I gott'a go, good-bye. Worst case scenario, South American jungles to forget about Hardy. Even worst case scenario, New York City to ambush him and leave his heart in shards while burning her soul into his.

The first; last night he had set up his room and recharged his cell phone. Today he had an orientation in New York for an hour around three for Caliber, and thought he would catch an early train after chatting with Dana. But before he could get out the door that morning to the laughing children playing in the great gazebo while the local fishermen set their blue crab traps against the angry face of Storm King Mountain, his cell phone buzzed out with a series of calls. The first was Kevin Slyer, he assured Kevin The Half Moon Inn was five stars. The second was Renee, the field rep for Caliber, Human Resources; not today Mr. Harding, come tomorrow evening at seven. The third call was from Vera Lopez's secretary; could you stop by Channel 22 this Afternoon Mr. Harding? They agreed on four o'clock. This had freed up his day, Hardy now felt the urge to have a little fun in the city. Maybe a museum and some gothic art before Channel 22. He had not been to St. Patrick's in a good many years, thought maybe he would do St. John's as well if time permitted.

True to his words with Kevin Slyer, The Half Moon Inn was truly five star, the Continental breakfast filling, the dinner the night before excellent. Kevin Slyer and Caliber spared no expense for Hardy. Since arriving the day before, Hardy, like a spy tends to do, was evaluating the new world around him. New York law-enforcement had been clumsy at La Guardia but it was obvious, The Half Moon Inn was under intense surveillance. The police too were playing games. Hardy recalled being deep in thought the night before at the strangeness of the behavior of his clock radio, not really understanding why the police in New York would want to start a feud. But he did know they were cops, U.S. Intelligence play at a level a thousand times higher, the FBI would not be so stupid or clumsy. Hardy was unaware New York State Law-enforcement had been stung by the CIA a few years back. He was equally unaware New York was almost as hot as Georgia in the wake of this spy affair.

New York would be fun. He had business, pleasure or obligations just about everyday in the city. When his calling would not bring him to the canyons of Manhattan there were old Haunts and friends to visit in Highland Falls, or on this side of the River in the hills of Putnam County. The Hudson Highlands being so special for one on a visit, though routine of scenery, haunts and friends when he was apart of it way back when.

As he stepped out that morning to the hopscotch playing of the children in the great gazebo to the rocking of the white boats in the marina across from the pier from where the fishermen plied their craft, while a freight lumbered down the tracks skirting the feet of the great mountain on the other side of the wind surfers. His thoughts were of Pam, Spiral, and who could have been the acting covert DCI..? Though Marty Bear did come to mind. *Scandal* he thought, *Too corrupt. But with cover in these covert operations one never really knows...*

It had been misty, foggy and damp in New York City on the fifth. He had been milling around 44th Street a block up from the U.N., stopping at some little deli and coffee shop to have a piece of danish, a cup of coffee, and read *The Times* for a spell. All the right embassy workers from the various diplomatic missions were in attendance that morning, including some old friends of covert cover from the Belgium Mission, filling the back and quietly talking in code while they sipped their morning coffee and yacked away shop talk of unclassified matters. The words spoken in code were for their old covert friend—a pleasant good morning and covert instruction. The weather had not been much better when the old man of youthful strive reappeared on the street, adorning a fold up umbrella, walking a few blocks up and disappearing into the crowd at Madison. He continued to walked in the drizzle for awhile, fighting the crowd and the other umbrellas which would bump his. He turned back towards First Avenue when he reached 60th Street, quietly milling about until he found the address he had been searching for above a gallery not far from Second Avenue, which featured Japanese erotic art and culture; a loft apartment and photography studio doubling as small living quarters for two erotic art students from Germany. He folded his umbrella, sliding it into the left-hand pocket of his trench coat, unbuttoned the coat and proceeded to ring the buzzer.

"Ack, damn it! Sally, you and Hanz play for a while. I'll get z'he door. Do not cum you two till I get back," he left the camera running and went to answer the intercom. "Who iz it?"

"Wolfram Strasser, I have a package from your Uncle Claus of Eastern Berlin, in our now beautiful unified Deutschland."

"Hanz, a package from your Uncle Claus?"

"Tell him we are busy, come back in an hour."

"Hanz said come back in an hour, we're busy."

"Hanz does not know me, it will only take a minute. Tell him I'm busy too. His relatives said nine-thirty on the fifth. Hanz is German, Germans should know better. No need to see Hanz if he is having fun? A small package, photos, I think..?"

"I will receive the package for him, come in," as he buzzed the door open.

"Thank you (German)."

Instead of the elevator the old man walked up the three flights, turned to the left and found the door. The first shot of the silencer when he opened the door pierced his heart. There was no need for a *coup dé grace*. The young couple making love like wild animals in the back amongst the music and rolling camera were totally unaware their comrade was at the door dead, lying in a pool of his own blood. A few seconds later they would both be dispatched into the next world by two shots each. There was a need intertwined in the wild love making to make damn sure their exit was final. The old man then gently pulled the plug and took the video cassette out of the camera. The dossier he had been on a hunt for by luck was laying atop one of their term reports marked, Gothic Architecture. He silently left, his gloved hands leaving no trace.

Once back outside he quietly walked a handful of blocks silently fading into the mist and disappearing down the subway at Fifth Avenue and 60th Street. Both the video and dossier would remain in the grip of his black leather gloved right-hand safely tucked away in a plain legal

Manila envelope. He took the N&R and jumped off at Prince Street, where he slowly weaved his way through SoHo to Little Italy's Mulberry Street.

Ronzi's is quiet little restaurant across the way from trendy Genaro's, intrigue and illicit honor seem to pour from its soul whenever a wary traveler or honor guest would be so bold as to enter into her foreign land of good food, culture and gangland mystique. Anthony met the old man at the door and seated him in the back. He ordered the pork chops Italiano, which meant he need to speak with Ralph Ronzi.

"Günther, my good friend, what do you have for me? Could you not just give your order to Emil?"

"This is more than just olive oil and tomato sauce, I wanted to know how your wife and kids are doing. Good. But I have something, something I wish to show you. It is delicate," and he took out the dossier and video and handed the documents to Ralph. Touching the video, his hands still gloved, he said, "nice boys, misguided. Having a little fun. I feel bad about the girl," and gestured with his hand under the table like a silencer, as Ralph fumbled through the documents.

"And this man Günther?"

"He is Don Fusaro's adopted Godson. He is a good kid. Damn good agent;" Ralph understanding immediately Günther meant spy, not FBI. "My sources suggest he is very valuable, I need to keep him alive. Don Fusaro-Debenadetto would frown harshly, I'm sure, should any harm come of him. The last picture, you recognize?"

"Yes." It was of Victoria Fusaro-Debenadetto Corizzi.

"Let Don Fusaro know the three this morning were on me. It is best you do or old Joe in Atlanta. I hope he liked the Beaujolais Nouveau?"

"He will... Now eat! You are always welcomed here old friend." And Ralph bellowed in Italian and instructed Emil, *shred and burn these, the same for the movie*. There was a metal pail in the back for just such arrangements. The video cassette in a short time would only be a glob of melted plastic.

Günther started on his lunch but turned after a few mouthfuls and spoke, "Vos is dos new dish here? Make me a little for later." But Ralph was deep in his thoughts of silence.

"Günther for tonight? I give you a whole dinner for later. Günther, the old men of Europe, they know of your games. Most do not want to play."

"Yes. I see...I know."

"The children today (meaning the college kids), how many? Three?"

And Günther just held up three fingers and nodded his head. "I am leaving for Europe in about three weeks. I will not be back for awhile for you and old Joe. The great game calls me once again. But I need contacts...Let Don Fusaro know. That is the price...."

CHAPTER
6

It was not just the airport, their paths had crossed that Sunday afternoon, twice, as journalists keep track of their quarries. Once at The Jefferson Memorial, where Hardy with the help of Dave had ducked her questions, ditching her, though the dis (disrespect) had not been all that bad. A slight giggle coming from Vera out of Hardy's brashness. The second time was after dinner at the bar at Runways, a trendy fashion café, which always drew a crowd and tended to have excellent food. Vera had all her questions in a line, only to have Hardy disappear to the men's room at the same time her cell phone went off, ushering her off to her hurricane in the Caribbean. Not much time for Hardy when one has to pack and catch a ten o'clock flight out of Dulles. It was a quarter to eight when she was dumped from Washington and sent off to exile to face a raging storm. What Vera did not know was a lobbyist for Savannah Telephone had spied both Hardy and Jennifer Lopez with fangs at Runways, quickly realized what a mess this would be for the two to chat. Miss Lopez had a reputation of being a gifted surgeon when it came to interviews. The fear of a candid slip of the tongue by Hardy coupled with the high tech sector of the stock market, he made a call to Jeff Dylan's, who was home watching the game. And who in return called the president of Channel 22 at the time, falling short but hooking up with his executive secretary. Vera was on her way to Puerto Rico.

Vera was raging! Never even got close to Covic, or where in the hell in the Caribbean he may be by process of elimination. Though on her pending adventure she just might stumble upon him on her own. Vera was seething at ten to eight, just about to explode when Hardy emerged from the men's room. It must of been Hardy! It had to have been Hardy! God damn that over sexed aloofness fool of a ladies man! Though she certainly did not let on to her inner emotion of gifted desires to strangle John Custer Harding! It showed, Hardy knew anyway. He had made a living at survival by reading peoples faces. He was also well aware as Vera call travel; eleven being a better hour for her exile, while Dave studied the game on the bar room TV, the chemistry between Vera and him was like nitro!

It was now New York and again Vera was about to explode. Hardy had many items of interest on his itinerary, as well as Caliber. He had made the studio at Channel 22 one of his stops just short of a handful of times since the first. Mostly to please and smooth a lady vampire, who was about to put a couple of silver bullets into an over sexed spy. Vera was well aware Hardy was trying hard not to offend. As requested by law-enforcement and the intelligence community, Hardy would be kept off camera, his comments off the record. But there were many interesting insights, views and misconception Hardy could make clear. The informal discussions still had a feel of two street fighters about to go at it with razors on the subway. Vera's feelings if Hardy were to be so accurate to pick them off, and he had come close: I am not your little rabbit! And this is not Hemingway's *For Whom the Bell Tolls*! Vera was in control in those sessions. Hardy was on thin ice, and Hardy know it.

Deep down inside Vera knew. She had reminded Hardy a bit of Monique, though mostly in complexion. But unlike Monique, Vera tended to be clear in thought, straight and down to earth. She knew this, and she showed it with her eyes, clear and crisp. Monique from her research had been a game player and a product of a shattered childhood. Her childhood had left Monique with many rooms in which she could hide inside her mind. It had made her a natural in the spy game. Vera knew she was different from the women Hardy had been with and drawn to in love affairs. Petite, hot! and very hot in temper, as petite Latin American women can often be. Vera was well aware she was bringing out the best in Hardy. Pam was more like Monique, it was obvious Hardy was failing in love with her. Vera's little scouting reports had made her furious! She did not take well to Hardy's attempted brushing aside her subtle undercurrent of flirtatious seduction. *Quite frankly, there had been no advance on her part, not one which could get her in trouble, or land a gentleman's hand on her knee. It was just his damn attitude,* were Vera thoughts. His attitude had made her explosive, and Hardy knew it. *Now, to only sabotage his little affair with Pam. And couldn't she not have stayed in Atlanta? And does Mr. Harding really need to know she is here in New York?*

It had been an informal chat true to what they agreed upon. But Hardy had pushed all her hot buttons! Thank God, Eric, the producer was able to come between them while two of her girlfriends and co-workers held her back. Their little informal chat had left Vera at the boiling point.

It was the end of the spy affair, Hardy had been making the rounds. By the time Hardy left Channel 22 the afternoon of the seventh, Vera had decided to endure John Custer Harding. From her spies and the talk around the studio, Hardy would be easy to find–old haunts in Highland Falls, West Point, The Half Moon Inn. Hardy would be around until January. The studio work was complete, at least complete to the point of not needing too many visits from an over sexed spy in love with a rival from Dixie. And God damn it! couldn't have Sherman done a better job a hundred and thirty three years ago! Miss Wellington obviously watches too many movies! Vera would endure Hardy and his little adventures on Metro North to the city. But God damn Eric! Did he have to mention to Hardy about seeing Pam Wellington the other day at DNN, New York!

"Well Mr. Harding, West Point is just across the river from where you are staying. I hear Cold Spring is nice. Will you be milling around West Point, Mr. Harding? Your Dad? Old friends?" Though Hardy was too busy shooting the breeze with Eric to have noticed. A subtle payback for another gentleman in arms who just saved Hardy's life. Vera was again absolutely furious! She watched him leave the studio and wondered why the intensity was so dangerous when the two of them were together? Was it really intensity...? Or was it blinding passion boiling away beneath the surface ? A Channel 22 company limo would ferry her home.

It is not so much a big star, as it is TV and knowing everyone believes they know you. *Thank God it is Hardy who must disappear for awhile and not me*, were her thoughts, as Vera climbed into the limo. The ride would tend to be pleasant, free of combatants. Vera was tired and a little bit of Hardy is too much Hardy. Now it was time to enjoy forty-five minutes of stress free comfort.

But her spies in the Southland had been good. It was the classic seduction Miss Wellington had played on Hardy–two brandy glasses, her rope slipping to the floor with the entanglement of their bodies. Vera had the inside gossip of all the dirt. And God damn that tramp! Chocolate covered fresh strawberries and all. Oh...she is a pro! But the ride, Vera could relax and giggle gently to herself now, not knowing if she would want Hardy even if she could bed him. The latter could be a real possibility if she put her feminine wares to the enjoyable, or not so enjoyable task. *Hardy will be gone soon, I will have other more pressing pursuits*, her thoughts.

But those trips to St. Patrick's? What in the world could Hardy be thinking when he kneels in the Cathedral? Probably asking God's help? He is in love, and he hasn't been laid in three weeks! Again, Vera sat quietly in the back seat of the limo gently giggling to herself. But it was obvious, Pam Wellington was constantly on Hardy's mind. God, he was somewhat obsessed..? Though Vera could not decide. But what was clear, Hardy had not felt this way about a woman in a very long time. Women can tell these things, Vera was no different. When she thought about it was obvious, this coupled with his attitude had lead to the intensity of their encounter and exchange. Vera was also well aware of the stories of how the great Hardy had been severely burnt in a love triangle a few years back. His friend Covic winning out and leaving with Monique to some far off millionaire's island in the Caribbean. Rumors had it that Hardy was left with his heart shattered, on fire and falling to the floor in lover's shards of fractured passion. A burning for the fabled Monique, who usually destroys more love, than she builds.

Reckless emotional women. Hardy falls for reckless emotional woman who play games and wheel panic attacks like hitmen wheel 38s. She could tell, Monique may have been fading from his soul but whatever they had or did not have would stay with Mr. Harding for all time.

And as the limo pulled into the drive, Hardy would not be such a bad guy, or date it not for his attitude...

Monique awoke and walked naked to the open window, the gentle late night breeze teasing her hair. Across the field the cool Caribbean wind blew the sugarcane to one side on its way to the black sand beaches below. Monique liked Martinique, the French authorities had been kind enough to look the other way where her lover now stirring in their bed was concerned. Covic had been restless again, the jarring of his massive hulk had broken into her sound sleep. Now the beast moaned, beckoning her back to his lair to tend to the needs of his naked form. A tear welled in her eyes as she watched the moonlight dance over the sugarcane, the breeze gently playing with both her heart and the golden field below.

Covic had been both her white knight and her pig, were her thoughts, as she watched the ruthless boar rail about in the white sheets of their canopy bed. It had been an intense love-hate relationship. Covic shifting from prince to unfathomable beast to Jeckle and Hyde within minutes for her viewing on many occasion. Minutes? His shattered character changed in seconds at times, a mare split seconds notice for her to get out of his way.

Their love making had been intense as well, going from one extreme to the other. From bliss to abuse. At times her climax was intense, extremely intense, to which she would need time to recover; again, she watched the pig stir. At the other times of Covic and his uncontrollable sick desires, she would become nothing more than his throw-away whore. His victim, surely rape would have been more pleasant...? Her thoughts, and should she slice a dagger through his heart before he wakes...?

Covic was still playing the games with the ladies too, two or three to his bed some afternoons when she would return. The price a whore turned lover has to pay to keep her lifestyle. Playing the game..? yes, oh but Covic didn't know a thing about romance. He did not know how to play the game when it came to romance. But he had money. He had his freedom now to toot a little coke and have his way with whores that come with the coke. The Feds could not touch him, the French now his reluctant patrons. The creep liked to fuck around, and he had many high class ladies of which to service him. This of course the mixture that would spark the intense jealousy inside Monique, turning her soul into white hot passion of a mixed desire to hate the one you love but to do so in burning intensity; *perhaps his flesh cannot stand the sex..?* It only fueled the destruction, keeping the intense love making and abuse between the two alive, as it slowly destroyed their lives; and another tear welled in her eyes.

She now stood there still at the window, the breeze tugging at her naked breasts. She watched the moonlight again wash over the sugarcane making shadows of long lost plantation ghosts in it's wake. Behind her the sick moaning of Covic calling out to her demise. She thought about Hardy, thought he would be killed. She wanted a life, she did not want to wait. She now realized she had to get away from the hell she created, nurturing it by her own weakness and fondness of an abusive relationship. She thought to herself, I had helped this illness, now this sickness grows? Though there are no counselors for the whores of outlaws. Monique was emotionally dying. As she gazed out across the darken field, in her soul Monique knew she was simply becoming nothing more than another one of her lovers whores. It was a return to her past she had hoped to have escaped through Covic. If the abuse side of the cycle of worthless whore and lover continued, she would be soon be dead.

Monique was a very beautiful woman. She knew how to play her feminine mystique to a man's desire; and how it would push all her beastly lover's hot buttons, fueling the cycle of her demise even more. God... Was she also to blame for her own destruction? Her eyes were now blurry with the wind, breeze and tears to water the sugarcane.

Again she thought about Hardy; she thought of the *what ifs* in her life of hollow regrets. Hollow be it for the lies she constantly told herself.

But it was the dinner party the Friday before last, Covic had used a phrase of such cruelty one should never use when talking about a woman of mixed heritage. It had been coupled with an endearing term of whore for Monique, the lady Covic ravished and was his only lover in the steamy Caribbean nights. Whores for coke in the daytime were only to keep the cruelty and intensity going. One should never use such language, especially if the woman is your steady lover, the lover you wish to keep. Monique was damn well aware of how vulgar Covic could be. She knew damn well he had used the "N" word behind her back on many occasions when she was not around. But that evening at that dinner party what little respect they had left for each other had gone the way of wind and the sugarcane. It was gone. The respect, the last little grain of respect had gone out of their relationship, and Monique was nobody's little slave girl either. That night it was painfully apparent she had to leave.

It was now quarter to four, she slipped back to his lair; "I can't sleep sweetheart, I need to get some air." He groaned slightly when she kissed him good-bye. He was back asleep and did not hear her, or perhaps more the case, he did not care. Covic just laid there in a sleeping haze of over tiredness and too many drugs.

It is most often warm in the islands, a lady tends to dress light. It was with the silence of one motion her flimsy peach dress slipped over her naked form while her right hand in impulse picked up her purse, which contained everything a lady needed, including her passport of which she would not need on her journey, and perhaps it was just as well. She would buy new panties and whatever else she needed in Paris. The last spy affair had taught her to pack light and always keep her finances separate from her lovers. Her bank account Monique would carry with her to her adventure along with the abuses and scars of Covic. At the airport she would slip a note in the mail. Why...? She could not answer that for herself. She was not even sure Covic would care, or if he would even read the letter between whores.

She had it planned since the dinner party, the moonlight and gentle breeze making needed love to her naked body had made up her mind that evening in the pre dawn hours. It was what her soul needed to make the decision. She picked up the car keys and quietly closed the door.

❖　❖　❖　❖　❖

He had caught Pam's expose on "Spiral" Friday evening and again on Monday, electing to watch DNN's special on Columbus Day over Maria Patino's special on Channel 44, though it was a tough call. Both days there was his lover calling out to his heart in code for all the world to see.

Hardy had known immediately on Wednesday at Channel 22, Pam had been playing a game: You are in New York and it does not have anything to do with me..? Though Eric was kind enough to save him from being Vera's dinner, ratting on her as well: *Her over energetic bad temperament may have something to do with your friend Pam Wellington staying in the city for maybe a month or two?* Vera did not want Hardy as a lover, but she did not want the competition to have him, at least not on her home turf.

Over the next two weeks or so it would be an endless series of phone calls between Pam and Hardy—breaking up is hard to do. Games of romance tag: I love. I want you. We cannot be together. We must never see each other again. You know I cannot handle it if we do? To Hardy's broken shatter-hearted discourse: "Pam, I need to see you." Knowing she had him. Knowing he had been had. Knowing he was in love with her. Knowing she knew it. Knowing Pam was playing a game, she was winning, and damn it she knew it! To the obscenities us men say under our breath about women when we know we had just lost a hard fought battle. Hardy gently put the phone down, and gently and affectionately called her a word he would dare not say to her if they were entangled in each other's arms. They would meet at the Hilton Saturday the 17th around seven for coffee and maybe a light bite to eat. Hardy would come away with blue balls and a heart pounding with desire. Pam was setting him up. It had also been obvious, she was in love with him. But love means nothing in the spy game, Hardy had been burnt before.

It was Pam, blue balls, and the desire to look for a beer buddy, which drove his soul after coming away short of a first down the evening of the 17th, leading him back to Saint Patrick's the following week in-between stops on his itinerary. And it was the ultimate spy trick of his last visit to the great cathedral, he had noticed he had been followed in, KGB he suspected? He did not know Vera noticed as well, nor did his visit go unnoticed by the clergy of the archdiocese: He looked up at my God and the massiveness of his cathedral, tears weiled in his eyes; "knowing the tears I was weeping were real but overlooking the real reason for my sorrow: I had not been laid in seven weeks, and that, in that one afternoon I was allowed to enjoy myself in the city meant all the world to me. I finally found one day of peace in my life in the turmoil of this spy affair. There truly is a God in heaven. I was also in love with a beautiful woman who turned my soul away empty to keep my heart blazing on fire." Hardy had found a drinking buddy in a small pub off Broadway near Wall Street who was kind enough to endure the weeping of his soul, laugh a bit, and educate him somewhat of the brewing geopolitical climate in and around the Caspian Sea and former Soviet states, which lie there in-between the Black Sea. Oil, a pipeline, and unrest in Georgia, Armenia, and Azerbaijan, which stretched all the way to Grozny. His first name generic; one never gives out his real name to spies, especially if you work on Wall Street and oil is your business.

"Sounds like you are still in love with her Hardy...?"

Before they would part ways Hardy would thank him both for his insight and understanding. The information Hardy would need in his pending adventure. A spy never turns away from honest geopolitical advice. The information was important. In the modem spy game this is so often how it works. You hand off information and you don't know why, only that you are suppose to. It was the same for the insights Hardy left with gentleman from someplace off Wall Street and Broad. Sometimes you just know: The higher power of psychology practiced by The West in the spy game in these years of the technology and information age. Hyperbole...? Yes. Always fling hyperbole at a bar. Hyperbole is important. Documents are saved for secure dead letter drops. But spies have to be careful with hyperbole as well, hyperbole can get you killed. Especially if you are the one who intercepted that which your tender ears should not have heard.

Hardy picked up his sport jacket and headed out to mingle with the light gathering of dry leaves amongst the business suits of the five o'clock crowd down on Wall Street and Broad. His soul was telling him to go, his heart was saying no. Maybe she is there...?

Vera had witnessed Hardys return to St. Patrick's the 21st, noticing his entourage of stalking KGB illegals, a handful of law-enforcement and press. But what impressed her about Hardy that morning around eleven as he gazed up amongst the pillars of the great church, was the emotion and sincerity in his eyes. An undercover Vera for a story of a lifetime suddenly found a warm soft spot in her heart for a spy about to be exiled off to some foreign battlefield for the cloak and dagger crowd for his own good, and possibly to his death. He was in love with a rival but he was a good man, this, even if conceit and a slight case of vanity were his personal demons. She quickly put together a scheme of her own to snare Mr. Hardy on her own terms, or at least have a little fun. Rivals are rivals, though most women respect true love when it shines in a gentleman's eye's. It had the last evening Hardy departed from Channel 22. *That night it was clear Hardy was in love. But not with me*, were her thoughts. But Maybe have a little fun.... ?

It was the phone call to Dana and the scheming of best friends, which would damn Hardy to a trip of emotional agony when he finally set out on his adventure. The consoling of best friends and best laid plans of mice and men, oh what a tangled web they were trying to weave. To Pam's tear felt verse of, we are damned even if we are in love. He has to leave, and I may have to too if I get in any deeper with the mob. Though Don Fusaro is a sweetheart. But the conversation was cut short before Leonard Cohen was able to pick off most of the details to a mild chuckle of his own, relating most of the hearsay scheming to Steve Summers who was trying his best not to laugh, or at least not too loudly.

It seems Miss Wellington was in love, something she had sworn not to do. Miss Wellington had also been dumped, something that never happens to Miss Wellington. And on top of this all, Mr. Harding was in love with Pam. Though a big enough man to admit it, and a big enough bastard to do the right thing, in this case—*Pam I am in love with you but we have no future.* Pam had been tossed. But Pam had a plan.

"The bastard dumped her Leonard?" While Steve was holding back both tears and laughs for his one time co-anchor.

"Shh, here she comes, I'll go talk with her."

"He did the honorable thing Pam..."

The steam rose high up on the Hudson, a misty cloud forming and settling about twenty-five feet off the water, as the morning sun illuminated the face of Storm King Mountain and The U.S. Military Academy At West Point. Emily had been kind at the front desk, Hardy could stay at the inn for as long as he wanted should his pending departure for the Gulf be pushed back a month or two. In any case it would fit in well with his plans. Hardy enjoyed The Half Moon Inn, and had found himself on a quest of his own to bring the one he loved back for an illicit honeymoon of sorts until his appointed time. January was still the month. Hardy enjoyed deeply The Hudson Highlands, and now wanted to share it with the one he loved. His trips across the river on the weekends to see old haunts and friends were equally enjoyable, this, even if the ghost of Monique had appeared at times amongst old friends in Highland Falls. Hardy now had a desire to share old friends with Pam amiss the scenery, history and backdrop of West Point.

It was now about nine-fifty, the sun felt warm against the back of his black leather jacket, gently burning the mist off the river as it rose. A new grouping of children were playing in the great gazebo and pier, as he turned and walked to the train; heading straight for the old station, then a hard right and down a few blocks to the new one. The sun and Pam played warmly and gently on his soul. As he passed by the old train stop, feelings of romance recaptured. Feelings of which he felt he would never respond to again wrestled with his heart. Memories of their fun in the meadow coupled with the love making that evening played a game with his mind, his manhood started to stiffen interfering with his stride; God how he loved her. The Depo was now a trendy restaurant.

Metro North was on time the 28th of October. When he stepped aboard at ten-o-five, it was Vera and Covic which consumed his mind like a ten year old with a Rubic's Cube, not Pam, though his manhood had left a spot to remind his heart.

Vera, for the way she exploded at him at the studio on their first meeting, and how she stalked him at MOMA, The Museum Of Modern Art, about two weeks later in her quest for insider information. As journalists overly obsessed with stories and women overly obsessed with romance of which they desperately desire, even to lie to themselves of their emotions of the victim they intend to bed often do. Often confusing hate for love with a desire for a good stiff cock. It was what Hardy had thought to himself. Which would be for the most part true to the situation; *She needs a good stiff cock to straighten her out—she needs to get laid.* Had it not been for the complex emotions of love for Pam, Hardy certainly would have made a play for Vera, a woman he was certain of not to have survived. It was quite obvious sparks flew between both of them when the two were in the same location at the same time—Vera hot as hell in anger with a strange sense of burning passion and desire paralyzing her overwhelming desire to choke the living daylights out of Hardy. Hardy had an ego, it was best Vera did not have the ability to read minds, or discern his thoughts of long distance as the train left the platform.

The truth be known, Vera had her spies in the business. She knew about his bedding of Pam, his attitude and that his conquest had turned into love. All the inside information had inflamed her passions making her furious as hell: *Pig!* were her thoughts picked off by Hardy in the lines of her face in their first meeting at Channel 22.

But it was the simplicity of Covic's secret that played mostly on his mind. Though it could have been the technology he had his hands on, which upset the French so. (The ten-o-five was now heading for Garrison, Hardy now fumbling for comfort in his seat, readied his walkman.) It had to do with his ex-wife whatever it was. Oh, it could have been any list of a handful of whores he was seeing but most likely it was Connie, Hardy's ex was big trouble. The technology..? Sure. But it could also be one of those geopolitical riddles which drive overly sane countries like France absolutely nuts—Furiously insane to the point of 9mms. Whatever it was, the Israelis were hot as Hell, though somewhat more subdued in their anger.

If it was not the technology...? then in this case Connie slipped, or slipped purposely, letting Covic find out one of the cabinet ministers or high ranking French politicians was a Russian agent, or ascounded with the jewels of King Louie XVI with the help of the government. Whatever the tidbit, the French Government was hot! Covic of course played a game with himself: I cannot recall. But he could, should it be convenient for him, further driving the French to the edge. Could it be our counterpart to Dr. Albright was really a Russian agent? Playing it both ways? World War II? Vichy? Jews? Old secrets never die, countries just learn how to deal with them. Covic had apparently stung the country of France, and upset the whole applecart in the process. Or he controlled an item they needed for their national security. In any case, whatever it was, it now threatened the role The French were to play in NATO, along with the allied planning in the Balkans. His little game with The French seemed to be also interfering with declared U.S. foreign policy. What was not clear was the role of Langley. So often in intelligence stings and snares, declared and undeclared policy are at times at odds: People play games. Covic was more money than spy, but Covic was CIA. The KGB did their best in Atlanta to play him, or portray him as a double. We used the secret for counter-intelligence? *which was obvious.* The French of course let off the hook after we eliminated our KGB problem here on American soil: Exposed, they are all dead now?

However, France's indiscretions had cost us one hundred and twenty three GIs in Kosovo this past summer when the beast, Milosevic had his men over run the 82nd Cavalry Signal Corp as they slept a day after the initial setting up of their intelligence gathering mission. The whole ambush was kept "classified", national security, but word did get back to us in Atlanta for use in our operation. The secret had netted Covic a hundred million and Monique. The secret had also turned deadly this past August. Monique had turned into quite a little gold digger to my crushed and tattered heart. Then we let France off the hook...? Human life means nothing in the spy game...Off the hook but at an extremely high price...? Covic is allowed to continue his game..? Or blackmail..? The whole turn of events played by the media as a huge diplomatic coup by the French, the heroes..? When in reality they really were actually taken out to the woodshed instead by The West..? Serbia reduced to half it's size, or about to be? Bosnia..? War.? About to be one..? Reduced to half its size, or about to be again? By way of France, and good American blood! God damn it! It makes my blood boil!

"Mister, are you OK?"

"Yes, I was just thinking a little too loud to myself. I'm sorry."

...The secret could be of use to me, if I could figure out what it was..? It could very well get me killed if I did..? That is for damn sure. Covic is still apparently running with it. If I do..? My biggest problem would be keeping my mouth shut when I get to Iraq. One never really wants to be too conscious of such spirits which can get you killed. And keeping away from Vera would be a must, she is too good. Too damn good for her own well being. If we did not find ourselves intertwined in bed, the heat and tension would keep the hate strong. She was certainly no angel. A lady maybe but not in bed. That I am willing to bet my reputation on, but not my life...and I still am consumed with Pam.

In bed Hardy was sure Vera was one hot total whore! His cock again began to get rock hard, as he fumbled through his ritual with his radio and readied *The Times* for his long ride to Grand Central Terminal. "Good morning, this is Wayne Talbot in for Tearse. Here's a quick check of what's happening: The frigate *Yorktown* misfires a missile hitting the Greek frigate *Andropolous*, six are dead...."

And as Hardy turned to page three of *The New York Times* he thought again to himself, *Langley is eliminating Greeks now. Just a tragic accident I bet... And that is how it is usually played out.*

Renee Jadot sat quietly stirring her morning coffee and half & half in the corner booth of The Poplanopolous Greek-American Diner in Astoria, Queens. She was just beginning to gray at forty-two. Patiently she sat pondering her thoughts of her two boys and daughter in state school at Delhi while she looked over her case load.

She had married young, the marriage lasting but a short time with pain enduring for another ten years due to an abusive ex. She spent most of her life working two jobs, preparing and doting on her three kids along the way; money to put them through college, a doting mother to make sure they were prepared emotionally.

It was about five years before when she had started her double life, though she had played along for many years at the psych-hospital and Social Services where she worked during the day. The FBI on occasion would use the talents of her and her friends but that was just candy coated hyperbole. The FBI subcontracted if you will, to The New York State Organized Crime Task Force for insulation purposes. It was state law-enforcement who they really work for as handlers to set the psychodrama for whatever sting operation they were working on. They simply would handle, or manipulate the subject by psychology into whatever undercover scenario best fit his talents. Undercover work, though Renee was not the person undercover. If she was lucky she stayed part of the background. Renee was damn good at her God given talents. It also is of great help when you have the subject's case history before you. You know what he likes, you know what he will do or not do. RN's who work as psychiatric nurses know case histories, often they know or have known of the person to be used in these assignments. Knowing a subject or person makes an undercover assignment easy. But Renee was also well aware of the darkside, the KGB do the same and recruit heavily in the psychiatric and professional community.

When she was younger she had been attractive in a liberal sort of way. Now days she could lose twenty pounds, her face graying and marked with lines, as it peered out from behind wide rim plastic glasses with thick lenses. At forty-two, she would no longer blend into a cosmopolitan setting. She now looked like an aging flower child, her politics more than slightly to the left of center.

"Good morning Renee, I hope I am not late?" Emily Rodriguez sat down stealthily opposite Renee Jadot, presenting just about a mirror image of her friend in her aging Spanish looks. Emily Rodriguez had work undercover for what she always believed to be the FBI most of her life, it was not until the Southern Spy Affair when they realized the true colors of many of the state groups; undue impressing of an FBI umbrella, which in the end tended to sting more cops out of stupidity than gangsters. Emily had an impressive and extensive background in social services. Renee had her coffee and a bagel already waiting. The morning would be both friendship and business. The FBI still feeling it best, there still was a need after the spy affair to use the people of The Shithead Division to insulate the Bureau from any situation from where the KGB could possibly mole in.

"The first picture you see Renee, is Carlos. Carlos is the number two man in the Ventura Cocaine Cartel. We do not know his real name. All indications are the Ventura group will be taking over the Cali routes. They are polished. They are more ruthless. Carlos was burnt pretty bad by the spy affair down south. The CIA, as much as we despise them, had forced Carlos over to the KGB, now The Russian FSB. Carlos is still heavy into narcotics. This time he has the blessing of the KGB, who are at this moment playing the various Russian organized crime groups back against the FBI. He is also, as I said, KGB. The Russians are playing some kind of game personally with Carlos. They seem to be letting him traffic narcotics on Russian soil and Eastern Europe so they can train him and play him back against U.S. Intelligence. Carlos's repayment for his abuse? He has a fondness for the peasants and far-left movements in Colombian and Peru. The money he makes from his empire someday will go to fund and educate his people. At least this is his dream before corruption takes its toll. It already has. Carlos is a pig. Too cosmopolitan for a Socialist, too much an eye for the ladies and the fast life.

The next photo," as she fumbled through the large manila envelope she had brought with her, catching one side of the photo on the paper fold as she removed it, "is of Joseph Covic. You know about Covic. He is a pig too, but he is our pig according to the FBI. He did pull the rug out from under the Mexican Mafia when the whole spy affair came crashing down.

The next photo is of his friend, John Custer Harding, 'Hardy' for short. His nickname. This is his lover Monique who he lost to Covic in a love-triangle."

"She is very beautiful."

"The three shared quite a little love-triangle relationship. Hardy for love. Covic for sex, coke and information. She is quite a little handful. Very beautiful too. Hardy and Monique have been in love off and on for most of their lives. Almost since they were kids. She was in love with Hardy, she went with Covic. I show you this because Mr. Hardy is going to take over where his friend Covic left off. He is leaving this spy affair and heading to..."

"Excuse me ladies, more coffee?"

"Yes please."

She tended to her service and before turning to go back in the kitchen left a pile of creamers.

"I'm sorry Renee. Hardy is leaving for Iraq. Where no doubt the military and the CIA will embellish even more on his legend before they once again kick him out in the cold. We want on board, drugs.

The last photo is of Pam Wellington of DNN. Hardy has real feelings for Miss Wellington. As you can see...."

"I watch her every afternoon on DNN at four. She is very, very beautiful."

"They got together when the story of the spy affair broke. Hardy really loves this girl. They had quite a little love affair down south. They are both now here in New York at this moment. We do not want this love affair to end, though neither one knows it." Emily's face now drifted off in time lost in the gaze of her last photo. Her features were gray and sunken. She played with the edge of the bagel and gently stirred her coffee for a few more moments of time-share between friends, to which seemed like an eternity to Renee. The kids now in school?" Emily asked. Renee nodded her head. "Good," Emily said.

"They do not even miss me Emily. They don't even want to come home for Christmas. They spend more time with their father these days. Bill has mellowed out, I don't mind."

"How is your French?"

"Not too bad, I spoke with my aunt in Lyon the other night."

"Renee, we would like you to handle Carlos, at least try to get his habits more friendly to our operation by power of suggestion. He has a flat in Paris and lives there a good part of the year when he is not in Russia or South America.

Hardy is the problem, he despises our type. I cannot really blame him, half the people The State Of Georgia used for their handling fell out KGB in The Southern Spy Affair. Renee, our colleagues down south were double agents at best. Renee, we have arranged for you to work at The Hotel De Paris, Carlos has an office there. If you are able to build his trust he will bring you in to where you belong; where we want you. He is leaning to Socialism. You are not but you are leaning left, he may take you in. Don't worry, you or I am not his type. You will not have to sleep with him. He may like Monique. Monique is in Paris. We would like for Carlos and Monique to play. Hardy is good in love-triangles, maybe we can get him to enter our little screenplay? Monique is no problem, Carlos will bed her. Though I would love to manipulate you Renee into this screenplay, big sister relationship? Motherly friend to confide in? We will see what we can do. Oh, Monique, sure. But we still want Hardy and Miss Wellington together. It is also what God wants. You will have to be very careful of whose toes you step on in this mission. The French may not take too kindly of us playing on their soil.

Renee, keep in mind if Carlos ever finds out what you are up to, he will kill you. He is no dummy, the KGB have been training him covertly. If you except this assignment, it of course will be the most dangerous of your career. Think it over.

We can arrange to move your aunt from Lyon to Paris. The old girl is quite a card. She would be your cover, you her's. The French Resistance?" Emily now sat smiling gently laughing to herself. "She knows the game. From what we hear she likes Paris too. Now you finally have a reason to visit Paris again."

Renee pondered her thoughts..."Maybe it would be fun to do the Louvre again...."

She sat level with George Washington's feet on the steps of Federal Hall, squatting seductively with a ham sandwich cradled in her sun dress. The unseasonable warm Autumn weather warming her soul. It was eleven forty-five, a gentle breeze played with her dress adding comfort to a lady trying to enjoy a dietary requirement for a TV journalist on thin cardboard rye with no cal cheese dripping with too much mustard. The ham was Virginian, the lunch itself could have been any number of mouth watering delicacies of road kill from a Georgia highway. The sun only cooked it more as she toyed with it between her thighs.

It was between thoughts of Hardy and how best to make love to Virginian ham between two pieces of cardboard with something yellow and sticky that at best looked like Silly Putty, when he appeared out of no where to slip his arm around her waist; his right hand free to discard the road kill between her thighs before it would turn her off from eating right for the rest of her career. He was sure her system would regret her dietary poison and respond appropriately the next day if not for his rescue. But Hardy's deed was not complete until he found her right thigh high up while he gently kissed the side of Pam's neck. They sat there, two lovers on the steps of corporate America, kissing and cuddling amiss the lunch time crowd of The New York Stock Exchange. Pam squirming a bit at the indiscretion of Hardy's right hand on her lovers thigh while the wind blew a handful of dry leaves about like a mini cyclone before them.

"I've missed you so Hardy," and she squirmed again at his lovers indiscretion, letting her lips turn once more to meet his.

"Don't talk, I need to hold you. I need a hug," and the cardboard snack tumbled to the granite steps below, though the pigeons in their attitude even snubbed the offering. "Let's go get a real lunch," Hardy said, as the dry leaves broke ranks and gently tumble up the steps to meet the breeze as they playfully tugged at her long dark hair.

This time it was Pam who transgressed in lovers passion, her right hand moving to where it should not while she soulfully responded to Hardy's emotional needs. Her lips were now on his, the kiss he would carry with him to the Gulf. He squeezed her thigh and let her passions play with his emotions. It would be the encounter which would carry them off to Tribeca and later beyond that to a session of love making at her suite at The Hilton, which would seal his fate for the near term future, if not for all time. It was the little romantic games women play on the souls of men with second thoughts Pam was working on Hardy. He, his doubts and desires to turn around in passion when the woman he loved was pushing him forward in life and romance. She the desire not to lose the man she wish now to spend her life with. Though in this case she would need to trap him first for his own good.

For Hardy it was Iraq and Pam, knowing love had no place in his world. Hating himself for now being in love. For Pam it was a desire to go on the afternoon's little adventure. She knew Hardy had second thoughts. Her desire now was to tease and keep Hardy on edge and his cock hard. He was deeply in love, it showed. But Pam was not going to be an easy mark for Hardy to toss this time. Nor was she since Hardy had learned she was in town in the beginning of October. She would weather Iraq and burn her soul into his heart for protection. Though the risk of hanging on a lovers cross should she fail weighed heavy on her mind: *You may leave Hardy but not without my soul burning inside your heart. I will be damned if I burn in my bed in Atlanta without your burning in your thirst for me in the Gulf. I will burn but you will be consumed by the flames of my memories, and of the love that awaits you back home.* With her thoughts complete, Pam released another volley of passion on Hardy's soul. *If I am to be damned, then so shall you. If I am to burn in my bed, than so shall your soul burn in the land from where life began.*

Hardy now read in her affection an emotion he could not quite understand, he took her hand and lead her across the street to The J.P. Morgan Building, kissed her and the two turned and slowly wandered down Broad.

"I went looking for you at The Exchange, Joseph the guard at the door pointed to Federal Hall. Ronda recommended a place down the street. Actually two, The White Horse? Or should we try The Wall Street Oven?"

"How?"

"I have spies too Pam, I am kind of in the business. You are doing a story on Richard Grasso? I heard. I knew you would be here."

"Next time you take me by the hand and lead me down the steps like a newly married bride, Hardy, remember, I play for keeps — Pigeons prefer rice on such occasion, not cardboard. Damn you, I am in love with you Hardy," the breeze was now making passionate love to her hair, as Hardy fumble for a response that seemed to choke his emotion right out of him.

"The Autumn air seems to have numbed my senses too Pam, lets go get a bite to eat," Hardy said as the wind now blew the lost leaves of Wall Street about, weaving God's subplot out on Hardy's future while Pam would burn him with desire that afternoon.

Up in Midtown that afternoon, in the hollowed halls of 1010 Avenue Of The Americas, Ray Jones was giving a lecture on how the phone industry would never again allow the CIA to use any of the former Bell Systems companies as cover for any covert operations, or allow their personnel to be used in undercover work. Though before he was complete in his insights the loud laughter of the industry elite and over two hundred managers of Digital Atlantic Telephone had cut him short, knowing full well everyone in that lecture hall were CIA.

It was one-thirty, Ray Jones was about ready to break the meeting for coffee and continue their light hearted disavowal of U.S. Intelligence in about a half an hour. Hardy's train had made it past Croton Harmon that morning all the way to Grand Central. There was no telling what kind of mischief he could get into in the city. It was best to break for a reconnaissance report before they finished eulogizing the spy affair. Hopefully Hardy was making love someplace where he could do no damage to an executive's stock portfolio.

It wasn't so much Covic had found religion when Monique left but a need to repent for the over indulgence of cruelty and the realization the coke and the whores had gone too far. He now realized how truly and deeply he loved Monique. He also understood in his dive into the pool of morality that morning, that his lover Monique needed her freedom and a stable life. The words he thought best described his feelings were written in modern folklore, or adult nursery rhymes, though being profound was not his department even if he did show signs of creativeness in his letterhead terrorism. The verse which had come to his mind went like so: *if you love someone let them go, if they return then they are yours...* Though he did seem to think there was more of this verse and planned one sober afternoon to research as such in the first English book store he could find on the island.

And it was of those thoughts running stark naked through his head when he entered the great sanctuary to visit the Pope while he sat quietly amongst his body guards holding court and sipping expresso with Vito Longo screaming orders to the cooks and waitresses from inside the kitchen. The invitation to join Don Fusaro-Debenadetto had come by way of a callgirl and failed model who had showed up one Sunday morning about two weeks after Monique had left. The Prodigal Son or not, business was business and the words whispered into Covic's ears between love making sessions, though somewhat tamer, and perhaps a little more sincere, were words of advice Covic needed to take seriously if he expected to have a life expectancy of more than a few weeks. The messenger was a damn good lay and a real nice way for Don Fusaro to say I love you, we need to talk. It was what he wanted in return that troubled Covic's mind and kept him distracted in their love making, which lasted most the afternoon, breaking up for a short while around two.

Her name was Julie, she was second generation Chinese American with ties to both Chinatown and Little Italy in New York and the suburbs of Atlanta, where she now lived. Julie Lee was quite talented. Covic tended to avoid the Virgin Mary types, and Julie would certainly never come close to Madonna and Child even if she were to convert, say The Act Of Contrition and do five or six hundred Hail Marys and Our Fathers. It was for precisely this reason they hit it off so well, with the sex in bed that morning damn near killing Covic.

Covic long ago had realized Monique would not be around forever, and if he ever got married or fell in love it most likely would be a callgirl. Though it was apparent Julie's skills went way beyond the bedroom. Julie possessed a certain beauty and cunning few of her breed could blend and wheel with such seduction for a cause in most times survival. She was the type to tie a man up in leather while taking both his fortune and his heart when she left his world to return to her's. Julie had a charming which would secure her a role on a social level, yet she was the kind of lady who could strike fear into a man's soul should he ever encounter her in a law office with a briefcase in her hand. The thoughts of which had sent chills down Covic's spine that morning after her flesh had left him briefly, leaving Covic laying paralyzed in his bed while she tended to whatever ladies do naked in the bathroom after love making. She thought like him and reminded Covic of a girl who read the news in Detroit at the height of his spy affair of intrigue.

Great minds think alike. If they fell in love that morning it was as much for convenience as it was for sex. The sex by the afternoon had damn near killed him again, even if he thought they had started out on a somewhat tamer note that morning. Covic was in love, though it could have been lust but with Joe Covic love and lust are of the same family of haze. It was obvious by her eyes and the intensity of her climax, Julie had felt the same. Though Covic was determined to next time keep her away from the silk neckties, and perhaps he should toss out the four post bed? The inner beauty of the two were of about the same in thought. Emotional bonding and intensity can come later. Money, and the sex was great washed across both their minds of about the same calculated thesaurus. Like the intensity of the lust, which had consumed both their flesh at the same moment a few minutes before. Both had found their soul mate, if the sex did not kill them they might even have a life together.

It was the seething and the loathing, the hate, which comes from not being able to be with the one you so desire. Realizing you had been the victim of your own surveillance and coming to terms with emotions that eat away at your very soul for failing in love with the one you despise. Knowing that he is sleeping with your competition, which had consumed Vera on this cold and gray Veterans Day. The industry information and the insider knowledge of the love affairs of Miss Pam Wellington, coupled with the general understanding consensus amongst friends that Miss Wellington did not play fair in affairs of the heart, had cut across the core of her emotional existence. Now she was bedding Hardy once again, the one shining star of The Southern Spy Affair. Sweeping away her chances of romance with her quest for journalistic integrity with a gentleman who was charming and more than attractive.

God damn her! God damn that over sexed ass! were her thoughts that were running wild through her head. It was not just D.C., or being yanked out of the hearings and tossed out into the Caribbean before she could do no harm. It was an accumulation of things from his attitude and rejection of the sparks which flew between them, opting more for a fist fight than romantic tag in the studio, to his high opinion of himself. Vera thought sure that day if she had a gun Hardy would not have made it to his next affair of intrigue. It was the flaunting of that pretend to be Southern Belle tramp on her own turf where she surely would turn up in the exposé she was going to do, which really made Vera furious!

It was of course the day before, which really churned her anger and made her blood boil. Vera Lopez had been a victim of a hand off of news and received the word Hardy had hopped a train in Cold Spring and would be at GCT in little over an hour and one-half. It was there that morning at the foot of grand staircase in the great hall of Grand Central Terminal, Vera Lopez staked out her turf and stood-in-lie-and-wait like a Spanish Mountain Lion waiting for her dinner to happen by.

But it was safety in numbers at the grand old train station when Hardy, her quarry, made his entrance on the newly renovated grand stage on his first step into The Big Apple that morning, only to get lost in the crowd and splendor of the hall. Hardy had slipped away from the jaws of one hot and extremely angry TV journalist. Ducking her with overly self-confident pleasantries, and *gee, Miss Lopez, you look very nice today*. Which only seemed to fuel the flames and add to the anger and sexual tension. To Hardy it was a flash back to Dulles, though he did enjoy the sight of her butt one more time. Unlike the singer, her's needed no work.

As Vera strung Hardy along with a mix of questions and hot Latin sexual desire, Hardy strung her along on his way through the great hall with a mix of smiles, *I like you too...* light answers of child innocents and gentlemanly expression of, *we could if I wasn't in love*, which only angered further a Latin lady mountain lion in desperate need of a firearm. It was somewhere near the entrance of the subway at the other end of the great hall, Hardy had felt it would be best and The Time Square Shuttle had been a well timed by chance and most evasive maneuver. He waved good-bye and left his lioness seething in an overly massive crowd for that hour of the morning. Vera had been left on the platform clutching only a clipboard that was void and did not contain any written quote from a spy but a handful of obscenities.

Vera had been doing the ground work all alone and had come by herself that morning hoping to patch things up a little with Hardy. Maybe have him on the show, or do another piece or segment on The Southern Spy Affair and the New York connection. She had come away from Grand Central Station with an overwhelming desire to buy a gun. She thought to herself, *daddy would recommend a 357 magnum.*

Though it was not until the afternoon around four when the field crew sent over some footage taken covertly of Hardy and Pam going at it wildly in various stages of undress in some no-named alley off of Chambers Street, when Vera exploded sending a coffee cup sailing across the newsroom to the out cove of the kitchenette shattering the company coffee pot with such force that the shelf above had given way sending the mugs of her friends to an early demise.

"That over sex pompous ass!" were the words she shrieked out over the newsroom. It was best the film crew were in a different part of the building, and one really cannot shoot the messenger were her thoughts. But it was also of the best corporate wisdom, the kid knew enough to drop the package and run. Though it should had been obvious for Vera, he had been long gone by the time the tape rolled.

And what do men fantasize on The Time Square Shuttle after just tossing a beautiful journalist? Vera felt the need, and it was the day before a paid holiday, which would make a nice evening to go out and she made a few calls. She had to work Veterans Day but the work load would be light.

There was an attraction between Vera and Hardy of which Hardy could not deny. Though if he did he might not survive the relationship. On the shuttle that morning Hardy fantasized about Vera, what it would be like to have his way with her in bed? If she was as gifted with her tongue in sex as she is on the air and would he survive the experience? And how he would love to take the chance if not for Pam. But it was anger and intensity, which filled his passions and fantasies most about Vera. There was something there. The feuds, though blood had become now sparing between adversaries on a quest of forbidden desire and mutual admiration.

Vera had an in your face style as a reporter, Hardy liked her honesty. The night before he had had a mixture of a dream with Bella LaGosi leading a Rock'n Roll Band and Jennifer Lopez singing backup. The silliness of the dream had both scared and made him laugh gently when he woke-up to Pam's naked flesh beside him. He had realized it was his subconscious trying to tell him something.

CHAPTER
7

Hardy was quiet over Thanksgiving Dinner. He had been unusually quiet since the day before. Pam was equally lost in her thoughts, though for different reasons. In their eyes they each could tell of emotions and thoughts unrest, as lovers who are one often do when their mate is estranged for some reason of importance. It is best to know at such times, though timing is so often our adversary. Their watering eyes just gently made love over dinner.

For Hardy it was the letter the day before, Col. Clay wanted him in Iraq before the end of the first week in December. He would have to leave the first. True to his instincts, his job in Iraq would only be his cover. He had learned as much from Savannah Telephone, though as time progressed throughout his life he had made a pretty good phoneman too. The timetable had obviously been pushed up. He thought, maybe because of the air war. Though most of the inspectors had been tossed out, now either in Israel or one of the Arab countries favorable to the West. Though in the eyes of the Iraqis the people of Caliber fell short of inspector and landed somewhere between nuisance and technician. This even if they were obviously CIA, a CIA class of spy in which to engage in a game. They performed some services the Iraqis needed, this, even if the folks of Caliber were well hated by the enemy. Primakov liked the idea as well; well needed adversaries for which his ragtag group of advisers could play against. The best KGB technicians the Gremlin could afford to send to the haggard beast and his Republican Guard. They were about the only KGB Primakov had left of such a level to where he could compete against Caliber, or the threat of Scott Ritter's friends and Richard Butler's Arms Inspectors. His agents had laid the ground work a few weeks earlier to have them expelled from his little frontier in the Gulf, and beast he was trying his best to handle.

Hardy's expression was blank, as slowly toiled and picked at the traditional dinner of turkey and fixings the Inn had laid out. The dinner by The Half Moon Inn was excellent, Hardy was still lost and deeply confined within his inner thoughts.

But it was with tears welling in her eyes for of the same and different reasons she looked at Hardy and said gently, "come on sweetheart, you can tell me." And it was there they both sat quietly transfixed in the same thoughts.

With Pam it was a flash back to Tribeca. It was actually after they left the steps of Federal Hall, which played on her mind. They had had lunch at The Wall Street Oven. Hardy her hero had come to her rescue once while she had found herself lost somewhere in the maze in the basement, which lead to the restrooms or maybe to the demise of those who gamble their lives on insider trading, caught inside a bad scene from an old Abbot and Costello movie. Whatever the case, alarm bells went off inside Hardy's head and he had found her wandering about the subkitchen about to pee in her panties. Pam had gone upstairs first before she went down.

Then it was after a get to know you lunch between lovers estranged and separated for a month of tearful "hellos" and "good-byes"; breaking up is hard to do. The Wall Street Oven had been the first time either one of them could enjoy lunch since the picnic in the meadow of purple flowers. Love so often leaves our insides like the by-product of a warring blender.

A short time later they had found themselves playfully wandering the canyons of lower Manhattan. And it was there amiss the tugging of playful lovers arms on sun dresses and old black leather jackets against a mild October wind they played about; past a big park with chain links surrounding it's perimeter, Pam thinking they must be from the anchor line of some great sailing vessel of olden days. Past The World Trade Center Complex while Pam played lost lover and tease, keeping Hardy true to his nickname. For as they turned the corner on Chambers Street, she not only was able to see the large lump running down his right leg but a glowing clear spot of embarrassment around his large bulge highlighting his tan slacks, which had told her she was winning. She carelessly let her fingers slide across his embarrassment.

And it was somewhere just north of The Twin Towers Hardy had stopped her game by pulling her into an abandoned doorway on some no named alley just out of view of Chambers Street and the bustling traffic and people near by. Where it was there their tongues met in a heated volley amiss a hail of passionate kisses being darted in and out at each other like cupids with miniature machine guns. Hardy in his revenge had her sundress up and her panties off, his fingers soaking wet with her pleasure. Her face was flush, and Pam was deeply in need. But this is New York, and their fun had been interrupted by a black man and his wife with their two year old son in a stroller. They all just laughed, the baby transfixed at one of these early childhood memories that shape our lives. In New York one can get away with making love on the streets.

But Hardy the eternal gentleman, Pam a notable face; tabloids, and a desire to stay out of them. He let her sundress down and Pam withdrew her leg from his side while Hardy stuffed the prize in his pocket. Pam could barter for her panties over dinner. But his intentions did not die without a fight, all the while of the exposure of their embarrassment Pam had been mounting one last attack with her lips on his. Her hands grabbed what Hardy prized most in this world giving it a playful lovers squeeze until Hardy let out a moan of mutual surrender. He had her prize stuffed safely in his pocket, though neither one knew who had won. To the mischief of their sin, God had felt it best they be both left unquenched and burning with unspeakable desire. And so it was they would stay in an erotic state of arousal of which they both deserved for the rest of the afternoon and most of the evening while they played, or tried to play lovers games in the corner of the bar at The Tribeca Grill.

As legends go he was somewhere between Hollywood and the Far East. His bar and grill providing a thin backdrop for two lovers separated for a month, though an eternity between souls. Thin because the lighting could have been dimmer. Thin? because the corner could have been more privet. But lunch had stayed with them. The bartender, a Colombian kid of about twenty five, sweet and noticing their condition, would only check up on the two when he was needed.

It was between the Chardonnay and kisses, the candle light, which interwove their lives with small talk, that games of footsie would go astray and they both would realize just how deeply in love they were with each other. The sexual desire of Chamber Street had never left them, but now was transformed. They found themselves more reasonable and mellow. Feelings of lust abandoned were now born of love denied. The wine and candle light now playing devilish games of torn lovers with their souls.

It was about ten amiss the burning of many desires of both flesh and heart that Pam used her cell phone to summon the company limousine to take them back to The Hilton on 7th Avenue. In the back they were *one* in most of the ride to Midtown. Their lips melting into one that evening to the many illicit climaxes of two who could have been kids on their way to and from the Prom. Little chirps of pleasure while Hardy let his hand find where it should not beneath her sundress. The traffic had been heavy, the ride to her pleasure had taken longer.

Hardy sat their quietly, putting down his fork and piece of breast he handed her the envelope. And as she read the letter her thoughts were trapped between her tears and lines of her anger, which would carry him off. She drifted back to that night and those few so special days of October.

They had barely closed the door behind them of her suite when their clothes laid in a ball shredded on the hotel room's floor, their naked flesh meshing into one: Hardy slamming his massive namesake into her over and over again to her pleasure. Their love making intense, their sex extremely loud and her climax, their climax had been shattering!

It had turned into an all night session of love making, it was somewhere around three in the morning with her thighs on fire; Pam had been a victim of Hardy's overly endowed tongue and Hardy ready to go again, that the bad news came forth:

"I have no more."

"You do not want to trust me?" as she nibbled at the softness of his neck, leaving a lovers notch on that which Hardy felt should be as tough as leather. "I have one someplace," and her flesh slipped from his side giving his manhood a gentle tug, as she escaped out of bed leaving Hardy now to make love to her naked form while she found her way across the room to her case on the vanity of the bathroom sink. The tanning lines of her naked flesh now dancing out to him, calling to him while they teased him in the shadows of the soft bathroom light, bringing forth both his soul and his flesh, as she slowly and deliberately made her way back into his arms. "My last one," and she kissed him and gently rolled it on his cock.

She wanted him now! She wanted him her way! The last time he had taken her from behind. This time it was her time! She was on top! She was in control! She guided his cock to the pleasure point, of her desire, to where she demanded it! to where she wanted it! and it was there impaled for all her pleasure she would ride him for all her life!

"When do you leave?" and she handed the envelope from Caliber back to him, her eyes too blurry with tears to have noticed the date.

"The first. I go out of the American terminal at Kennedy the first."

Hardy could not look at her now, his eyes too filled with emotion. Since the end of October they had pretty much been living together. His room at The Half Moon Inn providing a common law honeymoon nest. Her suite on 7th Avenue becoming only a stop-over and changing room for the items of a lady, which would not fit in a cozy honeymoon retreat.

Hardy glanced out the window to escape the pain of dealing with the good-byes of the emotions of his lover over Thanksgiving dinner. A cold bitter wind now played havoc along the banks of the Hudson whipping it's currents to whitecaps, as a tug and barge made it's way up the river to the angry face of Storm King Mountain dodging a wind surfer in a wet suit too oblivious to the barge or the bitter wind to care. The chilling thirty degree weather and the grayness of November all around only adding to their despair. Though lost for the moment, in his gaze Pam saw all eternity, their eternity. Hardy only saw gray and the harsh November weather. A squall of snow flurries now washed past the picture window making a haze of the tug and wind surfer. It was a stark contrast to the last days of October when they had found themselves skinny dipping out of silliness in the Croton River to the unusual Autumn heat.

Pam's thoughts where there too, lost somewhere between the barge and stark naked gray angry face of the mountain. It was of that day from where her silence was born of that crazy afternoon at the dam. It was the eternity of his gaze lost in the flying of the building snow that she would return to escape from that which she really should tell him. The letter, December 1st, it was not all that important now, she thought to herself.

She had taken the day off with Mr. Tomilyn's blessing. Their love making had ended around four. Hardy wanted to take the train back, pick up his rental and do a day trip. The weather was nice, the temperature again suppose to brush ninety. Though the forecast hinting at an early Winter's revenge the next week. At least the mercury back to where it should be in the 40s and 50s.

It was about twelve-thirty when the train deposited them back in Cold Spring. A short walk to the Inn, Pam stayed in the car while Hardy went up to the room momentarily. Like all women Pam needed a few things, which was remedied by a quick stop at the pharmacy across from the old Butterfield Hospital on 9D.

"Don't forget..." But of course she did.

The ride down Route 9D was pleasant, Hardy true to his personality rented another Sebring convertible. His style often was to let the top down and let the wind make love to his lover before he would. Though Pam did not need any softening of her soul, the wind now played havoc with her hair to Hardy's laughter, as he circled the glass all around her reducing the breeze to only tickling her scalp. It was one o'clock, the temperature was just shy of ninety.

The great face of Croton Dam startled Pam like The Rockies must of to the settlers of the 1849 Gold Rush. And as the convertible neared the zenith of the old wooden bridge, a black couple was taken by surprise under a tree by the gushing spillway of the old dam. He with his trousers down around his ankles, she with her dress hiked up high, protesting, denying him his climax in the glare of Hardy's maroon convertible. She forced her lover to withdraw moving her dress down to where a lady should be on a hot afternoon. Hardy and Pam just laughed, as Pam blushed and buried her face in his shoulders. The dam plaza had been deserted, they had caught two lovers by surprise. Hardy showed his heart and parked their car five hundred yards away near a grouping of pines, allowing two very hot and upset lovers ample time to escape their embarrassment.

It was not long after the tape went in that the small talk turned to kissing, as the warmth of the day and two lovers denied the flesh they so wanted washed gently over Pam's mind — *Two lovers so kind and generous enough to sacrifice themselves for me and Hardy.* And as the two retreated Pam readied herself and Hardy to advance.

The water gushed wildly over the spillway. A huge rainbow formed in it's mist, appearing, and dancing before them as they neared. Above the roaring water was the bridge suspended over the gorge from which the water flowed. On the side of the old dam next to the spillway rose a gatehouse rising a third up it's two hundred foot summit.

The first series of steps were blocked off, though not much of an obstacle for two lovers. Hardy took Pam by the hand and lead her up the incline aside the steps to the first landing to were they would turn and ascend three or four landings to the summit of the gatehouse. When they reached the top Pam leaned out over the rail to catch the rainbow, Hardy with his arm around her waist pulling her back to meet his romance. The rail was old, Hardy needed affection. He held her tight, the rainbow and the gushing of water only adding to the intensity of their exchange as they kissed. Neither one was sure who held the edge when they were finished consuming each other beneath the dancing rainbow of the spillway. Hardy took her by the hand and they both retreated down the steps to the meadow below, settling in thought and location near some old abandoned fountains about half way across the field.

To their left rose a great hill, steep and layered in tears like a virgin's wedding cake. Pam was not sure who lead who but it was Hardy who took her by the hand as they playfully ascended the tall grass, which lined the hillside. It was about the third or forth tear, Pam had been playfully giggling and playing with Hardy's butt all the way up, falling once and demanding Hardy's help while she laid pouting amongst the tall grass of the hillside, when he helped her to her feet and her hand by lovers skill found it's way to where it should not.

The ride, the unfulfilled black couple, the spillway and the playfulness of the day; he was ready, Pam knew Hardy was ready to explode. It's different for men, she thought, and Pam knew men well. The couple who had sacrificed themselves for us had really turned Hardy on, and in the scheming of her thoughts, Pam knew she had Hardy right where she wanted him. Noticing the condition of his mind beginning to spin of sexual desire, she gave Hardy one of these fuck me kisses while her hand again found his cock through his jeans, grabbing it and giving it a squeeze, as she landed on the ground with a plop. Her butt hitting first, as she laid back in the tall grass with her dress hiked up to her waist. Pam was wearing no panties. His condition was obvious while Pam played an affectionate game with her naked thighs and Hardy's emotions. For the moment she had just turned into both punishing whore and virgin bride. Both her words and naked flesh started to taunt him.

"You want me Hardy? I'll be your whore Hardy! Your big cock ache Hardy? You want me naked in the hot sun Hardy?" as she slipped the rest of her dress over her head.

"Pam, I...don't have any. I was going to do us up right back at the Inn," though the words just did not seem to make much sense, his head spinning in the desire of his manhood that was quickly blinding his judgment.

"You have to trust me!" and she reached up and unzipped him. *Damn Hardy was wearing a thong*, now her head was starting to spin amiss the fire in her thighs. Pam did not lose control, she pulled it down. "Take your shirt off," she demanded and gave him what men desire most from no commitment sex. *A TV journalist caught with a spy in her mouth* were her thoughts wafting through her head, and what a mess this would be to land somewhere in the folds of *The Globe*. But the risk was slight and she was well in control. Hardy was obviously losing control, and losing it fast. He plopped out to his heart broken disappointment with a slight sucking sound, he was in a very bad way.

"I want you inside me Hardy!" she demanded.

"Finish me!" were the pleas of a man turned into a little boy on his first time.

"No! Do me now!"

"Pam, I don't have any!"

"I don't care! Do me now! Trust me!" Hardy was gaining his edge back and Pam grabbed him and once more brought him to the edge with her magic, then releasing him just short of his climax denying him the explosion he desperately needed. "Do me now! I need you inside me! Trust me!" she pleaded.

Hardy was in no state to fight a losing battle, he laid her down in the tall grass and drove her home with all the intensity of a playful revenge he could mustard. For Pam the orgasm was not important. For Hardy it was a shattering explosion! which ushered him into a state of bliss most times reserved for the spinning heads of virgin school boys. The echo of his lovers howl reverberated across the valley like a lonely timber wolf crying to the full moon. They just laid there Pam recalled; Hardy locked deep inside her with his massive namesake throbbing and pulsating, delivering to her what she so desperately desired and dared not tell Hardy of: The game school girls play- and lady journalists, who want their spy to return to them one day.

And so now as a tear dropped on the fold of the letter from Col. Clay; Pam reading it a second time in disbelief or for insight, it was not important anymore to tell Hardy she was about three weeks late while he studied the snow flurries and angry river to lose his pain in the cruel face of the mountain on the other side. The two now becoming one in soul as they quietly finished their holiday dinner, hoping the warmth of their flesh later would ease their despair.

What had started out as flurries had turned into an early season noreaster. The tiny grains of snow and ice pelting the window panes of the Inn. Pam now laid partially atop Hardy, their naked flesh melting into one form, as she gently played with the patch of hair in the center of his chest.

"Will you have leave?"

"I will be away Pam for a very long time. Leave? R&R in Israel every six weeks. I won't be back in the States for a very, very long time. I don't know when."

"But he threw the inspectors out, the air war?"

"Col. Clay, they have work for us. Caliber will find something for us to do. Something is cooking... You know what I was thinking?"

"What?" and she gently kissed his left nipple.

"The day at the dam after we made love, then hiked down through the pines to go skinny dipping while the breeze blew the fall colors down around us. Then how the current carried us down stream. How stupid I felt when we walked naked back through the woods to get our clothes... I love you Pam."

It was a kiss lovers give before they drift off to sleep. The kind of kiss loving couples give after the children are in bed. Afterwards, Pam just laying there playing with his chest hair, listening to him breath. Hardy returning the affection, gently playing with her hair. His eyes closed, listening to her affection, listening to the snow outside blowing up against the glass, a distant fog horn of a tug in the foreground finding its way back down the river making love to their souls as she chugged along.

"Hardy, that day at St. Patrick's, you never told me what you were thinking of. Why did you go?"

"Oh, I like the gothic architecture. In the early years of this spy affair I was almost killed a few times. I credit God, or good luck for saving my life. Though I do not know why sometimes. U.S. Intelligence did a pretty good job at keeping me alive.

But religion is a double edged sword for a spy. I saw that with Covic, the people the KGB use will try to play your passions back against you. It really takes all the fun out of going to Mass. You always have to be constantly on guard. It does not diminish your belief in God, only you must temper yourself. Because of what I have gone through, I am Catholic, and secular. Being secular is a gift of wisdom from my Jewish friends.

Many times the KGB will have their Socialists mole into The Church, this includes Baptists and other denominations. They do this to handle and influence. The Roman Catholic Church is highly political. These Socialists will even at times try to manipulate the clergy with psychology for policy reasons. Get in their way they may even hit you with the spy spray or spy dust like they did to Covic to try to spin him out. In high doses it has an effect like a hallucinogen. Not everyone who has a vision of God is of the same spirit as the children of Fatima, or Lourdes. In the spy game spinning someone out with psychology and chemicals mixed with strong beliefs in religion is done quite often. The police arrive; he's nuts!

I'm a spy Pam. More than a spy, I'm a soldier. My uniform is that old black leather jacket and coat I wear. Soldiers kill in the service of their country. Spies send situations into motion to have people killed in the service of their country. It does not take away my belief in God, only that I am a solder, and I cannot allow myself to get lost in religion. It takes a lot of fun out of the magic and mysticism of The Holy Roman Catholic Church, I still believe in the Latin Mass.

The KGB move the people they control into the various churches out of guilt. It is there out of guilt they ply their treachery, while they kneel and pray to all mighty God out of guilty. They are the busybodies, the people who never could mind their own business. They try to move in and run things. Even try to get the parish priest to do things their way, not the way of the archdiocese or Rome; their way. In highly political spy affairs, they would even out of politics force the parish to change or word the liturgy differently to suite their cause. I guess one is absolved from sin if they practice murder by psychology and can get away with the sick deed without leaving ones fingerprints at the scene. Substitute a sin at the sacrament of penance and do three Hail Marys and two Our Fathers.

Me Pam? I am not a hypocrite. Confession? I cannot even confess my sins even if it were a heart felt desire. The walls have ears for a spy, Catholic priests are human too.

That day at St. Patrick's, the tears were for you. My tears were for the one I loved. Knowing we could not be together. The spy game is like the Gospel, and is best described by scripture:

Verily, verily, I say unto thee, When thou was young, thou girdest thyself, and walkedst whither thou wouldest, but when thou shalt be old, thou shalt stretch both thy hands, and another shall gird thee and carry thee wither thou wouldest not. John-21,18, I should have been a Baptist."

"I'm impressed Hardy."

"I am older now Pam, and my country carries me off to where any man in his right mind would not go. Religion holds no meaning for me as a spy, the verse does.

The tears? They were not just for you, they were for the turmoil I've endured and the pending hurricane, which surrounds me wherever I go. The KGB followed me into the Cathedral that day and sat behind me to harass me. When my tears started to flow so did their abuse. Like uttering an obscenity in the holiest part of the Mass when one is about to receive The Body Of Christ. I guess good Catholics can destroy a person's life without the threat of penance if one is a Socialist. I could not even find sanctuary in The Holy Church.

The tears? The tears were of joy. I was given a day of peace in my life and allowed briefly to be with the one I love. There truly is a God in heaven of which lost spies are forever damned to be estranged from. He saved my life once, what I am doing must be damn important, this, even if I must give up my life in the next world."

"You are getting too heavy Hardy, I'm glad God likes me," and she ran her hand across his chest and made love with her lips to the softness of his neck to return her lover back to the flesh, while a gale blew the snow up against the window panes. The draft now fluttering a lovers candle set up in the corner to feed their intent.

"Hey can we talk? What's going on Vera? What is on your mind?"

"I have to get out of here. New York is just getting to me. The piece I did on the spy affair down south, a lot of hostility."

"John Harding?"

"A little bit. It is just his attitude. I do not know how to respond to him. One moment a friend, the next an enemy. Then at times he reminds me of my father. He mixes me up inside Dan."

"The people down south really abused him Vera. For their own good, his friends listed Hardy and Covic as Russian agents to give them cover. Until the truth was uncovered they were well despised. Extremely abused too. Covic may be a pig but Hardy is an old time Catholic deep in culture, not religion. *The devil with you*, often their attitude. He must of picked that up from his daddy. He looks twenty, he thinks like a sixty-two year old."

"That is how I feel, he is a good looking guy for forty-two but it is like he is living in a time warp, It confuses me. At one moment I fantasize about him as a lover, the next I want him as a father. Then race. I guess my subconscious tells me his type of Catholic is prejudice but Hardy is not. He could care less that I am Puerto Rican. It just freaks me out, confuses me inside. And now the work I have been doing has made a lot of enemies. People are jealous, I need to get out of here."

"Hardy was Covic's unwitting accomplice, he paid a price. He had been hurt bad from this mess. He also belongs to another lady at this time. I know Vera...I have seen the competition. I have been in the business a long time, national needs correspondents. I can pull some strings, get you out of New York. The little work you did do in D.C. did not go unnoticed. The powers to be liked it. That is the word anyhow. Hardy? No guarantee, and he belongs to another."

"All is fair in love and war. Hardy? He is really not the reason. I mean you have seen the intensity, something is there. I cannot lie to myself. But...I have to get out of New York. If you could...?"

"You would be bouncing around Vera. D.C.? Yeah, on occasion, but you do not have the years to call D.C. your home. Most likely? Bosnia, Kosovo, Brussels, Moscow, London, than to the MidEast. It would either make you or burn you out. I think it could be done..? Your decision."

"I have to get out of New York, Dan."

"I will see what I can do Vera..."

"Carla, ask'a Joni to come see me."

"Sure, Vito."

"And I want'a you to work'a tonight you do'a that for me? Now get out of the kitchen, it's 'a hot in here. I will be at the bar."

"Sure Vito."

"Joni, come here and sit, I poor you coffee. I know, no expresso; Sara. You like'a this lady friend of Hardy's?" Joni nodding in agreement, as Vito Longo continued, "people like this lady reporter, I like'a this lady. She has class, a good kid. Hardy really loves her. You'a friends with her now?"

"She called me once, we are suppose to go out when she gets back to Atlanta. I like her," and Joni quietly took a sip to hide the subtle competition of her and Pam where the affections of Hardy lie.

"Good, you let me know about this lady, it's important. She needs anything, you need anything, you talk to me. I take care of you. OK? Good. You'a good kid.

Today? I need a few things. I pay you for the day. I pay you what you make in tips. You take my car, when you get done, the day is yours. You like'a my car..? Good. Suzy cover for you tonight."

"I will not be back for a..."

"You don't worry, my car, she'a rides'a good. You pick up'a can of tuna fish for Covic. We play a little game. He talks too much but every time he does it helps me out. What can I do? We play'a game," and Vito laughs. "He be'a OK. A game. Vito would not get you involved like'a that. Now, you go! Have fun! Oh, but'a Joni, I treat you like'a my own? I know about'a you and Hardy. You leave'a this love affair alone. You do not'a ruin this for Hardy? Huh...? He'a really loves'a this girl. You do that for me...? Good! Go have fun!"

"Carla, call'a the deli for me. Ask'a Joey Caccio to a call'a me back. Ask'a Joey to stop by this afternoon. You do that'a for me? Good, you do what'a you do later," and Carla put down the tray and napkins and hurried to the quiet of the office to place the call. The place settings could wait a few minutes.

He gently played with her dark hair, as she laid quietly naked sleeping next to him. In the seduction of her early morning dreams Hardy was quietly tossing over the wording of his next love note. Often he would get up early and walk to the village for coffee, leaving a note of affection on the end table by the door to warm Pam when she awoke.

He had seen it once outside a city garden café with the understanding coupled with the wisdom of an old-timer, the young lady was as beautiful and as cute as the inscription she belonged to. Though because of job requirements and a foreman's coop(phone company car), the coffee and schooling of romance from Ziggy had to be cut short. Hardy never did see or meet the young lady of his dreams that morning. But it was a top a pole that afternoon that he filed his memory away, he now signed all his notes of affection to Pam, I love you, you're pretty and smart too.

But as he tugged at her locks, she started to stir. They stayed in bed, which was best, the snow had still been piling up. Her dark hair now somewhat shorter and softer than when he found her gnawing away at two pieces of cardboard and Swiss (though the putty could have been American) at the feet of George Washington. The reminence of her Savannah tan now highlighting the mocha color of their twin cups of coffee room service had sent up. If not for her sleepy shinny blue eyes she could have been a Spanish princess walking out of a scene from El Sid. Though it must of been the crossing or short circuiting of wires in his brain between his love for Pam and his sexual frustrations of desire for Vera, who he deeply felt could use the over endowment of his manhood to correct her attitude, which brought him to this point of crisis in his thoughts. The condition widely known in the craft from which good phoneman are born is referred to as cross battery. Though Hardy did come to the understanding deep down in his soul should he ever let Pam go, he would surely suffer a condition a phoneman would call as open tip side. Something akin to playing with half a brain removed inside one's skull. If the lady did not kill him, he most likely would only be left with the ability to hum. Still, over dinner the night before there was obviously something Pam was not telling him. Though denial was putting a quash to thoughts of, *I bet it's a boy?*

Hardy now found himself in an obsession of thoughts in the waking minutes of sips in-between his morning coffee while Pam's naked form went to and fro from the main room to the bath taking care of whatever beautiful naked lady's needs are in the morning, and how to continue their love affair from different corners of the globe? If not for the sight of her naked form, perhaps a tear of separation would form in his eyes. Though since Col. Clay's letter arrived Wednesday, his eyes always seemed to be moist with emotion.

Pam had now been done teasing him and wore a robe now in the bath, as she finished her morning ritual. Outside Hardy watched a gale blow the snow up against the panes of their second floor window while Pam slowly drifted back to bed, her robe dropping to the floor as her naked flesh slid in next to his. Her hand now finding what she so desired but no longer needed between his thighs. "Let me help you with that..."

The shower now ran wildly like their love making a few moments before. Pam to make up for the secrets she kept from Hardy had made their session fun as well as intense. Men love wild loud love making, Pam did not disappoint Hardy but now found sanctuary from her embarrassment in the bath. While Hardy now was left to lick the sweetness of the wounds of his erotic torture of an angel turned whore, who had played both a head trip and an exceptionally loud orgasm on him before she would slip away and tease him from the steam.

Hardy in their moments of trial separation had felt it best to surprise her on her return by slipping on an orange thong. He had taken a side trip to the Poughkeepsie back in October when he had learned Pam was in town. He had found the gentlemen's lingerie nestled somewhere between teddies and ladies G-strings at a shop called Sweet Dreams in the mall. Hardy is use to going to where most men dare not tread. To mustard the nerve for such expeditions is not contrary to his being, though the sales girl did do her best to illicit a blush while Hardy thumbed through the gentlemen thongs, briefs, G-strings and something that looked like a silk jockstrap. In the end it was not Hardy who had blushed.

He could hear the shower running now, it would be a long shower. Pam would make him wait for her return. It could have been their love making, or the orange thong but whatever it was his thoughts had drifted back to Monique, though he could only remember the bad times. And though Pam was of the same cloth, Pam was not Monique.

She had destroyed his life, Hardy at about the same timing returning the screen play to Monique and destroying her's. Hardy could not deal with it, deal with her, or had the desire to do so, or the need to do so. He was now in love with a beautiful lady journalist, losing himself in Pam eased the suffering of a lifetime. Hardy had not the will, the courage, or the heart, should he ever see Monique again. And as the steam rose from the shower; a lover in the mist, Hardy could only recall the bad. His orange thong now only half filled of the pain of a lost lovers bullet to his soul. Had it been Pam's ghost emerging from the steam to be lost in his arms, his thong surely would have been too small.

She was with Covic now, his odd couple partner. Covic was a pig but a pig with a big heart once his guilt kicked in. Which was about once a week after a three-way, or a night on the town with his whores. Monique did put up with it, or would put up with it, were his thoughts, not knowing or really sure what her payment in return would be. Or what redeeming qualities she saw in Covic, if she saw any at all. Or if he would ever really change. In any case, their lives were now apart. The cord had been cut, Monique had chose to stay with the afterbirth.

Hardy slipped the orange thong off and hurried to join Pam in the shower before the water cease to flow.

It had turned warm that Monday morning turning fourteen inches of snow deposited Thanksgiving night and Friday into about ten inches of slush. There was no hurry, check-out was at ten and they would catch the ten-forty-six out of Cold Spring that morning and spend the night in Pam's suite at The Hilton.

Across the river Storm King Mountain rose high above the water covered with snow while another freight lumbered down the tracks at her feet, teasing the sunlight in the glare of the snow as she made her way south. There was no traffic on the Northwest passage, which had proved so elusive for Henry Hudson, only leading him in his day to the wilderness of the mighty Mohawk instead. The snow had even kept the wind surfers at bay. Though with warming temperatures, nuts in wet suits would surely return by noon. On the pier play two small children with their gray haired nanny while a couple of fishermen with a bait pail fussed with their line. Across the cove moving hastily towards the children from the empty marina that looked like a floating ghostown, the Victim of the pending winter season arriving early on Thanksgiving, were a couple of trumpet swans in search of a breakfast of stale white bread. Hardy and Pam closed the door of the Inn and turned away from the pier and their future, as they slowly made their way up the street disappearing down the tunnel at the end of the block and emerging out the other side of the tracks. The Depo was closed until noon, so they slowly made their way a short distance to The Foundry Café, stopping only once so Hardy could remove about four inches of wet snow from his collar. Hardy had been the victim of an old oak and a mild breeze; *perhaps we are all one in nature?* of Eastern philosophy and melancholy honeymoon endings. The hardwood did not miss his mark, the old oak had deposited on him well.

They were two lovers, two silent lovers. Two lovers who were about to have their world torn apart. Beneath the tears of moist eyes, warmth of desire and one in thought, while music of Glen Miller, Artie Shaw and Billie Holiday filled the café. It had been much the same all weekend, Hardy and Pam just staying in bed most of the time, their naked flesh melting into one. When they did rise for more wine, cognac or ice water, Pam would slip on one of her silk night shirts, Hardy his thong; Adult play things to keep the atmosphere light and soften the good-byes amiss the laughter and the tears. Though most times the lingerie did not stay on long; Pam now as she sipped her coffee against the tunes of Glen Miller replaying the scene of her and Hardy naked in front of their bedroom window watching the noreaster play havoc with the river Thanksgiving night. He had been wearing only that damn orange thong when he took her from behind, cupping both her breast with his warm hands, her hair pushed to one side while his lips and teeth gently made a meal out of the nape of her neck. Only the sounds of lovers moans and the chirping of mini orgasms could be heard that evening. There were times when soft words of lovers had been exchanged, even breaking through the tears to lively conversation but for the most part the sighs of mini orgasms was about the most dialogue they had had over the weekend. Too often too deep in love to talk: Words too painful to speak. Only kisses and silence.... silence and kisses: Thoughts too understood to convoy. It was amongst the stirring of her coffee that the entire weekend had manifested itself in the café that morning.

Iraq would be safer for Hardy, his fate and appointed time changing daily depending upon the emotions of which Mafia family were angered by the headlines of the morning papers. This, even if Don Fusaro to repay a debt was looking out for him. There comes a time with adopted fathers, or second daddy's, when business is business. Hardy would be relieved of much stress once he was safely on his flight out of JFK.

For Hardy his entire life he had been an endless victim of tragic love. There were many, with Monique making a guest appearance and showing up every couple of years to sow havoc in his world, or torture his soul. He would get over Pam, though he lied to himself. At least he could; though he thought to himself, Pam was the best thing to have ever happened to him. Get over Pam? He would try but in this case there was a fatality of which either he or his soul would not survive. He would deal with it, were his thoughts rifling through his head while he gazed teary eyed at Pam stirring her coffee quietly. Though he knew he had lied to himself again. He was damned and remembered the punishment and crying of a darkened hallway, as his dad told an uncle to never lay hands on my child again.

He had left a bag at The Half Moon Inn, a beige shaving case with green trim, which the Inn keeper had been kind enough to send down to the Hilton that Monday night. When you are on the go you travel light something Hardy had learned early on in life as an army brat. His shaving kit contained a variety of personal items a gentleman and spy would need. It was now safely tucked away in the luggage he would carry; one large brown gym bag, all packed and ready to go waiting by the side of the suite's main door.

Pam was making some last minute adjustments on her makeup in front of the bathroom mirror, a glow surrounded her like most in her condition. She did not need any makeup. Nor had her glowing condition serve notice on Hardy's pending status as a daddy. It should of but the hand-off was not received, Hardy was too busy absorbed in his pending departure for the Gulf. A fumble of intelligence of which Col. Clay would have canned him for. Hardy was quietly sitting by the phone waiting for the courtesy call from the front desk to advise him the limo had arrived.

Outside several floors below on the bustling crossroads and walkways of 7th Avenue mixed in with the hordes that make up the crowds of New York, were an array of law-enforcement starting with the NYPD, The New York State Organized Crime Task Force, along with the FBI and uniformed and undercover cops of both the NYPD and New York State Police. All of which blended chameleon like into the crowds of 7th Avenue and the diverse city landscape, except for one uniformed cop directing traffic up on the corner of 57th Street. Though even the cop directing traffic and the metermaids of the traffic and sanitation division were undercover.

The ride to the airport was much the same as the ride down on the train, the weekend, Thanksgiving or breakfast at The Foundry; silent understanding, silent affection, silent warmth while their forms melted into one in the back of the oversized Lincoln Town Car. Staying that way till the airport and up the escalator to the ticket office and baggage check. Pam's head most times resting on his shoulders, her arm catching his, her hand finding his. Her murmured words finding their way whispered into his ears.

On the escalator were an army of travelers going up, an equal or lesser number retreating, descending going the opposite way with an equal number of mix expressions and emotions on their faces. Kennedy was extremely busy that morning. December 1st, the Holiday Season, the first week after Thanksgiving, JFK could have been Macy's. And as diverse as two lovers being pulled to different parts of the earth, so were the masses at The American Terminal that morning. There were tourists dressed in the usual tourists uniform or profile along with learned travelers, Ph.D.'s on a seminar to nowhere. There were businessmen vying for first class and little kids with disposable Kodak cameras creating a handful for mummy and daddy. There were people from all walks of life, and twice that many nations. There were Japs and a delegation of Chinese heading to taste British tea. There were a family of French ready to make friends with the Chinese, hoping to advise them of British beef, or a better wine than Chilean. There was an old German with his grandson crying on his knee in the lounge atop the terminal. Near by a young Arab man with his even younger Irish bride of not more than eighteen, and obviously extremely pregnant. Her blue eyes shining and illuminating the baggage check-in line and adjacent lounge, her belly big enough for twins with her pretty face and flowing blond hair catching the eyes of a handful of single men before they realized her condition. Secretly wishing at the sight of her beauty that it only were they, who would have spent the night to which her body would blossom.

One by one the weary and the excited, the dull and the eccentrics, the young and the old with the virtuous of all creeds lined up to check their bags and take the next step to somewhere. In the line now could be found the old German and his grandson. Not far off the Arab and his young Irish bride mixed in with a handful of tourists and a couple of businessmen with twice that many Chinese. Caught within the folds of the light hearted were Pam and Hardy.

After a few minutes the next two openings for claims and baggage appeared; the old German and the boy were on the left, the Arab and his young bride were on the right. One bag, apparently only hers. Hardy and Pam watched him kiss his bride good-bye, hugging her close till his brides bag cleared the metal detectors and made it through the doggy door on the conveyer belts to the other side.

"FBI FREEZE!" as two very large agents came out on nowhere to slam the Arab to the floor! Only to have the young Yemenite whip out an electric car door opener from the pocket of his sport jacket "BOMB! Everybody get down!" screamed again, as the booted steel foot of a third agent stomped down upon his wrist! A fourth gently prying the remote detonator easily from his maimed hand.

His Irish bride had landed in the corner wailing: "You bastard! You fucken creep!" while the tears flowed out of her sockets like waterfalls. She was to personally deliver the CD player now tucked safely away in her bag in the grip of the U.S. Customs Agent behind the doggy door to Uncle Yourself during her brief stop in London. The bag not staying long in the grip of the customs agent before it was dropped in a hard steel container kept around for just such arrangements.

The old German was still laying atop his grandson when the three FBI agents lead him away to chants of God is great! death to America! and Zionist pig! A fourth remained behind. It was now apparent to Pam and Hardy who out of magic or levity had found themselves out of the line, landing somewhere in the corner of the lounge at about the same time the terrorist crashed face down into the floor; two FBI agents had grabbed both of them by the flesh of their arms. Then whisking them away to safety in what felt like an airborne assault to where they both stood now shaking of both momentary terror and adrenaline rush to the stone face federal agents in the lounge who had saved them for questioning instead of shrapnel which never came.

In the lounge that morning were almost as many cops and federal agents as there were passengers, including Port Authority Police and airport security. The New York State Organized Crime Task Force almost out numbering the FBI, a gift of Don Fusaro's friendship Hardy must put up with wherever he goes. They had tagged along and felt it more than appropriate to lend the FBI a hand.

"John Harding? Pam Wellington? Come with me." Which was more to be expected and somewhat special, the other would be travelers would be taken to the main room to be debriefed while the jet would be fully unloaded of cargo and parcels and delayed for an estimated two hours, which meant maybe tomorrow they could board. The folks at Kennedy now had to make a fine tooth going over of every inch of the plane. An inventory would follow of every item—a jet should and should not have.

In the corner of the roped off section as the agents lead Hardy and Pam away sat the Irish bride uncontrollably crying. Coming to the realization her husband would have sacrificed both her and what the nurse at the hospital said were two very healthy twin girls waiting to be born for his holy war. The forth agent was stern but understanding, he now had a willing witness.

"John Harding, Pam Wellington; Special Agent Heartgrow, Special Agent Ryan. John, who knew you were taking this flight? Don Fusaro-Debenadetto? The Israelis? Anyone in Atlanta? New York? Any contact with the French? Countries of North Africa?

"Pam, how about you, anyone.... ?"

CHAPTER
8

Harry was a nice enough guy for a serial killer, always polite and courteous. Harry was also unstable like most of his unfortunate breed or brethren, who fall victim to such anti-society habits as murder tends to be. Like the many before him who hated mom and were too confused over their erotic sexuality and lack of understanding of such, which comes with maturity and a healthy sex life, Harry did not pick up on the KGB subtleties which mask themselves in undercover work. His subconscious did and he started his career as a serial killer quite by accident on his first date with a street walker that had been previously scripted by some Ph.D. in psychology, who had both an in with The Shithead Division and his patrons in Moscow. The FBI do not employ serial killers, the FSB did. The doctor of course was a different kind of double agent. Harry by midsummer had been trained by a series of rewards and punishments. Sex if he was good, guilt if he misbehaved or missed a que. In the end the message was *kill who you were suppose to and enjoy your sex.* If not, the spider people knew about stuff of your childhood and they will hurt you. The doctor also had well placed friends in society: And Mrs. Crawford, isn't it a shame about so and so's kid? Your daughter isn't one of the kids I see out at the corner at ten at night? And how is your husband doing at Loral these days? Sounds very interesting. Oh, your nerves, kids, I went through the same. The doctor prescribed something for me back then. Let me think now...

The doctor was only one of a few in his craft Moscow had targeted, his work with the FBI and their Shithead Division of local and state cops had flashed up on their data base. Doctors are human too. Most of his brethren knew about the darkside and were good people and professionals, who were well equipped and prepared by education and placement of their lives to guard against such treachery. The ones who were intelligence assets Langley was able to protect. It is a little shared secret no one really talks of, psychology and the spy game. Nor could the professional community let their ranks be ransacked by the assertion of every paranoid schizophrenic who thought he was part of a CIA conspiracy or that his doctor was a spy. But the truth is the weak hearted are used in the spy game, as Harry was. Just another throw-away unconscious agent assassin. The ones who did not catch on became the Harrys.

But a reputation of law-enforcement and good undercover work, the doctor needed no help in finding an army of psychological socialist Cretans as handlers. Make poor bastards like Harry jump through a hoop like a circus dog. They were mostly college kids, all the pot and coke one could do if they helped the doc out and played his little undercover game. Oh, don't worry officer, he is mine. Something could always be worked out in pretrial, and usually was. The doctor had ties to the FBI, the college children were naïve. The doctor and his Cretans, the people Harry would refer to as spider people, the people Hardy hated, were the brainy types the KGB would use to run operations against our government. So smart they were stupid. So aloof and snooty they make your skin crawl. They were the head in the clouds type, who in reality have their head bent over backwards stuck up their own ass. So gifted with intelligence that they were ignorant of normal social behavior, or the common sense one learns in pre-K of how to tie one's own shoe at age four. Understands Freud and advanced micro molecular electronic theory, yet cannot raise their own children, or change the oil in their car. Hardy knew the type well, despised them with vehement furor. Ignorant of normal social behavior, and most times trapped in the spy game by their own inequities. Work undercover for the FBI, and handle some Poor confused kid to kill people. As Hardy would say, "They were dangerously dumb too." Your typical Ph.D./KGB agent and self-assigned—self-absorbed social worker type for social causes, who felt it best, government should be managed by doctors and scientists, not by our Bill Of Rights or Constitution...

"And so gentlemen, the murder last week was the seventh since April. The same MO applies to all three locations: Atlanta, Athens and Savannah. Our man is on the move."

The modem spy game is played by psychology, mind control and paranoia. Paranoia, for so many times if you do not respond to the psychology, the KGB make the threat real. *Could their be any left? A cell?* Were the thoughts of Special Agent Louis Johnson, a strapping black man and former college basketball star of six feet five, as he listened to the GBI wrap up their briefings on the Georgia serial killings. Special Agent Johnson was now reflecting back on both the briefing and his exchange of words with John Harding many months before.

Agent Johnson had chased Hardy around over the years in The Southern Spy Affair thinking he was a Russian agent, coming to the realization a little too late that Hardy was an American agent. Then having the unpleasant task of playing The Shithead Division back on the KGB and narco-traffickers to the demise of their careers, and some, their lives. His assignment had given Special Agent Johnson broad powers. It had also taken the full might of the Bureau to force the cops the state task force was using to play themselves back on the enemy, his reports often landing on Senator Hatch's desk.

In the end, it was Hardy and Covic who did most of the bulk work in the spy affair. The Sicilians realized the treachery of the KGB spies and the little undercover games they played with the police; a tradeoff at their expense, most were eliminated. Spies. Spies get to have all the fun, or at least pull the carpet and send things into motion. The dirt of the business which must be done, his thoughts, and he could not prove it anyway. Most were killed? but not all? again were his thoughts. The briefing by the GBI, and an unlikely rise of a serial killer from street walker to high class callgirl. Then, how quickly the change in the killer's diet. Though...the MO did stay the same.

And then his thoughts drifted to Don Fusaro-Debenadetto, and why Hardy wasn't killed or why Don Fusaro was so hell bent for election to protect him? And what does Hardy have going with the traditional Mafia? Not all the bad were eliminated..? The KGB too..? Recruited KGB on American soil? Hardy knew the type well. And now, so did he.

Hardy believed and so did Agent Johnson, coming to the realization just after he almost baited Hardy into a fist fight with a federal agent; Special Agents do not play fair all the time either. But now Hardy's discourse rang through his brain word for word: Socialist kill little children! Murder by psychology! Children slaughtered for policy or a spy game!

Makes you sick. Get some poor confused drug ridden insect to do your dirty work! He could hear Hardy screaming out the words in their interview. God damn outlaw for the U.S. Government! Sometimes he wished he never heard of John Custer Harding. The interview had taken place over three years ago. It ended with an exchange of subtle blackmail; federal charges against John Harding to Hardy's suggestion of his undercover operation being somewhat compromised followed up the next day by a conference call between himself, Special Agent In Charge John Blacke, Director Freeh and DCI George Tenet, who was the Deputy DCI at the time. Hardy had won out. Hardy was obviously CIA, this, even if no one would admit to owning him. Don Fusaro wasn't such a bad guy but Agent Johnson at the time longed for the old days when Don Fusaro was no longer a hitman for America and Atlanta would return to a simple game of cops and robbers. As for Hardy..? Nobody blackmails the FBI! though Don Fusaro-Debenadetto did stay a free man. But now Hardy was gone and it was quickly returning once again to a game of cops and robbers.

Agent Johnson looked at his watch and hoped he now had time to make it back to the office before four-thirty. It was December twelfth, the report from JFK and Louis Schrillo's office had just been sent down by secure fax. He wanted to read about Hardy's most recent classified adventure before he went home to join his wife and three kids in their suburban middle-class neighborhood of Atlanta.

The windshield wipers slapped wildly on the front screen of Agent Johnson's car, as a steady cold rain came pouring down. They were on low, one of blades pulling out of its bracket, challenging the other and making the ride to the crime scene more difficult and slower. Agent Johnson had used his own car that evening instead of opting to go back to the office to use one of the Bureau's or his wife's. Across his mind was playing a series of thoughts of Hardy, of serial killers, of KGB covert operations aimed at handling spies or destabilizing America.

The object so often is to get someone else to do your dirty work. Could there still be some KGB around? God.... it is so different when you leave the world of legal or declared agents. Shadowy, scary as hell. God damn creepy, makes your skin crawl. Little children lying on the ground dead, like shattered shards of broken glass of picture windows in a protection racket to secure or recruit some agent for a foreign government, most times Russia. And God damn Hardy for turning things upside down and making me think like that! God...I've had it played on me myself. Instead of Loral or General Dynamics; Gee Louis, isn't it unfortunate what happened to that girl in the papers...? Was she free spirited? Oh, I'm sorry, I know, the FBI cannot even comment on such things. Just sad. Oh, by the way, how is your little girl doing? I bet you are proud of her? A junior now? Wow? Good kid I bet? You know I saw that piece on the six o'clock the other night, God, it must be very interesting what the Bureau does on cases like that? Your little girl, seventeen, very pretty. Does she go out a lot?

God damn Hardy, why did he have to start this? Couldn't the damn CIA find enough KGB targets to hit overseas? This looks like the place...

The cold rain had tapered to a fine mist when Agent Johnson pulled on to the dirt service road of the old aqueduct to glaring lights of the crime scene, which highlighted his rust red colored old Buick in need of repair. In the lights could be seen the wandering of two groups of state and local law-enforcement. The first grouping was on top of the aqueduct, the second at the bottom of the embankment tending to whatever cops do when a dead body is located and foul play is involved.

"Detective Masa, this Agent Johnson of the FBI."

"Oh, I know Louis. Long time. Clark, write Agent Louis out a ticket, unsafe driving condition."

"The hell you will Robert! Good to see you, same old Rob. What do we have here?"

"Another one. No ID. Strangled and stabbed through the heart. Young, twenty-five to thirty. Good looking young girl. Panties over by the tree where we set up the floods. She was wearing a *T*."

"Rob, Clark, take a look at this," one of Detective Masa's men said as he opened the file.

"Guys, Agent Johnson."

"Mary Santora, age 27. Part-time model. Some gentlemen's magazines. A couple gentlemen's clubs. Here is a list of publishers. Divorced, a three-year-old daughter. Sometime escort. High-end clientele. For the most part a good single mother trying to make money on the side. When we found her she was, or I should say wasn't wearing an expensive cocktail dress? Party dress? I will have to have one of the girls fill me in on the right term."

"Hooking?"

"No Rob, we think she was just out with friends, B&B Disco out on Artery 80. You know, the strip everyone parties at?"

Route 80 was a six to eight lane highway which ran between Savannah and Bloomingdale.

"Another callgirl?" Robert Masa. asked.

"When she does, did, it was strictly through an agency. Very top-shelf this lady was. Highend hotels, conference centers. She did a lot of work at the Marriot and Crowne Plaza in Atlanta. Businessmen, jocks, politicians, execs. A lot of money the girls said since the Braves got hot. Nice girl. Needs money. Husband left her with a quite a mortgage. 20 seconds on TV. Network, sells soap. Just out to have a good time last Friday evening. What do you have on the new one..?" and Detective Burrows handed the file to Detective Masa..

"Not much. The usual way. No ID this time."

"He's getting careful, how many does this make? Eight?"

"Nine. Number ten was found this morning in at Atlanta," and Detective Masa looked at Detective Burrows and guessed his next question. "The same," he said, as he handed the file to Agent Johnson amid the ground fog and the fading mist of the crime scene. The silhouettes of their colleagues dancing across the fog in the lighted, treachery like ghosts ascending to heaven. "What troubles you Louis?"

"We can talk later...But the first one was a streetwalker. It's...just something does not fit. Tomorrow, I will stop by your police station. I have to get home, maybe hit Penny's. I have to get the wife something for Christmas. I'll see you tomorrow."

And so it was in late fall of '98, at very dawn of winter after a brief lull, beautiful young women started disappearing all over Georgia, turning up on the roads and right-a-ways between Atlanta, Savannah and Athens.

"We owe Mr. Harding a little payback. Pam Wellington is a very attractive young lady, emotional too. Does Harry like the news? It would be useful to know what John Custer Harding is up to on his little adventure in the Middle East. Have your people steer Harry to DNN. Pam has lots of friends, she likes to talk. A victim of reckless love now. Maybe she needs therapy? Harry and her could meet?"

And with that the online chat ended....

CHAPTER
9

The stopover in London was brief, though it had been good to see Trevor again, if only for one evening of bullshit and twenty-five-year-old Port. The connecting flight to Riyadh had left on time the following morning.

Christmas had been quiet, a simple dinner of turkey and fixings shared with the guys of the 82nd Airborne in the mess in the compound. Which held both the facilities for Caliber and the comings and goings of The United States Army. Hardy was, however, able to sneak down stairs to the phone room Christmas Day to clip on Col. Clay's line and place an overseas call to Atlanta; perks of the business. Besides Col. Clay would toss it off and it was all in the game. Hardy was sure it would cost him somewhere down the line.

But it was on the twenty-third of January, Hardy received the call by way of his beeper. He had been somewhere in the middle of an oil field outside of Kuwait City leaning more towards Bahrain, which was also part of his district by air, working on a set of three different censors for air quality, noise abatement and seismic movement. The devil wanted his due. Christmas Day had caught up to Hardy, Col. Clay's secretary asked Hardy to forget about the CEV, wrap it up, how did you do at the cell site earlier? and he would like to see you immediately.

"Hardy, I have a little mission for you to go on. If you could maybe you could delay your leave until you get back?" Col. Clay looked up from his papers and across to see Hardy gently nod his head. "These papers just arrived, we are going to play a little game with the army. I would like you to drop this package off in Brussels for Gen. Clark, than go see your father. The KGB or FSB, whatever they are called, should not notice you."

"Sure."

"Hardy, I have to bust your balls."

"Christmas Day?"

"No, I can explain that. I am glad you called your girl friend. Hardy, it has gotten back to me from my sources, Miss. Wellington may be having your baby."

"God damn her!" Hardy said firmly, though not very loudly with his eyes grimaced. The intense anger showing on his face.

"Did you know?"

"No," this time the word and expression said softy and quietly, the momentary anger fading from Hardy's face.

"Well it could be problems Hardy. In any case, drop this off in Brussels, then I think Gen. Clark has some errand for you to do. When you get back stop in and see me, then take leave. Tel Aviv I believe is where everybody goes. Hot little town I hear. Leave this afternoon. Oh, and when you get back, bring coffee for everyone."

"Milk no sugar....?"

Yevgeny Primakov sat quietly looking over the latest intelligence from the Gulf his deputy had dropped on his desk, taking his reading glasses off once to clean them and turned to his aide Ivan Patwijec for some quiet analysis.

"This could be trouble Ivan;" turning the last page and handing the folder back to Patwijec. "We could track the girl?"

"Which one?"

"All of them. I have known the Americans too long not to look the other way while I get kicked in the ass."

"Could be nothing Yevgeny?"

"Could be. Czechoff would know. But who I really need to get in touch with is Marcus Wolfe. He still plays the game in Germany? Can we still trust him? I have not seen Marcus for many years."

"A former spy master and intelligence chief. He was a good Socialist. I believe he still is. Big problems with reunification. I will see what he is up to. Still handling and managing a few cells, I believe."

"Contact them both..."

"Stella."

"Yes Col. Clay."

"Come on in and bring your pad. I think Hardy will be just the right man to mix it up with the FSB."

"You mean SVR? Col. Clay?"

"Well, whatever the hell the Russians call themselves these days. That will be your second memo to Riyadh, they are to be call KGB regardless. Too many people do not know who we are talking about. In any case, it is coming up on four-thirty, Hardy should be on his way.

Bring your pad; two short ones. We'll have some fun. I will get you out of here by five. Promise."

It was all but about twelve minutes when Col. Clay finished and looked up at Stella. "Well that is about it, type it up tomorrow."

"Hardy should enjoy the change."

"Well, state side when you become involved in these things law-enforcement always throws in because the Mafia angle. The mob mentality. It's like a sergeant in hand to hand combat. Hardy was banged around pretty bad in Atlanta. The spy game is an officer's game; a chess game, though our guys do not play chess. They look out the window of their quarters and view a gridiron or a battlefield, the Russians play chess. But there is a difference, we cannot have sergeants dropping bombs on each other. Maybe the FBI can, we can't. There are reasons why we have Officers and use men like Hardy. We have to think first."

"Yeah, I know Ben. I see it in Jack."

"How is Jack, Stella?"

"He is doing good, back home with the kids. Southern Command has been nice enough to work it out that only one of us is sent overseas at a time."

"Anyway, get out of here, call your husband. If you have any problems, use my phone. I will see you tomorrow."

The old churchyard in Wales was sleepily deserted, as a warm glow of light and a handful of flurries from the silver shrouded sky anointed them while they walked along in a biting mist through the churchyard cemetery. He had come for Hardy, interceded for Hardy, listening to the child in his adult innocence. And as they strolled along between the frozen frosted golden tuffs of tall grass in their eternal ritual of guarding the headstones of another age, the bitterness of the cold did not pierce his flesh, nor the essences of the ghostly realm of his counselor clothed only in his holy garments and robe of another age. Hardy in his Southern best reached out to reflect upon his wretched form shown before him lifeless in an Atlanta homeless shelter on the silver morning's heavens about two o'clock high in the bitter steel cold English-Welsh winters sky.

He spoke to Hardy of courage; of God and country; of the nobleness of his young deed and quest. He spoke of deliverance and righteousness, and of the understanding that the crusade of his mission not only frees America of her bondage inflicted upon her by her enemies, but of the bondage of the many in the free world and the third world, and that he must always do what is right and just: Render unto God that which is God's, he spoke. Render unto America that which is of the goodness and beauty of her realm. But it was with the touch of his warm hand while at the same moment another dove's flurry anointed his forehead melting away to a tear just below his brow, that he spoke the words that Hardy knew before his visitation; that most who play the great game must someday pay with their lives like he and of Our Lord who sent him on his quest at the dawn of this age. For surely few are left to ripen on the vine in the great game. And than he blessed him...

"Touchdown will be in approximately twelve minutes, please fasten your seat belt," and than she repeated her message in German, as it once again bellowed out over the PA, whose level was turned up way too high.

Hardy had returned to the flesh to awaken that April morning to find a St. Christopher's pendant lying near his clothing which laid in a heap on the floor and an old black gentleman, who's heart had not survived another evening amongst Atlanta's homeless.

St. Joseph Of Arimathaea was no where to be found, though his presents still filled the great hall of the homeless blessing the old black man on his final journey. The crucifix on the north wall now seemed softer and more merciful—more redeeming—more demanding of those on this earth that Hardy should be fed and sent on his way to complete that which he was brought into this world for.

That afternoon one of the old-timers had spotted Hardy as he was on his way to pay his last respects to a friend he never knew; a man who substituted his life for a screen play of the living world he knew not of. Old Brendan took the lad in. The truth, he had been looking for Hardy, the lad, as the old Irish splicer would call him, since it came down among the retirees that the beast had fled town and was now somewhere in the blue waters of the Caribbean skinny dipping with Hardy's lover and love.

He took him in and it was but three weeks later to the day that one of the lads in corporate, for they were all laddy boys to the old Irish telephoneman, broke down in a tear filled confession which lead to Hardy's redemption two weeks later. Sending him off once more to his crusade of God and country and to the arms of a Miss Pam Wellington. The lad at corporate did narrowly escape being shot, though the severe beating he received was recanted at Mountainberry's with the post script of his confession being he rightfully deserved it and he counted himself lucky.

And Hardy reflected and pondered his thoughts of that evening and of the next day with old Brendan. He had been with St. Joseph Of Arimathaea, walked with him while viewing his own dead flesh as it laid lifeless in the shelter. He had felt only warmth in the bitterness of the dead in the biting cold of the old church graveyard, his flesh lying still of life or sleeping being played out upon the steel silver gray sky. A reminder of man's mortality.

Perhaps all eternity is of that one last final blast of adopimine upon the receptors of our brains when we give up the ghost? Old Joe was happy and at peace that night in the shelter before he retired, Hardy quietly reflected to himself. For Hardy there was no question of life after death; he had been there, though it was a short fall from heaven. It was pleasant, and his patron was pleased.

But he also know the psychology; we study it because the Russians do and would play it back against our agents: The Jerusalem syndrome. But there is something to religion, Hardy deeply believed; he had been there. And it is always best when one serves his country in the jaws of death to be level with religion. Balanced with God and the disappearance of fear which comes with the belief you will be all right; It won't be me this time. I will be okay. Another? Combat? Safety in numbers. Though now, Hardy was on his own. But there is something in religion Langley quietly sends down along the rumor mill. For should a man have a religious experience or finds himself woven in scripture, it gives the agent a will to live. And there is something about religion; if only all eternity is that final burst of adopimine; it is for the dying. And his thoughts recanted again: Buddhism, though he was not; the right balance of faith. The Jerusalem syndrome: Games in the spy game and the desire to stay alive without doing one's self in by running around the Holy Land in white bed sheets.

There is something about science and religion, he thought, as the wheels screeched down! And a good dose of adopimine never hurt anyone—people tend to live longer.

And in the loving benevolence of this world and of the next, we are all but mortal. We who toil in the shadows in the cold of the free world of the shifting tides of politics and ideology of the raging storms on earth that seek to drag us back to the dark ages of communism or the inhumanity of the age of Dickens: Are there no work houses? No institutions! The balance of society in the measure of humanity. We are all but angels in the struggle of one cold war into the next. Though it is nice to be save, if only for your appointed time of your end. *All spies and saints have demons.*

"Thank you for flying TWA, please watch your step while leaving the plane," and once again she repeated her message in German.

The gate was busy in Brussels, as Hardy hurried onward to baggage and head on to a collision of who he should not, nearly knocking the manila envelope out from his tight muscular grip!

"Oh no!" and a flurry of damn it's and lessor obscenities filled his mind. "Miss Lopez, what a surprise to see you!" he said in a warm condescending voice of a man who just found himself too close to his stalker.

"You fuck!" she replied, and she was in no mood to play games; Hardy slow in realizing the honesty in her anger.

"I love you..."

"Security!" though they did not respond to either English or Spanish.

"Woo, wait. I thought you did this purposely. Please. Please...wait..."

"Look Hardy, I just flew in from Berlin, I have to collect my bag and get over to NATO Headquarters, something is heating up in the Balkans. They have called a news conference for two A.M. Eastern Standard time."

"Look, you have time. I have a car waiting...It's where I am heading Vera—they may not be able to start without me."

"You fuck..." but this time she smiled.

"We can chat in the car, I did not know you were overseas now...."

"Mr. Harding, Gen. Clark will see you now," and Capt. Credo showed him into the generals office draped with an American flag on one side and a NATO flag on the left. The windows were frosted, the glass; leaded. On the right wall was a small library, the left; shelves filled with items of family and past personal pride mixed in against the mahogany woodwork and a desk, which held the same as well as important documents. The general rose quietly and appreciatively to shake Hardy's hand.

"Good evening Mr. Harding."

"Good evening Gen. Clark," Hardy being both gracious and firmly polite as the two shook hands, while Hardy handed the general the envelope.

"Mr. Harding, what we do is important. Mr. Harding, what we are up to is a game between us and Caliber. It is a game but it is an important game. You know this?"

"Yes," Hardy said, his reply spoken softly and firmly.

"I have read the reports from Atlanta and Washington, I am impressed. I strongly believe you will fit right in. Now, how is Col. Clay?"

"He is doing well general."

"Good. Mr. Harding, there are reasons why I have Col. Clay and his secretary as liaisons with Caliber. Good people Mr. Harding. Mr.

Harding, Col. Clay has been a liaison for us to the civilian sector in the past. He really knows what he is doing. You are not army, but..."

"I understand general."

"Good. Now if you wait outside, Capt. Credo will have something for you to do. Oh, and Mr. Harding, you are to visit your father. That is an order."

"Thank you general;" Capt. Credo showed Hardy to the door and returned to Gen. Clark's side, who had just unsealed the manila envelope and thumbed quietly through the packet returning to the top page and reading the heading quietly to himself: TOP SECRET— Updated CIA maps.

"This is why I delayed the news conference Freddie," Capt. Credo quickly glanced down to the papers and looked back with quiet immediate understanding to Gen. Clark without the breaking of silence. "Have Sgt. Hurley shred these," and he returned the papers to the grip of Capt. Credo. "He is to be told his assignment is classified. He is not to talk to anyone."

Hardy had entered the back of the press conference about a handful of questions before closing and quietly sat in the back clutching the sealed envelope and seal small brown cardboard box containing the circuit board Capt. Credo had given him. There are perks which come with the business, which some had not paid there dues upon rising to the level of their position. It was therefore duty noted by Hardy of Vera's handicap of attending such functions. She was but a mere seat away from Hardy, though twice as much to the door. Leaving her only a wobbling chair to stand on to ask her final question. Which would also be cut short to close the conference. Height was also Vera's handicap. But the brushing off of the disabled during a news advent does tend to make the handicapped unpleasant in mood and disposition. Hardy knew enough to keep his pleasantries to a warm friendly and genuine "hello." Though Hardy's soft conversation was friendly and generic, it was Vera who did not pick up on the deception of strategic ignorance and ambiguity. Hardy held his cards close to his chest. Though he did file away in the recesses of his mind a line or two of intelligence from Vera. She would be in Pristina about the same time as he, and what's more, she would be bouncing around the entire European theater of operation.

But closing news conferences, jet lag and the frustrations of a rookie new comer aboard in the press pool, Vera had a need for coffee and someone to vent her soul to of the sins inflicted on her. For it was not his charm she had lead herself to be a victim of but the gentle smile of their now found friendship. Hardy lead the way to the commissary. Vera was in need of a friend, could not hold her secrets in this state women often find themselves in, and Hardy could, and certainly thought to himself he could use the intelligence. In this case a freebie, the only exchange would be her good knowledge, understandings and frustrations while she blew off steam.

The smell of illness greeted Hardy like death's devil with his cry of a goulish millennium ago sent to cide the earth of those who were now ripe of the vine when he opened the door of his father's apartment in Brussels. A creepy little nurse who he did not trust as far as he could toss her unholy unkept form showed Hardy to the bedside of his dying father. Who did his dying best to turn and greet his son amongst the IV, narcotic drip and the sick purr of the oxygen & breathing machine. His father was yet unable to view the kindness of his son's face, giving Hardy a moment to step back and compose himself an extra second or two to dry his eyes and deal now with his father's wretched form looking more like that of a Jew or a Pole from a Nazi death camp of fifty years before.

"How are you son?" his soft reassuring voice comforting Hardy. "I still have a few more days left in me. Don't cry Hardy."

"Dad, I didn't know," Hardy's eyes were now welling up moist, an Officer's son's discipline keeping the tears at bay.

"You did too good a job in Atlanta son. Had you known, the KGB would have forced you to choose between your daddy and your country. I kept it from Dave and Bonnie for that reason Hardy.

The doctor Hardy. I went for a check up, all was fine. I went back six months later and I had prostate cancer. I knew. I am being eliminated Hardy." Col. Harding could see the anger building in his son's eyes. "I always check. On the security clearance Dr. Swartz turned up an Israeli double. Ours, mostly ours. Jerusalem knows how to play the game, they know the rules. We use his practice a lot. When I received word I was terminal we checked further; NATO, they use him a lot for their people. The doctor seemed OK, one of his health aides turned up KGB. Like the one by my side. Give the right answers; No pain. ...The needle son. The needle most likely had the culture wiped on it."

Hardy was absolutely furious! With an overwhelming desire to snap the neck of his father's torturer.

"No Hardy," and his voice faded to a low revenge. "My people and NATO think I can handle it; handle her. I've played this game before, I most likely will take a few if not all to the grave with me. Son, this old soldier is an old man, let me play *deceiver* on my death bed. Better me, than you, Dave or the grandkids.

"I saw it all in the sixties son. I was involved. The KGB eliminated both grandmothers, than handled the Mafia to give both grandchildren a Sicilian Kiss Of Death at the funeral of one. It is better I die son," and Hardy could see his dad labor under the fatigue of his internal executioner.

"I'll come again Dad, you're tough old bastard. You'll last another six weeks."

"I am going back to Georgetown son to stay with Dave, Bonnie and the kids. They have everything set up. We have the KGB set up. Gen. Clark has past word you have a job to do. You are to do your job. I will not hold it against you if you are not there when I am buried."

Hardy was choked with emotion, a tear welling and spilling down the cheek from his left eye, as his dad grabbed his right arm firmly.

"Promise me that you will do your job son. Remember what I taught you—Your country comes first."

Sometimes a man sins and has to give his life in the spy game. Better to die a hero, than a coward. Better a hero, than a trader. Though Dad had no mortal sin in war or cold war. There is a certain kind of absolution that comes with God, country and honor. Dad's sin was having a son too good at what he did best. Dad's honor was giving his life for his children, their children and future grandchildren. A cold warrior to end. The great deceiver on his death bed, ready to dispatch evil and his torturers to the nether world for the condition they render him; hell to those who break the rules of great game. A soldier and spy should go out of this world by a bullet, a ricin dart or a heart attack, not by some cowards cancer. Hardy knew what his daddy was going to do, Hardy had done it before, played it many times over. Some secrets once told render the spy a security risk by all sides: He knows too much. The agent and to whoever he shared the intelligence with must then all be eliminated. Hardy had promised his dying father before leaving, and the tears of love or guilt did not roll but the fire of revenge burned angrily in his eyes. Whatever Dad bequeathed Hardy by his covert action after his death, Hardy would finish his work and send the sad lot to their untimely slaughter. On the plane ride to Tusla, Hardy recalled the band of mob controlled carpenters who set up outside the door of his little B&B before Don Fusaro-Debenadetto stepped in; Dad may not make it, but I sure as hell will! were his thoughts. Hardy had way too much work left after The Gulf to die in his own spy affair. The revenge would keep him busy and alive even if his country ran dry of work. On both counts it would be impractical to think either vendettas or the spy world would die for the rest of time.

What was left on the military flight? Pam, the baby and should I call her? And knowing damn well if he did the KGB would go after her. They would anyway. She has been compromised, so had he. But...And it would have happened sooner or later.

Once the wheels screeched down Hardy was to look up a Major Davy, of Her Majesty's Royal Infantry Guard, or something like that. His NATO liaison, who would give him a change of clothes and point the way. Though Hardy was still way too upset over his dad and promised himself to be polite to the British. Trevor had taught him but not well. Atlanta was Dixie, Brits faired about the same as Yankees to Johnny Rebs. In truth it was Hardy who should have been paying more attention to Trevor, not Trevor to a transplanted Yankee in Dixie. The mistakes we make, which often come back to bite us all in the ass.

I like the Brits, were his thoughts, it is just they do things so different than us in these affairs of intrigue. Now I play on a neutral ball field, kind of like the Army-Navy Game. God help me if I end up in The Tower Of London over this. What the hell was his name? Major,.? Major, oh.., here it is, damn paper looks like it when through the wash, Major R.A. Davy. *What kind of name is that?* he thought to himself, as his head crashed into the ceiling. The landing had been a little rough.

It was just over dark when Hardy abandoned the Humvee in a deserted potato field just inside NATO controlled territory, driving the last three quarters of a mile with the lights off before he crossed over into the no man's land on foot to find his way into the hills of Pec in the cover of darkness. Major R.A. Davy had assured Hardy, the Yank, a Captain Gillett, would receive his new dog tags in a few days. They now adorned Hardy's neck and felt unusually comfortable under his combat fatigues. His change of clothes and press ID were in the backpack for his trip out of the hills. Hardy had opted for GI cover on the way in. The circuit board, though similar to the satellite TV links he had serviced in the past, was somewhat different and had U.S. Army written all over it. This, even if it did not say so outright. His only friends to keep him warm that evening were a cell phone, his classified military communications gear, a little bit bigger than a cellphone and his side arm, an army issued 9mm Beretta. The only weapon he would carry with him on the dark cold lonely journey. When he got within ear shot, he would give the special forces guys a toot with the communications gear. *But that most likely would not be till tomorrow*, were his thoughts. It would be a long cold night. The air war was just heating up, and Hardy felt he could make good time if an F-15 did not do him in before he tried to get some sleep around two A.M. Hopefully by the next afternoon he could hook up with who he had to.

His work and assignment was both a game and a technical field call of importance. It was obvious to the powers, especial the British and our own forces, that Milosevic knew we were putting a man in. Another dimension of the game was to see how well the enemy could spot, track or intercept Hardy. A spy goes on instincts, Hardy was but about seven or eight miles in that evening when he noticed it. Hardy had too been known for his caution, he would not sleep much that evening. Hardy had known since The Southern Spy affair if he ever entered the Balkans, he would be a big game trophy for both the Russians and Milosevic. Rest that evening would be tense at best.

Hardy had made good time that evening finding time for cover and sleep. He now found himself awake at five-thirty to trudge on ward again. It was about four thirty in the afternoon that he found himself encamped at hill #131 according to his map. *By his instincts and his telemetry he should be in ear shot of his mark, if not able to see the Green Berets by sight alone*, he thought quietly to himself. He typed in his coded message and received his reply to advance to the base camp on the ridge at four-thirty the following morning, and not to advance should he be delayed in his coming past dawn. Which was just as well, the air war the night before and that afternoon had been intense, Hardy could use the rest and welcomed the advice of the group captain to get some shuteye and leave the worry of the enemy to his men. They had Hardy in sight and could easily cover him from the ridge. Though it was best not to give away his position, or theirs if possible.

The by-product of Hardy's assault to their encampment was to monitor the efforts of the Yugoslav Army in their efforts to track or capture Hardy, something Captain Strauss recorded in his log as being feeble at best. Though it was obvious Primakov had had the KGB leak Hardy's activities to the intelligence unit Milosevic was using and had pride in during his failed coup against Western foreign policy. By the time Hardy was ready to leave Kosovo it would go down for as a huge intelligence coup for both Washington and Whitehall over Russia and her dying satellites in Eastern Europe without firing a shot or playing a spy game. Though the A-10s certainly played havoc on the enemies supply lines while the F-15s and F-16s took out their command and control centers. High-tech ruled! The same would be said for Hardy.

Hardy knew but he didn't. A game always follows a spy. He would not know how important his little vacation was till he return to Kuwait. The only thoughts he had that evening was to get some sleep, hook up with the Green Berets in the morning and make it out of Kosovo alive.

The air war was extremely intense, sleep would be difficult. Hooking up with his friendly allied torturers very possible. Leaving Kosovo under press cover at the Russian controlled airport in Pristina deadly and damn near impossible. On all counts his adventure would only really begin when he reached his objective in the morning.

Darkness comes early in the winter. It was cold, the shelling extremely intense, Hardy wished he had whiskey but thought about Pam and flavored cognac instead.

It was still dark that morning when Hardy made his way straight up the loose rocky face of the mountain on a near vertical climb, arriving at the base camp about a quarter after five to have a body builder Ranger grab him by the belt of his backside and toss him a few feet inside the encampment.

"Welcome Mr. Hard-on!" though he said it with hushed intensity and a body language of exclamation and ferocity. "You have a gift for us, and we have a parting gift for you on your way out this afternoon. But time for some breakfast and Captain Strauss would like to chat with you. You will be dining with my CO," and he helped Hardy to his feet and lead him down a goat trail of sorts to the camo tents and the silence of his colleagues.

"This is the card that blew. You can see the burnt mark. Games Hardy. Either the enemy; Russia, or our own people for whatever reason. If you are crippled the opposition will take a swipe at you...? In any case what you are replacing is suppose to do a little bit more;" Captain Strauss could now see in Hardy's face inquisitive avoidance and moved to let him off the hook. "Classified, Hardy."

"Thank you Sir," Hardy said quietly and more like a civilian of which he was than a soldier.

"Hardy, breakfast is canned but it is not bad. Could you do me a favor and take care of this while I have my sergeant make you up a meal?" and Captain Strauss looked over to see Hardy nod with approval. "After that Hardy, have your breakfast and hang out with the guys till about ten, then I have orders to have you do something for me; actually for yourself. Come see me after breakfast a little past ten; ten/ten. Give me time to do what I have to," and again he watched Hardy nod with approval. "Great!" this time spoken by the Captain with serious intense silence.

The circuit card was similar but much smaller than a D4 Carrier Channel Unit card. The installation easy, the housing of the equipment had not been damaged by the intense foreign spark of electric current. Hardy had brought with him an adapter card to facilitate the adjustments of the option rocker switches, equalization and level for the analogue portion, the digital half for the most part was preset. In any case it was best to line it up once, then pop the card in and out six or eight times and possibly give away their position electronically to the enemy by their efforts. All went smoothly and Hardy was back in the tent eating a gourmet canned breakfast by six-thirty while Captain Stauss had one of his men; half sergeant, half technician try it out. It work better than expected; the new card did more. Hardy received a double breakfast for his efforts. A repayment of sorts for a civilian, better than a medal and a lot more energy for his way out that afternoon.

A full belly, a pat on the back; though Hardy would have clocked him if he mentioned a gold star or att'a-boy, Hardy went to hang out with the guys for a few hours.

"Stella, did Kevin Slyer's office call?" Col. Clay spoke gentlemanly over the Meridian Telephone intercom to his personal secretary with fatherly affection.

"Last night Ben, I was waiting until you were free. I will be in a second, I have the folder from Brussels," and Stella moved the picture of Jack and the kids to one side with her tea and picked up the papers and walk the twenty feet to Ben's office.

"No, Ben, the gossip from Caliber is this is a huge spy affair, and still is, regardless of what our friends across the Potomac admit to, or don't admit to. At least that is the gossip relayed to me of what Kevin Slyer was told by someone on Capital Hill, maybe The White House? Apparently something is flaring up again in Atlanta and Whitehall has a man in helping out the FBI. That's the gossip Ben, I don't think it is a game. You know the game and rumor mill, I think this tid bit is real. Anyway, here are the papers from Brussels and the update on Hardy is that he is still in Kosovo and still very much alive," and Ben grinned as Stella place the remaining files on his desk.

"An orange thong, God damn that kid!" Ben said firmly but with force and humor. Have Hardy go on leave when he returns and leave his report on my desk when he gets back. If he lives. When he returns from Tel Aviv have him come in and see me. A little fatherly kind of talk. He is not going to like what I have to say. How is his dad Stella?"

"Bad, very bad Ben," and Stella sat down for a little mid morning break and chat with her adoptive father."

❖ ❖ ❖ ❖ ❖

It was about a quarter after ten when Hardy entered Captain Strauss's tent gently shaking snow off him.

"Hardy, I am glad you left me a few extra minutes. How'd things go?"

"Great, great group of guys."

"Good. Now here is your assignment," and Hardy looked down to read the title of the worn paperback: *Diary Of A Nazi Spy.* "You are to read and complete chapters four, five and six before you leave. You've played the game, you understand how these things work. Pretty good book too, copyright 1956, still holds true today. Hardy, only chapters four five and six.

And then that nice young strapping sergeant you had a run in with this morning and his buddies have a going away present for you. Use the sergeant's tent and keep warm while you read it."

"Thanks Sir."

"Oh, and by the way, you did good work this morning. The system is up and running. You most likely have already saved a few lives. Our boys anyway. That last A-10 that went by.... Well the enemy is not at all amused. Be careful when you leave. Good job."

It was snowing harder when Hardy left the tent and walked down to the sergeants facilities to find the warmest spot he could for his assignment next to a dead smokeless kerosene stove, which gave away the secret of how they enjoyed such warm meals in better times.

The three chapters had amounted to a half a page shy of one hundred and ten, where Captain Strauss found his Penthouse bookmark of Pet Bonnie Jane wedged just under the bold print of chapter seven's heading when Hardy return the novel around three that afternoon.

"I like your bookmark Captain Strauss."

"One of those collector cards. I keep the Playboy for myself. Have a good read?"

"Yes Captain Strauss. I understand. Took my time. Kind'a like to read the whole thing."

"Don't. Look Hardy, you are not military, but that is pretty much an order."

"OK."

"English, tell Bully to come in here," and he turned to Hardy, "Sergeant Bulwark and the guys have something for you Hardy."

Sergeant Bulwark entered the tent a short time later with a handful of his buddies holding a box of Class Act condoms with a red bow on them. Inside the box to Hardy's surprise was not rubbers but a vibrant purple thong with the name Ralph embroidered on the silk fabric.

"You fucked up Hardy. I am sure you have rubbers. Use them next time! You have been compromised," and the lines on the face of Captain Strauss showed both anger and humor. "Bully, see that Hardy is wearing Ralph when he is leaving the camp this afternoon. And gentlemen, see if Hardy is as big as the girls in Atlanta say he is. Hardy and Ralph are to be one when he leaves the camp;" laughter is not allowed when the enemy is looking for your position, though there was a silent hysteria before and after Hardy changed.

"I feel rather small Captain Strauss, it was an orange thong that left me compromised and father to be boys. And she does give good head," Hardy added softly with firm intensity. All humor or not, the enemy was out and about. Silence and the soft spoken was best.

Hardy, its your call. You play the great game. My advice; be a bastard!" were the words spoken by Capt. Strauss with soft tone intensity and much seriousness.

"How was the trip in Hardy."

"Walked mostly, hitched a hayride. Made good time."

"It is snowing pretty hard right now, be careful on the way out. My advice, change into your press cover when you get close to a large village. You know enough to bury the army greens. How does Ralph fit?" Captain Strauss looked up to view Hardy nod and blush with embarrassing approval. "Bully! show Hardy to the perimeter," and with that Bully and his buddies escorted Hardy to the beginning of his journey and pending demise in Europe. Though one never knows with Hardy, and all prayed in the region that evening of those who live and dwell in the hollowed halls of intrigue and war that he would survive, while Hardy's quiet thoughts as he made his way down the snow covered pass through the Balkan hardwoods were of the fragrance of Paris and that he would enjoy France.

Dave Harding was just getting ready to kiss his wife good-bye and head out the door to work when a stressed out uniformed ASPCA officer knocked on the door.

"Good morning, are you Mrs. Harding?"

"Honey, what is it and Dave came to the door. I am Mr. Harding."

"Mr. Harding, have any of your kids been feeding the ducks down at the creek or at the Potomac?"

"No," and Dave could see by his eyes this was more than dead ducks, which he had read about the week before in *The Daily Star*.

"Domestic and wild water fowl have been turning up dead by way of poison Mr. Harding, I know your kids are good kids," and Dave could see by the pale face of the shaken ASPCA officer the powers to be were thinking poor man's bio-terrorism. "Mr. Harding, The National Park Service and the CDC in Atlanta are also investigating, if you see anyone suspicious down by the water, give us a call, will you?" and the only thoughts shown displayed on Dave's face adding to the stress of an ASPCA officer on a national security case were of Dad, Hardy, and the scum really want information.

"I sure will officer," and the honesty showed on Dave's face with the understanding he knew more, and he knew why. Bonnie standing besides Dave showed only confused comprehension and terror on her face. The words *Oh God*, though not spoken, clearly could be read in the lines of her face, which no longer looked thirty-seven but fifty-two.

"Have a nice day Mr. and Mrs. Harding..."

From a distance through the snow it looked like the steeple of a church or a mosque on the horizon. Further off past the steeple black smoke billowed from the night before, just before dawn actually, Hardy seem to recall. But now the A-10s were quiet. Hardy was now standing on the edge of a farmer's field and took a few steps back into the safety of the woods and slipped off his backpack with change of clothes and a press ID from *The Washington Star*. Though if he ever got caught, the copy boy some day when visiting Dave and Bonnie would surely put a 9mm into his head. Hardy quickly changed and thought over what kind of questions he should ask in his pretend interview. But what mostly played on his mind as he found his way across the field was how to get from point *A* to point *B*. Point *B* being Pristina. He had now been three days out of the base camp, and as good as he was with a map, he hadn't the foggiest of where he was. He did not know Slavic very well either.

The bombing had been intense the night before and all the next day increasing in viciousness as the afternoon wore on, as a shaken Vera low on Prozac viewed an unshaven Hardy hop off a gypsy convoy through the café window, the only unbroken piece of glass in the city of Pristina. Coffee and cigarettes seem to settle her nerves, a substitute for Prozac and a mild trade off of sleep, as she watched a worn torn Hardy dazed from the stress and the carnage of an hour's ride out of Atlanta to nowhere which took six and half hour's to Pristina on a peasant wagon being pulled by an imported green John Deer Tractor. Above the city of hell an array of allied eagles gathered looking for the carcass to reap those who were now ripe of this earth, though mostly they only sought to devour the beast. Vera took a sip of coffee, a pull of her cigarette and wiped the moisture from her eyes of the dead bodies, which now lined the streets of the friendly terror in the skies to find the courage to confront her antichrist. Though what she really saw through the window that evening was marriage, as she watched Mr. Harding stumble into her café and into her life.

"I cannot escape to Times Square this time, and we need each other," and he leaned down and kissed her. Vera responded out of need and intensity found in the taking of forbidden fruit, as Hardy moved his lips to the right side of her neck just below her ear. "It's John Marshall of *The Washington Star*," and he whispered, "I don't know but I am tonight."

"I have a flat Hardy, we will save each other."

"We're British now...?" Hardy whispered and she took him by the hand and lead him out the door and across the street, both checking the sky first.

Their love making had been intense and now she laid astride Hardy, half on him gently tugging at the small patch of hair in the center of his chest. Stopping briefly to reach up with her tongue and kiss the side of his neck.

"And so what happened Hardy?"

"Well when Covic left with Monique I ended up with a few things. The next thing I know, a beautiful gripter moves in next door. Anyway, this chick was so good she almost got shot. The mob thought she was a cop. She was not cut of their cloth. She is of mine. The mob thinks sleeze, at least those on the narcotic level. She was four years of good quality school with little money from home and a lot of coed. Not an escort, but had she been born with an over abundance of beauty she would have been a five hundred dollar an hour callgirl escort. She was beautiful just the same. I know talent when I see talent, conditions were I could not sleep with her, so I started to train her. Anyway, after the mob tried to hit her she moved out. They wanted their own con-artist in. It did get back to Don Fusaro, he lost a player for the attempt on Bernadette. When you are a spy and you start training a player, they are your agent. Don Fusaro went wild. Opps, wrong family. The opposition then lost a half a dozen or so. Kind of a belated St. Valentine's Day Massacre."

"You know for a spy Hardy, you talk too much. But I kind of like being your lover tonight. Tonight we are. I owe you, you almost did not make it to Times Square that day. Hardy, I know about Pam. We saved ourselves. I know the rules to the game. Tonight we are in love. Now tell me, who is Ralph?"

Hardy reached over and ran his warm hand up to firmly cup her breast, kissed her and said, "the Special Forces guys know about Pam too."

"Oh...You know you really should call her," and she kissed him, reached down between his legs to give a yank and slid herself atop his namesake.

Hardy's climax came about the same time a cruise missile exploded at the airport on the outskirts of town, Vera's a few seconds later to the boom of an F-16 smashing the sound barrier. Hardy had stayed erotic and erect, having multiples to Vera's intense delight and fear of the terror in the night before they both collapsed into each others arms. Ralph laid lifeless on the floor. Hardy didn't need Ralph that evening but could have used the namesake of the gift box. Vera was on the pill, foam, or something.

"So Hardy, how does a world class spy train a world class gripter if you cannot share your big cock with her."

"Well, the term is *master spy*. The reason she was in the game was she could have scored over a million dollars if she could have gotten her pretty little hands on those documents. She would have also gotten a local businessman from Athens off the hook while she was doing it and received a nice little bonus to boot. The druggies screwed it up on her, I will not even talk of them on the same level of Don Fusaro. Don Fusaro-Debenadetto is the Godfather. Those creeps who almost put a hole in my gripter were not even of the level of Mafia mole. Spies... aah journalists," and Hardy could see Vera start to smile and laugh quietly to herself, "of my level like con artists of her level. Sleeping with me was optional. They screwed everything up. I'm here, she is over there; too late now. She would have been both; world class spy, and world class gripter."

Vera slid up on her side, propping herself up on one elbow and kneaded one of Hardy's nipples; "I may want you for myself Hardy, you like kids? Just kidding, I'm protected," and Vera made light of a situation, which made her world class trophy squirm with both desire and nervousness. Knowing next time he will not receive a thong but be joining Ralph lifeless on the floor. Courtesy of either Bully or Col. Clay. Vera's humor showed light on the first time her lover broke a sweat, leaving his one weakness exposed; his over sized cock. Which she now had tightly in one hand. "Now that the war is over," and Hardy knew she meant theirs, not the one shattering the night outside, "maybe we can see each other? Hardy, I have needs. I've been bouncing around Europe. I left my husband years ago. I know the game. We could use each other? You have a game, one you have to play," and Hardy could now see his one time enemy was consumed with a burring desire of *like*, as well of sexual needs to be fulfilled.

"You know the game?" and he gently stroked her dark Spanish hair. "And you want to play? And you know I must play the bastard?" and he gently kissed her forehead.

"I know the game. Yes. And you really should call her. I like kids, and was that a question mark after your word bastard?" and Vera gave a firm but gentle tug of his over enlarged cock.

"Damn you..." and Hardy closed his eyes and prepared himself for the intensity, which started to triple when Hardy realized she was starting to do for him what gentleman prize most, while at the same time sealing their contract and new found relationship with her warm moist intense seduction. Vera was paying Hardy back for The Times Square Shuttle. Hardy gentle played with a lock of her Spanish hair and drifted off into ecstasy.

The Shiloh Ambulance made it's way north on South Road, stopping at the light and turning left on to Hackensack. Then going a few blocks to Vassar and up two lights to where it would turn into Swenson, giving the two man crew and driver the needed extra time to prepare their charge.

"Welcome home Dad," his second daughter beaming next to Dave. "Dad the kids missed you, getting older, and they will understand. All things considered, you look pretty good. How was the flight?" and Dave and Bonnie showed the crew to where dad would be spending his final days, as they rolled Col. Harding down the dimly lit but loving hallway of their Maryland ranch.

"He is alone today. No Miss Lopez. Col. Ogelvic said he is worth a lot on the chess board. Moscow says let him board."

"A lot Mikhail?"

"Maybe a Putin. Orders, let him board. Big game brewing. If we win we win big. Maybe not the old days but Washington will stumble. Not even interference, let him board," and with that the two Russian intelligence officers watched Hardy climb aboard a six seater at the Pristina airport heading to Greece by way of Albania. It was the trade off of the bargaining of chess pieces between enemies, which saved Hardy's life that morning—or a desire not to lose ones Queen in the first round of play before breakfast. Czech...Hardy was on his way.

CHAPTER
10

Christmas was good to Special Agent John Blacke, his shinny new espresso machine brewing a fresh pot of coffee in the corner of his office next to a large box of chocolates and the small wooden tree stand holding their coffee mugs when Agent Torres and Henry Chatsworth entered the room.

"Steam me a cup of tea will you John when your Christmas present has run its cycle. Keep this pace up and you will need another new coffee pot by Easter," though both Henry and John were now noticing how quiet Robert Torres was.

"Hey, it's not a coffee pot, it's The Gorfino Premium Espresso Maker. Make's damn good cappuccino too. So what's up Robert? nothing from the wife for Valentine's Day? or did we blush in Victoria's Secret?"

Robert was still well deep in thought but not too deep to have missed Agent Blacke's humor, and removed his right hand from his chin, smiled and just said softly, "I will make it up to her when I return to Georgetown; a little milk in mine, John.

Hardy should be finding his way to Pristina at about this time? Maybe a little longer stay?" and his hand returned to his chin. "Col. Clay will most likely break the news to Hardy when he gets back from leave in Tel Aviv. The very end of March maybe? If he gets out of Kosovo alive?" and his hand again spelled out his inner thoughts, or their workings on his face.

"What do you think Henry?"

"Keep me informed John if you could. Right now I would like to concentrate on this doctor and serial killer."

"You think he is *handling* him?"

"I think this doctor is KGB. I think this doctor is a little more connected to the Russians than the Russians would like. They usually try to keep their covert actions extremely insulated. But the spy affair, kind'a fudged everything on The Gremlin. What do I think...? I think this subject is our man. I think this doctor is going to send old Harry sniffing around Miss Wellington, give her an emotional complex of one mind structure or another. Maybe bump her into therapy, handle her? And she is having Hardy's baby.

But then I thought about it last night just after I hung up with my embassy in Washington; so he handles a confused killer or two. But he likes lads with documents? the last spy affair proved that, and this doctor is apparently the one who got away. What if...? What if the good doctor was to come across something in the realm of spying that was just way too good to turn down or let get away? And a wee too bosom to Moscow to boot. What do you think Robert? and two lumps of sugar for my tea."

Agent John Blacke was now looking inquisitively at both Henry and Robert, as Robert handed Henry his tea.

"Hardy has not called Pam. If we hold out a lamb chop for this doctor we better be damn careful. There are some documents we do not want to go over. The snare would have to be air tight around all the embassies and consulates when the time came. If we do John, Henry, we have to think it out slowly and very clearly."

"I think it would be worth the danger the damage could cause. Moscow knows we are working with you, if not Langley, maybe Whitehall. I am sure we could dig up some little tid bit or British biscuit between us. Even a deception, the doctor would fall for a deception. How would he know?"

"The Russians would know. It would not play past the Russians," as Robert looked over to see John Blacke in agreement.

"It would not fly Henry," John said, adding a bit and asserting his position of responsibility as lead agency with his voice and demeanor.

"Oh, the Russians would not buy it gentlemen but by the time they received this little pork chop, we'd have the doctor. Then who is to say what the national security value of this piece of paper is. Moscow gets junk, we nail a creep to a cross. What do you think Robert?"

"I am so consumed with Hardy's new adventure Henry, than this, and few other items," and he took out a picture of Renee Jadot from the file he and John had shared earlier that morning and handed it to Henry with the narrative. "I have a lot on my mind Henry. This lady could be real problems for all of us. Than this doctor. Hardy will be awhile on his little adventure, longer than Hardy thinks. I think we should go slow with this doctor. I think he is already ours. I think he had been had as soon as we made him. I do not want this guy to get away. I want this man snared; hook, line and sinker. Than we let John's people finish him and his operation off."

"If Moscow bites we could play him back?"

"That is what I am thinking John. Moscow is not going to bite for trash. What do you think Henry?"

"We need something good Yanks."

"Robert, what is new from last week regarding Hardy," Special Agent In Charge John Blacke asked CIA liaison Agent Robert Torres in a voice that bellowed and beckoned to be heard even if it went against his intention. His voice had a quality that traveled, and would have, if not for the sound proof room. The Gorfino Espresso Maker again brewing another perfect pot of coffee, while Henry Chatsworth fumbled with his tea with his stumbling hands during the daily mid-morning briefing, a by-product of the spy affair.

"It's confirmed, Hardy has just completed his little service call, he is now trying to find his way out of Kosovo John. In Brussels he found out his daddy was given a case of cancer. It seems no one plays the great game fair anymore. The KGB John are exploiting his father's condition.

Like most of their covert operations they must keep themselves well insulated. The people they are using to torturer his dad are not of the same level as those of the directorate, which supervise such actions. Hardy's dad is an old conjuren, he is a legendary Cold Warrior in his own right. Moscow cannot physically talk to their people, I believe they will fall for the deception. Col. Harding will die but he will take a few with him when he goes. Remission? Once he gets back state side. Then when they realize they have been set up, they will kill him out right. Most likely the narcotic drip piggybacked in his IV for pain. It is what makes 'Günthers' John. If you live the great game hardens you. I only track the players. Behind the scenes; manipulate a piece or two. That is not my job either. I am your counter-part John. Hardy is my quarterback on the team I root for every week. If I can help him out I do. I study the great game, Hardy plays full contact," and John could see Robert was upset yet in control with a face of mourning for a colonel who has not yet died and a colleague he will never meet being sculpted by the brutality of the great game, which make men killers of all those who put on the shoes of the *deceiver*.

"With us it is soccer," added Henry. "John Custer Harding is already a 'Günther,' John. I saw it in his eyes before we introduced ourselves. A little covert mission of my own around Savannah. He told me to 'fuck-off.' The Colombians and the fifth their money buy were brutalizing him that day. He did not know which side I was on.

But my people are quite impressed. At least that is the word faxed down to me. This time direct from Whitehall, via Brussels. Hardy is and can play with a lot of finessse. And I owe him one John, to keep from getting shot myself I went along with the chicanery. Good cover, the goons think we are on opposite sides. But he is there now and I am here. But it is good to file these memories away for a time when they may be needed."

"We are all spies John, just different types," Robert tossed up with an insert of Georgetown polish and common sense. A lot of different cops, there are a lot of different types of spies. Some more deadly than others. All are 'Günthers' at some level. Hardy could not do my job though he possess the knowledge. I could not do his. We do not even talk to each other at Langley. Small talk; weather. We are terrified of what the other will say. Get one another killed.

We all know it. I am glad I am here in Atlanta." Robert looked grave, which comes with a sense of doom every time a colleague tells you something classified. Knowing after you learn the secret you never wanted to know in the first place, it was best to play on and make a good living rather than retire and fall to the curse. Most died for one reason or another a short time after they retired. Robert was forty-two, he had many more years of unwanted advances from the intelligence file marked "classified," and a strong will to work on until they called an ambulette and carted him away to an old age home for retired spies. If he was lucky he had thirty-five years. The reality was that the enemy would most likely kill him by fifty the same way as Hardy's dad to try and find out what they could about The Southern Spy Affair. Talk if you wish not to feel any pain, and maybe an extra few months with loved ones.

"It is about the same for us John. Every time someone at SIS wants to share something with you, you run to see if you can find the cyanide tablets. Scary as hell; *I don't know, I don't want to know.* If they tell you anyway it is because you need to know. God I hate this business! What a rush if you are winning, better than football, my football. Tear your heart to shreds when things go wrong, or when things have to be done. I am sure you have a pet cemetery out back in Langley, Robert for when things have to be done? Classified John, and the wording of your subpoena would have to be word perfect. Isn't that right Robert?" but Robert looked too grave to really respond. "Gentlemen, now let me toss out this little screenplay my people in Whitehall tumbled over for our serial killer fond double agent doctor...."

"And so gentlemen, that is pretty much the little snare my friends across the pond wanted you and Robert to look over. And John, my contact at SIS wants you to know his contact at Scotland Yard apologizes for telling your Agent Quacken he was not fit to be a bobbi," Henry looked up to see John in a little puzzlement. "Oh, the surveillance. We monitor our problem children too. So upset he just started talking to us,"

Henry now looked over to see Robert evolved from his grave mood to mild laughter and amusement.

"Who is Bobby?" Robert asked to a bit warmer gloom and thawed out humor, than had once been reported by *ESP* when the meeting began, to see both Henry and John take the whole situation in stride, and certainly humor is best before you sink your teeth into some wayward double agent profiler. Sad but it certainly is best if you can laugh when you watch some KGB mole have his life self-destruct before you. Robert like the input Whitehall had sent over and would be in contact with his people at Langley that afternoon.

"Gentlemen, this one patient this doctor has has a lot of material. My agents are keeping a close watch on him. He likes us, he does not really care for the doctor; on to him. How would we handle the dead letter drops? Your people Robert? Henry?" John looked over to see Robert and Henry become suddenly extremely serious.

"John, for myself or any of my people back in Washington to use an FBI field office for an undercover assignment like this would be extremely dangerous."

"That is right John, it could bring down your whole intelligence community. There is a right way to do these things and a wrong way."

"John, for Langley to get involved we have to have total deniability. Dead wood, sometimes we use an army base. Classified John, I cannot tell you. Do you have any agents you can throw away?" John could see by the look in Robert's eyes he was deadly serious. It was the look of death from a fellow agent that even chills the spine of a Special Agent In Charge. The ancient battle of intelligence—vs—law-enforcement suddenly entered the room and reared it's ugly head. Special Agent In Charge John Blacke was out numbered two to one."

"Gentlemen, this kid John's men have under surveillance is kind of a prodigy according to our double agent beast handler, he catches on pretty quick. Is there an army base close by? Fort Benning? The area he would have to use would have to be open to the public, yet the MPs would have to be able to challenge the rights of your people. Ours? Or the FBI's? The U.S. Army would know what to do with it. This is their domain. Kind'a a damn good reason to have a British base on American soil. This is your one weakness Yanks, you're too damn strong and too damn proud."

"Henry is right John, and I am too damn upset to even talk right now. Do you even realize just how sensitive this whole affair would be?" and Robert was visibly shaken at the mare thought of proceeding further to a conversation and discussions of frame work, which would take them all into deeply sensitive and extremely classified matters.

Robert in the back of his head still held delusions of grandeur of making it to retirement someday, the instant graying of his hair and aging in front of his friends told him he would most likely be dead by forty-nine. Looking over he could see John extremely upset and Henry not faring any better, though Henry with his British luck had made it to retirement age.

"This kid gentlemen," Henry piped up, "is strong enough to cut the cord from the beastmaster, but he is also smart enough to shred the documents if he cannot unload them to U.S. Intelligence. I could try but he does not like my personality type and my British accent, he most likely will think he is being false flagged. Bright kid, hates the good doctor. Cannot really blame him. Not after we had our friend Harry surface," and Henry turned to Robert for confirmation.

"That is right John, if the kid does it he has to do it himself. The problem is he does not know how."

"'Operation Vortex' if things go wrong gentlemen," Henry chipped in.

"Not this time Henry, this is relatively small. It almost happened last summer; Hardy, the mob was going wild. I have heard Henry you dealt with 'Vortex' in Germany in the seventies."

"I dealt with Günther at that time too. Messy, but it had to be done."

"What is 'Vortex' gentlemen?" a pale looking Special Agent In Charge John Blacke asked to the understanding Robert could not answer leaving the strategic ambiguity to Henry.

"Dead bodies John. Günther did most of the work in those days. Every time the mob would get close to a lead they would run into a dead body. Either ours or theirs. When you gotta go, you gotta go. In layman's terms, we could not let their people get too close to our operation. The mob tends not to play the gentleman's game fair. We even had a handful of dummy operation for those clowns with clubs to uncover. I guess in America they would use baseball bats? A lot of dead bodies in that spy affair. Germany did go our way. Pretty much paved the way for the Wall to come down fifteen years later. Your boy has a few things, it won't be 'Vortex' but it will be serious," and Henry looked over to see Robert quietly please.

"John, I do not know, I do not want to know. I cannot even talk about my thoughts. What Henry just told us sounds a little like a controversial movie I saw with my wife years ago. Every time the guy had a lead, the person would turn up dead. Sounds pretty chilling Henry, are you in therapy?"

"No, but I could use some more tea."

"The hell with tea, lets get lunch gentlemen!" John Blacke said loudly, which should have been heard through the sound proofing. "Gentlemen, my agents suspect Miss Wellington knows she is being stalked. They will keep her safe and sound and pampered too until her over hung lover boy comes home. Bastard hasn't called her! Oh, by the way gentlemen, I have a piece of dead wood, and he is playing for his life right now," and three walked out the door to go down the street for a noon time bite.

Agent In Charge John Blacke was in an especially good mood the following morning when Henry and Robert came in for the daily briefing.

"So how'd things go last night? brain storming, any ideas?"

"Henry and I stopped at O'Brien's and had beer, talked vaguely and veiled about some ideas and thoughts we both had. We understood what we exchanged. Spies of the same breed tend to be on the same plane of thought. Henry as you can see, John, is rubbing off on me."

"Well gentlemen, I had a few thoughts of my own. I have two of my best senior men working on it this morning," John had just finished when the Meridian when off and Jennifer was on the line to advise him Special Agent Miller had just called in and needed to talk with him immediately.

"Oh...I see. That is too bad. Take the rest of the day off, have your partner cover the kid. See me first thing in the morning," and with that John Blacke hung up.

"Agent Miller advised me that when he went to interview the doctor about the spy affair, the doctor lunged for a stiletto letter opener in the office and he had to lay him down. Another team is on the crime scene, I told him to take the day off. His partner Walker will talk with the kid. Just one of those things. Do your people think they may have any openings at Langley, Robert?" Agent Blacke had finished to see them all look grave at the fortunate turn of events.

"Harry now has handlers without a brain John. Pam Wellington will still need to be baby sat," and Henry after he finished looked withdrawn but secretly happy with the turn of advents. "The KGB may move in now for a little more *hands on* for the kid. We could set a trap. We will not catch them at that level, and if we do a week later they will be swapped back to Moscow," Henry said, and he looked over for some consoling from Robert.

"Henry understands where I am coming from John; I have my own set of classified thoughts to worry about. We still need to keep an eye on

Pam," and the meeting turned morbidly silent, while the Gorfino Espresso Maker churned out another pot.

"Are you Robert Nathaniel?" and the college child quietly replied. "I have to ask you a few questions Mr. Nathaniel.

Dr. James Smith was your psychiatrist?," and the delinquent had enough sense to keep his answers to one word.

"Did he ever mention any advisory role he had to the FBI? Did he ever try to recruit you as a Russian Agent? Did he ever mention the names of any of his other patients? Where were you last night?"

After a blitz of one word answers a shaken Robert Nathaniel finally got up the nerve to ask why? Answering the college child's question was optional but Agent Walker went ahead. "Dr. Smith is dead son, I needed to touch base with you," and inside the FBI agent felt sorry for the boy. "The cord has been cut, find yourself another doctor if you need one.

One last question Mr. Nathaniel, do you own a shredder?" and with the nod of Robert's head, he said, "thank you," and left.

With thirty five years as a Special Agent comes the thick skin to deal with the unpleasant and the handful of fuck ups we all inherit in our lives. Agent Miller only had one brandy before he went to bed. He usually sleeps sound, that evening would be no exception. He was glad he was retiring in April, and liked golf. The letter opener had just laid idly next to the doctor when he laid him down. But the eyes; he could have gone for it. Sure the surveillance, but the surveillance is classified. He had earned his retirement that afternoon, and John Blacke knew he would have no trouble with Agent Miller keeping his classified secrets.

CHAPTER
11

A single box of Belgium chocolate adorned Stella's desk along with Hardy's report and Col. Clay's coffee. Hardy was already on the plane to Tel Aviv, in the note he asked Stella to thank Col. Clay for the extra two weeks of leave, and the paid vacation he just came from in Europe. He also responded and conveyed his deep affection to the two; Dad was holding his own, and word had gotten back to him in Greece, his father was doing much better in Maryland. Though two weeks or not, Stella felt sorry for Hardy for what he would face when he returned.

And in the Disco Of Prayers, Prime Minister Ben Netanyahu's friend and one time lover, sharpened her skills and readied her lipstick for her mark to come in the door for some fun and R&R. Zaporah had been both a callgirl and a soldier in the Israeli Army. At five-eight with her dark hair, beamingly beautiful green Jewish eyes and European features, she could have been a model in her younger years, and was. But not of the type the religious sects would be of the breed to find her in. Though sex aside, they were not of the cosmopolitan schooling either. Cosmopolitan was Zaporah. Ben wanted answers, Zaporah's lipstick was sharp.

...France...? and a few other items of intelligence were the thoughts of former spy master Marcus Wolfe, as he readied his insights for an old friend. Maybe a bombing? Paris, Brussels, Amsterdam, Bonn, Berlin or Moscow? Blame the CIA, blame Hardy. He will be running his operations on top of Carlos. Narcotic Trafficking and South American power. Unfortunately we just cannot find high caliber talent in the spy game in these troubled years. But Marcus continued to brain storm; there will be documents. If Hardy gets a hold of them it will be a mess. The French...? The French will let Hardy play. Blame Washington if something goes wrong. Most likely let their own people tag Hardy along and secretly hope they do not kill each other. If Hardy gets lucky? he will play them back...Back on me...And had Marcus Wolfe not been alone, a secretary, friend or lover would have seen how upset he was. But the Wall was now down, talent lacking, and the need to do things the real, real old fashion way was obvious. If he failed, he realized immediately he would lose the children of Socialism he was raising. Though finding semtex and good quality weapons was difficult in this day and age. And so Marcus sat and thought, readying the sublime, a report of thoughts to be sent to an old friend in Moscow. The real, real old fashion way...And just how to accomplish the communiqué?

...France...? and a few other items of intelligence were the thoughts of Ben Netanyahu, and God, I hope he likes Zaporah.

...France, Renee Jadot, Carlos, Marcus, Ariadne/Americain Technologies, Lockhead, Newport Naval Base and Sen. Coyne of Rhode Island along with a Colombian owned company call Laredo Cable of Texas were some of the thoughts playing on the mind of both Robert Torres and Henry Chatsworth just before they entered into their morning ritual at John Blacke's office. And what not they should tell the Special Agent In Charge of The Atlanta FBI field office, with the friendly understanding that Britain and America would both love to run the show. Henry was a friend and colleague but Robert certainly would love to have the better hand when the game ended, so would Whitehall. And getting Hardy laid any more times than needed was not very important. Robert Torres would put a call into Jerusalem later that afternoon, he had enough on his mind without worrying about a beautiful ex Israeli commando.

...France, Hardy and I hope he does not take the news too hard, along with; if I ever get my hands around the throat of Kevin Slyer! were the thoughts of Col. Clay. But before he picked up the phone to ring Stella, a mild snicker and smile consumed his face. Hope he has a good time with Zaporah, I hear she is pretty hot! Four years in the Israeli Army, Special Forces, four years in a strip club and a pretty damn good callgirl too, I hear, and again he gently laughed to himself. "Stella, I need you, bring the file from Caliber marked Brussels," and he hung up the receiver and gentle chuckled again. But then his face became grave, poor Hardy, and he quietly reflected and waited while his friend and assistant came in.

"Hello, is Bin there?" the young Arab voice said in broken English before letting on he was calling from London.

"No, I believe you have a wrong number," he responded, knowing the peace talks had moved too smoothly from one level to the next, leaving little choice but to sacrifice one of the young teenage boys in the village square where the Hasidim meet. "I know of a 'Bin' in Damascus of my family name, perhaps you call there?" and after an exchange of thank *yous* they both hung up.

The coded message had sent chills down the spine of Ibraham, inside he despised the blood shed and the sacrifice of the brethren of his young. Had he not been an Israeli double himself, he would have surely picked up the phone and called Shin Bet. But Ibraham had also smelled KGB that morning, and was well aware of his own CIA past. There is a price to be paid to expose or set up an opposing piece on a chess board; lbraham was high up on to food chain, the other team would lose a few players. They now will pay with their lives for dialing a deliberate wrong number, were his thoughts, as he hurried to his own study and personal library to think over his next move. Though before taking Mark Twain off the shelf to improve his English and American slang, he thought Zaporah, and oh, what a vice I am in.

lbraham knew how closely the Israelis watched, most of the time he was their man, Zaporah his agent. He wanted what was best for his people: Peace. Growing to his maturity in his beliefs, philosophy and understanding by a gifted childhood, which lead him through the best schools in Cairo. He was of the foreign policy breed, unlike Hardy, his mark, who knew the technology and always understood even before national security ease dropping or caller ID, there would at the very least be a DLI on his line.

"Hello Hardy old boy!" Trevor's voice booming over the disco music.

"Hey Trevor! Buy me a pint."

"Damn Yankee. Hey Hardy, that kid from Yorktown got shot."

"God, that was sad. Well, you know, there is a right way to become a spy and a wrong way. His daddy worked at The Department Of State, had an uncle in Atlanta. Started swapping documents to the Russians, thought he would set them up and we would bring him over. The Russians had him for breakfast. We forced him over, he tried to play deceiver and the KGB stuck him with a homosexual lover."

"Happened in Berlin."

"Sucked him dry, kicked him out of the nest in Moscow?"

"Apparently old boy."

"Tough break, glad the Chinese did not get their hands on him," and then, Hardy became serious and direct. "Trevor, I'm from the school, if it is not your's, you don't touch it. When you rise to my level of writer..."

"Your a writer now old boy?" and Trevor gave a little British snicker.

"Well... you learn along the way, a little common sense and honesty are always the best cards to play. Someone like me...? I would put a bullet in my head before I went over. And this Cold War is dead; other laughable spy jokes of note. I've done that much damage to the enemy, I'd bump myself off before my toes walked barefoot in the snow in Moscow. Sad about the kid. A breakdown would have helped him. God, when they sink their teeth into you, you know it."

"Well old boy, the war may be over, the bloody game plays on. Poor lad," and Trevor's mood shifted with a smile to that of a sly British fox. "So my friend of intrigue is only a writer now?" and Trevor's British humor showed through with amusement.

"Well...Yeah, thought I'd play that game for awhile. Oh, a little freebie for you old friend. Hot from the Balkans," and Hardy took out the interview and article from Kosovo. Ghost it for me, will you? Send me my fair share of whatever it is worth."

After a few minutes of a fast read skim, Trevor looked up and said, "'You know Hardy, this ain't bad. If you ever get booted out of the nest again, give me a call. Try a book in the mean time. And the word is old boy you may."

"Not going to happen."

"It may."

"Caliber is good cover, not going to happen, and if you ever ghost my book I will have you shot. British humor or not," and Hardy was now amused at the boldness of his British friend.

"It be a friendly game of spy old boy."

"So how's the BBC these days, and God she is hot" Hardy had glanced across the disco to see Zaporah sharpening her lipstick. "And on the Sabbath too."

"I work for *The Weekly Empire & World Report* these days Hardy. And the word is she is hot! She is also a player Hardy. I suspect you are her mark. Benny apparently wants answers. Benny apparently is also very happy you will be playing on French soil this time. French? At least that is the gossip my girlfriend at 10 Downing Street received. Covering a meeting of Tony Blair and Robin Cook. Downing Street is her post. So what's the game?"

"Fuck her, let her wait. Oh...I'm not sure yet," and the bartender came by. "This pint is on me Trevor."

"Hardy it seems to me a writer could go places a technician for Caliber, or an agent of any of your intelligence services could not. It's the game I play. Good cover, *real cover*. You would of course have to have one or two small works published. I could bloody help you with that old boy," and Hardy could see by to sculpting of the lines on Trevor's face his friend was serious and concerned. "Retire and write fiction. Easier life. That's what the greats do. And God she's hot! You know Hardy, you are starting to look your years now. A tumble with our little Israeli Girl

Scout could be the best thing for you," and Hardy could see Trevor's mood now a bit more playful.

"Writer? No I'm a phoneman, real cover Trevor. In my heart I will always be a telephoneman. I am also starting to subscribe to the school of women being nothing but trouble. Too much sex lately. Too much of the opposition fucking with my head."

"Which one?" and Hardy smiled. "Too much Ralph I suppose old boy."

"You've heard...."

"Is it true what they say about Jewish girls?" Hardy said, her naked flesh still teasing him, Ralph's orange cousin keeping the bedding company on the floor.

"Israeli girls do it better," she replied and it was clear to Zaporah, Hardy too knew how to play the teasing devil's lovers game. I like American boys but I have to be back in Jerusalem for work tomorrow. Why don't you come with me? You stay for awhile?"

"I like this suite sweetheart, only the best for friends of Caliber."

"But Hardy, the commute," she said with some sabra seductive pouting. "When you leave?" and she gave him one of those kisses that make one's namesake steel.

"Am I really your mark?" and then he answered her question. "The fifth of April I have to be back with Caliber in Kuwait. We have almost a month. And you do not have to do me again if you do not want. I know how you think Zaporah."

"Oh, and I know you Hardy."

"A little game between pros?"

"OK, a little courtesy between *Pros*. I like well hung American boys," and he kissed her and settled in with his new found wife for about four weeks of temporary marriage.

"You did a good job with Zaporah, Hardy. The word has come back from Washington, nothing but hyperbole is what the Israelis felt you fed her. And boy is she hot about it!" And Col. Clay looked up with beaming pride and Yankee humor at Hardy's conquest: That's my boy! One of my men. "How is your dad doing Hardy?"

"Better Col. Clay. I called Dave before I left Israel."

"I'm glad," and then his expression changed. "Hardy, you fucked up: Pam. I know, you know the game. We want to kick you out of the nest. You have money now..."

"God damn Trevor! he set me up." Hardy said firmly and forcefully but with respect to Col. Clay.

"The novel Hardy; four five and six, it is pretty much what we want you to do. We have a good cover story for you planned. If you stay here I have to bust your balls. You've played the game before, go on a little adventure. Start with Malta, or Algiers. You know how these things work, you'll find your way. Retire, make it easy on yourself; semi-play. Same thing may happen here as it did at Savannah Telephone. Though I suspect a different game this time. Pam was really just the excuse we were looking for all along. A blessing in disguise for me, and I like you Hardy; second son, you know that. You have everything you need this time to make it. No more homeless shelters or confiscated documents as collateral from Friends who skip town with old lovers. And you are smart enough not to replay your past. I let Trevor know where he could find you John. You know to game Hardy, go on a little adventure. This time around have fun," and Hardy could see in his bosses eyes both fatherly concern and playful amusement. "Well...You fucked up Hardy. You know, you really should call her. Then burn her!" Col. Clay said with intense seriousness and warm amusement.

And then Hardy said, "I did, I have, and do I really have a choice?" and he looked over to his friend and boss for guidance but all he really caught was warm friendly low spoken laughter.

"No!"

"I'm sorry lbraham, they know."

"You were the best Zaporah. My son will be running the escort service. It was good cover for me, Ph.D. and always had funds to go back to school. I am glad it is you Zaporah. Better you Zaporah. Better me than one of the children."

"You have relatives."

"No, you know. The CIA, you. I have to cover my friends. The children of the streets, they do not understand. Jerusalem, Washington, Moscow. They only see pain. I want what is best for them. I want what is best for you too. Like my own Zaporah," though lbraharn would not want his little girl in the business, either business. "You should be the one. It would mean a lot to me."

"It will force me out in the cold when I do."

"Go to New York, Zaporah. Now, its time."

"Good-bye poppa," and with that, she fired one silent shot into her friends heart. Even with loving friends when duty called ice ran through her veins. It was one, she had time and studied the book case to remove *Every Spy A Prince,* lay it by the body and replace it with Mark Twain.

"What do you have for me Ariel?" and Gen. Sharon laid the dossier on Prime Minister Netanyahu's desk. "Damn her. My best girl, maybe my best agent and she comes back with third hand American BS. God, this Mr. Harding is a card. Forty-two, plays like seventy-two. An old conjurien at the tender age of forty-two."

"Well...Benny, you're not much older. The only problem is this tender old conjurien would probably survive a ricin dart. And who cares? His playground is going to be Paris. Pay his airfare, we owe the French one," and General Sharon looked over to see his boss and prodigy smile and gently laugh.

"All the same, it still could be real problems Ariel. Covic drew us in towards the end. Embarrassing if some details come out. But he likes the Cathedral Of Notre Dame. Send him a little love note and let the French pull their hair out. I have the Golan to worry about, you Lebanon; Washington knows. Give him a kiss and send him on his way."

"Zaporah could have a reoccurring role Benny. You like Zaporah."

"I like Zaporah, good fuck too. That was the idea. We ended up with hyperbole gifted wrapped by Col. Clay with a *I love you too*. Hardy has had a little too much Zaporah, though I could use a little more. The wife understands. She knew this before she married me. And we need to know."

"This kid Benny spent many years out in the cold. He has money now, keeps in shape. Be a different game. He also has a lover back home having his baby."

"Yes, I know. We do have people at DNN we can work with. There is a little spy game apparently still going on, the FBI eliminated some doctor/mole the other day. Sloppy, could have blamed us. The report here advises us Whitehall and Langley have a man in each in Atlanta. Its upsetting really, I do not know who I hate to play with more, the British or the French, and Langley really knows how to stick the dagger in and twist it. Let Zaporah reenter the script again, keep the back door open. In the mean time, lets see if we can pick up where the Russians left off with a friendly game of spy. Miss Wellington's father was a Jew, maybe she will help us out? We need to debrief her. Family friends, a friendly game of therapy. *Bennies* for the baby. We'll help her out, but we need to know. Enforcement in the states must be all over her life, our people could piggyback on the surveillance. The bugs are already in place. We have played with the FBI before."

"Well...our young phoneman burned Zaporah, Benny."

"I would not say burned Ariel but he did win the match, and Cranes Stationary on Burgundy letter head with *honey I left you, sorry Kiddo, the marriage is over, and I love you too,* is not very fair. Zaporah wants a rematch. I would like to taste her flesh again too. And Ariel, Zaporah is also now out in the cold. I owe her."

"Where is she now Benny? I will send for her, let her hang out in Europe."

"Greenwich, Connecticut, a small place off Round Hill Road."

"Does she have any kids Benny?"

"No. Mid thirties, works out three hours a day. Likes to play, likes the role. Good times. She has been burnt bad in her life Ariel. She is damn good at her assignments. I am surprised John Harding had it that easy. She is tough. No kids, wants it that way. Lost one. She has been hurt. That is what makes her so good and dedicated. I owe her one Ariel. Go pull her out of Connecticut, have her hang out in Bonn. If it is France, next week it is Germany."

"I trained you well my friend. I will take a walk over to intelligence and see what I can do. I have some people in Scarsdale I can use. White Plains, New York, is not too far."

"Yeah, Ariel, go over to the Mossad, hang out, make a nuisance of yourself like you always do. Let them know the frame work. A little operation, keep their people busy. Hobbies, we all need one. And Ariel, thanks."

"I will yank her out of the States Benny."

The fax Emily Rodrigues received from France was brief, about two pages altogether with a short encryptic note from her friend and soul male, which innocent *doubles* often exchange leaving Emily with a warm understanding her friend was faring well. Renee Jadot had by the first week in April nurtured a warm and loving motherly relationship with Monique. Both now worked for Carlos with Monique more then willing to play the role she knew best for her new found mom.

In the communqué it was obvious Carlos controlled Laredo Cable and the documents according to Renee floated everywhere about the room and office; Carlos not really understanding the importance or the gravity of his criminal venture. But the names showed true on that piece of electronic magic from Europe; Ariadne/Americain Technologies with a couple of French cabinet ministers and the name of Sen. Coyne standing out most of all on that piece of paper. A few months and they could nail the operation to the wall. The one problem, Newport Naval. Double agents with competing agendas with intelligence do not like to send memos to the local FBI field office. But this was quickly remedied by Emily with a black magic marker and a simple note on the paper in brackets: Personal, Renee Jadot, before she sent it up the maze of bureaucracy to her boss at The New York State Organized Crime Task Force to be further censored along the way.

We want him bad! were her thoughts along with, intelligence is going to have to eat this one! Which for anyone who dwells in these worlds of intrigue knows one should never even think such thoughts, let along brag and gossip about such competition between friends over white wine in the lounge at the neighborhood four star friendly restaurant. There would be hell to pay, and there was. Intelligence was listening, the operation was important and Carlos would not get away. But the soil was French, and spies have their own way of dealing with messes of mixed jurisdictions. The FBI would know by that afternoon, black ink or not. They would, however, not be very pleased or in the best of moods, and weren't, when the New York office received the gossip over sight from Atlanta by way of Langley. The shit was going to hit the fan but in the mean time and pending next few months all at the task force in New York would have to endure the silent boiling of their Special Agent friends. The FBI were not at all amused.

"Welcome to beautiful Malta Hardy. You'll love the waters." Trevor's sun lit humor teasing the soul of his old friend on one of Gods mornings atop café patio over looking the crystal blue waters of the Mediterranean. The Greco-Roman architecture trying to soothe his friend's anger.

"Trevor, so help me God if I ever get my hands around your throat!" Hardy said with the warm friendly anger of, I owe you one pal! "You know Pal, I had a nice little home and friendly scam going in The Gulf before you set me up. *Hardy fix this trouble, on your way back from to Balkans, bring coffee.*"

Trevor could see Hardy was still quite angry. "Good to see Kevin Slyer let you keep to laptop, you'll need it," and Trevor could not keep himself from laughing. "Here is the main number to *The Weekly Empire & World Report* with the editor's name and extension. Every once and awhile file a little piece with Larry Mearl. If you have any problems you know how to get in touch with me. They know you are freelance, filing a story is optional but the cover air tight. Good luck Yank," and Hardy could still see Trevor consumed with amusement.

"You had this planned all along, God damn them!" though Hardy was not really amused. Apparently the local FBI field office in Atlanta along with the British and his own friends in the intelligence community including Col. Clay were paying Hardy back for his over hung cock and over done mischief of the last spy affair. Hardy did not know Trevor and Henry Chatsworth broke bread together many times over the years back in London. Hardy did not even know who Henry Chatsworth was. But it was obvious Henry Chatsworth knew of Hardy.

"Good luck on your book Hardy. I would recommend you hang out in Algiers for a couple of weeks before you enter France, get the feel of the place. Something to write about," and with that Trevor finished his tea, said farewell to an old friend and hurried off to catch his flight.

All Hardy could say was "good-bye," the rest of him was frozen speechless. John Custer Harding for most of his adult life played deceiver, not deceived. This time he fell for the deception, and fell big.

"God damn her!" was the first obscenity Special Agent In Charge John Blacke or Henry Chatsworth had heard out of the mouth of Robert Torres since he arrived from D.C. last summer. Though Robert's profanity was much more mild then the wording of key perverse phrases coming from Agent Blacke's vocabulary, as the two looked on to see Henry's eyes so angry he could not talk. "I was so wrapped up in this serial killer," Robert continued, "this situation of Renee Jadot had escaped me. Overlap, I should have overlapped," though Robert looked over to see John still too angry to speak in a fashion befitting an FBI agent and Henry still to angry to utter a word with eyes that looked like they would like to reach across the Atlantic and throttle some wayward lady undercover cop by the throat!

"I will make the calls gentlemen," John Blacke said as he melted into his desk chair with a three hundred and fifty count aspirin headache with a side of Tylenol.

CHAPTER 12

The evening was cool and damp in Atlanta when Joni Cone and Dana stopped by to inquire how the mother to be was coping.

"How are you doing Pam? the bastard hasn't called you yet? Hardy," and fire showed in her eyes of a burning lost, a deception of a relationship years ago up in flames and a situation of a sister in arms in need of the one she loves.

"Bastard," Dana chipped in and looked to Pam to give loving support and understanding. But with a real desire to just sit and give a group hug to a mother to be who really needs one.

"He called last night, we talked," and she looked over the two. "I knew the rules to the game before I became involved with Hardy. It is an understanding. He is better off now, never want again. Monday he is going to wire me a full years child support so I can get going on the nursery. He is over there, gets a little, no one special. I want it that way. We cannot be together. I do not want him to nail himself to a cross for a relationship that could never be," and suddenly her expression changed. "The baby just kicked. Must be a boy. Just like a Hardy attitude, or is a Jew like daddy. God, Dad hated that expression; Must be a boy," and Pam turned, picked up her Orange Pekoe Tea and viewed both warmth and deception from her two friends. Dana being tied to one of her ribs, if not born from one, Joni on a subtle mission of her own. And though the hate was real regarding Hardy, the intense competition between sisters of the sensuous for the affections, or trophy sex of John Harding would be evident and clear should he ever show up in Atlanta again, which he would someday.

"I will fix us some more tea," and Joni hurried off to the kitchen to leave Dana consoling an overly pregnant Pam, whose size lead to thoughts of deception of her baby's pending birth; what type? or how many? and is the doctor playing games?

❖ ❖ ❖ ❖ ❖

"He is being a bastard to her Joe," Julie Lee saying to her lover Covic, as she slid up naked next to his naked form in his new body. Covic had had a revival of sorts, though a tad short of St. Mary's and an arms length from Buddhism. He had finally found the right whore in his life. And if not for their checkered past, they both could easily run an Atlanta PTA meeting. All things considered, they were still both exceptional in bed. The near death experiences of their sex only added to their loving and stable relationship. The only coke the two share these days was of the soft drink variety, the rum was now kept locked. But the sex still extremely good, lack of health aides or not. I saw Joni the other night, Don Fusaro's girl on the inside. And I can even command a bit more these days Joe should you kick me out, a gallery of the girl next door types means higher fees for me and the business. But I want you for myself, you too? You happy Joe? I keep you satisfied? No more three ways?" and she gave a yank of Hardy's alter-ego and slightly deflated competition.

"No, you are all I need but I would still fall short of the church crowd. Though maybe once and awhile for insights of the old days, every once and a while we need some spice. Three-ways are fun, you are a pro; honesty sweetheart. I'm the pig, Hardy the bastard. I trained him well, or he me," and he eased down to kiss his whore and loved lover, her naked form more than earning her keep. And was it babies he saw in her eyes? or her in his? Whores of mixed sex or not, there was no denying their love.

"Am I your Spice Girl Joe?" and by the grip on his cock and the looked in his eyes, she could see she had him more then just *by the balls*.

"Sweetheart, you are pure cinnamon and sugar," though it was his diet which was filled with the candy.

"Don Fusaro-Debenadetto says if you want me to treat you right, and keep you from straying to acquire what men want best, you are to share the funds you raped him of with Hardy, bastard or no bastard, should he ever need it. The Don said you are to look out for him," and she gave a warm tug of his pulsating six inches. Viewing the shafts top, it was clear, he was ready. "Me? no more pepper in your diet Joe," and she took him all the way. A lover, a friend, a five hundred dollar an hour escort. Covic just closed his eyes and prepared himself for another brush with his maker.

For Monique, Carlos was just another under hung cruel outlaw with a huge ego and excessive appetite for drugs she had to play steamy coke whore and erotic dancer to. Not knowing who she deep down despised most, Carlos, or her manipulative adoptive mother who essentially forced her into the cave of the slimy beast. But their was no denying her calling, or the tragedies of her life and childhood, which made her so good. Monique was the best in the business and in a twisted sort of way of the abused, she relished and reveled in the sick and perverse of worthless sex. By the third week in April in the year of Our Lord 1999, she had the beast jumping through flaming hoops like a little circus dog. Something the narcotics trade in Colombia, his handlers and controllers in Moscow, or the networks of Eastern Europe were unaware of. Still she knew the role and understood the importance of her seductive deception of a killing loving sexual relationship. Secretly, deep inside, she wanted Hardy, or she wanted to die.

"Monique, more mail for the Americain file. See if there is anything more in there for or from Sen. Coyne. Oh, Monique, Carlos is in such need this afternoon, stress I guess?" Knowing full well her people had the ladies all over him at lunch at his favorite café on *The Champs Ellysees*. "Maybe you and Carlos should do something this afternoon? Keep him faithful, he really cares about you," knowing what her wicked stepmom meant in sugar coated breath, was, take the cruel beast out, give him head and spend the afternoon as his whore. And oh dear, you really can handle more then one? Be it men or women. Still Monique bit her lip; needed money and prepared herself to keep her Paris home and lifestyle secure by her God given talents and gifts of her craft. *Someday life would be better, no sign of the business and maybe a baby*, were her thoughts as she readied herself for cruelty. Her entire life she needed love settling for the animal instead. *Oh, but Cados was so good in bed.*

North Africa; and loving the despising of those with ties to terrorists of an American spy, for all in the modern world of terrorists paranoia of Americans who spend time in Israel with beautiful cosmopolitan Israeli women, he must be either Satan, a spy or both. This time they were somewhat right, though Hardy fell short of the legal variety a sheik or one of his monsters could prove. All the same Hardy was watched before he boarded that plane bound for Paris. The truth be known, and it wasn't, Hardy did a scene or two from *Casablanca*; mostly street bazaars to mix it up a bit and piss people off. You always have the edge when the enemy cannot think clearly. Or find themselves in terror of just being terrorists. Hardy is of the philosophy of that we all bleed red blood. Blood being holy but lack of blood being dead. Regardless of whether one is from Syria, Iran or America. When one is dead, one is dead and perhaps our maker does not care if it's St. Mary's or Mecca. But fear is both felt by Hardy and the enemy. The difference is spies tend to use common sense and don't sweat. A certain quality, which comes from the comfortability of ones own psychology and an over abundance of near death experiences in ones life. One really has not lived till one has experienced the rush of enemy ricin darts, 9mms or has been poison a time or two, Hardy use to tell himself. Though his right side was somewhat better than the year before last when he almost succumbed to the enemies treachery; treating himself for a month to avoid a ricin dart on the way to the doctors office or worst.

Double agent types, the Renee Jadots of the world, of who he knew not of. Give you information one minute, ricin dart you the next with full employment for life by law-enforcement. The only value to have these people in the game for Hardy was to set them up and play them back on the double agents, who were controlled or fell in the sphere of influence controlled by Moscow. Spies such as Hardy do not need handlers, though they do serve a purpose when they are played back on the ones who really deserve it!

But now North Africa, Hardy did not have handlers but he did have terrorists. A by-product of a steamy affair with an ex Israeli commando, which obviously ended too soon, and obviously was pick up and tracked by the enemy. One of those situation of when a gentleman tosses a lover of who he will really need in his life, like at the present moment.

Hardy had done a little too much Parisian in North Africa before Hardy had a chance to fall in love with Paris. A subtle change was in the oft. Though a good case of healthy paranoia did sweep Hardy when he found his way on to Air France; and did they have a plastic explosive problem? Like some have with cockroaches out of place in a pretty pleasant abode of comfort of an upscale city apartment? Hardy left his new found friends with digital watches and plastique in North Africa to fall in love with Paris that morning, though he was sure they would meet again. Something about a police roundup in Algiers and a summery execution of about fifty or so. I guess they felt they had been set up? Another gold star for Hardy, though he was really not sure if he really deserved it, or if it really belonged to him. But God would Zaporah be proud in any case.

The plastique was Czechoslovakian, the report on John Blacke's desk read. The flight had arrived safely in Paris. On the wire from the secure fax from Paris over glass, Interpol seem to indicate they had more.

It was Sunday, the second of May, spring time in Paris consumed Hardy's thoughts, as he sipped wine and picked on cheese in the warm Spring air nurtured by the French sunshine pulling through the high clouds not far from The Hotel Dé Paris. The breeze was from the south, gentle and warm, further easing the torture of his soul of the phone call to Atlanta from Algiers. The call had still been reeking havoc with his life, even after two weeks time and a safe flight: Pam, I'm going to be a daddy again (Monique deciding other wise the first time around), and damn her. Pain, severe pain, even after a little fun and tumble with a Prime Minister's callgirl. *Easy on the cheese, and maybe take the rest of the bottle back to my suite,* were Hardy's thoughts. And God, she is beautiful. All French girls are beautiful. Paris streets are beautiful. Monique and I am going to be burnt bad by Pam; Pam with the same thoughts back in Dixie. Though his luck could change, he could come face to face with Vera, though Vera was suppose to be in Bonn at the moment. Paris sunshine, and depressed moods of lovers with razors ready to remove men's souls. There was a darkness of the day along with Paris love, another floated amongst the flowers and the breeze. Would Paris be trendy in fashion of spent ricin darts and shell casings?

Not far off in his world of collision, a stark raving mad Latin gent was going berserk while his whore and Hardy's one time lover tried to soothe the beast. Both her and her adoptive mother not sure if it had something to do with the recent bombing of the Chinese Embassy in Belgrade, or the communiqué received from Belarus by way of Moscow. Though Carlos's rage was of a local concern and when the name Harding was blurted out in both English and Spanish, the sudden and momentary panic attack was evident on Monique's face; a sudden rush of love, death (his), betrayal and childhood games they continued to play into their twenties between the sheets in Inns, soft apartments and adult establishments. Illicit pursuits, needed to keep one another alive while they counted the days to betrayal. Carlos had seen the change in direction of his kept whore's disposition, counting the change in direction of his concubine's emotions in all that is rotten in Colombian fifth disguised in loving charm.

"Who is this man!" Carlos screamed on the phone. "Two weeks! He's been here for two weeks! Don't tell me about that!" He screamed in Spanish coming back with, "Where did he arrive from!" and "Don't tell me you don't know!" couple with some sort of Latin obscenity and a reference about some South American soccer star shot to death in Bogota the Year before.

Monique was upset, both Carlos and Renee could clearly see that. Carlos assuming business, Renee understanding the truth of the core of Monique's panic attack and her sudden dive for the Prozac bottle. Which up until that moment had been kept safely concealed from Monique, who suddenly and unexpectedly blurted out the word "bitch," which Carlos just assumed belong to the chaos of the afternoon. Renee was able after the last breakdown to remove Monique from the room in time to keep her from saying wording, which surely would have sent Monique to the place to keep a baby she decided not to have company. Exceptional talent in giving head or not, Carlos would have killed her.

John Custer Harding had apparently hit most of the cafés and shops Carlos had under his control in the short time he had arrived in Paris, while French law-enforcement tagged him along upsetting the entire drug trade. For Carlos it was more than just cocaine; a trade off of sorts. Moscow was now using these people in the spy game. Drugs in, drugs out, technology out and off to Russia. While Primakov played Carlos back against the western investments he made; a flourishing economy built on poison of a snow that destroys young American lives and a money, which devours a political system and corrupts a little place in New York called Wall Street. Carlos had no idea who John Custer Harding was, or that one man's slut was another's love of a lifetime. He wanted Mr. Harding dead. He expected him hit by the first of June! were the last words Monique heard Carlos say over the phone before she was almost forcefully removed from the room by Renee. Her hysteria being understood by Carlos's hot Latin temper: She knew who I was and what I did before she slept with me. She likes my coke, she likes my cock. She will got over it. I kill, I've killed before. Just a bad day. I treat her right tonight, and Carlos shuffled the files, opened the whiskey and prepared himself to go back to his usual confused thoughts that floated around the room like the documents Primakov would love to have a look at.

He sat quietly sipping French coffee at the café directly across the street from The Hotel De Paris. It was one-thirty, the sky was turning steel, though a refill or two would fit in before the showers would force him inside. The viewing was better about the sidewalk and light street bustle across from this small but five star hotel. And perhaps a light bite to eat while he waited with his refill. More polite to dine a bit if one is receiving free coffee, though the wine was good but best not to buzz on this afternoon. Though with life's discipline the wine would not be much of a problem. Be it a glass or a bottle, and oh, he thought, the French, so good. Consume, and lay the wine down. But the edge, it was best that afternoon if he kept his edge about his wits. Coffee would be in order, and it was, showing up with the waiter just as the two young east Germans pulled up, got out of their car and went inside. The Hotel Dé Paris. From his table he could see the two stop and talk with the concigliier at the front desk. A sweet older lady; he was sure. Judging people from a distance comes with maturity.

And he thought to himself, *the old networks had been a buzz since the kid arrived, knowing at age forty-one one is only a child in the spy game,* not knowing that Hardy had spent his forty-second birthday April second, making love to a beautiful Israeli agent. *And Carlos Sanchez, obviously a different "Jackal" with a similar name.* A little subtle message from the old folks at the Gremlin who want my child dead. *And well, well, Marcus sends a couple of Boy Scouts for a little more hands on regarding the value of Mr. Harding's piece on the chess board. What shall I do..? But now then, the Préfect of Police watches too,* and he glanced across the street to see the unmarked Saab. Though he was not good with autos, and he should have been, and thought to himself, could be French domestic, police just the same. And perhaps a little interference for the American child, though he would probably hold up better to a poison dart at his age than mine, and it was clear to even him as he spoke the thoughts inside his head, that American football had certainly rubbed off on the old man. The Nazi rubber was what the South Americans had referred to him, they were in white shaken pale fear to call him scum bag to his face. And as he watched the whole screenplay unfold across the street his thoughts consumed his own mortality, though immortality had been with him most of his life. The French, do they really want me...? Than he finished his lunch and readied himself to leave and thought of his next move.

"Friends. It is important to me Hardy that we be just friends. He does not know. Too angry, too hazed, too out of control to understand my panic attack. Blames himself. He knows I am emotional. I will tell him you are not attracted to me. I will tell him you are in love."

"I am Monique," and she could see in his eyes the fire of another, knowing he was not passing off some line of reverse involvement to explode the flames of a death love between them. Whoever she was, she was real and Hardy was choked when he tried to continue. "He sent you Monique?"

"Yes, I am his lover. I am also his whore;" her emphasis was on whore. "It was understood right from the beginning. I played the game to get noticed. The French like naked women, maybe a little bit more. What life do I have Hardy? Then a lady undercover agent or cop, I do not know which, she pulls me out. I work at The Hotel De Paris, Carlos notices me. She knows Hardy, Renee knows. She knew from the start! That bitch!" Monique looked over to see anger in his eyes of an understanding she know not of. Hardy immediately realized he had been set up.

"She is French?" and he thought of the treachery of his ex-wife and her connection, pausing to give Monique enough time to answer.

"She is American, French-American. Has an old grandmother to look out for. That is her cover. It just does not fit. Hardy, I have played with the FBI, something is wrong here. She had been holding something from me since she plucked me from the whores. Businessmen Hardy. You know me, still upscale, still young enough."

"Still very beautiful too Monique," and Hardy looked up into her eyes to see a silent thank you. *The years have been kind to your beauty Monique,* was the understanding of his wording before Hardy continued. "Where in America is she from Monique?" knowing instantly someone back in the States had a double agent problem, and that someone in law-enforcement had their own little screenplay for him to play out, Monique being their first pick for the leading lady. It was obvious were his thoughts, this little adventure being courtesy of Caliber, the FBI, Whitehall and Langley. Monique was someone in law-enforcement's way of stepping on some toes. Carlos a trophy, policy change or one more accommodating in Washington or London a trophy. Hardy himself a trophy; *your man is into drugs, no I will not get out of your operation now. You go fuck yourself. Bold. But a very stupid move. Trophies all around,* were some of the thoughts picked up by Monique while Hardy tried to hide what he knew; the whole kit and kaboodle regarding Monique and her wicked step mom. "Cop class?" he asked, Monique knowing he meant class like in Navy ship.

"She is a cop," and she glanced down at her watch. "Hardy, I must get back soon," and she nervously took another sip of her wine. The lounge in the café being quiet, calmly calling out for more conversation; the seductive of French culture.

"I am your mark, and you have to leave when you are instructed to spend the whole day in bed with me? I could not anyway Monique, I love her that much. Oh, I've had a tumble or two but I can't. Not with you. And it's love between you and me Monique. Not in love but love; regardless of how it was manufactured. A false love of foreign psychology of a spy game. But it is love. A love of understanding of the destruction of our lives. A love of friendship Monique. A tragedy of love understood. I love you enough Monique not to engage you. A sober love Monique; a stable love of friends. We will always have that magic time so long ago to reflect on. Love but not in love. Friendship but not crucifixion. A love of life, not of lead of 9mms sent to finish off what they could not before. Lie, tell him we are no longer in love. We are not. But love. Lie. I am in love Monique, Kiddo, Pam, I love her like I have never loved anyone before in my life," and suddenly Hardy realized he had just thrust a stiletto through her heart. "She is the same as you Monique but different. I thought she was different, thought I'd try a different personality type. But I was wrong. I was deceived. I love her. She loves me. She knew the rules to the game in the beginning. We can't be together. A tumble once and awhile."

"But not with me...?" and he could see in her eyes both emotions and anger of being robbed of her rejection before Monique continued. "Give up the game Hardy, make it easy on yourself, write, retire. Go back to America," though in her thoughts Monique did not want Hardy to leave her in France to rot. *Take me away Hardy, don't leave me in Europe to die,* were her impossible thoughts Hardy read on her face before he turned to her and spoke.

"I am your mark, we spent the afternoon together," and Hardy took the equivalent of five hundred dollars in francs from his wallet, "I hear the shopping is good in Paris?"

"A freebie Hardy, Carlos is my money."

"OK," and Monique could see Hardy had not meant to offend her.

"Good-bye Hardy," and as she watched him walk away she thought to herself, *he looked so cold the last time on the boulevard in Martinique when he watched me dial Covic from the coin phone, I felt so cold. If anyone can be cold in the islands? I was. He was. He is who he is. I am who I am. So cold when tragedy sculpts your lives.*

Julie Lee stretched up on her tippy toes in front of the bathroom mirror to fuss with one of her earrings wearing only a bright red thong and matching bra, slowing teasing her beast into good behavior. Though his condition was obviously beastly, and she thought to herself before she glanced at her sundress, *God, I could use it. A few more of these Sunday morning therapy sessions he'll be ready for the church crowd. We both will. After Mass we can fuck like wild animals, or before. Take the edge off, won't know who we are, or what we do. Now what part of the country would Joe like? and which country?* And her internal laughter almost showed through her thoughts, as she watched her beast watch her thong clad flesh in front of the mirror from their bed.

"Honey, come here, I need you."

Oh, I know you do. And I kind of like Buddhism but The Church would be good cover...

Julie slow and seductively made her way over to their bed to slip into the loving and waiting hands of her whoremaster. Covic gently using his warm loving hands to slip the thong off before her naked flesh slid in next to his. Her bra had been the first to go on the trip into bliss from the bathroom; a one motion seduction of silent words spoken, *God I need it bad Joe, and I know you won't disappoint me. We'll change your life forever when we are finished. If we survive?*

❖   ❖   ❖   ❖   ❖

They almost didn't survive, silk neckties again. But when the heavy breathing stopped Joe reached down and gave his whore a kiss more a kin to the first time at a church under threat of shotgun. Though the way things had progressed since Julie showed up at his bedside back in October, Covic would not need any encouragement for the positive change in his life. Further expanding his thoughts before he spoke of the pleasure it would be to play a little trick on the church crowd now and again. As long as they rose early from their sleep to see their maker before they went off to church to see their maker. When they made love they were one with God, near death experiences and all.

"The word is *Love*, the South Americans are real hot over Hardy. Baby are they hot. France, I think? Some wealthy coke bandit called Carlos. Only he wants to fund his own revolution, a United States of Colombia and Peru with a little Chile thrown in. Carlos has help from the East, that's why Hardy's involved. I know some people, bad people. This cat Carlos is upsetting the whole applecart, both; intelligence and enforcement. Wants Hardy dead by June. I'm here. But common sense Julie, you do not put contracts out on spies," and he leaned down to kiss her while she played with his over abundance of chest hair. Though now she was use to the gorilla type, she kind of enjoyed it.

"Joni said about the same Joe. The Don's toes have been stomped on. The Colombians are on thin ice. East Germans apparently hit Vicky. Word is Don Fusaro is like a wild man. And Joe, I really do not like being the go-between. Joni. There is just something I do not trust about the women."

"I thought you two were friends?"

"Well, we are but she has been acting a bit odd whore lately."

"Hardy fucked her, could be the curve ball she's throwing you. They were an item a very, very long time ago."

"I did not know that. Maybe?" and Julie's face charged with concern. You going to see the Pope, Joe? I want out of this mess Joe. So do you. I would say Iowa, too much out of a mob movie. How about the Pac Rim? We could do Vietnam. You to Church, I to Temple. Buddhism is flexible. Leaning West Market wise anyway."

"No...The Don and me have too much in common these days. The FBI would most likely grab me one foot into Dixie. We'll play this game a little bit longer. North Africa? India? I'm flexible sweetheart. Russians in Eastern Europe, Caribbean is getting too hot with Hardy mixing it up with Carlos. Like a best friend who is a bad influence on you growing up, always getting you in trouble. Should be the other way around, and was. Hardy is paying me back. In any case, Hardy goes out with a bang, I'll be next. Can't let it happen."

"But we can't stay here either Joe?"

"No."

"What do you mean he has been shot!" Carlos raged in a mix of broken English, Spanish and French, as he watched Monique go to pieces at his rage in the front room office space before his. Carlos turned his back and continued but waited momentarily to find out from the other end it had been a professional hit, though not orchestrated of his breed. "You come in and tell everything. Pierre! God damn Pierre!" with some kind of profanity in Spanish. "These scum bags really hurt me this time Munuel," and he hung up in time to see Monique damn near shattered on the floor.

"You scared her! What the hell do you expect!" Renee now with her arm around Monique trying to stop the carnage of tears and shaken emotions.

"Get out of here! Get out of here both of you!" he screamed, secretly hoping they would change their minds in a half hour. Renee would, Monique took the rest of the day off.

The twenty-ninth of May, he repeated to himself in whispered Spanish, *he is still alive and I lose one of my best lieutenants...*and he gently slumped down in his chair, the stress reminding him it could have been a gunshot that had knocked the wind out of him that evening while he waited for Renee to return.

"He has been like a wild man since you arrived Hardy. I needed to talk, so I looked you up. A freebie if you want?" and Monique watched Hardy pour her a glass of Bordeaux Sec.

"So you just left, and no, I do not want a freebie but Pam did get me into wearing thongs," and he watched Monique laugh in amusement.

"An Officer's son wears gentlemen's lingerie when boxers are more appropriate to your upbringing?" and again Monique laughed.

"The psychology being the whole world can kiss my ass Monique. After what we have been through, you too," but the *You too* spoken softly and with affection followed by the pain of his father's torture. "Spies are suppose to be a bit kinky, writers a bit flaky. Play the enemies passions back against them. Don't like baseball, must be a Russian plant. Likes West Point Army Football, must be a trick. Isn't that how it always is? You end up fighting your own more then you engage the enemy. You? You escape me to find a promised life with Covic. You escape Covic to trap yourself with me. The twenty-ninth of May, I'm still alive and the spy game starts to Rock & Roll already. Someone is looking out for me. Seeing anyone else besides Carlos?"

"No. Hardy, you are a writer now?" though this time Monique was serious and was unaware Hardy was trying to get out of the business.

"I'm trying Monique. Not much different. They come out of the woodwork looking for me just the same. Just float around, get ideas. Trevor. Trevor has some freelance items of interest for me to jot down a line or two. Then the book. You know me, good but Joe was the creative one.

And Dad, Dad's dying. Creeps. When he dies part of me will have died," and Hardy intercepted her pass of compassion and comfort firmly and gently pushing her away with his hands by the waist. "Please don't Monique."

"We always deep down desire destruction Hardy. Love our abusers, hate our lovers. Seek to destroy the healthy, desire to be one with the flesh of the beast. A bigger orgasm will make it better, and I am better than his last whore. Surrender the baby of the deserving, desire the offspring of the pig. There comes a time when therapy is not even Novocaine. Or the spoken dysfunction is worst than root canal. Not even for old times sake?" and Hardy could see in her eyes the pain shining in his.

"No, I have my own root canal. Part of me is dying in Georgetown right now. Told to stay, duty, and desire to be with my dad. 'Your country comes first,' he told me. Ordered me. It was an order. Dads a colonel, you are in the Army. You follow orders."

"You still play the great game. Orders?" and Monique wanted to take him in her arms and comfort him like the baby she gave up.

"You should go now, he'll be looking for you. No freebies. Not for me, not for you. We all pay in life for what we receive, what we throw away, or what we desire. No freebies, better a bullet kill me then a freebie in your arms. I'm in love Monique, could I stay in Atlanta I would not want. It was a healthy love, would still be if I could be there. She is having my baby, I wired her a full years support so she could ready the house," and he looked over to see he had just put another bullet into her heart, as a tear came to his eyes and rolled down his left cheek.

The parting was speechless, love exploding all around the room like a war zone or a cupid with a submachine gun; love lost, love gained, love denied, love of the new in this world, love of the old, love of the tossed away, love of the taken, love of death, death of love, emotions so dangerous they resembled a multi car pile up on The Deacon in New York. By the time Monique closed to door to his suite behind her, silent tears flowed from both their eyes. A good-bye was appropriate, a silent understanding of the unspoken instead left them both in the courtesy of their own thoughts.

"Good evening Madam, is Carlos Sanchez in?" and a dazed Renee Jadot from the stress of to day looked up to see a handsome old European gentleman come in from the night air to inquire of someone of the nocturnal world, though not of this office; Carlos spending his nights with the ladies or with the men of the drug world.

"No, he will be in at nine tomorrow. Come back then," Renee replied, but it had been a bad day and her attempts to shake off the gent fell short.

"Oh, but I see. I have these files regarding Ariadne/Americain, I must be sure Carlos receives them."

A flustered Renee Jadot tersely replied in her attempt to get rid of the old gent (it was nine at night, and Renee had not the need to play games after such a brutal emotional afternoon), "Oh, you can leave them with me."

"Oh, but I need a receipt. Too important, could you please?" the gift of the old conjurien now adding to her anger.

"One moment, I will get the file," and Renee stood up, walked over to the file, fumbled through the papers momentarily and turned to go back the three steps to her desk.

The first silent shot pierced her heart. The second, unneeded, piercing one of her lungs on the right side. Günther's hands for the most part had stayed concealed in the pockets of his old black leather coat until they and the nine millimeter equipped with silencer were needed. He simply picked up the file from the floor and said good-bye to Madam in French: "Au revoir Madam."

CHAPTER
13

"I guess this little adventure goes the way of intelligence," John Blacke said to Henry and Robert. Robert gently laughing to himself.

"Don't look at me John, I was here. No overseas communications. Have your men check," Robert replied, and John could see both Henry Chatsworth and Robert Torres both gently laughing with amusement. Both looking like the cat who swallowed to canary of an advent they knew would happen three weeks before, regardless of their overt desire to do it themselves. There are reasons why there are Günthers in the game.

"Well, this young lady," John Blacke said, knowing her greying forty-ish age, "should not have been there in the first place. She apparently got what she deserved. State groups, God damn state groups. At my last workshop at Quantico we discussed the problems we have with state groups and overlapping jurisdictions. France, God damn French soil! I received a nasty little telegram from the State Department this morning, would have loved to have seen what New York received. Apparently the French do not like American undercover cops, or that type, being shot to death on French soil. They are, however, impressed by our Mr. Harding. Been there about a month, has most of Marcus Wolfe's networks in Paris exposed or set up. French law-enforcement will nail them on narcotics if they cannot get them on spying with a P.S.—*If he fucks up, you and Henry get the blame, Robert.*

"Hardy's making waves, the boys at the Gremlin are a bit hot again. So the war's over, now we do it for nationality instead of ideology," and Henry looked up to John and Robert and continued, understanding they were closely following along. "France in a vice, the Mirage is a good fighter, and, could you share the technology? More tea gentlemen, and ascounded with the documents? Dead letter drop time," and Henry looked over to see Robert eager to chip in his insights.

"Bet the French are glad the documents were not left behind. Carlos may be in a rage (and he was) but the French are happy. This Latin thug most likely had French law-enforcement held at bay by those documents. Did not even know it. Had the French government by the balls, now their law-enforcement can move in. The Balkans fiasco, bet they hope we come up with the papers. They owe us one. What do you think Henry?"

"Be a trade off Yanks. The French will behave, like us, British beef or not, and the only mad cow is in Moscow. They would really prefer for us to come up with the docs. Robert, you better recommend to your people, intelligence should have your bases in Germany be on the look out for someone wanting to unload documents. Hardy's Guardian angel has them. Hardy or Günther, the usual suspects. American Bases and NATO should keep an eagle eye."

"Let's do lunch gentlemen," Special Agent In Charge Blacke said, though John had been told to lose a few pounds.

Stupidity is when you think your life is being scripted by old Magnum PI reruns, or that your childhood sweetheart and recently disengaged lover actually cares when you watch her from afar dial the number of the beast. Knowing you are on a covert mission of your own to retrieve her worn cold heart, spending what little money you have left for housing on the folly of love and reckless emotion. A bigger cock, yes, but Covic had more money. The creative one who could not spell, yet could put the words together to keep from taking a mob bullet, make a few million and make his best friends love his personal whore...Fly off to Whore Island, and return to exchange death with a nice old black man in a homeless shelter. Why would she look me up in Paris just to kill me? Is she so insensitive of the irrepairable damage she has done to my soul? Better it be a hired bullet from the gun of Carlos, than by a kiss of Monique. Though her's are more rapid fire; lethal, like an Army Green Beret cutting down a house. Cutting everyone in half while he does it. Vera, Zaporah and a baby I cannot be a father to; children to come back in twenty years time. The offspring of a spy affair to shoot you with a 38 for not being their when they needed you. Perhaps whiskey, though whiskey is not my death. Cognac, but cognac is too good to kill one's self over. Brandy or Monique, what's the difference? Too much of either will kill a man's soul. The poison the year before was better; never a gripter around when you need one.

Mist and mystique, it is ten and the shops of The Champs Elyees are just opening up. French lingerie and Pam. Something for her, thongs, she likes thongs. Maybe one from me for her to keep? Orange, the Dam. I cannot be there but I want her. I'm selfish, even if our life is a series of flings, babies and unfulfilled commitments of lovers and tossed victims of need, I want her. Black, black lingerie for her, I like black. Though color and tricks of intensity and pleasure. The pleasure that comes with the sanctioned affection of one of our whores or lovers, or the pleasure you feel at the moment of death when it is one of the ladies of the enemy. Pleasure, and we are all whores. Sometimes the enemy plays fair, and I am the biggest slut of all. Though I would not speak of myself in mixed company as one. I am a whore, not whoremaster like Carlos, or beast like Covic. I am a whore, and damn proud of it! Had I been born of the opposite sex with an over abundance of beauty, I would know my calling. Pam knows. And I would always have available funds.

"The three black thongs and the two rainbow ones. The gentlemen's section?" *and God my French is terrible....* as the nice young hostess pointed the way with a French hand that said forget the panties, take me instead.

Orange, European size, oh here it is, American 34. Pam will like this, remind her of her talent and how she trapped me; how she made me a bigger bastard then I was. Babies in the spy game to be played back on a loving father twenty years in the future. But Freud tells all us of the breed of spy, it is mom who they will hate. Love, and what's the difference? I will be dead just the same. Of a 38 or a shattered heart, what's the difference? When one is the one is dead. Babies, babies like Teddy Bears, Pandas are better. In any case, a baby should have one.

"Excusez-moi, avez-vous Anglais?"

"Oui."

"Merci, merci. I will take these," and Hardy looked up to see the pretty French maiden overlook the faults of the clumsy American. Is there a shop near by that sells little stuffed bears for babies?"

"Oui," and she explained to Hardy in better English the direction to the preferred shops, than most in New York, or the good old boys of the southern drawl of Dixie.

"Ugly Americans, I don't think you are ugly Mr. Harding. Where are you staying? I could have it sent over'? American boys are known to blush when buying for the ladies. But you buy for yourself, oui?" and she tried in vain of her unwanted French seduction to make the invading enemy blush.

"Oui, mademoiselle, it is how this damned Yankee found himself shopping for a Teddy Bear," and Hardy looked over to the receptive seduction of lingerie hostess. For she looked more like a hostess then a lady of the shop, with an intense understanding of a gentleman with the wish of seeing her dressed for the part of lady of the evening. And surely she modeled what she sold. But times being what they were, Pam, Monique and a tumble too many, Hardy just paid for his penance and said, "Merci. Merci beaucoup," the second part of his departure being in appreciation of her attraction.

"Au revoir Mr. Harding," she said with a smile with thoughts of Pandas, lingerie, and maybe a little undercover work? while she waited for law-enforcement to swing by: *What is this passport number? Oh, a Mr. Harding and boy do we have a file. And perhaps Interpol? And do the British really have to pull this? They have enough problems with their beef. Does not really mix well with our wine anyway. There is a reason why us French have attitudes.*

The scream that morning should have been heard by Hardy on the other side of The City Of Lights. It had brought the local Paris police running down the streets and up to the fourth floor offices in The Hotel De Paris to see a panic stricken Monique falling to pieces by the body of her wicked step mom. Only to be followed in a few moments later by Carlos in a blistering rage! All things aside, Carlos was a gangster and the hot Latin had a lot of questions to answers being the likeliest suspect for the death of an undercover American cop. Who he mistakenly thought he could trust with his most nefarious insights. Carlos rightfully thought he had been set up, which he had been. Leading to such a blistering rage that the Paris police took him out in handcuffs to be released at some later date, which to Carlos's understanding may be never. But never being if innocent, South America. Which further enraged him at the Paris police station's version of booking.

"Au revoir Monsieur Sanchez," one of the finest of Paris was heard saying to Carlos just before he slammed the cell's door shut.

"How did you get in?" Hardy quietly closing the door to his suite of a French version of an American Hilton behind him. "I thought the TV was next door. I should, could use to improve my French."

"Renee is dead, the police took Carlos away. The guy at the front desk remember me from the other night, saw I was upset and let me in. Thought I was your lover, wants to be mine. Tricks of the trade Hardy."

"We were once."

"You want to be again?"

"No. Do you want a drink?"

"No. Prozac, and the bed is comfortable!"

"It is. You can sit on my bed as long as you keep your clothes on. So what is next? Back to the States? Find work in Paris?"

"Float around a bit. Like the Louvre, fell just short in my younger days of the runway. I'll survive Hardy. Joe and I kept our finances separate. I had some back up funds when I came to France. Carlos paid good as long as I gave him head. Glad to see him shipped off to South America. That is my guess if the French can't charge him, just toss him out. One Covic to another. Joe treated me better, just had a more intense appetite for sex. I'm young enough Hardy, I could make a movie. You want to make a movie with me Hardy? We could practice our lines? I'm a bitch Hardy, I'm upset. I am more angry at me then you," and Monique looked over to see Hardy just finishing up pouring himself a glass of French cognac, annoyed at the insert and turn of complexity in his life. More angry at the need to comfort trouble that had looked him up at a Paris café a month ago, than the need for an old friend to be comforted.

"Complex feelings, I probably would not be able to respond. Hung like a horse until I hear your name, then I show up two inches shy. Love. Regardless. Love messes everything up. The past tense, I'm in love now. Pam understands betrayal of the flesh. If I want to have a reoccurring role in her life I must avoid old flames and betrayal of the soul. She'd cut it off. Which for her would leave her enough left over to share with the girl next door. You I'd come up an inch short and six ounces under scale. Reality Monique, we would end up killing each other, or being played back against each other. Complex feelings, just turned forty-two, a kid in the great game, too old to be your leading man. I do not want to be your lover either Monique. The days of romping around West Point with motorcycles, leather, no clothes and Farrah Fawcett haircuts are over. Mine is kept short. A Bastard's cut, always will be. I love you enough to be one."

"You really are one. I come her for consoling because my wicked step mom has been shot dead and you put a bullet through the last asset I have; my sex. You loved my sex once. A freebie Hardy, the file to Ariadne/Americain was missing. The French seem to be happy, less paper work. Do you have it?"

"I was with you last night. But spies, drugs and documents, sound interesting. And the French don't want them?" and Monique could see Hardy was becoming quite playful over the demise of her boyfriend and the death of her wicked stepmom. "Hey look, what would I do with documents?" and Hardy tried his best to keep from laughing.

"Bastard!" and Monique was hot with both sexual desire and the need to throttle a former lover by the throat, as she watched Hardy pour her a glass of aged cognac. "What's next?" and she could see Hardy throttle back his mood to a more seriousness one, more appropriate for their impromptu liaison.

"The countryside, maybe the Bordeaux region. I have really upset, people in my short little stay in this town. Expensive too, need to save a bit. Do not want to throw everything away. Maybe an inn, chateau, though a chateau may be more." and he turned, took a sip and turned off the TV. News, and the wording was reeking havoc with his thoughts. Monique now could see he was becoming serious. "I almost did triple-x work Monique. After the thoughts afar on the boulevard misfortune was that bad when I returned. Homeless. Before I turned things around, the mob was so upset with me they would not even let me make a porn movie. The KGB; a real mess. I do not blame you for the misfortune, twists and turns and the tragedies of your life. I just do not see the need to fall into each others arms so we can die in each others arms. To fulfill another's romance novel so they can cry over a tragic ending of their making? and say, God, what a great love story they had. Then watch them pretend they did not script it. Especially if it is the enemy's novel. I have had enough tragedy in my life Monique, so have you," and Hardy looked over to see his one time she-devil now about as sober as he was about the situation. "Renee. As soon as you told me, I knew someone in enforcement had a double agent problem. You and I in the same town at the same café table, and the KGB are not using some Socialist psych-handler back in The States to try and script our lives? If I flew to New Delhi, you would have been there. I write my own love stories these days Monique, you should too. If we are to be together we write our own script. It is not what I want. Is it what you want? Do you want to die in someone else's novel? Or be forced to put a bullet in the one you love? I'm getting burnt out from love Monique, I go to Germany after this, pay for my fun. I'm sorry. I have a lot of work here in Europe, Moscow wants to kill me. A handful of terrorists in North Africa want to pay me back. I suspect I got an att'a-boy I did not really deserve. People we upset."

"How is Trevor doing Hardy?" Monique making a strategic insertion of friendly distraction.

"Trevor set me up, a friendly deception. Deceived for once, I'll pay him back. More cognac?"

"I could use some, skip the medication tonight," and she handed her glass to Hardy. "They're hot Hardy. Carlos and the paranoia of the drug trade. Lieutenants, whores, police, documents, they are really hot. Could I stay here tonight...?"

Changing diapers for less then potty trained toddlers was a far cry form sneaking into Syria for a little mischief, or taking out a Hezbollah camp with C-4 in Southern Lebanon. But by the beginning of June Zaporah had become well adjusted to the role of live-in substitute mom and enjoyed the company of Danny Weinstein and his wife Barbara on their sprawling Greenwich, Connecticut estate. In the beginning it had been hard to find, nestled deep in the woods on a long dirt driveway off North Porchuck just down the road a little from the Wild Flower Sanctuary. Zaporah had spent the better part of one April morning circling around Old Mill Road, Round Hill Road and Porchuck looking for to right turn off. Then finally just by accident running into Danny as he pulled out with his BMW 318I convertible. Though after a quick turn around, some morning coffee and some rugala overlooking the Japanese garden and goldfish Pond, Zaporah was all unpack and settled in. Greenwich MONY could wait and Barbara could more then need a hand helping Zaporah get settled into her living quarters. The help being South American, a language problem, and Zaporah was as much a friend as business. It had been a Thursday and Danny had called the office down on 700 Steamboat Road to let them know he would be in Monday, Friday being his once a week train ride down to the city and Wall Street. Zaporah was well needed and would fit right in; world class nanny and security detail all rolled into one. Though with two young children less their potty trained, there would be many an afternoon until Yossi showed up when Zaporah would secretly wish she was back again in Southern Lebanon handling C-4 instead of poop.

But it was the first week of June that upset Barbara so when Yossi Cohen showed up at the door to carry her soul mate off to Bonn, Zaporah was more then just a Nanny and friend. But Israel, Ben Netanyahu in a jam, the election, Islamic terror being exported out of North Africa by way of Iran, and something to do with some kind of rematch with some over hung American spy. God forbid he was a Catholic. He was. But was he circumcised? Zaporah assured Barbara he had been and ask her not to take out the knife and ceremonial wine. There would be no need for such ritual. But no, he did not keep a Kosher household and she would try to live with the crucifix above his bed. She further assured Barbara she would close her eyes when making love.

Leaving the kids would be hard, in the very short time she had been in Greenwich they had grown deeply attached. Zaporah had told her friend she would miss the weekday afternoon trips to the trendy new mall in White Plains and the friendly lunches at the Kosher restaurant just off Central Avenue. America had been a short stay but a very warm and friendly one.

Hardy had awoke in not the best of moods; drugs, guns, and South American contracts. Monique had spent the night in the next bed over, the hotel being kind enough to supply two beds for each room of the class Hardy was paying for, saving him from spending the night in the bathtub. Monique had returned the favor by being courteous, she had been kind enough to wear one of Hardy's T-shirts, complete and clad with her own panties to bed the evening before. *Hardy would have to put up with my legs* being her thoughts. But now she teased him from the bathroom mirror wearing only one of Hardy's Van Huessen dress shirts with little else on, her fun being cut short by the ringing of the hotel room's phone.

"Hardy, Trevor old boy."

Hardy still waking up and suffering a lack of coffee, just gave a grunt while Monique continued her seductive harassment from the bath. "What Trevor, it's early, I haven't had my coffee and I have an unwanted houseguest."

"Rumor is some nut in the States put a contract out on his own life to start that little adventure you found yourself in in Kosovo. Politics, thought the war would start and the agent would be eliminated! Backfired! The guy is still alive. Big win for Gen. Clark too."

"Who cares Trevor? The spy game is nuts. You call me from London to tell me bullshit?"

"No old boy, the word is Milosevic is caving, Gen. Clark is not going to lose one ground troop. Good for your boys, good for ours."

"No ground troops? What was I doing in Pec? Trevor, I'll believe it when it is signed, the truce. Rumors, gossip, and nuts? I heard a story once from Don Fusaro, ah, hold on—God damn you Monique! Put some clothes on! Sorry Trevor, old *items* die hard."

"You get laid?"

"No, tossed her, took the second bed. Would have taken the bathtub had I. Anyway, Don Fusaro told me some Don or chieftain in New York needed to get a man out of the city once to whack some guy and a blizzard hit. The hitman went off the road, froze to death or left the car running and did himself in. The guy lived. It happens. Folklore after that. The guy had some kind of reverse Mafia curse. Made men in the mob were afraid to hit the guy, kept getting people killed. It happens. Suspect he was one of ours. We do it for effect sometimes. You know, *ouch*, a calling card, a little message. Do not hit this man. P.S.—*Uncle Sam loves you*. It happens Trevor. So the war is over, what else?"

"Algiers, the fifty or so who met their fate had apparently left their friends quite upset. You better be careful Hardy, this cell is by way of Iran, may want to drop an A-bomb on you this time. You were the American, you get the blame, spy. They know."

"Not my fault Trev."

"They don't care Yank. Be careful. You received the gold star. Watch your ass Hardy."

"Monique too. Trevor, have to cut this call off, my worst nightmare wants to get dressed. I want to be out of here when she does. See ya Bud."

"Good-bye John."

"Oh, and you don't like my ass now Hardy? If not a freebie, a rematch just for sex? I could use it this morning, at my peek. You want to go?"

"No, mine was seventeen, been there. No more flesh to love, or love to flesh. You're on your own, I'm out of here in a few minutes. Hold on...

"Yes."

"Hardy, Trevor again. The word from my gal at Number 10 Downing Street from her Jewish colleagues is Zaporah; terrorists. The Israelis want her in. That's all, gotta go. Be careful John."

Hardy laid the handset down and turned to Monique, "I have one too many rematches to play out Monique. Love or flesh, body or soul, neither one of us would survive. You don't strip in from of me, I won't leave Hallmark cards with *Heart & Soul* inscribed on the inside where the love is."

"You really are a bastard Hardy," and Monique lifted her confiscated former flame's dress shirt above her panty line for a little *fuck you revenge.*

"Get dressed."

Emily Rodrigues had been like a wild woman since the news of the murder of her best friend in Paris had reached her offices in Midtown. Over the next few days after the news of her friends untimely demise, Emily had found herself on the phone screaming at every district attorney she could think of from the Atlanta, Athens area of Georgia to the various county district attorneys in Southern New York, ending up with a nasty little spat on the phone with Westchester County District Attorney Jeanne Pirro.

"Well, didn't your people have him under surveillance when he was with that tramp from Atlanta? I want this man charged!"

"Emily, that tramp is a highly respected TV Journalist and anchor woman, who I deeply respect. They made love at Croton Dam, their frolic was out of view of my peoples lenses.

I don't care, my best friend is dead! I want this over hung creep indicted!"

"And you think he did it! When you know Paris police had him under surveillance with Monique Gaudinier in a hotel in Paris that evening? Emily, what am I suppose to do? The FBI sent me a little memo a few months back, hands off Hardy. Well..."

"I do not give a fuck," and profanity for Emily was as foreign as her deceased friends operation, "Find something!"

"Emily, I will charge Hardy with walking around Europe in a purple thong and snow jogs but I have to check with the French first for..." and by the sound of the slam of the handset on the other end of the line, it was clear Emily did not take too well to Ms. Pirro's humor in light of the pending wake of her friend. And God, I hope the body does not smell by the time it hits American shores.

How many times must a man be crucified for falling in love with the wrong woman? And does she have to play havoc with my soul like this? Peak or no peak, a reverse strip tease of burning desire of the unexplained. Unexplained, for I do not know what it is that I feel. My peak was a tortured teenager of wild sexual fantasies with no lover to remove what God so desired to explode and come forth from me. Only for Monique to show up in my twenties too overly endowed with God's grace to keep us separate in each other lives. Leading us to tragedy ridden liaisons for the rest of our sexual lives. Of love. Of hate. Of indifference. Of Scorn. Of revenge. Only then to return and burn in sexual desires with our souls of which we both were born of this earth without the gifts to deal with the silly intense games of romance we play on one another. And God Damn her! for stealing a dress shirt to play out such classic scenes of seduction, which will only lead us to blissful destruction. Throw your panties on the bed you whore, watch me immolate myself with your desire while you tease me in the ritual that I begged you not of before. I loved you at West Point! I loved you when you stripped naked for the gentlemen understanding the misfortune of your tragedy, which brought you forth from those gentlemen's clubs to find comfort and security in my arms. I loved you as Mary incarnate. I loved you as the teasing whore! I loved you when you burned me to find life and security in the arms of the beast. I hate you now. Put your clothes on Monique Gaudinier. Leave me here to burn one more time when you walk out of my life. For when you walk out of my life, you will be no longer in my heart. Destroy another's soul my childhood virgin, though I had not been your first in that time so long ago. Nor was I your first mark when you returned to Atlanta to burn the inner workings of my passions, and leave me to rot while you lunged for the arms of the beast. Get dressed Monique, let us both move on with our lives. But perhaps, it is I, who should be the first to brake the ice of departure?

"Monique, I will be back at five, hope you are not here sweetheart. Lock the door behind you."

"Hardy. Hardy..?"

"I have to go sweetheart, I'll see you," but she knew she would not.

"Hardy, wait," but the words were muffled by the running water of the shower. "Hardy!"

"Gotta go," and it was hard to tell which sound a naked Monique heard first, the cold closing of the door to romance, or the ringing of the telephone.

"Monique, is Hardy still there?"

"No Trevor, he just left. I will tell him you called," and a wet naked Monique, the intensely hot scorned lover of lack of romance, hung up. Leaving Trevor hard at the other end at just the thought of what his American friend tossed away. *One should always have a little in the morning*, were the thoughts Monique read on Trevor's mind. Reading thoughts of long distance had become her art.

"Good morning; Mr. Harding, room two twenty-two."

"Oui Monsieur, what can I do for you Mr. Harding?"

"I will be leaving this afternoon, I wish to pay for the room till tomorrow."

"Oui Monsieur."

"Should my lover return this evening, could you advise her of when check-out is?" And please Monsieur, please do not let this young lady know where to find or get in touch with me."

"Oui. Pardon, Mr. Harding, a Monsieur Downing just called for you from London, said it was important."

"Thank you, I will call him back," and Hardy handed the gentleman his American Express Credit Card and waited a handful of the bits of the intelligence we all take for granted in this world. A good spy, is a good observer.

"Here you are Monsieur Harding.... Monsieur Harding, there are reasons why us French are known for being discreet, you will have no trouble Monsieur. Monsieur Harding, the Paris police were about this desk a little while ago, though, how do you say? not your adversary? But you Monsieur."

"Thank you, merci Monsieur. I have to leave. Merci, merci beaucoup."

"Au revoir Mr. Harding."

She rips me apart whenever I see her. Setup, and Madam got what she deserved. Monique; the only quality in the life of tragedy which consumes us both is she feels the same pain I do. I immolate myself, the fires of hell burn her insides to the intensity that drives us all to the edge and beyond. Like a Sicilian red, a hearty Italian wine. A Bolla you save for a pasta dinner with family, knowing you are too afraid to even uncork the bottle. Not knowing if it is death you consume, an omen, or the pouring forth of good times. With each kiss of Monique I would burn in everlasting intensity. Knowing hell of the flesh with Monique would be better than heaven of the spirit. Yet with each kiss I would slowly die; the poison which comes with the understanding death is the link between you. A Sicilian red in a French body with a creamy tanned bronzed African skin of good breeding the good ol' boys of the Deep South so despise. The extra virgin olive oil and the young balsamic vinegarette to begin a meal of close friends, only to find love is not a virgin and the bite is real and only cider vinegar. The disappointments in our lives of the ones we love, only to find out our respective situations are the breed of death of the meals which kill you. Or the innocence in secrets we hide only to uncover sorrow and lack of good human understanding. I should have flown to a New Delhi and traveled north to Kashmir to find what Buddhists seek of words that escape this Roman Catholic boy. But the Louvre and perhaps it is better I run away from Monique in The Cathedral Of Notre Dame? But for now the Paris subway will do.

"Excusez moi Monsieur, pourriez-vous dire ou est Monsieur Harding?"

"No, Mademoiselle. But...Ah Monsieur Harding said he will be back later today."

"Merci Monsieur."

And Monique hurried off to her one time office to hand in her resignation to one of Carlos's Lieutenants. Trust, now lack of trust since wicked step mom met her maker. The gentleman at the front desk had been very gracious leaving Monique with a warmth of trust instead of the cool deception he had worked on her. There surely are reasons why the French are discreet. Hardy would be back by three to retrieve his belongings, Monique would show up by five for dinner, leaving her the whole day to start over and re-plan her life. By five-fifteen that afternoon she would realize it would be one without Hardy. But it would be the most innocent deception of all of an overly eager young girl at the front desk upon Monique's return to inquire of Hardy which would hurt most of all, cutting her to the core: *Your sister Pam called, the baby is healthy and should be born sometime in July.*

CHAPTER
14

The report laid in triplicate on the desk of Agent John Blacke's new red oak desk while Henry poured two cups of coffee and a tea with one and a half lumps of sugar with a slight spot of cream. The morning wake up bews would be cool enough to drink by the time the three finished the report.

"The arrangements my men have worked out for Miss Wellington are working well, playing right into the hands of our investigation. Agents Reading and Tenza informed me this morning they have come up with the forensics on Harry. I intend to have him taken into custody this afternoon. Any problems with that Henry? Robert?"

"The good doctor is out of play, why not? Robert?"

Robert put down his coffee and turned to both John and Henry, "Why not? Harry pretty much is just into DNN. No mad doctor to manipulate the brains who push Harry's buttons. He is pretty much only a news junkie. Pam is surrounded by friends, the Israelis seem to have the idea. Yank him out John, charge him. Henry, how are your people doing in Atlanta?"

"The traditional spy game Robert, making progress. Slow, but we will play what is left back. A matter of time. That is all," and Henry turned to Robert.

"Well gentlemen, Hardy is our boy. John what do you have for us before I leave, I'm off to Bonn for a couple of weeks. Documents, the brass need to know."

"A legal operation Robert?"

"I do not know, Henry. If Hardy has the file, he would know what to do. It really depends who has the file. By what the NSA sent down over the weekend, it is clear the Russians do not, or Marcus Wolfe for that matter. God, I have never seen them this upset before, wait till Hardy moves out to another part of France. If I have to mount a legal operation, it will have to be done out of our embassy in Bonn. Berlin is not ready, the little outpost they have there will never do."

"Your operation Robert?"

"The affair is my baby, Henry. I am worried a bit, South America was really where Langley broke me in. Different game in Europe," and Robert looked over to see John Blacke in amusing concern.

"I guess that is why Washington sent you down last summer, Carlos has gone berserk gentlemen. Interpol has a file on Carlos about the size of what Pollard tossed the Israelis fifteen years ago, and the French cannot find something to charge him with. Tomorrow Carlos gets tossed back to Colombia. My guess is he will be back on the first plane to Europe as soon as his plane touches down on South American soil. God is he hot! My guess gentlemen, Germany! Oh, by the way gentlemen, the men Carlos was using in Paris do not want to let Monique Gaudinier out of their employment. Monique can take a hint, and one does not leave such employment until the threat of death by gunshot has past. If they feel they have been set up she will have to fuck everyone of his lieutenants. She may have to anyway, the scum would like to try and got under Hardy's skin; *look what we did to your virgin!* Hardy likes whores but has had enough of Monique. Sad; but it would hurt. The South Americans are also all over Hardy's old pal Joe Covic. He apparently controls some people who control a few routes. They want Hardy dead. They want Covic to do the job."

Robert looked up from his report, angry and upset, hoping his trip to Bonn would not be in vein, or too late. "Do they know about the DEA angle John?"

"No gentlemen, but it was the DEA angle which saved the backside of Mr. Covic last year."

"The trade off of intelligence and law-enforcement, John?" Henry chipped in.

"Pretty much Henry. Covic has balls, both these boys do. Found himself the right whore, turned his life around. Too bad, probably be killed."

"Don Fusaro know?"

"He will, Covic's girlfriend is sort of a liaison in an old game of *Indian telephone*. He will very soon. Don Fusaro is going to go berserk. I intend to leave Don Fusaro-Debenadetto out of prison if he behaves; serves his country. He will be off the wall by tonight or tomorrow.

Henry smiled in nervous amusement and said, "I will let my men know. I have a man in at Longo's, Vito is amused to find us British love Italian food so much. Really do not want these lads to shoot the wrong spy, God that would be a mess," and Henry looked over to see the other two join in with a bit controlled stress laughter.

"Robert, I want you to send word to Jerusalem, I do not want the Israelis stepping all over my peoples toes. Hardy, and why is Jerusalem so hot now?"

"The tailend John, they played Günthers for awhile. Hardy had made himself known in North Africa, he has captured the eye of some terrorists. The Israelis want in. The French too. I am sure Jerusalem would love a little leverage over Paris..." and Robert broke in speech at the knock at the office door.

"Boss, another dossier from Interpol. I gave it a quick glance, I think you three should give it a read."

"Thanks Jennifer," and the three took to their work assignment by way of a Special Agent In Charge Blacke's secretary, which would bring the session up to noon and closing time.

The bar crowd was tense at the favorite watering hole of Joe Covic. The Black Beach with her bikini clad ladies walking all around had an assortment of thongs and G-strings flowing all about the background in front of the beach where most of the lovelies went topless. The Black Beach was where Covic held court, made his contacts and did his business throughout the drug world underworld. A little South America in French Martinique.

"Señor Covic, you like your money? Sí? You like your whore? Si? You like your life? Sí? Good Amigo. We talk. You like the goodness of God's gifts better then your friend Hardy? Sí? Good Amigo."

"Who are you friend?"

"Carlos Sanchez is a friend of mine, you friend make trouble, si?"

"So?"

"Hey Gringo, you like life? This man to die. Carlos, he think you do the job, si?"

"Hardy is CIA."

"So Gringo, you kill this CIA."

"Hardy is a CIA spy, not covert operative. Big difference Amigo. No. Then we kill you Gringo."

"OK, my life or his. kill him, Hardy's people kill me. OK, big bucks Amigo. Not you, someone higher up on the food chain. I play at Carlos's level, he sends you. He can kill me? but I can hurt him? and he sends you?"

"'You fuck Gringo."

"Someone higher up, Carlos have a brother...?"

William came into the disheveled office of Emily Rodrigues to drop the file on her desk, which look as much a mess as her outward appearance. The wake had been intense, leading her anger to even greater intensity. The kind of anger, which blinds overly sane people into actions of which they shouldn't, if in the *reasonables* of which brought them into this profession would ordinary keep them from making such mistakes. Emily slowly read the file, beamed with anger and amusement of a tid bit in a witch hunt, and dialed her friend at The Manhattan District Attorney's Office.

"Philip, is Robert M. in?"

"The big M. is out today Emily. What's up?"

"This report of the shooting of the two German kids and their whore off 60th Street back in October, they found something with Hardy's name and a partial fingerprint?"

"Emily, there was no positive ID on the print. The FBI think the kids were into poor man's spying."

"The document?"

"Mr. Harding's, Emily. Believed stolen."

"We need to talk, I want him charged," and Emily's anger raged inside her before she continued. "Then contact Interpol, have him pulled out of France, Germany, Belgium, wherever!"

"Emily, the FBI has sent word, hands off. Both Atlanta and Federal Plaza. Look, Emily, I believe your people or ours had him under surveillance at the time, he cannot be two places at once. He was the victim, not the gunman. Hardy does documents, not guns Emily."

"He is tied to it, I want the man charged! I will be over this afternoon."

"Good-bye Emily," and Philip Roma prepared himself for heartburn to arrive after lunch as he hung up the phone.

Shooting a balloon, his ex, and pig or not, I can trust Joe, were some of the thoughts playing on Hardy's mind in his search for another Paris café to escape Monique and plan his move to Bordeaux. Joe, for Joe was the subject of intelligence left on his gift from Kevin Slyer, which had also been coupled with an encrypted memo from Trevor Downing. Both Whitehall and Langley wanted Hardy to be aware of how upset Carlos was, and of the pending turn of events involving his former best friend: It's either him or you.

Shooting a balloon was a term taught to Hardy by Peter DeMarco back in his early days in the Specials unit of the phone company. Sometimes you come across a circuit that does not exist anymore, and thus the term; shooting a trouble on a circuit which does not exist. As crazy as it sounds it happens. The fire company in Athens came to Hardy's mind. Some Cold War siren installed for a week in 1960, only to have some old timer thirty years later wonder why the hotline to the siren does not work and call in a trouble report. You arrive, you find the wires, you find the paperwork with the design and you start to try to put it all back together. Finding out three weeks later from the Business Office it was officially disconnected a week after it was installed in 1960. Leaving the repairman with the silly feeling of having spent an entire month working on something that does not exist. And that apparently was what Langley had done with Covic? Given him a riddle that does not exist anymore but enough of a skeleton to drive the French up a wall. Hold them at bay, and let me go on my little adventure? And of course he received this from my ex-wife between the sheets from her contacts in New Orleans and Montreal? *We fucked you thirty years ago, now disconnect that secret Joe!* Between the two of us we then had everyone by the balls. Still he has half, I have half. Bring the two of us together and shoot us both? Well, at least we covered each other well? But there was more on Hardy's mind; the French apparently had one foot on a freshly waxed floor and the other in a bucket of mud. Their law-enforcement were not at all happy but they did seem to let Hardy play his game. American death in Bosnia covered over by the French lack of concern for a U.S. Army Signal Corp deep in territory where they should not be. Fucked by the French, covered over by Washington; State Department and a bigger picture. What was the other half? Joe's half? But in his heart Hardy already knew; being conscious of intelligence Hardy did not wish to be told would only force him to send situations into motion of a cover my ass letter to Caliber, or to one of many who play the game in Washington. Surely Trevor would be forced to do the same?

Disconnect that calling card Joe, it was only good for a week. Oh, and by the way Joe, you go the other way on this we will kill you. Love and kisses, Langley. P.S. Whitehall says "hello."

I'm going to be a daddy. God, and maybe twins. Two I know of, one covertly? A son covertly? But a covert baby? Jill from The Athens Post, she's not but there have been many Jills in my life, and rumors abound. Bet it's a girl? the covert one. The old Monk of Georgia, keeper of the rumor mill, a covert baby, and of course she moved to Tibet? Pregnancy by enlightenment?

Sure there have been more than my fair share of Jills and a couple of Moniques; though none as painful. False threat, no baby, stomach pains and I am always this emotional when I return from the doctors office, coupled with you bastard and you fuck. Only to show up a year later in Paris to try and murder me by love, lack of love, consumption of love, or love injected into a life that does not want love leading us to our over dose of love: Crucifixion by affection. There have been too many Jills and Moniques, the Right to Lifers should picket me full time. I should list them on my passport. Twins? and a covert baby to come back someday from Tibet, Japan, Madagascar or Kauai to slice me through the heart when I'm sixty-five. Good stationary; I love you, please save my life. And if you can't, take my heart and child support and tell the child how much his daddy loves him. But love him to death, to my death. Your daddy could not be there but he did save the world for you so you could have life. And a covert sister some place. Could be, and overt twins.

"Monsieur Harding, I think you will find the rooms quite attractive. Our hotel is small but we keep our rooms, how do you say? like an American Bed and Breakfast. You should like, oui?"

"Oui, Monsieur. Is there a telephone?" And Hardy was glad the hotel manager broke his confusion of thoughts.

"Well, I will need liaisons. If you want Hardy dead, OK, $250,000. I do not work for free. Hardy is my best friend, it will most likely cost me my life someday. $250,000, I will set it up, the hitman will want more. A deal?"

"OK, Señor, a deal. Señor, your bar is as shadowy as you Señor. I should kill you just for lack of lighting. Gets some lights Señor Covic. Hey Amigo, I know a good electrician. You like? I kill you for light bulbs if you double cross me. Sí?"

"Who will I be working with?"

"Juan Miguel is Carlos's brother. You fuck with him Gringo, you fuck with Carlos. He like me Señor, he no like you. Sí."

"Sí, Amigo. I know of a lady, a lady his brother will like. A peace offering, a liaison. Juan like the ladies, Amigo?"

"Sí."

"Good. Now this lady is not just any lady, high price call girls to the stars. Hollywood. Coke connections, rich and powerful; expand business. Honor amongst thieves. I trust her but I don't. Good lay. Good liaison. The same for Juan Miguel. Sí?"

"Sí."

"After I set it up, Julie and I leave from Panama, the canal. I trust this young lady, we have slept together. But not with $250,000. Sí?" and Covic looked over to see his friendly South American viper nod his head. I deal only with Juan Miguel."

"You know me think Señor? me think you set us up Gringo! You come to Colombia Gringo."

"Then fuck-off! Better yet, trust Bernadette. Go to Colombia?" Covic looking over with amusement, gently laughing to himself. "You think I am that stupid Pedro? That is the deal. Bernadette owes me, she will do it. I will send her gift wrapped this week."

"You know what I think Gringo? I think I come back when this is over and kill you anyway. How do you say Gringo, *lose face*?"

"Now fuck-off, and run along. I don't talk to errand boys." and Joe looked over to see a sudden shift in pocket movement. "A...a...aah I like guns too Amigo, so does Julie standing right behind you. Damn good with the Eastern Arts too I might add. Now, Fuck off!" and Joe's last two syllables turning his Colombian viper sheet white and scurrying away from his villa in need of some island rum.

His desk looked about as war torn as the election he was about to lose. Washington, and an Israeli public not at all happy with the pace of the peace process, or the direction of the government. The wind was shifting, more moderate and gentle for the wings of Doves. Though with a fifty-fifty split in her populous, her security was still guaranteed. But one of a security more accommodating to peace.

"Ariel my friend, what do you have for me."

"Besides the bad news Ben? Well he was, or is one tough bastard. A quiet man but tough man. Fair. Will not see the future your way but maybe not the wrong way...?" and Ariel paused for a moment and continued. "I have moved Zaporah to Bonn," laying his file on Ben Netanyahu's desk he continued. "The American agent, Hardy, he has made the networks of Marcus Wolfe as mad as hornets. Primakov by way of Marcus by way of the drug networks of Carlos Sanchez, who are doubling in the spy game; since the Wall came down Moscow cannot find good help in the spy game. The grassroots level of espionage has always found itself riddled with such vermin, Ben. This man Harding has made everyone as made as hornets. Mexico City reports the Colombians have put out a contract on Mr. Harding, they want to keep him from moving to Bordeaux.

"What else?"

"Shooting in Paris, there are documents floating around."

"God, I would love to have our people get a look at them."

"And there is more Ben; Little Italy, our consulate to U.N., their field people," and Ben understood Ariel meant Mossad on to ground in the streets of Manhattan, "they seem to think Mr. Harding's old patron from Atlanta will let it go through this time, has the South Americans beaming from ear to ear."

"Too bad. I guess business is just really business for Don Fusaro-Debenadetto. Even for second sons. Too bad. Instruct our people not to interfere...on American soil. Europe is our playground, he will like Bonn."

"Next we have hot tempered Hezbollah trained Iranian leaning terrorists of North Africa, apparently Langley or Whitehall set them up with Hardy playing a semiconscious role. They all decided to come in out of the woodwork to take a peak at a spy. Hardy playing the terrorist trophy, even wearing some funky, kids call them funky these days, blue jeans with a mess of hippy holes in them to attract attention. A new version of the gray man. They came out Benny. What followed was a summary execution of about fifty or more by the Algerian Government. They blame Hardy. This cell also has ties to the group of Hezbollah in Southern Lebanon, who we suspect are responsible for the death of the child Zaporah lost years ago. She wants in Ben. Worst way. Likes Hardy, will pay him back. But the friends Hardy is attracting; well it is personal. Documents too. She wants in."

"What is this with Trevor Downing you have highlighted here?"

"MI6/SIS boarded a Liberian registered tanker off Gibraltar, seized 120 million dollars worth of cocaine heading to Naples to be shipped to Milan. Sent the wire services bullshit, a little white lie of only finding two and a half million dollars of cocaine before they scuttled the ship and sunk it in relatively shallow water. Playing a little game with the lads the report said. They want to see how bad the Colombians want their lost white gold. Carlos is so upset Ben, he is medicating himself with his own remedies. He is back in Bonn, the Americans called it right. The BND are keeping an eye on him, Zaporah too; with the who has the documents game? The Germans would kind of like to have our friends in Washington leave now that the great game is over and the next cold war has not been officially named, word is we are all rolling to China. And...Mr. Harding has apparently upset the Chinese as well. That little gift he brought Gen. Clark from Col. Clay, well..."

"God Damn that Nazi! Didn't he know we had a couple irons in the fire regarding Beijing! God damn that man!"

"Yes...Ben, he knew. Apparently wanted to stick it up both our asses at to same time. Forced us to pull out of the satellite deal."

"That fuck!"

"Relax Ben, it will be Ehud's worry," and Ariel Sharon paused a bit. "Now last...the ladies in Atlanta are getting along well. Pam does not need therapy but she loves to talk. The mob has a girlfriend in on the inside asking all the right questions, the FBI quietly chuckle away listening to all the gossip. The doctor is playing games, could be twins. Her doctor is not a Jew. Hardy may have a covert baby boy someplace. Got back to Pam Wellington, upset her but if you want to have a life with a spy you have to put up this shit, her words. She expects a few surprises along the way. She like us, her daddy. She knows we are listening too. I have some people our agents can work with at the U.S. Attorneys Office in Atlanta, we have the market cornered in law. That is about it Ben. Oh, the FBI took the serial killer out of play. We suggested it, the FBI bit. Good idea either way."

"Just do not let the Americans know, Special Agent In Charge John Blacke will go wild. I know this man."

"They do, he won't. Assurances from The State Department. Now let me wander over to intelligence and make a pain in the ass of myself and leave you to lick your wounds. Let the next man worry about this mess Ben. He's been there, he knows.

"Get the fuck out of here Ariel, go find a Villa where we both can cause a little post election mayhem. Shalom, now get out of here."

The old gift of Kevin Slyer's Pulled through again. Trevor, and the Gibraltar aftermath. Better check it one more time. High-tech in a turn of the century Paris style American Inn. God, Pam tore my heart to shreds today. Could almost see her on the other end of the line. Dialing Atlanta from Paris these days is as easy as calling next door in the old days. God, we've come a long way. Twins? Who is playing a game? Pam or the doctor? Damn women...Now an E-mail from Vera, Berlin; won't be there any time soon. She is safe, good in bed too. I've become a daddy one too many times now. One I know of, unless twins. One covert, obviously, and he looks like me? Time to shred the old heart again.

...Here we go; magic screen, oops, who left that? ...Hello Langley, glad I cannot trust Joe anymore? Bernadette, and glad you are in Europe. Hazbollah extremely hot, stay away from Cyprus. Be careful of Greece and Turkey...This screen will disappear into outer space in fifteen seconds. Good morning Mr. Philps... Has to be a way to down load one of these magic E-mail and blackmail Langley; thoughts that can got one killed. Covic has the idea let him do the job. Hardy is over hung and misbehaved. Yea, DEA to you too. Sorry I blew your cover pal! Monique. Owe you one rubber (friend). You can handle it Joe, drug Cartels never believe the truth. Their people make lousy spies too. Love and kisses, Hardy...

Let's see...Dear Trevor, like Persian girls, going to be a daddy. I want out of the old game. And by the way, did you get, opps...receive the piece I wrote? How did you like it? Send me the check if it makes it in. Trev, keep a careful eye out. France is buzzing, all of Europe I hear; terrorist in the game big time. You're second prize, unless Zaporah reenters the game. They hate us more, but you Brits do make better Snakes. Been hanging out at St. Pat's too much. Yea, I know, I love you too. Trevor, who the hell is Henry Chatsworth? and do I really want to know? I always like to get to know a man before I let him set me up. Pay back is a....

Well, lets put the old toy away. God, and some people think laptaps are better then sex. And the opposition rendered me a psychosis on paper back in Dixie. Laptops and sick puppies. Who reads this stuff anyway unless you have to? ...Good, done. ...Let's get out of here, things to do.

Monique, and The Café Dominique, my new haunt. I wonder how long it will take for her to find me? Christ, Carlos is almost as bad as the mob. Not long I'm sure. She will probably even like this place. More comfortable. Hope she keeps her clothes on. I hate to come home to beautiful naked ladies laying on my bed when it is against my better judgment to sleep with them. Forty-two, at forty-two you play the devil and watch them burn in their desire at their passion peak. You do when sex can kill you and you're a daddy in Atlanta with a mistress in Berlin and a temporary ex-wife about to show up in Bonn or Hamburg, I'm sure. Sexual peaks, mine was seventeen. Wish I could be reckless again. Monique, anyone but Monique. Vera was hot and down to earth once we got over the intensity of almost killing each other. But Monique, you're so damn deadly to me sweetheart, I know you feel the same. Why entangle our flesh just to die in each others arms? Love but not in love. Love but in love, I'm in love with another. An overt daddy to boot. Love, I love you enough not to engage you. Somehow I suspect you feel the same. But there is another power driving your soul, I saw it at the café that morning. The "what ifs" coming back to haunt you. The "what ifs" were never meant to be. Help me escape and leave me alone. If we ever sleep together, I will never leave Paris alive. You know that in your heart.

I'm a terrorist trophy; Vera my intelligence officer, Zaporah my live-in commando. Pam the mother of my child, and you wish to damn me between your legs. Better I die letting a terrorist try to drop an A-bomb on me while one of my lovers shoot him in the nick of time, then have my passion squeezed and my heart crushed between your legs. Have mercy on my soul Monique, have mercy on us both...Damn phone...

"Yes."

"Monsieur Harding, a parcel from Malta at the desk with your name on it. Send it up? Oui?"

And had the desk man had the ability to read one's mind as spies who go on instinct can often give the illusion to, he would have read concern of letter bombs being batted about by demons of too much and too little romance inside Hardy's head. It took awhile but Hardy did come to his senses.

"Who is it from Monsieur?"

"A Monsieur Trevor Downing, Monsieur Harding," but Trevor was in London...

It was sunny out, a warm Paris sun and mild breeze blowing about the early summer season. Hardy had retrieved the package from the front desk and left it in the bathtub while he went out for lunch and some deep thoughts of what to do with an unwanted, or unexpected parcel. The bathtub would be best; the fourth floor, would probably just blowout the wall. Healthy paranoia, too small to be a nuke. Trevor in

London, Caliber safely tucked away in the Gulf, Zaporah would send love and kisses from Jerusalem, well, maybe not. In any case if one could view Mr. Harding around one o'clock on that Tuesday afternoon, it would have been reported back to Langley and Whitehall, and it was, that our hero not only had demons on his mind but complexities of hazardous substances, especially ones that kill; and the more benign ones, which only remove ones hand or two. With all this on his mind, it was further reported; Hardy seemed hungry, a tad lonely but with a wish to duck the surveillance of a tragic old flame and disappear into the safe bosom of a new haunt, The Café Dominique. Which was located the other side of The Champs Ellyees, a few blocks down from his old haunt; somewhat smaller, warm but shadowy with a small streetside sidewalk café. Where he would be found by an old spook sipping a cheap version of the prior years Beaujolais and gently tugging on some fresh fruit and an assortment of fine French cheeses.

"Good morning Mr. Harding, may I sit down?"

"You mean afternoon? Sit down next to a young pup like me?" he asked with slight bewilderment. "But I like German, you speak good English, What do you want? And who are you?" and it was clear the old German could see the puzzlement on his face.

"I am your Guardian Angel, Mr. Harding, and was even in Atlanta for a time. Morning? because you look like you just woke up. Did you receive my parcel?"

"It is in the bath, I have a terrorist problem."

"Well, well, you sip old Beaujolais when a better wine would be appropriate..."

"Sometimes you just know..."

"Sad about that American undercover cop who was eliminated at The Hotel De Paris a short time ago. Too bad, on French soil too. It is very sad when Washington cannot keep track of her wayward children. Stepped on a few toes at The Department Of State. Dr. Albright is livid. Sweet lady I understand. And that poor emotional young lady this undercover cop adopted as a second daughter," he said taking a pause. Then Günther Von Müller looked over and about to Hardy's eyes with grandfatherly concern, viewing the intensity and deep pain of the emotions of demons, which carve the faces and lives of rookie spies. One is only a pup in the great game at forty-two, though Günther would not hold up well to a ricin dart. Yet Hardy in his youth was young but not quite rookie class, Hardy a step or two above if not more, and he wondered how he had made it this far before he continue. "Your exploits are legendary young Mr. Harding. I have followed your saga. I am too old now, I stick to what I do best. And who cares at my age?" and

Günther smiled warmly and paused again for a moment before he continued. "Now then, I seem to have come across this file from Ariadne/Americain, I suspect you would know better what to do with it?"

Hardy was quiet in thought for a moment or two, glancing down to the file once or twice tucked partly in the folds of a *Paris Daily* before he spoke. "I see. It might be nice to take a peak...The young lady..?"

"It is a shame to throw away such a love affair young Mr. Harding. Your love life is legendary as well. Such a shame, and she is now an indentured servant of the South Americans for awhile. She could be useful? If you do not bed her, string her along. You know how the game is played. She has access to more, you know what is important."

"I see," and he poured the old German a glass of wine.

"Old Beaujolais, this wine Mr. Harding can kill you. Sometimes you just know," and Günther laughed mildly. "You remind me of me forty years ago. I was good, you are better. I have been following you for sometime. Oh, we have never met but you are kind of like a son to me. The close call you had in Savannah? That was me. The gentleman almost bumped off my charge, you were my charge, my responsibility. We all knew how important your work was, I was there to see that you made, or that you lived peacefully in the arms of Our Lord had you the misfortune to fall into the wrong hands. I have been there young Mr. Harding, now when I come I bring you gifts. Gifts of life, gifts of death, or silly papers I have no use of."

"Been there?"

"Fifty-nine to sixty-four. What a mess. Strung to Israelis along, played them pretty bad. Oh, Nazi past but I like them. Not too much of a sin. Philby really. Fucked us all back in those days."

"I like history, how? Vague tones, I understand."

"Oh God what a mess. From fifty-nine on. They had spun Philby out to do a job. He had in the past been a liaison between the intelligence communities of both London and Washington. But these were troubled times. The political clouds off on the horizon were dark, black and ominous. Like seeing a big black funnel cloud coming out of the sky. I'm an American citizen Mr. Harding, I have been to the Midwest. Kim Philby was not as strong as you or the others. It looked as though by the time sixty-three rolled around that Moscow would win everything. Lock, stock and barrel. The South China Sea, Eastern and Western Europe, unleash a Socialist agenda on America. Which my adoptive country would not be able to contain. It was ominous, scary, like the Blitzkriegs my people would do to the allies during the War. Kim Philby wanted to be on a winning side. When he went over he set up Dallas and the scandal in Britain. Toppled the British Government. I'm an old man Mr. Harding, dates, dates sometimes slip my mind. Most times someone like myself does not want to remember. You too?" and Günther looked over to see Hardy nod his head in agreement of how best classified matters should be handled: Complete memory loss. Though, there are times when it is important to remember. "When Philby went over we almost lost everything. Damaged relations between us and the British. All the West really, Mr. Harding. But not a total loss. We held."

"Held?"

"Yes, we held. And you know now I am telling you this for a reason. It would have been a disaster in Atlanta had you failed. The same for this little game. But we won too Mr. Harding. After sixty-three the Russians had fell short. Over extended, leaving all the players set up. Both us and the British simply asked the right people if they had anything to do with catastrophe? There were a few that year. The Russians were over extended, like Moscow in the winter, we played their people and networks back. We turned the whole failure around. It laid the ground work for Europe in to late sixties and seventies."

"And that is my history lesson? Like a big game of *Risk*?"

"Yes Mr. Harding...Sometimes we all lose a game or two. You may this time. Eastern Europe is hot. It was not enough to win, now we are laying the sword to their throats. Moscow is already insulating herself through Beijing, a new cold war is about to be born crying into this world. The subcontinents are up for grabs. The Socialists of Eastern Europe yearn for a return to the old days. There are many prizes out there. It is important you understand how important your work is."

"Even when you lose?"

"Yes Herr Harding. You must absorb the loss and turn it around. Sometimes it takes many years down the road to over come misfortune. Langley cannot bring you into their bosom for a fatherly chat, so they send old Krauts like me."

"And Dallas?"

"He was a Russian agent, and was, since he had been a babe. He was not the brightest of Cold War children either, Herr Harding. The Mafia. But temptation, had the West been able to play him as a double, we would have had some kind of a low grade agent deep within an evil police state. They gift wrapped him and sent him back to us. Stuck him up our ass. We knew we would lose that game, they saw through the deception on that terrible November day. Well...you know the rest. Philby."

"Me?"

"Good breeding Herr Harding, though my Jewish friends do not care for old Germans to use such terms. Your daddy; you were ours since you were a babe. Sad really, there were others that day. A window above or below, the hill. Sad. What Is even more sad is that we lost and had to endure the cruelty and suffering of places like Eastern Europe. I am German first, though maybe not now. We all pay penance in life, I was fortunate America was mine"

"So if I lose..."

"You turn it around. The East wants a rematch, they are insulating themselves through Beijing, or will be very soon. This being the reason for your Gen. Clark sending them a little wake up call."

"Love and kisses, your crew from campaign finance?"

"Yes...exactly. If you are going to lay hands on our politicians, then we are going to fuck with you," and Günther looked over to see his adopted son snicker and smile mildly. "Good boy, Herr Harding. Now.. Your old lover, she wants a rematch. Your choice, you know what to do. Her South American friends have been keeping an eye on you, they will be sending her by soon. Hang out and stay for a while. Before they kill you, they will want information. I know the game, I know where you are heading. Same for you regarding me. And what we could exchange we do not need to know. We both know better. Common sense."

"OK, and you will be in the shadows?"

"It is the game I play best. Now.. Au revoir Mr. Harding, good-luck my son."

Hardy had had a lot on his mind that morning leading him to his rendezvous with an old German ghost. Much more thought upon his head to digest in one simple lunch time café meal and he pondered to himself as he watched Günther Von Müller fade away down one of the alleys to another unnamed street, that perhaps it would be best to stretch the wine and cheese out while he waited for Monique to just happen by. *But documents, what should I do with the documents?* were his thoughts as he gazed across to street to the art store in wait of summer time seduction, though not of a U.S. Army Base but of the fuck me eyes of Monique Gaudinier.

Perhaps it was anger? or the weather? The mad rush of adrenaline of a blood hound on a scent of revenge? Opposing psychology of political means? Or just plain stupidity? that distracted Emily Rodrigues when she stepped in front of the speeding MI6 Metro Bus just off forty-third and Sixth, while she hurried with lack of commonsense to The Manhattan District Attorney's Office. Many tried to help, New Yorkers being somewhat warmer than previously reported by the press of the jealous in the past. But aging gray haired middle aged ladies do not stand much of chance when their flesh meets bus doing fifty or better. The news team from Channel 14 who arrive short time later assisted in the retrieval of the legal papers, which floated about the sidewalk in a trade off of pressing stories and intelligence. You can have the whole story if you keep your mouths shut for a short time. And where had they heard that before? The clean up of the blood was left to be fought over by The New York City Police Department's EMS Division, and her Mayor's finest, though somewhat short of Playgirl, Firefighters.

"Jennifer..."

"Yes John."

"Have Agent Reading come in and see me. I wish to send Don Fusaro-Debonadetto a little message."

"He is late from lunch John. As soon as he returns I will send him in."

"Oh, and Jennifer, tell Henry Chatsworth and Robert Torres I want to brainstorm all Monday. We'll set up a little thinktank of our own for a week or two. I do not want to lose Mr. Harding."

"Oh, boss, before Agent Reading went to lunch, he did want me to mention to you of his concerns. John, he is not sure which cards Don Fusaro-Debenadetto is playing, but he did make clear he will speak with you when he gets back."

"OK Jennifer, let me know as soon as he comes in..."

Secretary or not, with secretary to The Special Agent In Charge comes insight and responsibility. Jennifer may as well have been an agent. When she went home at night she was considered undercover. Her friends pretty much said so outright, though words of such assignments never needed to be spoken. Seldom were, and at the present no longer are. Though if the need be, they would be. Jennifer had not only the trust of her boss but of the entire FBI field office. She know her role, both roles, extremely well.

"Would you like to sit down? I have a better bottle of wine coming."

"You knew I was coming?"

"I knew I was being watched. Carlos has changed his mind? Instead of killing me, he wants to bed me?"

"I have come to save us both. I now have permanent employment whether I like it or not. Renee was a cop, I must of known, being their thoughts."

"So you want to fuck me and hope I make the same mistakes?"

"Hardy, don't. Don't be like that."

"We make love, we destroy each other. You know that. So which way do you go this time? Enforcement? or intelligence? All the people you sided with in Atlanta were double agents at best. Almost cost us Dayton."

"Hardy...please.! Please understand. Covic was a pig, he still is if I know him well enough, but his work with the DEA was important. He controlled so much! All those people, your scum double agents who were my friends would have been slaughtered. You were a tough kid, I knew you could handle it. One life Hardy, you're alive, and so are the rest!"

"You almost killed me back then, my father is paying for your sins and my gift. I ought to put a bullet in you myself."

"Hardy, please understand...Please, life, your life, you are alive. My future, I had no future with you back than. And these people law-enforcement were using were good undercover operatives. Please Hardy, I had to choose."

"You killed my father! and will have, unless *The Good Lord* intervenes. You almost killed me. You almost derailed Dayton, and I almost had my ass shot off because we had to fight Kosovo. You almost started a God damn war!"

"Hardy, please...!"

"Excusez moi Monsieur, your Chateauneuf-du-Pape. Your refill of fruit and cheese will be out shortly. Would Mademoiselle like to order anything?"

"Non Monsieur. Merci beaucoup."

Somewhere between the time the waiter brought Monique's glass and the arrival of the new cheese and fruit platter, the intensity faded. Dissolving to gentle tugging and playing of wine glasses, than slipping further to quiet thoughts in-between the picking of grapes and the tugging of cheese.

"Where are you staying..?"

"I found a smaller hotel, more like an Inn. More like the Bed and Breakfast we made love in in Savannah."

"Like your place Hardy? back in Atlanta?"

"Yes. The new place is comfortable, more reasonable. I have money now but I still do not wish to live above my means. You would like it."

"Does this mean you are taking me home...?"

The communiqué from Marcus Wolfe was brief, though the concerns deeply troubling, sending Yevgeny Primakov by impulse to summon his old friend Czechoff by way of his own communiqué through the dying facilities of an out dated intelligence community. The exchange took place over glass, though the inferior grade fiber optics, which the West still allows for export. Glass being somewhat more secure then copper, most of their exchange of secure on line dated was received and disseminated with the least amount of interference of Western ease dropping surveillance.

What was apparent between the two was the setting up and exposing of all their networks in France by an American agent, a Mr. Harding. Carlos had demons, and the Americans were playing both Carlos and his demons back against him. There seemed to be a dual prize here for Western intelligence; narcotics, and the dismantling of not only a spy ring but one of Primakov's covert operations as well. Mr. Harding had to be stopped before he moved out of France into a larger Europe. Or at the very least, be controlled, or sent to a controlled demise. If there were any chance of retaking Germany into a sphere of Socialist dominance more conducive to Russian intelligence, the American and British operation would have to be stopped.

Furthermore, it was discussed between the two of the need for a face to face meeting between Yevgeny and his old friend and former colleague Marcus Wolfe, coupled with a desire to have more hands-on handling of their agent Carlos Sanchez. Or at least have him tempered by a group of their operatives who actually knew what they were doing. Carlos was out of control, the Americans were making him even more so. In their terms: Nuts. What was also quite apparent was the lack of amusement Langley and Whitehall had over the Gremlin's desire to use another agent who bore a similar name to the legendary terrorist. Messages are exchanged in these games, Washington sent theirs back by making the new Carlos straight-jacket material.

But the communiqué did end with a discussion of various ways to lure John Custer Harding to Eastern European soil where the old KGB still had a strong foothold and could easily compliment operations. And possibly, a bomb, a terrorist bomb. One which would kill many and could be blamed on the Americans: Your man is involved with terrorists, now fuck-off! We will not rewrite the treaty. Where there is a writer, or technician, or whatever this Mr. Harding was, and is obviously CIA, then somewhere in Washington there are documents with his name or coded number on them. In any case, a real mess for the Americans. Even if the CIA are the best in the world at keeping a lid on their own generated conspiracies. This man Harding had to be stopped, Czechoff was instructed to look around for a friendly terrorist cell. There were many in Southern Russia, both friendly and unfriendly.

The meeting between Yevgeny and Marcus Wolfe would take place next month. The cover being a seminar of the old days, a reflection of Cold War fun and games. He would just have to keep Marcus away from the Americans and the British delegation, and hopefully the two could find time to dine together that evening? After dinner, in a secure library, the two could discuss and toss over ideas to where this Soviet style scripted American lead terrorist attack on Eastern Europe would take place, how many deaths would be required, and how not to leave their fingerprints on this terrible crime Washington was about to be framed for.

After thinking through the entire operation frontwards, backwards, sideways and upside-down, Yevgeny then prepared a list. It was important his wife have an abundance of Russian Vodka, French wine and Beluga Caviar for the evening. But in the meantime, maybe pick up a box of chocolates for Dr. Albright for when they were to meet in Davos for some informal talks next week.

"John...?"

"Yes Jennifer," John Blacke said over the phone, breaking his rhythm with his friendly coconspirators.

The file from The State Department on Sudan arrived. Mr. Rubin sent word; you can go along with the extradition of the six terrorist from the West African nation of Senegal."

"Great! Thanks Jennifer. I will come out and pick it up in a few minutes."

"Good news gentlemen! Thought we would help Mr. Harding out."

"Taking out Hezbollah's command and control group are we?" and Henry just laughed with gentle amusement. "My people did their part last week, boy are the South Americans hot over the sinking of that tanker."

Robert just quietly smiled in agreement, "good job John. I am off to Bonn in a couple of days. Washington is buzzing; the last intelligence received from the NSA upset everyone from the Pentagon to Langley to The White House. Our analyst went over it two or three times to verify.

Primakov would like to have a peek at those documents floating around. Buy us some time, buy Hardy some time if he does not take a ricin dart? It will be a damn good chess move to have these six terrorists locked up on American soil."

"Solitaire?"John Blacke asked.

"Be best. They could most likely use the services of a good Jewish lawyer when the do arrive in America," and the three just laughed mildly at Robert's humor. "Where?"

"If we can work it out, Thursday, Stewart Air Field in New York."

❖ ❖ ❖ ❖ ❖

"Too much wine, too much wine can kill one. Come on, I'll walk you home..."

"Not my place Hardy, lets go back to your room. No sex, talk. OK? You fix me a cup of coffee. I am not that buzzed, and we need to talk."

"OK...If we ever make love again, we'll get good and drunk first. OK?"

"Grand Marnier, or your best XO Cognac."

"A deal," and they slowly made their way down the cobbled stone street past the art store and the flower vendor. Lost but not lost. The Café Dominique was a nice place to be lost about on a warm sleepy Paris afternoon.

It had been hot over the past week, hot even for Martinique. Hot even for Caribbean standards, hot even when the gentle wind blew the cool ocean breeze through the second floor window of their Villa across their naked flesh. Joe had had a tough week, stress, and the need to be a perfect whore with his perfect whore. At Julie's advice they baby oiled themselves to burn their perfect bodies into one; Joe's new one, Julie's gift she had been born of. But stress, and the ominous teaching pouring forth from Cosa Nostra in Atlanta; the need to release and be whores in one. The stress leaving him limp while Julie tended to her lover, her true love; gently stroking his chest and kissing his neck and bringing forth the emotional pain.

"It is what he wants Joe," and she could see the gloom in her lover's eyes. Joe Covic had never been so affectionate in his life, or besides himself with grief. For the sensitive side showed through, the one he always hid, the one Hardy knew not of. The Beast being a gift, and a gifted performance of undercover work. But he was who he was or what he became to be, and he now found himself in the arms of someone equally as bad, or as good as him. And as good for him. The right lover, and the right whore to be entangle in his flesh for his consumption and life; their life. The need to make love was obvious, his condition equally obvious. He settled just to be a little boy in his mother's arms, Julie giving him what he needed most that evening; affection, and the desire to be first time teenagers again. Small weddings with no family to keep the elopement from. And had he not had such a reputation to protect, perhaps he would have broken down. But Julie seeing his innocents, comforted him one more time before she continued. "Joe, I have never seen Longo's in such intensity of darkness and omens. I picked up Joni and we left. I was afraid to hang around. Joni could not wait to leave. It has to be done. When it is over the Don said you will be free. That is the deal."

"It is going to change everything Baby. It will completely change our lives," and Joe continued to run his fingers through her long black Chinese hair while their naked flesh melted together. "We leave tomorrow for Colón. From Colón we fly to Madrid."

"Did Bernadette get along with his brother?"

"They've been fucking like wild animals since she arrived. She is good, the best in the business. A real Pro. A real whore too. Tomorrow night we meet at the club, his club in Colón. A covert rendezvous. $250,000 for me, $60,000 plus expenses for the man I hire. An even $100,000, I wire him what is left over. Trust amongst thieves. Bernadette is the go-between. The next day she walks across the first bridge on the canal with $350,000. Juan will watch her walk over, Juan will watch her walk back. Juan will keep Bernadette as collateral until the job is completed. Bernadette controls my networks, Bernadette likes to fuck, Juan likes to fuck Bernadette."

"You trust her Joe?"

"No but if I lose Bernadette, I get hurt bad. When this goes down Baby, it is going to change our lives for good. Are you ready for it?"

"Yes. I love you Joe. We are two whores Joe; it will be nice to be two virgins again."

"Is this what you want?"

"Yes," and she started to give to him for free what others could not buy: Love. "The bridge Joe?"

"Cops, insulation. Wants to make sure he is not set up. A paranoid bastard. The way he likes the ladies Bernadette will probably be wearing a G-string when she comes across the bridge."

"Share? Wouldn't you like a three-some for a going away present?" and she gave his cock a gentle tug.

"No, I have you. You are all I need. You ready...?"

"Yes, a new life. I'm ready," she said, as Julie's naked body sat up and leaned over Joe, giving his neck little love kisses on each side. "I'm ready sweetheart, and so are you," and Julie slid down and impaled herself atop his cock for the ride of both her life and his. Giving him the release he so desperately needed all that week that the stress had robbed him from.

"I like it, nice digs. Going to your demise in style."

"Your coffee."

"Oh, come Hardy, you mean you would not fuck me if you came in and found me laying naked on you bed with my wings spread out in warm affection? A naked model on your bed?" And Monique looked up to see her playfulness was hitting a nerve of her former lover. "Not even for old time sake? We don't have to make love Hardy, we could just fuck, and, I know what you like and how you like it," and Monique could see both anger in his eyes and a bigger than average bulge in his pants. Hardy was always hung, his condition was even large for Hardy.

"Close but no cigar, I have control. Drink your coffee. When you are finished I will call you a taxi."

The wine had been kind to Monique. French wine having such a bad reputation with the ladies who find themselves with the wrong gentlemen. The wine was working, so was Monique: A freebie. Though Hardy was not but had found himself with much more material to write should he ever decide to dump Trevor and ghost for a publication which would make old ladies blush.

"You're in need, I could finish you off first...?"

It was dark that Thursday evening around eleven-fifteen, dark even for upstate New York when the flight from West Africa touched down amiss the intense heavy security at The U.S. Airforce National Guard Base at Stewart International Airport in Newburgh. Under the lack of light of the new moon, the six would-be assassins of spies and terrorists of humanity would be flown by helicopter to Manhattan where it had been decide by the Justice Department the arraignment in U.S. District Court at Foley Square would best serve the free American public.

It had been a gift of life to John Custer Harding by both the Atlanta FBI field office and their colleagues in New York, who wanted to make up for the troublesome meddling of some out of control cops on French soil. It had also been a thank you from The Department Of State to The Department Of Justice; geopolitical concerns would take front burner, law-enforcement would be sensitive.

It had been oppressively hot in Panama that July second morning around eleven when Bernadette started across the span with a green and black gym bag in hand. Smooth, it was smooth, her behavior that would be reported back to several Western intelligence agencies. Smooth to the handful of the hired henchmen of Carlos. Smooth, and smooth walking into the arms of Joe Covic and Julie Lee.

"How'd it go?" an apprehensive but cool Joe Covic asked.

"I gave him a good lay before I *ice-picked him*. Death always makes the orgasm intense." And Bernadette paused briefly, "distracted him, the G-String does it every time."

Covic just smiled. "The launch is just a little way down, let me help you with your bag."

"The ship?"

"*The South China Star*, a Burmese registered tanker. Not first class but you have roughed it before;" Joe looking over, just smiling again at the very beautiful young lady he had the pleasure to have trained through the many years of her erotic life.

"I think we will all like China Beach," Julie chipped in. "Hanoi seems to be warming to Capitalism. $350,000 for a kill, Bernadette, you can share our bed. Or buy your own. Don Fusaro sends love and kisses, the only people you will have to worry about if you return to The States is the FBI."

Bernadette just smiled, they could see it coming, "OK, three to a bed. Then we all go back to Mass. OK Joe? You earned it."

"That is what I want for my birthday, a three-some. A threesome for three hundred fifty thousand, it sounds fair. Then we all go back to Mass. Julie said Buddhism is flexible, and I like French."

"Champagne when we all get aboard, when we reach international waters. We sail the other way, maybe Greece on the way over..?" Julie added, and they all could see Bernadette was hot. They all were hot of the day, the deed and of the intensity of their affection. "And Juan Miguel?"

"He told them he wanted to be alone. I left them something from Don Fusaro-Debonadetto next to Juan for when they find the body."

"Corpus Christi."

"Corpus Christi."

"Corpus Christi."

CHAPTER 15

"What do you think Robert? will he have any problems when he gets to Germany? Different game?"

"The drops John, about the same. There are people he can work with, we have people in place in Europe to help him along if Hardy needs it."

"Rogue cells?

"No, not really rogue cells. Inactive cells. Some new, some left over from to 1980s, the 70s. He will have people help him out should he run in to trouble."

"In this country?"

"Yes. We have some inactive calls in America."

"About to same for us John, we still have quite a bit of old MI6 left in place in Europe. Our people and yours use to work together quite well in the old days, use to fit together hand and glove.

Your people Henry, did some magnificent work in to old days, I have studied them." Robert chipped in with admiration of a student, who cut his teeth on the learnings of old MI6 spy affairs. "I leave for Bonn tomorrow, any tips for me Henry...?"

Paris and demons. Paris had been filled with old emotions and demons since Hardy arrived. Even having an old spook look him up to advise him of the need of this guardian angel to keep Hardy safe and alive for when he should enter hell at the end of his life. It was mostly demons the spies of the high-tech world picked up on in the inner workings of poor Hardy's mind that morning. Mostly demons; demons of the enemy, demons of French law-enforcement, demons of the sick and informed minds of this world. Demons, only demons. Demons of French crossed bred terrorists, who in their twisted mind thought everyone who did not subscribe to Islam was the antichrist.

And it was of such thoughts, demons, which consumed Hardy, as he made his way out for some fresh air and a short day trip of the Paris sights:

It was good she liked the coffee, two cups and a taxi, and, God, yes, we have to talk. We need to talk Monique. Documents and a mess. Documents and the need to stay longer in Paris. Documents and old lovers. Documents and babies in Atlanta; an impossible situation. I could not go to you even if I wanted to. Love and fatherhood. Emotions, mistresses, babies, and temporary wives. I cannot go to you Monique, too much has happened between us. It is an impossible situation. Regardless of what old ghosts say, who cannot make up their minds whether to save me or shoot me. An impossible situation. Emotions, and you would only leave me once again to feed myself on rice and beans.

Triple-X movies...I could not even be your leading man. There will be no need for me this time. But should we Monique, then lets make them pay. Though I have already paid many times over in this life for falling in love with the wrong girl. X-rated movies and more to eat than just rice and beans, there will be no need of such employment this year in the life of this spy ...And writer. But Paris, a setup, and being forced together; if we have-to we make them pay! And who is pushing your hot buttons these days? with Carlos deported to hell I hope? We make them pay.

Your love? Death in your love?

I desire to be with another, though with life's complexities of the spy game, I blur the lines and cross over to pursuits of the flesh to bury my pain. Surgically separated from loved lovers, I go to Germany soon to damn my soul and pay for my fun. They are the same as I, I am a whore Monique....

Thoughts...? We are never alone in our own minds.... And God, I am glad she cannot read mine. Though she shows her affections or ensnarements on the outside, wings spread open wide, her naked flesh upon my bed and the need I have to stay celibate for the right lover. Zaporah, Bonn and magic screens, the right lover waits in the next country over while I am left here to wander the streets of Paris to hide from the flesh which would consume me and damn my soul.

The Paris fresh air, and not too hot on a summers morn.

Documents, damn documents! An old lover with access to documents. Documents to trap me, illicit love to kill me. But documents and an old ghosts; string her along Hardy, you know the game. String her along, if you don't bed her. 63 and I'll kill you if you fail; turn it around! Wisdom to drive young pups like me insane. The insanity of it all.

Bed me Monique what do we have to lose?

Our lives. Or at the very least, our sanity and emotional stability.

It was a terrible Paris morning amiss the loving warm sunshine of the city of lights. To Hardy everything and everyone seemed dead, the loving sunshine only adding to the thoughts of what a gorgeous day it would be to bury or wake humanity. Sickness of ill treachery of humanity with those consumed with a spy game to kill or destroy for respective foreign policy; Primakov, Marcus Wolfe and some lad, as Trevor use to call them, named Czechoff. A crazed drug narco-terrorist and spy named Carlos coupled with past thoughts of how law-enforcement in Georgia tried to destroy Hardy's life to save their own ass at the expense of his heart. An old lover, NATO troops, MidEast stability, Dayton, and PacRim intrigue, let alone the pending mess he was to enter in Europe and Eastern Europe. Law-enforcement; state groups and corrupt county officials in some Georgia county who fell shy of FBI quality but still try to *false flag* in any respect. Sacrificing human life and the stability of loved relationships to save themselves or trap and manipulate sexuality and illicit affairs of the flesh at the expense of humanity. The corrupt county officials having one reason for their treachery, the state undercover groups who at one time the FBI had pride in their work, having a second reason; undercover work played well when you were ghosting or moonlighting for the KGB. In any case, crush or destroy the meek! Trample over the good! Destroy the healthy in this world! And piss on Gen. Clark in his demand for sixty thousand NATO troops! We can justify it with a bigger sting operation! Cut the county creeps a deal! If we lose the bigger picture we can raise our children in fifth! Fifth is the world of which brought forth the perverse who wheel sick and illness; the end will justify the means! And God damn them!

The complexity of John Custer Harding's emotions did not go unnoticed by either Whitehall or Langley, group think-tanks and discussions broke out in London, Washington and in Atlanta over Mr. Harding's darkness that morning. Documents, did he have them? though they suspected he did. Günther, a shadowy ghost of yesteryear. And would he survive a rematch with Monique, and at what expense? Would it justify his engagement with an old flame? Was there really that much more to take or steal from Carlos? The complexity of the situation had upset all in the West Paris, and high level cabinet meetings. French law-enforcement, and North Africa replayed. Hardy, and let him play his game; Washington and London get the blame should anything go wrong! It could! But the West, and Paris comfortable in playing a doubles game of good cop/bad cop to the world; let Hardy be.

What bedeviled Hardy that morning was not satanic verses being sung by French song birds guiding him on their wings of death but lesbianism. Monique and lesbianism. Sick minds and the destruction of beautiful healthy lives for a game; for as to save one's ass, for as to save the quasi good and the quasi sick in this world. One to sting and save one's ass, the other to sting and destroy a few lives to save one's ass for greed. My enemies enemy is my friend. Both sick of the illness of filth.

Before the Southern Spy Affair ended both the cop of the *middle ages plague* and drug vermin gangster had found bliss in each others disease arms at the expense of Hardy and Monique: Save each other, filth begets filth, and piss on humanity. Fuck the bigger picture! There will always be drugs! Wall Street would stumble! And if we destroy these two and save ourselves with some quasi pretend production we can justify it'! Damn it, we have to!

It was lesbianism, Monique, and God, if we sleep together I hope we will both survive, were his thoughts while Hardy tumbled through the different types of this sexuality in both tearful thought and amusement. They had been through it before, would deal with it again if they had to. Hardy being an understanding spy, educated and learned of the streets with a Ph.D. of life along the way. Complexity of thought to even confuse and deceive his own people in London and Washington; a gift of lesbianism played. A gift of lesbianism on one's mind. A gift of the destruction of young lives, which leave *deceivers* and their beautiful counterparts with many rooms to hide within their minds for when the sick come sniffing around. A gift of the three different types of Lesbianism had played on Hardy's mind:

Bio; life's predisposition.

Environment and childhood; the make up of young life experiences, which shape our lives.

Lesbian Chic; the desire to service another woman to please your lover. Often going hand-in-hand with cocaine and a party: It is his fantasy, I want to make him happy.

Though in the turmoil of the upheaval in a spy game when the Deceivers, players and whores become so battered by the abuse of the sick minds of treachery they blur the lines of sexuality, worth, common sense and desire, what is right...? Hardy had seen it with Covic, he had seen it with Monique.

The ending of his complex thoughts that morning, as he boarded an English speaking tour bus, were, that he really did not want to deal with it, or Monique. Though it did not stop one silent tear drop from flowing from his eyes. A tear drop of the destruction of innocent lives. A tear drop of the destruction of beauty. A tear drop of the exploitation of the healthy out of jealousy and greed to destroy another's soul so that one could live. A gift of what they both had gone through. A gift of lesbianism.

Civility in the spy game, though he thought, there is none. The old gentlemen's game had not been played very fair in the modem affairs of intrigue, and had not been now for many years. The generations of such having died out long before Hardy was born. *The brutality of it all, are any of us worthy of life?*

The city of lights, The Eiffel Tower, Notre Dame, The Champs Ellysees, Hardy may as well have been home watching TV:

In Atlanta they would not let Monique and me be together, congressmen, big cocaine money to blur their common sense of the special interest who put them there. The Chinese, and working with the enemy. Damn Monique with a brutal beast, bash Hardy around and maybe he will go over? Maybe we can force him over? If not to the Russians, then perhaps the Chinese? Bash them both, brutalize them to their core but save my corrupt ass! I have children and an electoral public at home to worry about! And fuck Gen. Clark, the man should be happy with what I gave him! Let the Russians retake all of Eastern Europe, the Czechs cannot vote anyway. Robin Cook, Tony Blair, Dr. Albright, Mr. Holbrooke; fuck them all. I have phone companies to worry about! The Chinese can fight it out with the Japs over The PacRim!

But now, now they want us together. I guess silently hoping we would kill each other. Not knowing that in out hearts we both know it is true. C-Span, even in Paris, I get C-Span, and I got better dialogue from Romper Room when I was a kid. The House is a zoo, circus a better word. God, what are we paying these people? Too much for a circus show. Too little; the South Americans seem to make sport out of buying American politicians. While the Russians and Chinese squeeze them by by their corrupt balls for being the dishonest fucks they are.

Monique and I cannot talk, or we lose half of Capital Hill, the three hundred and change on the one side who really deserve to be taken to the woodshed.

Monique and I must be lovers; crucify ourselves in our bliss unto our death so The House can have everlasting corrupt life. September, the hearings, God, I am glad they are over. Monique and I together...And was this just an oversight of some zealous cop? Some zealous dead cop now. Or is the ugly face of Washington corruption reeling its ugly head? Kill them both! C-Span. One cable channel in English, C-Span! God, I cannot wait till this tour is over...C-Span....

It had been a minor trade delegation to Tehran Czechoff attended covering joint oil ventures, expanding Yankee imperialism and what to do about it, and terrorism; officially evil. Unofficially it depended on what and who the targets were. Though such dialogue is never spoken outright about such trade delegations, or at any meeting, regardless of how high or how low the matters of state were. Terrorism is not condoned. Though at the cafés in the open Tehran market bazaars one could freely speak his mind about such issues of evil. America being evil, Russia being the lesser of the two. Though in friendship with the devil, it was further harder to discern between the competing Western intelligence agencies who was more evil? There were two devils; one major, one a minor devil. They broke bread and decided it was best though words were further not spoken outright, that the Great Satan America should be made to stumble if at all possible.

Czechoff had found the right man who knew the right groups who know the right terrorists. He also had the inner inside track of the right ear and was looking to sharpen his sword on a leading Iranian journalist. Who's demise would further soothe the right ear and inner soul of his friend, the ruling President Of Iran, Mohammad Khatami. Czechoff was assured some kind of explosive device would be found and sent off to bear fruit at the end of the harvest in Europe: A time to reap. My enemy's enemy is my friend. This man Harding was obviously CIA Spy as opposed to operative, what's the difference? But wait, I have a thought...And maybe his holiness and divine president is in today...? Both Czechoff and the Mullah hurried off with different thoughts on their minds about a similar out come to tragedy, which to the Mullah's train of thought would be Gods divinity and work brought to bear on this earth by angels in the flesh of mortals. The same but different. Iranians tend to worry about Iran not Russia. Many years of religious bloodshed tends to deprogram clerics of The Koran leaving them pragmatic where once only Allah filled the void. Religion for some, like Razi, was only in title. Razi had a better idea.

His name was Rahim, his friends called him Razi.

"How did you get in?" Hardy asked though he knew the answer. "It's been a bad day, I wish you would keep your clothes on."

"I could have been on top of the bed, naked and spread eagle instead of underneath the covers. Your bed is comfortable Hardy."

"You fit in with the surroundings."

"Like your place back home?"

"No, more like Savannah. What's going on?"

"The French police are all over The Hotel De Paris. I think they are going to shut the office down soon. You made his lieutenants as mad as hell today, what did you do?"

"Took a tour bus, then hit about six more of his haunts; the magic screen, I was left somewhat of a gift this morning on my laptop. Think they dropped *speed* in one of my brews today... Really that crazy?"

"I have never seen them this upset before Hardy. I scrambled to get out of there. *Speed*, well that explains your disposition. Sit, relax, we will stay up all night and make love. Make love Hardy, not fuck, I'm being nice. Relax, come-on..."

"Speed, the bus, I may as well been at the game."

"You never did like baseball."

"No, but when I bump an enemy agent they know it. Full body cheque; ice hockey in New York, right-tackle on the football team. Baseball does not drive my soul, knocking the enemy into the next county does. In Europe, the next country. Though *speeding* really play's havoc with your soul when you come home to find old lovers naked in your bed. So you just stopped by to tell me you will be out of work, the enemy is mad as hell, and to torture my soul with your naked flesh?"

"I brought you something Hardy," and Monique sat up in to bed, though modest, the sheets covering her breasts and handed Hardy the file containing the papers. "Atlanta. I owed you one Hardy. You want me, you can have me too."

"I'm in a nasty mood to be making love, the speed, maybe it was in the sugar? I don't know. I will be up past one tonight. The papers, can you get more?"

"The office is chaos, like a monster without a head since Carlos was tossed out. They are druggies Hardy, not spies. They double with a wink and a nod from Moscow. They do not know what is important. I can get more before the Paris police move in with pad locks and shredders. We will have to move fast. Chaos Hardy. Stress, that' s why I am here naked under your covers. Stress, I had to get away."

"A vacation?"

"An afternoon vacation. OK?"

"OK? But you can't stay."

"You're speeding Hardy, strip, climb under the covers. No sex, we'll just lay naked. Stress Hardy you need it."

"I can't."

"Then what."

"Hot bath, relieve the stress. Plan my next move."

"Candles, if you're going to take a hot bath, you need candles. Like back in Atlanta," and Monique looked up and smiled. "I brought some. So what is your next move?"

"I have to leave Paris. The French are doing their part, I'm doing mine. Stay longer I will be shot to death. I have a whole other list of his sore spots to hit. Time to move. The documents are going change everything; more complex. Torn between priorities. A lot on my mind."

"Strip Hardy, slide under the covers, we'll talk. You need it. Group hug minus the second dancer," and Monique looked up to see Hardy smile. "Hardy I am damned to be your reoccurring mistress throughout your life whether I like it or not. One law-enforcement group or another, one band of runaway spies or another, someone out there will always be throwing us together or ripping us apart. Pam must know that...?"

"There comes a time in a gentleman's life, Monique, when a man responds to the flesh he should not and goes limp of the flesh of intense love. The complex feelings us men always run from. The complex feelings I have had to endure, face, come to grips of and consume when whiskey should have been more appropriate and damning. I cannot perform anymore. With Pam, sure. Vera, yeah..."

"But not with me...?

"I don't know..."

"You're speeding, the shaking will stop when you are in my arms. Come on in," Monique said, as she moved the bedding to reveal a perfect body that had driven some overly sane gentlemen crazy in the past. "Let me soothe your flesh."

"I can't.."

"We'll just lay naked Hardy...."

"Robert, welcome to Bonn. Bill Kennedy, I'm the chief of station for Germany. How was the flight? Good. Oh, the limo is right over here."

"The flight was not bad but this is my first time in Germany. I majored in South American affairs. I was stationed in Panama and Ecuador for awhile."

"Most of my file is back at the office Robert, here is short brief for you to look over. Quite a game brewing. The intelligence gathered from the NSA seem to suggest The Gremlin is pulling in terrorists to upset the whole applecart. You said your man may have documents?"

"Yes, we believe so. Ariadne/Americain, a couple of American lawmakers, a handful of French Governmental officials. Technology transfers. Primakov wants them bad, we believe our man may have them."

"How bad?"

"Ricin dart bad. Eastern Europe is swinging back left, the Soviet old guard wants to take control of what they lost. Uprising?"

"Tell me about it. Russia sure is not making it easy to be friends. Your man?"

"If he has the papers he has to drop them somewhere. I want to meet with the top brass of the likeliest bases. Hardy will most likely make his self known, then drop the papers. Most likely will need to meet with an officer before he does. Point the way, show him the drop point. Or maybe even a face to face exchange. I do not know. I am here to make sure Hardy does not get away, or his papers before we send Mr. Harding on his way. Terrorists?"

"It looks like Moscow would like to have these people blow something up and blame your man for it. Here is the report, your man is stepping all over their people. It really is their jugular. Desperate."

"I knew about North Africa, this is something knew."

"Everyone is hot Robert. Moscow feels if they win this one they can make us be more reasonable in the Balkans. Bad blood since the face-off at the Pristina Airport. The West flexing our muscles. Turkey, Greece, the Balkans all secure. The strait ours. Though Turkey. Moscow bogging down or about to in the Caucasus. The Russians are upset, and they have us breathing down their necks. Can't really blame them."

"The Russians have a terrorist problem. The Russians are playing it fast and loose with their over abundance of nukes. The Russians get what they deserve."

"I agree. But all is not mellow after the Cold War. Blackmail it is. Damn blackmail!. Give us money or we give tribesmen in Uzbekistan atomic bombs to play with and send them to somebody else's backyard."

"Eastern Europe?"

"The political swing is not too bad, a Trojan Horse of sorts. A little to the left, a little to the right. It is just the people they have been placing in office are all controlled by the old guard KGB. A real nightmare for us. The spy game plays on. Oh...Here is another file for you, we will talk more when we get back to the embassy. Oh, by the way, Havel's been compromised."

"That is too bad."

It was by the small brook, us Americans would refer to as a creek. Zaporah would set up on a park bench every Thursday at about eleven to feed the ducks and wait for Yossi Cohen to happen by in the small park just outside Bonn, simply called Zeckendorf Gardens. The park was peaceful, slightly wooded and semi-private. The kind of setting one could find two lovers making love under the veil of pleasant seclusion of a sleepy small town German hideaway nestled in Bavarian enchantment.

"Good morning Zaporah. Such a peaceful place, not all in Germany is bad."

"What is new Yossi?"

"Your Mr. Harding is in France; women problems."

"He does not know what women problems are yet."

"The rematch is yours Zaporah. He is a big trophy to the Iranians. John Custer Harding is pulling everyone in. If the Russians cannot set him up, then they would like to have him for a weekend or two, suck every ounce of intelligence they could from him. The KGB had gotten burnt bad in Atlanta."

"You want me in France?"

"No, you would have competition; old flame. I don't want that. Not this role for you. He has documents, he has to drop them. If he goes to Brussels, he sets up NATO, no one in the West can afford that. He has to come to Germany."

"Where? Munich?"

"No, you stay put in Bonn for awhile, we have problems in Munich. The Russians have arranged for it to be easy for Hezbollah to have their surrogates in North Africa move to Munich. Jerusalem, tacit ambiguity. The Trojan Horse, the Russians are holding back. Russian Jews. Most likely more Russian than Jew. I do not know if we want them. Jerusalem said we do. So we play the game and fuck them in the end. Moscow quietly pointed out these clerics of North Africa are not hunting Jews. A terrorist is a terrorist, but for now we play the game."

"Iran?"

"Iran is going to fuck us," though Yossi profanity was quiet and respectful and Zaporah was understanding, having had used much worst wording in the past to describe the enemy she hated. "Moscow is playing a game with Tehran, we play a game with Tehran. Hezbollah still murders our people in Southern Lebanon. Regardless of Iraq, Iran will do what Iran wants."

"Nukes?"

"We believe Tehran has them. If not warheads, the little ones that can hurt. If there is such a thing as a little nuke?"

"So what's game?"

"Moscow most likely will want Hardy near by when a bomb goes off to suggest a subtle blackmail over Washington of the problem they have with their people working with terrorist. Foreign policy will be forced to change, Mr. Harding would be eliminated. If the game is still played fair. A-bomb...? I doubt nukes."

"Moscow?"

"Moscow still supports Syria. The Gremlin is still sore over the way we stuck it up their ass with the technology Pollard grabbed from the Americans. The Bible Code, you want the other half Yevgeny? read the holy scriptures. God were they hot; Russian Jews first," and Yossi looked over to see Zaporah laugh in quiet amusement.

"So for now?"

"Stay put. You like Zeckendorf Gardens, your lover comes soon."

"Oh... Is he going to burn in his desire..."

"You like babies Zaporah..?...You are thirty-five now..."

❖   ❖   ❖   ❖   ❖

The bit stream picked off by the NSA, decoded and sent over to Langley, The Pentagon and the NSC at The White House was brief but to the point: Czechoff's trade mission to Tehran had been a complete success. The text of his communiqué to Yevgeny Primakov was approximately two and a half pages. Encrypted in the text was the nefarious in chilling details, yet well disguised and of no value in world courts or the give and take of head of state exchanges. A smoking gun, or one that was about to be loaded without the outward appearance or fingerprint of a gun. Tehran liked the idea Primakov had sent by way of Czechoff. It was also reported in the narrative compiled of the full analysis sent over by Langley that afternoon to the NSC, Tehran apparently had a few ideas of their own. The terrorist falling under the KGB sphere of influence, though Tehran had hands-on control of their Party Of God freedom fighters. The signs were ominous. The Russians had been quite unaware their communiqué had been picked off, or that a more nefarious motive and mission may be afoot by those they thought they could trust in Tehran.

Back in Moscow Yevgeny Primakov brooded over the choice of locations for his deception and stumbling block for the West to negotiate around. What city? what site? what location? and how do we arrange to have Mr. Harding present?

"Robert Torres? Grace, I'm the staff secretary. My cover, I am second in command in charge of the station. Bill Kennedy wanted you to see these files. You are familiar with how to use our computer system? Good. We keep a lot on paper Robert. Lose a disk, you lose everything. Lose a couple of sheets of paper, sometimes the KGB mail them back to us. There is something to be said about doing things the old fashion way at times."

"Bill mentioned shifts in European politics?"

"A little to the left, a little to the right with the exception of Austria. The big problem is Moscow has been quietly moving their own people into power since the Wall came down."

"Nazis?"

"A little bit. Moscow sticking up our backsides. The Gremlin still supporting the extremes. Nationalism if not ideology. We may have won, the game plays on. Intense here in Germany at times. Havel's been compromised."

"Bill mentioned that."

"Oh, before I forget, this is the report from Col. Clay at Caliber, you may want to take a peek at it? Just be careful with the data bases, unlike Washington, we really have to worry here in Bonn. It is that intense."

"And the systems? Any problem with me roaming around?"

"No, but I would recommend any secure communications you wish to have with Washington, it would be best, or to go into Clementine. We believe the Russians and for that matter the Chinese, are locked out of Clementine. Clementine II, is DOD. Good luck Robert, I'll be back in an hour. Thanks."

It was shortly after midday prayers and just after his talks with close advisers, most of whom were all of a high religious order, the report from Razi was third in line that afternoon. The number one point of business and of interest was the thrusting pain of an Iranian journalist, who did not wish to conform, or in poor judgment upon the teachings of an Iranian God bestowed on mortal men, questioned the wisdom of the current Iranian administration. In effect, questioning The President Of Iran, which of course is like questioning God, Allah himself. The journalist would be dealt with.

Next on his pallet was the fate of one hundred or so Iranian Jews suspected of spying. Further suspected in the supporting of freedom of written expression for one wayward Iranian journalist, who like they use to say in the former Soviet Union needed to be reeducated. Spies or not, they were Jews and Iran could expect a good payout from Jerusalem in either case. Though war seemed unlikely; Iran still being the main counterbalance to Iraq.

Last was the Razi report; His High Holiness President Mohammad Khatami just smile and nodded his head. What better way to play the two great devils against each other, then have an atomic bomb go off on Russian soil with an American agent to blame. The plan was quietly, silently and tacitly approved without anyone saying a word, though much of the details were jotted down in freehand Arabic.

Unbeknown to the Iranians, they really did have an Israeli spy problem. A tiny video cam above the conference table recorded every word scripted and was immediately sent back to Aman headquarters, where it was sent up the chain of command to the head of The Israeli Mossad, who happened to be Ariel Sharon. Gen. Sharon by luck or good fate just happened to be in the leadership at the time; the shared rotating leadership of the intelligence community of a small state being one of the stumbling blocks of Israeli spying.

Being severely bitten in Lebanon years ago, Gen. Sharon had the data analyzed and shared with his counterparts in Washington. Who later that evening would call and invite all to share in a video conference by way of secure fiber between Washington and Jerusalem to decide what to do next.

From the bed Monique could hear the running water of the bath. Hardy, and the stress of the day pouring forth from both the faucet and his soul. The hotel was more like an Inn, Hardy having good taste in lodging. A gift of a good childhood, a loving family and a desire to find a warm soft place to cuddle, if only with himself. For he had endured much abuse in the past. The room was a mix of aged French off-white lace and antiques. In front of the bay window draped by Victorian curtain coverings of transparent veils overlooking a garden sat a café table in case the special couple, the guests of this Inn wanted to dine in naked. Clothing in love being optional. It was very romantic and soft. Upon the café table atop a white lace tablecloth sat a clear pitcher for water or fresh cut flowers. It's clear handle hung down like to pride of a naked man; oversized, and somewhat out of proportion. It reminded Monique of Hardy. He was always too well hung, and even when he tried not to be he still looked out of proportion. God having blessed Hardy with about three inches more then what man needs in this life. At least the illusion, though at times of love making it had felt like more than six.

It was time, the speed had run it's course through Hardy's body. From the bed Monique could see both the flickering of candle light and steam rising from the bath. She moved the bed coverings to one side allowing her naked mocha colored flesh to escape while she floated across the room to the ice bucket and open bottle of apricot brandy, swinging by the café table on her way. Monique filled the pitcher with ice water and turned to go into the bath with a refill of brandy and a backup of ice water. Hardy just looked up to watch the steam and candle light dance over her naked mocha flesh, as she sat the ice water and brandy down, kissed him and gently lowered her flesh on his amiss the splashing, rising of steam and candle light of her spy's therapy.

The snifter too full; the mix of ice, ice water and steam adding to their eroticism while they played about the steam and candle light. The ripples of the water casting erotic shadows about her flesh. Monique knew all the right spots to run the ice cubes along his flesh while they gently splashed about in the hot water somewhere between making love and playful sex. Hardy arching his back with his muscles tense every time Monique brought him to the edge of no return. Only to stop him and tease him more until he pleaded for the sweet consumption of her body. Till he pleaded that his cock be allowed to find its way; his way.

To the edge, until he pleaded to have her soul. Hardy's huge namesake left erect and pulsating, begging for *merci*. As Hardy himself was. With a lady who was both damning his soul and saving him to be damned again in her arms. Monique would play Hardy's reoccurring lover if she did not kill him in the bath.

...But first the plea, then came the consumption of flesh that sent poor Hardy over the edge and further damned in romantic eternity. Monique had reentered Hardy's life, Hardy had entered Monique.

Only two glasses sat besides the antique pedestal bath tub with sterling and gold leaf fixtures; one over filled with brandy, the other ice and water. They would share. Monique, the gifts of her flesh; Hardy his cock. A shared erotic afternoon of two years in the making. Flesh always taste so sweet when the kisses and love bites taste of fine French cognac or brandy.

For French law-enforcement it was difficult to know which one of the two lovers had the more intense climax. In the bath the flesh of two naked lovers melted together playing in the hot water, candlelight and steam. Even the large puddle of water upon the floor was out of reach of their surveillance. Though their love making had been loud. Well...The French, the French know of such afternoon delights. The two police officers just smiled and thought of their wives.

CHAPTER 16

The smell of death was more pleasant that morning, Bonnie having placed a fresh bouquet of flowers on the table by the window sill of thin beige curtains, which over looked the yard where his grandchildren played. The scent of mixed cut flowers with mums and roses played the room cheerful for Col. Harding's daily interrogation by his sweet soft spoken sympathetic torturer with sugar coated shit breath for their friendly and deadly daily exchange.

"Oh...Col. Harding...I like you, you are so cute," Gladas forgetting Col. Harding was sixty-seven and not four or five before she continued. "Tell me about Tet, you were decorated? Bronze Star? Wow, must of been some memory? That was sixty-eight? Cold War and Vietnam War, must have some memories...?"

Col. Harding's breathing that morning had been somewhat better, allowing him to turn and confront his torturer with old conjure praise and deception; his smile gave it all away, Gladas thought quietly to herself. "Oh, Tet, it was really very little, just a collection, an accumulation of the war. Gave the medal to the kids to play with. It was nothing really."

"So modest Col. Harding, come on, tell me?"

"It was Georgie Niles. Died, Georgie should have been the one to have received the medal. Second in command. Nice kid."

"Oh, that is so sweet. Do you keep in touch with his family?"

"No...But his wife was not as pretty as you."

"Oh...What a sweety. Sixty-eight.? Tet but trouble in Europe as well. Do you recall anything about a World War Two Class submarine the Israelis bought from the British? You know, Cold War, Europe, Middle East. This sort of stuff just festinates me. It started with a *D, Duck* something. Or *Ducker*...? Sailed from England, went down on its way to its new home...?"

"No...I...I was stationed in Nam, all over the South China Sea. Are you sure you did not get confuse with The Pablo incident?"

"No...This was a submarine Col. Harding, oh, you are such a dear. I can see you are starting to tire," though her expression was *I want to kill you, you old creep.* Dear Gladas had two twin brothers who moved to Canada in sixty-eight to avoid the draft. A third, the star of the family lost over Hanoi two years before. Col. Harding did not know but he knew her. Her personality type to a military man like himself was as abrasive as sandpaper—extra course. But the conjurian was sweet all the same in his response of *make love to an old man like me, experience, I think you are sooo cute and I am not dead yet.*

"No... I did not get to Germany until the war was just about over. Seventy-three? Seventy-three I think? ...Oh... I'm sorry. I get so tired so quickly" And Col. Harding turned a bit to one side and closed his eyes briefly.

"Oh, you poor dear. I will let you rest. Are you in pain?" But Col. Harding just gave out an old conjurian moan, which past the deception. "Oh, good;" knowing he was but accepting *No* as the answer. "Well, well, maybe I have too much of a drip, let me adjust it a bit so you can be more awake. So you can enjoy what is going on with your loved ones. OK? You can handle the pain? Good. But for now I will let you rest. You take a wee nap, I will be back in an hour. OK?"

"Bye, bye sweetheart," and Col. Harding just rolled his eyes closed to take a pretend nap and prepare himself to endure the pain. Unfortunately, Gladas was of the lower cast of spies who pretend they are not when they know they are. Being low on the food chain comes ignorance and naiveté of what can happen when one mixes it up with an agent of Col. Harding's class.

Col. Harding really was saying good-bye to Gladas. Though it did escape Hardy's dad which of the two would polish St. Peter's Gate first. Col. Harding was well aware of his sins during the war and suspected he would only receive the assignment to polish such Godly enjoyments. A kind of heavenly KP. Though he did secretly hope Gladas entered into the arms of Our Lord, the thought of spending each others company together in eternal hell was excruciating, about as painful as his cancer. Though being a good Catholic, he knew better. *Hell should be fun, hope they keep the liquor cabinet stocked.*

Monique like most women who want the affections of a man does not play fair. So it was not so unreasonable or out of character for Monique to be wearing only stiletto heels and a G-string in front of the mirror, playing to the the rising of the steam from the shower when the phone went off next to Hardy while he was just waking up from an evening of love making with an old flame he shouldn't have.

"Hi...How's the baby?"

"I'm due in about two weeks."

"I love you" and Hardy looked to the bath to waive Monique off of the importance of the call to her understanding annoyance and anger. "One or two babies?"

"One Hardy, my doctor was playing games....I need you."

"I wish I could be there," and Hardy looked to the shower to view Monique in the understanding of the fragile ground of being the other woman she was treading on; though quiet and respectful. I am not alone Pam... I'm sorry. She is meaningless."

"I knew this, what we would have Hardy, at the Dam that afternoon. I wanted you, I wanted your baby. I have your baby—just like you, attitude, he has been kicking a lot. He'll be just like you."

"He?"

"My doctor said it should to a boy. Gave some nonsense of showing up too big on the screen. A boy Hardy."

"God." And Pam could hear on the other end the last line she spoke had ripped Hardy's heart out before she cut him short and saved him from his tears. Spies are not suppose to cry she thought to herself, and whoever she was, she was no match in Hardy's heart or affections for Pam Wellington.

"Unconventional Hardy. It was what I knew when I conceived. You don't shoot blanks, I had you by the.... and the timing for my needs was perfect. Unconventional Hardy; it is what I knew in my heart from the beginning. It is my lifestyle; TV, and moving around. It is what I want, but I want you too."

"Look.. I feel terrible."

"I can hear you Hardy, it's why I cut you off. Don't speak what we cannot say. For us to be together you would not be able to do your job. You would be killed, or I would be killed. But we can be reoccurring lovers. Lovers, we'll have a life together. Lovers, we'll count the days till we can be together again each time we separate. OK, unconventional and lovers...?"

"I love you Pam."

"I have my spies too, how was the Israeli girl?"

"Oh God, you know."

"Harold in Jerusalem."

"She was fun but she is not carrying my baby. I love you Kiddo."

"Hardy, I was raised in The Bible Belt, but Dad is Jewish. I may go with him to the MidEast."

"Israel, it is a good idea Pam. I'd like to see you, I don't know if I can work it out. And I have a terrorist problem. It would be safer for you and the baby not to see me—But God," and Pam could hear Hardy's voice crack with emotion on the distant French phone connection, "I need to see you. I need to hold the baby in my arms."

"Don't Hardy, we are both crying. It's hard for me. Benefits, money. I can, unlike most single moms, handle it on my own."

"I take fatherhood seriously Pam. Regardless of what I must do, or the life I lead. It is not how I was raised. All I wanted was a stable life and 2.5 kids with a two car garage," and Hardy's last discourse went through Pam like the shooting of a man fifty-one times to keep a lid on a scandal. On the other end Hardy could hear Pam start to breakdown. Though his soft spoken words did succeed in keeping a lid on a sweet warm illicit romance. He could hear Pam start to gently cry a bit. "How is Ted? And you have to be strong sweetheart."

"Mr. Tomilyn sends his best. Said he wants your help with the U.N. should you and him ever find yourselves in New York at the same time.... Hardy, I have to go. Painful affections, the baby is starting to kick, and I miss you so. I don't want to cry.."

"I love you..." Though the last words spoken were not suppose to be a mutual disconnect but they were. Or perhaps the central offices and tandem telephone switching stations in both Atlanta and Paris could not handle the overload of heated passionate international romance. Monique was for the most part, except for a string of sorts and some high heels, naked in the next room over in front of the mirror pretty much in full view of Hardy. Though she may as well of been in another European country, or adorned the three hundred and thirty pound frame of a washed up madam. To Hardy as he put down the phone and placed the handset back in the cradle, Monique wasn't even there.

"Do you want to talk..? The phone Hardy, I am standing here naked in front of you and it is as if I am not even here."

"She is all I ever wanted. It was a good love. You and I Monique, we only destroy each other..."

The rage on Monique's face was more then evident, as she slipped her best Paris fashion dress over her head and marched out the door. Leaving Hardy to ponder his everlasting love/hate relationship with a woman who keeps coming back in his life to kill the one she truly loves. Monique could be the worst type of woman at times, and was, when she slammed the door behind her leaving Hardy alone to be at peace for the moment.

There were three sides to Monique, Hardy had been in love and in hate with in the past. The erotic dancer and sometimes fashion model he lusted for. The understanding lover and playful childhood erotic playmate he deeply loved; it had been a combination of the two who seduced him with her mocha flesh in the bath the night before. A body to die for, a playmate and lover to give your life for, and surely Hardy would if he had not known Monique's other side and had he not been in love with a lady from Atlanta who now had Hardy's offspring, or was about to. God, he thought to himself, there was no lady more beautiful in sex, love or heart and soul, then when Monique slipped naked into the bath with a refill of brandy and ice water to take him over his erotic top. There was no woman he despised more then the destructive mistress who used the tragedies of her life to destroy the enemy she was sleeping with, then when she slammed the door behind her. Hardy was not the enemy, Hardy did not know if Monique in her troubled twisted life knew the difference anymore. He just sat, lost in his thoughts for a few minutes and picked up the phone to dial Atlanta, finding out from her voice mail the woman he loved had just left.

"Hi, (Hardy's voice cracking with emotion to the ears of French eavesdropping equipment) I just wanted to call you back... I love you... ...Look, I have a terrorists problem, it is extremely dangerous sweetheart. If I don't make it, you let the baby boy know he was made in love—Not love child—made from love. Regardless if whether I make it or not, or if I can be a father to him. You let him know his daddy loves him....OK? ...I gott'a go, I'll call you tomorrow. Bye."

When Hardy hung up the phone he had no way to know the baby could not wait the full nine months, or that Pam was already on her way to the hospital. His only thoughts were of babies and of twisted sexuality of old lovers he needed but not sexually, though she damn near drowned him in the bath.

Colors of the rainbow, a droplet of water, fiber optics and light reflected through romance, one healthy, one destructive. Hardy just turned over and went back to sleep for an hour to relieve the many emotional pains which were tormenting him.

The knock on the door had awaken Hardy about forty-five minutes into his post wake up nap. Angry, though not sure, he wrapped a towel around him with thoughts of what does this...Though his obscenity was cut short by the second round of masculine knocks.

"Capt. Credo..." and Hardy immediately noticed the intense importance of his arrival. Capt. Credo simply placed two fingers on his lips and motioned for Hardy to be silent. "Would you like to come in?" Hardy said, as common greetings were appropriate and Capt. Credo just smiled, the warm glow even highlighting his bald head in warm friendship.

"You know why I am here? My friend back in Brussels wanted me to stop in and check up on you. How is your brother Dave?" Though Hardy knew the real reason why he was here was for the documents, having silently nodded his head at the first part of Capt. Credo's opening remarks. Knowing his friend back in Brussels was Gen. Clark and, even though the general liked Hardy, it was no concern of his if Hardy got shot, though he just assume keep his younger spy alive. Hardy was well aware Capt. Credo did not know his brother Dave. "Look here Dave, I mean Hardy," and Hardy knew he was playing a game while Capt. Credo's two fingers pointed to the text of a letter of some frivolous value, who's text had encrypted in it the understood written instructions of what Hardy needed to know. Hardy had seen it many times before in the mannerism of a senior in the game of wisdom when they wished to get across their point in brief direct elegance. Hardy immediately and instinctively focused his attention.

In the text it was clear they were being watched by more then just the French version of the FBI. Carlos, the KGB and a few others were keeping track of the movements and love affairs of John Custer Harding. It would of course be impossible to unload the documents directly to Capt. Credo; it was summer, he was lightly dressed with no bag or brief case. Fred Credo would certainly take a bullet as soon as he walked out the door. In the text was encoded a town in Germany, which was the small home of an American base. It was the obvious the drop point of choice should Hardy be able to arrange his whereabouts and at the same time keep himself alive. Though with his friendly fingers on the text just before the word document, Capt. Credo interrupted Hardy's train of thought. "Please call me Fred, Hardy. My friends call me Freddie, I prefer Fred," though in his lighthearted soft spoken manner, Hardy understood it made no difference to Capt. Credo, and wondered why at his age he was only a captain? But his fingers gave away what Fred Credo had on his mind; the words *documents* and *more* stood out from his subtle body language begging for Hardy's response.

"I think we can work it out. I'll have room service send us up a fresh pot. We can sit and chat a while, God, it is great to have one of Dad's old friends stop by. Dad is ill by the way. Oh, I have one problem, my recent lover is extremely mad at me...Just in case she returns," and Hardy smiled warmly.

We can retrieve more documents, and Monique wants to kill me, complicating the document situation, was the message received by Fred Credo before he continued, knowing the rest of Hardy's disposition of the English language was pure hyperbole and BS. "One lady ready to snip a few inches off Dave, I mean Hardy...The other having your baby in Atlanta. Be careful Hardy. Oh, my friend back in Brussels mentioned he had looked up your records, went through a chubby stage as a kid..? He said your dad did a good job," and Fred just smiled.

Hardy knew instinctively why Pam did not answer her phone when he called her back, Fred Credo having tipped him off in his verse spoken in code, and he thought to himself just as the coffee arrived, perhaps he should have had the front desk send up a bottle of whiskey instead. "Look, they sent up bagels, croissants and rolls too, let's eat. Dad taught me right Fred; Coffee first. It will go on my room."

"By the way Hardy, my friend back in Brussels wants you to know Atlanta and the big orange *T* is why you are now a writer."

"It's been a long time Fred, let's eat," both knowing five months in a spy game is a lifetime. Both knowing many good new friends in such affairs of intrigue only make it a short distance before a ricin dart or 9mm sends them on to the land of Purple Hearts or into the arms of Our Lord.

"The general likes the idea of the thong Hardy, he may issue them for all his men. Everyone can kiss our ass..." though the tones were spoken quietly, both men were well aware they were being watched.

Brunch had been pleasant and warm, Hardy assuring Fred Credo his baby would be all right, the spy affair had become known in the give and take of their conversation of phrases whispered in code, as their baby, or the baby. Fred in his own intelligence gifted way, assured Hardy that his baby was in good hands but it was the importance, even the urgent, picked up by his cadence of Fred's vocabulary that Hardy realized he should really not waste any time in the calling of friends in Atlanta. It was clear, the baby was about to be or was all ready in this world.

Hardy alone in his thoughts just wondered to himself and planned out of what he should do next. Spies tend to be calm in times of the emotionally intense. He still had Monique to deal with and a need to procure documents. Monique would not be in the best of cooperating moods should the timing of Hardy's good personal news over ride her personal objective of building a life with him.

Documents first, were his thoughts as he thumbed his way through his wallet in search of Dana DiMaggio's phone number.

Dana DiMaggio had not been home, Hardy returned to his wallet rolodex to leave word with production at DNN. On the other end it was clear the colleague of Pam could hear Hardy's voice crack with emotion, and subtle insurances were given that his heart would be past on to Pam, though which hospital he did not know but not to worry Mr. Harding, in any case, the Baby and Pam would be in the loving arms of friends and family.

Hardy hung up with the Jewish saint on the other end to retreat from Atlanta and invade his laptop for the latest gossip, finding out Carlos was in Bonn brooding and nasty while his men were all over France buzzing around as mad as hornets like a beehive, which had just been speared by a couple of rocks and a 2X4 from a band of less then brilliant twelve year olds. Word had gotten back to both London and Washington from Paris, French law-enforcement had never seen these people so upset, and Paris wasn't at all amused. Something to do with Trevor Downing having men in on the ground in both Bordeaux and Lyons doing just about the same as Hardy had been doing in Paris. Usually only about a few minutes before French law-enforcement came through the door to turn the café/drug den/spy technology transfer point upside down and costing everyone dearly as they did. Trouble Makers! The Americans and British make the best trouble makers! The French were upset and documents to boot!

But what was clear was that Trevor Downing had his men in on the ground, there would now be no need for Hardy to do Bordeaux. Documents were the game. Hardy had them and could procure more. Monique was the game they all played. She was not suppose to be there but she was and Hardy could handle the rematch if need be.

There had been more of a game with Monique from the very beginning, regardless of the sins of undercover cops or the placement of Monique by the manipulation of American cops who were double agents by the enemy or by the making of her lover more of a beast then he tended to usually be. For Covic had changed for the better as soon as Monique was out of his life. The KGB, and the making of an undercover DEA agent a monster to force his lover to Paris, Caliber countered with John Custer Harding.

In any case, documents were the game. Old flames needed to be bed and the travel brochures of Germany were calling out to Hardy. He would have to move, they would have to move fast. For all of France was about to explode! And Hardy silently wondered to himself of his next move; both, calculated and sexual. From the meaningless text of a meaningful covert commuiqué came knowledge of the whereabouts of an Israeli lady of their special forces, as well as some sightings of a hybrid Jennifer Lopez with fangs in Berlin. Vera would make a better liaison with NATO. Vera had also been quite a lady in bed. Hardy had hit it off pretty good with Vera Lopez once they the gotten past the stage of trying to kill each other. The game, they all knew it but an important game with a new soft spot about to be born in Hardy's heart that morning at St. Vincent's in Atlanta. Hardy closed the magic screen and put the laptop away.

❖ ❖ ❖ ❖ ❖

"Hi, you're back early?"

"The Paris Police closed the office down. They will let me back in tomorrow for some personal belongings and...Well, they seem to be playing a game Hardy, took a few more of his men away."

"Dana called just a little while ago, I'm a daddy Monique, natural, eight pounds six ounces. She did good; Robert E Harding, the baby will take my name. I'm glad it was natural, my covert son I believe was a c-section. I have to call her in a little while Monique."

"Robert E., it's racist."

"It is Southern Pride, it is West Point pride. Pam's daddy is a Jew, the Good Old Boys will cut her some slack, me too. Pam is paying me back."

"'You have one hell of a nerve! Telling your black lover your half Jewish princess had a baby with a Confederate name for diplomatic purposes to please you and a band of Southern bigots! God damn you Hardy!" though Hardy could see Monique was also filled of amusement with her anger.

"I'm a bastard Monique not a racist, I don't discriminate. A man has a right to love, a man has a right to hate. But you know me, I am not an extremist. If I kill, I kill as a soldier, most times I do it like a spy. Chess board. Monique, I like the name, it is why my middle name is Custer.

"Do you love me Hardy? I...I'm happy for you but..." and Hardy could see Monique's position in his life had been threatened. Knowing since his lost trip to Martinique and the homeless shelter, there would be no real placement in his life for her, only a steamy bath or some French silk sheets on occasion.

"I don't know...? I'm tired of almost being killed by you. Dad was given a case of cancer because I would not at the KGB's request die in your arms, and because I am too good at what I do," and Hardy looking over could see one very much in love and sorry lover for what she had put him through in his life. *One deception leads to another and another, soon we destroy the ones we love for the lies we need to keep to save ourselves.* And Hardy wondered to himself why electro shock therapy was not as common as the common cold.

"God, I am so sorry Hardy.." and Hardy handed Monique a tissue, her eyes moist and about to spill over.

"Eighty-four, after we finished playing like little kids on my visit to Highland Falls, I knew something was on your mind. Why did you run away from that diner we stopped to eat at and then lock yourself in your old baby blue Volkswagen Bug? It stressed me out, I did not understand it at the time. Even back then you were deadly with your emotions. I would rather face a 9mm than one of your panic attacks Monique."

"God, I am so sorry Hardy..."

"Me too."

"We are lovers?"

"I don't know? Heart seems to count in these affairs of passion."

"I play Hardy with my emotions and panicked stress, you play with love, what's the difference?"

"I'm a daddy, and I am not playing games anymore. I have killed too many people in the service of my country to really care anymore. I simply send a situation into motion. I met an old spook the other day, he scared me. I saw my face in thirty years. He no longer does documents, he likes silencers."

"She deserved it."

"All human life is sacred. I guess some of us have to give up life in the next world so humanity can survive?"

"So what will we have? You and me?"

"All I ever wanted was 2.5 kids, a ranch and a two car garage; life is messy. You and I can have what I offered my other lovers, and the mothers of my children. I suspect I know who the mother of my covert son is. We can have an unconventional relationship built on complex feelings minus the deep love I feel for Pam. We like each other, we're good in bed. Love..? I don't know. I have had my insides kicked out where you're concerned. A lot of pain Monique," and Hardy looked over to see Monique in about the same state he was in.

"The bath, you were not making love to me..?"

"No...Another played on my mind when we were splashing around."

"I'm so sorry Hardy."

"I had room service send up some coffee and tea, sit and relax."

For the most part they sat quietly for about fifteen minutes, Monique understanding the complexity of the mornings emotions. Hardy transferring from melancholy to extreme happiness of fatherhood, at least of a son he truly knew of.

"Hardy, I take most of my work home at night, when Emily was shot I took what was important. I have the entire office on disk, all of Carlos's affairs," and Monique reached down and retrieved seven or eight formatted computer disks from her perse. "Here, they are yours."

"Thank you," and Hardy accepted the peace offering and continued, "Signed documents would be better. You know...Who created these? When you go back tomorrow, see what you can grab of importance which is signed."

"Do you want to cuddle?"

"I don't know if I can Monique, I would be making love to Pam."

"We'll try..?"

"OK, we'll try...Do you remember a girl I use to date by the name Joni?"

"Yes."

"Well, she was the girl on the inside at Longo's, Joe had the brother of Carlos killed. Him and the lady who took your place just disappeared. The Panamanians want him for questioning according to what is leaked to me from Interpol."

"Well...I guess Joe owed you one, owed us both one," and Monique gently pulled Hardy down to the bed for an afternoon of affectionate cuddling.

The cuddling had been less sexual, less combatant, more affectionate, just what Hardy needed that afternoon. Lasting till about three, just before The Paris Police called to let Monique know she could go back in the office and retrieve her things; letting Monique know by the lighthearted French voice the French were playing a game. And it was just as well Hardy thought, it was extremely hot outside and the *air* had been on the fritz. Affectionate friends or not, it was becoming a bit sticky. In any advent, Pam should now be awake and this daddy desperately wanted to call Atlanta to see how she was fairing. Not knowing the wording he should use, understanding the reality of the situation and fumbling through his lines as he listened to the familiar ring of an American phone system.

...Good, hot dog, hospital, got through "Maternity, room 404 please."

"Please wait, my screen,...Oh, Oh Miss Wellington has been moved to a private room, room 827, the extension is the same. I'll put you through."

Pam had been awake and waiting for his call. Pam too had been rehearsing her lines for when Hardy called, which she knew by motherly instinct that it was Hardy. "Hi."

"Hi Honey, how is the baby?" Hardy's voice filled with more than the cracking of emotion, he had been dealing with personal betrayal and the turmoil of Monique when Pam answered the line.

"He's beautiful...He looks just like you..." and Pam could hear a sniffle of emotion coming to Hardy's eyes before he responded.

"I love you...Pam. Half my life I don't recall, the other half is Classified. I guess our baby is Top Secret? Atlanta, the same with my work with the press in New York; off the record and extremely sensitive. We cannot talk about it, or the baby. You got me booted out of Caliber, Classified. Though the Army likes the idea of thong underwear now."

"I'm sorry Hardy...But he's beautiful...!"

"My benefits from the phone company are better then yours, put the baby under my medical. You should have the information from the fax I sent you awhile back. Did you receive the support?"

"I do? I think...? I'll look for it"

"Good."

"Hardy, Paris?"

Hardy could feel the threaten concern Pam was feeling on the other end. Knowing honesty is always the best policy, knowing some situations are not classified but sensitive just the same. Though the meadow, Lake Lanier and Longo's afterwards couple with the feed back of how upset the FBI were, it was best to fess up about his Paris affair of indifference. Knowing the indifference was explosive, knowing how Monique could push his hot buttons, but it was Pam on the other end of the line who sensed the change of directions and prepared herself for his confession.

"Monique, Pam. We both were setup. And long distant phone lines have ears, some all not friendly."

"You betrayed me Hardy," though Pam's statement was intense it fell short of exclamation.

"I did but I didn't. Our relationship is professional," and Pam knew instinctively Hardy meant both spy and whore. "She is a pro Pam," and French law-enforcement knew he meant both meanings as well. "She has something I need," and Pam knew Hardy meant documents; Daddy and the news business. But in the games of Western intelligence, Paris Police simply wrote down about John Custer Harding's huge over endowment and extremely intense sexual appetite.

"I can forgive an Israeli commando, or a competing journalist Hardy but..."

"I know.... I love you," and once again Hardy voice was filled with emotion, though Pam could discern the over riding guilt and his desire to beg for his forgiveness.

"Well, Catholic boys know what to do, I want to see blisters on your knees when you return," and Hardy could hear Pam laugh with amusement and the seriousness of the underlying anger. "Hardy, remember, possession is nine tenths of the law, I am the one who has your baby."

"OK, I will stick to women in uniform or journalists with fangs. I'll behave, life is messy; I love you."

"I love you too."

"Unconventional?"

"Unconventional."

"I love you, I will call you and the baby in about a week. Bye."

The knock on the door was intense, not sexually intense but intense. Hardy had been expecting Monique, and though it was a lady's knock, it was an intense knock. Not one of panic, nor one of pain, or one of anger, or one of life and death, it was a knock of urgency. Which was unbecoming of Monique, leaving Hardy in his brief walk to the door to wonder way?

"Hi, come on in. I ordered dinner for both of us."

"I'm scared Hardy, not for me, for you. The French police were playing games, here," and Monique paused to hand Hardy the papers. "They knew just what I needed, left them for me lying right on the desk."

"They also know just what their people do not want to surface."

"It's God damn spooky out! We're being watched! Aren't you scared?"

"No...I've been through it."

"You walk out this door tomorrow with these papers you are going to be shot! Hardy it's damn scary out! Why! God damn it! Why! Why are you like this! Doesn't anything bother you!"

"We are all cowards Monique. It is what my daddy taught me. In the beginning, when I saw my first combat twenty years ago, I was terrified. There is no such thing as a hero, only cowards. We all live in fear. I am terrified right now that I will not be able to make this drop. Men respond out of fear. It is fear that drives men to do what must be done in the heat of combat. It is out of fear of what will happen, which make sane men nuts to die in the arms of their country. What kind of world will we have for our children if we fail? It is fear which drives our soul. We are all cowards."

"Will you ever lose your nerve Hardy?"

"Fear. I hope not..." and Hardy paused for a bit more in quiet reflection and of thought of their current situation and entanglement before he continued. "It is best you leave tonight, I'll send for you..."

"If you make it...?"

"If I make it... I'm a daddy, if possible I would like to be around for my son..."

"And your covert baby...?"

"Yes, both kids, unless there is more...?"

"Fear."

"Fear...."

CHAPTER
17

Zeckendorf Gardens was quiet and still on that extremely warm late July morning building into an afternoon us Americans would refer to as a dog day. The water of the German creek was still, the last ripple fading away with her friends. Zaporah had just run out of bread when Yossi showed up.

"Good morning Zaporah, I brought you some more bread. Your friends, they swim away?"

"Yes but the swan was nice, ate most of my bread. They are very beautiful. Like me, you know the story?"

"I remember you before you were of age to enter the army."

"What have you brought for me today?"

"Family photos," and Yossi handed Zaporah the five or six stills of the problem children of Lebanon they would soon hunt. "Big problems sweetheart, Jerusalem won't say. People are very upset."

"This one, the second photo, far left, I have seen him before. Lebanon, Gaza, I'm not sure?"

"Northern Israel, he has made the crossing. The firefight," and Yossi could see Zaporah's eyes become extremely intense. "He is higher up on their food chain now. Do you like Germany?" and Zaporah nodded her head. "Well, maybe you and me we tour the sites? Munich."

"How?"

"Motorbike, I just purchased a new one," and Zaporah could see the second half of his line was spoken louder and more fun giving as cover for the ears of a pair of young Belgium lovers who just happened by. "This one uncle here in the second photo, he is a very, very smart and cleaver man," meaning this was the one and he was an extremely dangerous man.

"The classic?" and Yossi just nodded his head to the intense eyes of Zaporah who had lost a child of that raid many years before.

"You think you can handle a motorbike Zaporah?" knowing she damn well could.

"As long as you are driving Yossi."

"Whatever our friends from America are planning," and Zaporah knew he meant the CIA. "It would be better if he did not attend the party;" meaning dead. "He does not get along well with my side of the family," and Zaporah just smiled and paused before Yossi added, "You get a chance to save your fiancee before you marry him again;" meaning Hardy. Though the look in her eyes told Yossi, Zaporah did not know who she wanted to shoot more.

"I'll leave you here, I have to get back and see if Uncle Joe McDougal called from Jerusalem," meaning the Mossad was suppose to leave something on-line for him to Zaporah's burst of laughter.

"You have a Catholic in the family Yossi..?" and Zaporah could see Yossi starting to turn red of his own humor spoken in code.

"A convert from an American Black Irish clan," and Zaporah could see Yossi still quietly laughing over an Israeli agents poor choice of words in his attempt to communicate in code. Though it did workout, Northern Ireland is a mess and it reminded Zaporah SIS/MI6 were involved. Competition and Palestine 1947, though it all happened way before her time. Still a rival spy service is a rival spy service, and just like her long lost temporary husband knew, the British play to win: Your people were caught doing something very naughty and, no, I will not stop gossiping to your next door neighbors, and please go easy on the youngsters; meaning the stone throwing brats of The West Bank. All and all, when Zaporah did take a moment and finished laughing the choice of wording regarding an Irish Catholic uncle of an Israeli Jew with Spanish lineage, did seem to fit quite well in Yossi bumbled attempt to tell Zaporah he had to call the Mossad.

"Go home Yossi, put a call into Rome too," she quipped, seeing Yossi starting to turn red in the face again, seeing how he really wanted to get out of there.

"I'll see you later sweetheart."

"Not if you have an Irish Catholic uncle you won't."

"I have to get out here, bye." But the humor did not fade as Yossi did, Zaporah was still left with mild thoughts of amusement. Fortunately the Belgium couple had gone skinny dipping with the swans or making love in the bushes at the other side of the park leaving room for silly humor and bumbled lines to be mixed in with the deadly serious work.

Hardy had hung out for about two weeks since the birth of his son and his long lost lover Monique had left that hot Thursday evening. Most days were spent writing an article or two for Trevor, or ghosting for some fictious travel bureau back in the States. For the most part he kept busy writing, dining in and building his cover. Even calling out for an escort on a couple of hot afternoons to further build his legend; secretly hoping French law-enforcement would not try to blackmail him. Pam was understanding but Monique, and should he ever desire a normal life one day he had to keep himself from becoming too much of a whore. But it was the torrents of hot Paris rain coming down in buckets on the morning of the twenty-eighth, which spoke to him so clearly within the thoughts of his mind; I'm being watched, the down pour, good cover and it was time to move. Hardy had been pre-packed and simply went down to the desk to pay his bill.

The traffic was light on that Paris street that morn, Hardy waiting in a darken doorway during a French monsoon waiting for his taxi to come down a French version of an Upper Eastside avenue, maybe Madison or Park. Waiting while he watched a well dressed North African man in a rain coat watching him. Waiting, while he looked around to see two more agents close off another escape route of his entrapment. Waiting while he watched two more close in from the north end. Waiting while he thought to himself that the call to the taxi company only sent his ensnarement into motion. Waiting, while he watched his executioners lighten the noose around him. It would come from the agent directly across from him, were his thoughts. Though his frame of mind was so intense he over rode reason or his body's need to cry out in cold sweats or momentary panic attacks; it was in motion, kill or be killed. Hardy had been through it too many times before, only this time he was out numbered five to one. *9mms he thought, 9mms would be the weapon of choice. French law-enforcement obviously pulling back to let it go through and cast a wider net with a bigger catch. Take the hit on the documents and blackmail them on the State level for running a spy operation and gunning down American agents on French soil. That must be what they are going to do? at the expense of my life. God damn them.* Though Hardy's thoughts were running a mile a minute while he prepared to wake himself. There was just something missing. *God damn it, something is just not right,* as Hardy watched a taxi come driving slowly down the street. Looking over he saw his would be assassin stirring, startled, roused a bit, a heavy set bald European gent with an umbrella pleasantly forcing him to one side, sharing the warmth and comfort of the doorway from the safety of down pour.

The taxi was his and Hardy made a mad dash for it's safety hoping only the rain drops would pierce his flesh. Hoping at the very least he could toss the documents inside. Hoping and crying out inside his tormented head to God! as he suddenly watched the North African agent clutch his chest and fall to the ground as the burley but handsome

European made his way over to the cab with his umbrella to share the ride. Both getting in at the same time, the Englishman being extra careful with the tip of his umbrella.

"Edmund Chambers, Mr. Harding, hoping to catch you before you went to the airport." Though they were not going to the airport. "I work for *The Weekly Empire & World Report,* Trevor wanted me to review the rough notes of the research you were doing;" meaning he was sent to save his life. "Trevor did mention you were still to file your reports in the usual fashion, the text is to be forwarded the usual way;" meaning the drop was still on.

"Nice umbrella," and Hardy looked down in the cab to see it was also equipped with a small trigger and CO_2 cartridge for the ricin dart along with the sharpened needle pin tip.

"The poor bugger seemed to have had some kind of gas attack. Some Bromo he should be all right. Must of been something he ate the night before?"

But Hardy seemed to have noticed whatever his flesh consumed seemed to have occurred just as the taxi pulled up. "Are you sure he wasn't having a heart attack?" and Hardy just smirked at his new found friend.

"I don't know Mr. Harding, I'm an Englishman not a doctor. He seemed to have had a lot of friends on both ends of the block, I'm sure he'll be all right."

"Poor bastard," and they both mildly laughed.

The Hotline rang about ten in the evening Moscow time, to the explosive red face of a tough street fighting Russian president, Boris Yelsin: *Are your people working with terrorists? My people tend to think an atomic explosion on Russian soil would hurt your people more.* Humor aside, the wicked wild tempers of both presidents were legendary. It was but a few moments later when Primakov realized the betrayal of the Iranians, turned pale and lost his usual intelligencer composure. The President would like to have a chat with him. It was ten at night, and Boris had had his usual two Vodka nightcaps before talking with his friend and adversary in D.C., the fur was going to fly! Primakov was visibly shaken. If there were to be an American finger print left on the tragedy coupled with the desire for the Iranians to play dumb while they well insulated themselves with former Soviet Islamic radicals, then a nuclear exchange would be expected.

Washington, London, Paris and Moscow were all boiling. The Israelis sent a little subtle message to both Tehran and Baghdad; one of their American built F15E fighters with the new and improved software package violated the airspace of not only both countries but both cities.

Which was a feat in itself for Baghdad, given the on going American and British operation and air war. The entire world had it's heart in it's throat with the Israelis simply conveying to their neighbors, *if we go you go, and do you really want to flip this canoe we are all riding in?*

Primakov was well on his way to being fired that night. Working late, before he walked over to confront the Russian legend about his fuck-up while he was well on his way to the Russian version of an American woodshed, shithouse, or both, he pour himself a Vodka, and secretly hoped the days of Siberia were in the past. Atop of all the anger, confusion and chaos that evening, the American spy still had the documents Primakov so desperately needed.

"Good morning Zaporah, how are the ducks today?" Yossi's warm and friendly voice reassuring her everything was going well.

"So what do you have for me today and, please, Yossi do not make me laugh anymore about the dreaded Black Irish," and Zaporah showed her amusement had still not worn off over her good friend's poor choice of wording.

Yossi and Zaporah had a close friendship, had he not filled the void of a big brother lost in seventy-three, the two could have become lovers. Israel's existence had shaped Zaporah's tragic life.

"More family photos and gossip. Poor choice of wording but our friends in London will be calling," and Yossi said very quietly, "the British are in Zaporah. Northern Ireland is their internal problem, quite a few on both sides rocking the boat, trying to cause trouble between Washington and London. We stay out of it but the British are on board." Yossi paused, looked down and opened the manila envelope, handing the new photos to Zaporah. "Do you know her?"

"The face...Very vague. Maybe..? Who is the black man she is talking with? The background, looks like Berlin?"

"Her name is Vera Lopez, the black gentleman is her liaison from The Institute Of Electricity Of Culture & Foreign Affairs. It is a Washington thinktank."

"CIA?"

"We think so."

"An African American CIA agent..?"

"Good cover. Jerusalem believes Langley is recruiting heavily in the black community. You really cannot blame them. With The Cold War over, Africa and South America are up for grabs. It is only common sense that the CIA would go after educated people of color. The white community do not know or understand the politics of these two subcontinents," and Zaporah understood the misterm of Africa fit better. During the turmoil of The Cold War priorities had to be addressed first. Yossi knew this, and knew Zaporah was a gifted student of such world affairs. In the circles of which spies are run and bred, it was common knowledge that all in the West were retraining their sites on the importance of the two great but forgotten continents.

"The girl was one of Hardy's lovers? He mentioned her name."

"Yes, she is a journalists, maybe an agent. Since the meetings with this intelligence officer, most likely an agent. Hardy and her had a fling in Kosovo. They bumped into each other a couple of times in Brussels. They met in New York. There is something there," and Zaporah understood Yossi meant romance. Though the silly games in these affairs, Zaporah just readied herself for the emotional competition of these needed affairs of the heart. Knowing from experience how to defend herself against breakdowns of the tragic or unpleasant. Looking across to her, Yossi could see her defenses kick in, or be called up to active duty.

"She's pretty. The black gentleman?"

"Leon Hess, a little bit more hands on from Langley. Get Vera ready for the lifestyle. A lot of stress when you rush a subject into deep cover. He is there to let her know what she is up against, prepare her."

"Guardian angel?"

"No. The Americans do not do that anymore. Not in a legal undercover covert action. They do have people they control who do. Spies."

"Like Hardy?"

"Like Hardy but with silencers. The offices in The Hotel De Paris; Hardy's guardian angel. Yeah, they don't do that anymore. And other myths of the spy game. Whitehall, Langley's remote. Partners in crime attached by a string of fiber. It wasn't us, it was the British, and Tony Blair has a better line of bullshit then Bill Clinton," Yossi just looked over to see Zaporah trying to keep herself from laughing.

"It might be fun to play with the British again. God, they get us in so much trouble. Better then the French."

"Apparently they are still fond of ricin darts. Here is the report from Paris of the other day. John Custer Harding has taken a fondness for umbrellas.

And Zaporah just smiled and read the report: *God do I want to bed him...*

"We leave for Munich August third, Zaporah."

The setup had been obvious, the Englishman and the American even changing the conversation when they became too close to the reality of the sensitivity the Brit had left dead on the sidewalk across from the small hotel Hardy was staying at. They both apparently did not know how well the cab driver understood or could speak English. He had dropped Hardy off at the train station, of which no jet planes were spotted. The Englishman went on to a Paris museum of art. Now he simply retold his story to the Paris police who had found it best to list the cause of death as a heart attack. But still, the setup was obvious; both of them.

Marcus Wolfe was quiet that afternoon, as he read in his Library and moved about his PC. He had friends of North Africa in Munich to correspond with, a couple of old cells of Socialism to run consisting of both young and mature veterans of The Cold War who yearned for the old days; members of a forgotten cause who now went underground for communism. He had both active cells and inactive cells in Germany and Czechoslovakia, with points both West and East to manage. On his desk a decoded communiqué from Yevgeny Primakov along with a text he needed to code to be sent to one of his agents involved with the handling of Carlos Sanchez.

If their plan were to succeed, there would be a need for Mr. Harding to be in Moscow at a certain date and time. Marcus Wolfe was now putting together the framework to have the subtle manipulation take place. Carlos Sanchez would be needed if their plan was to work. Carlos Sanchez was quickly becoming a liability, his over zealous indulgence in the narcotics trade having compromised their French operation. Which at the moment was now overexposed and about to be shut down, or the people of Carlos played back on the agents of Marcus Wolfe who handled and used them. If they could not stop, derail or setup, what had now come to look like a joint American and British covert operation, people would need to be eliminated. The problem was that Carlos was holding the front door open for the South American continent. Carlos was safer dead but should they win the game they would need him alive. In any case, it was clear as the Americans would say, the French operation had been well bird dogged. With Langley's man Hardy now with more documents, than he possibly could use. Whitehall responding by sending an army of agents to Bordeaux and Lyons to free up Hardy and take over where he left off. All the while the French are saying sarcastically, *please don't take these documents: And God, I hope they don't surface!* France was a mess, and what's more Hardy escaped elimination while a close personal friend took a ricin dart. The Balkans; if he did not stop the American lead effort, France would go the wrong way taking with her his political power base.

In the communiqué Carlos was to be made to understand how serious the situation was. Carlos was to behave. Marcus further instructed his agents to make sure Carlos had both a leash and collar on him. A choker would be appropriate. His outbursts were to end. He was to be told they were not to happen again: Hardy, and the British weren't the only ones who still used 9mms and ricin darts. In any case, if they lost this one, the chances of recapturing Eastern Europe, or placing people into office who were more comfortable to Socialism in his lifetime, or theirs, would never come about. It was serious, gravely serious. Like losing a backup channel on a secure data line during a national security briefing. Their security; the security of an ideology without a country, a life's work down the tubes. Carlos was to behave.

It was about the time of Hardy's near death experience, just after Trevor placed a call to Atlanta to advise friends that Hardy was still alive and employed by *The Weekly Empire & World Report*, that Dana conveyed a subtle blackmail up the line to Mr. Tomilyn by Pam regarding the father of her child. Though none of Hardy's activities could be reported by the deal worked out by the FBI and national security consideration conveyed further by the NSC at The White House. Though every other issue of intrigue spun off his escapes could. And if Mr. Tomilyn wanted the inside dope, then perhaps two more weeks of maternity leave coupled with a month's vacation instead of the corporate gift of three weeks were the order of the day. The baby, and God would Pam like to see Hardy. Or perhaps, as Pam conveyed through Dana, she would be more comfortable and pampered at Channel 44? A pay raise would arrive the following day.

Well...There is a right way and a wrong way to go about these things. Pam is right, and I could use the scoop. The UN and the budding media wars. Pam had Hardy but I have Pam. By the end of the day it was noted by some on staff that Miss Wellington's blackmail was working. Mr. Tomilyn, though having a love/hate relationship with Hardy, did like the spy. If he could out fox Channel 44 with the good news of the addition to Miss Wellington's family, then great! The folks at DNN reported back to production, they had never seen Ted Tomilyn in such a state. Babies! Good news for all! If not a pay raise, happy hour at Dudley's would be catered and free every Friday night.

It was reported back to Pam the following day by Dana, the visiting groupies and elite of the news world had never seen the people of DNN, friends and coworkers in such a state. Babies! Happy Hour! And blackmail for everyone! Who needs a union when you can negotiate such contracts!

It was, however, further reported back to Channel 44 the following day; everyone at DNN was extremely happy!

In truth, happiness filled the air of the entire news industry to the point people were coming down with influenza from happiness. And take an extra bonus to help you get over your cold in the Caribbean! Happiness, though Channel 44 were getting sick, while Channel 22 were only becoming ill.

But it was of another aspect which caught Ted Tomilyn's attention, he had problems. He had developed an over abundance of problem children from the spy affair with politics more then just a little to the left. He knew. Reports had to be filed objectively and the irritant of the public was showing. Let alone half of Washington who made sport of taking shots at the liberal press. Something had to be done. Miss Wellington's blackmail was cute, appropriate in terms of social blackmail, hell, businessmen do it all the time, but what was more important was that she was right. He needed Hardy, and Hardy put the fear of God into these problem children who now threatened to consume his baby. DNN was his baby. He could use the breaking news Miss Wellington could deliver. He could use the help at the U.N. once he yanked Hardy out of Europe after his mission was complete. He could use Hardy.

Monique had just been leaving her Paris apartment to join Hardy that Saturday evening with hopes of hooking up with him the following day, the first of August, when two German men shoved a gun in her back and escorted her to a black Sudan just around the corner. In the luxury car she was blindfolded and told to keep her big mouth shut, as educated thugs often do. They drove for about forty-five minutes. Monique suspected she could be in the countryside, though somewhere in Paris was a better bet. When they finally came to a stop she heard the click of an automatic garage door opener with the faint sound of the garage door ascending upward, the muffled sound trying it's best to make it through the expensive cars insulation. But it was not until she had been sitting blind folded with her hands tied for about an hour in some generic room with no smell or sounds to identify it to her soul, that she was released from her bonds to find she was in some medium sized office conference room to which she screamed an outburst and was rewarded a wicked slap for her efforts!

"Shut up!" and the second slap was worst then the first. "Keep your mouth shut and just sit there;" Monique could clearly see her opposition was of the breed best not to betray. Though the second command was not said loudly, but was said with such definition that one knows enough to behave. "My friend will be in a short while, we would like to ask you some questions. If we wanted you dead, we would have shot you. You are a piece on a chess board, we will pay a price for your office trip. We would pay even a greater price should we kill you. We could, your decision. For your troubles we will pay you what you made an hour before Carlos came into your life, plus damages. Me or my friends do not like to slap beautiful women. Sit here and stay quiet. There is some water and coffee over there, get up and move around if you like. The door is locked, the room is monitored; both video and voice. If you need to go to the ladies room you will be escorted. I will be back in a half hour," but before he left he threw the switch and sent the coffee into motion. Smiled and said, "a little civility in abduction."

"She's been slapped around, she'll behave."

"She senses it, Helmut will have no problems. Look at her look at the mirror."

"Two-way, she knows."

"I just want to hear it from her, that is all. Give her another fifteen minutes."

"I left her some fresh coffee, tea, muffins, creamer, let her have some time."

"Good idea, in the meantime lets review these papers."

"Give me a minute, let me pull up a chair."

"Monique, where did you get the papers?"

Monique was scared but the encounter though chilling was less then life threatening and she did not know how to answer, or who she was answering to: *Who are these people?*

"The ones I gave Hardy?"

"Yes."

"I owed him one, The Paris Police were playing a game. I took them and handed them to Hardy."

"Did you know he was almost killed?"

"No. Is he OK?" and it was clear to her beast handler, nice guy or not, that her emotional concern was extremely evident, though a bit over done.

"He is OK. Now, was it Hardy who took the first file? Did he kill Renee Jadot?"

"No, he was with me that evening."

Her German interrogator was deep in thought; chess player thought. He was older, heavy set and balding, a sweet man—As long as she did not play games. Attached to his eye glasses was a hearing aide, so it was all not that uncommon for subjects not to realize his friends in the other room were instructing him to further continue his questioning. Which ranged from questions of the spy game to wall coverings and drapes of the different living quarters Hardy had had in his life. As long as Helmut was told to keep her going he asked the questions to keep Monique talking, always keeping a tight stern eye on her due to her underlining rage. After about an hour he left the room and told her to ready herself. He would be back in a short time to drive her home. Though Monique hoped he did not mean sexually. Rage or not, Monique did suspect she would be returned home safely.

"What do you think?"

"Honest. The questions were not too threatening. I think Günther Von Müller. He slipped Paris Police for an afternoon, I think Günther."

"Documents?"

"Sure, Hardy has them. Günther passed them to him."

"Paris Police?"

"Thinks they are playing a game."

"They are, we are."

"Well that is about it. Background information is helpful. Helmut slapped her pretty hard, she will behave. She will think Russian, I hope. Smart girl."

"This is very sensitive to the French Government, I appreciate the BND helping us out."

"We do not mind helping out French intelligence, better this way. The word my people from Berlin wished to convey was let the Americans and British have their fun. Better the documents get lost in some Washington, D.C. archive, then turn up in Moscow."

"We are taking all ideas into consideration, I am glad they are lost. I am glad we know who found them and how he found them. On behalf of my government, I thank you....Now, maybe you get Monique back home."

"Sure."

"Oh, have your men be careful, here is the latest intelligence from The Paris Police. This little abduction probably saved her life. They saw it all. The enemy is spooked."

"I wish we could show her this."

"I know, we can't. Let her think the worst. But make sure she knows your men are prepared to see action on the way back. She'll freak, healthy paranoia....Now get her back home."

"OK."

"Oh, aah, have your men give her one more good slap in the face. Bait her if possible. Let her think the worst."

Pillow thoughts...It was the sweet dream of stressed out pillow talk when Monique awoke at six-thirty to the crashing sounds of a garbage truck coming down the street like a French Godzilla while servicing all the apartments on the block. Whatever the case, the need for extra sleep or not, it was best she get going. Hardy had sent for her by mail the day before, before the intrigue of the evening before. Monique just stumbled out of bed to find her way to the bath room, her cheeks still smarting. She had nice cheeks, Hardy use to look at them with fondness. Though a little make up on the bruised one and she'd be fine. Maybe an hour, then she would start out to find her way to the North of France.

"I have a problem John," John Blacke looking over to Henry Chatsworth sipping his English tea, the Monday morning meeting a bit lonely without the strong quiet Robert Torres. "My people in London want me in France for a little more hands-on."

"The stragglers?"

"The leftovers of this spy affair have a lot of material to unload. With poor Harry out of play they are pulling in the creeps to do the document thing. Your people have them under intense surveillance, my people are playing them back. You should be OK."

"Yeah, Henry, I cannot believe this. Dr. James Smith, *the document company*," and he looked over to see Henry laugh.

"Well...That is usually how it works. Those who have the most to lose get stuck with the most to move. Poor buggers."

"When do you leave?"

"Tomorrow. Once a week, once every two weeks, I will be making the trip across the pond to Atlanta. Paris, I will be working out of mine. Whitehall wants for me to pay a visit to my friends the French tomorrow evening."

"Visit the American Embassy too Henry, I have some people there. Hardy."

"Hardy, we almost lost him the other day...."

I don't drink coffee, I drink tea my friend.
I'm an Englishman in New York.

—Sting

"Englishman In New York"
Nothing Like the Sun
Virgin Records, 1987

CHAPTER 18

It was a warm moist Paris night when Henry Chatsworth left The American Embassy that evening, walking a few blocks and turning to go down a side street to make his way to his living quarters, an apartment a short distance away. Trevor had been on his mind, the replaying of the operation in Bordeaux and Lyons had consumed his thoughts. He was totally unaware until he felt the piercing pain in his back while he crumbled to the sidewalk to watch his assailants quietly walk away, watching his life slip from within his mortal body as he readied himself to meet his Maker.

Hardy had rented a car at the Paris Train Station and slowly made his way out that day to the North of France. He had made a reservation for food and lodging at a very chic, quaint country inn by to name of Le Chateau-Borghese, which was just outside Douai in a tiny village named Chernbord, where Monique was suppose to join him. It was two o'clock, Hardy had taken his time and thought he might sit have some coffee and maybe go through the shops. He had till eleven that evening to check in and Monique was not expected until sometime on Sunday, though she could surprise him and show up Saturday night. In any advent he had a day or two to play with, but the events of that morning, he would pass on the wine and settle on some coffee and rolls. Le Chateau-Borghese was but a short distance down the road, he had plenty of time and he needed to prepare himself for the tour of the chateau's vineyards, the over burdening and extremely proud proprietor demanded to give to all his guest that Trevor had warned him about: *But be patient Hardy, the gentleman is an extremely nice guy and he is someone we can work with. He has helped my people out in the past.*

Lunch was good but the coffee seemed stronger, bitter, and Hardy knew as soon as he started to get up from the table he was in trouble. He had to get out of there, he had to get out of there right away. Hardy was upset, though not overly so. When one does this sort of work, and one spends a good part of his life out in the cold, one tends to get use to someone always dropping some sort of chemical or drug into one's beverage. But this time it was different, Hardy was in pain, and he secretly worried about what they had used on him. Or how long it would take for the poison to do it's damage; Monique, and I hope I survive until she arrives.

Hardy could feel his muscles tighten harder and harder. He thought heart attack by deprivation of blood to his soul. The pain was building, starting like the aches and pains of the flu but increased with intensity. His car was a good distance away parked on a small tree lined hill in the village. Should he make it he had an extra large bottle of pain medication in his bag. He would, it was still early, the magic screen. Once at the chateau he could retrieve the right information or have it forwarded to treat himself.

It was when he turned the corner to view his car about five hundred yards away that the mushroom cloud when up raining shrapnel all over the crowd of people from the village carnival, which had forced him to park so far away from the village café. His rented auto ceased to exist anymore!

Crippled, Hardy did his best to make it back up the village in a fast walk short of a run as not to attract too much attention, finding his way out the other side of the village and down some country road. Walking was a chore, running was still possible. By the end of the day when the poison had set in, walking would be damn near impossible but still capable. Though the poison seem to affect his right side, his leg numb, but it was his right arm in total chaos. By the time he crawled into an old wooden tool shed up on a small hill under a shade tree just inside the vineyard, the spasms of his right arm had snapped his elbow out of joint. Hardy was in extremely bad shape with the poison playing further havoc as it ravaged his internal organs. He just laid there and begged for mercy. Though within the excruciating pain he was able to keep his wits about him and keep his thoughts clear and alive. He had nothing to treat himself with, though had he made back to chateau he could have found the necessary means for a poor man's medical. Seeing a doctor would be elimination by medical condition, Carlos would have insisted on it. French doctors have children they love too. In either case, Hardy would have to treat himself. Hardy was alone, Hardy was dying.

The report from AP simply read: Two Islamic fundamentalists were taken into custody outside Mogilev, Belarus by both Russian and Balarus authorities with a large quantity of narcotics and a small amount of firearms and explosives. The men were reportedly from the Groznyy area. In truth the two men were Iranians, the large amount of narcotics;

two grams of cocaine. The small amount of explosives; Russian built assault weapons and a small homemade poormans Atomic bomb.

The breakdown of the importance of the Russian nuclear industry as a subtle blackmail to the West had come back to haunt Moscow. The deception was picked up by Western intelligence, and was being reviewed by both Whitehall and Langley. The Israelis once again violated to airspace of both Iran and Iraq. No we don't have them, Dimona's a sham. Fuck with us you'll lose your capital. *P.S.*, our missiles can hit Moscow. The West was boiling! It was also quite apparent, the Russians had something to hide and did not want to lose this game.

John Blacke was wild that Friday afternoon, even having to be restrained by two of his agents when the news of the death of one of his best friends he had come to know in such a short time had reached his desk. Henry Chatsworth had been found stabbed to death on a Paris street, apparently on his way home just after visiting The American Embassy. Special Agent In Charge John Blacke was frothing at the mouth at the news. When his men finally calmed him down there would be a series of calls, which would have to be made. The first to Robert Torres in Bonn. Jennifer sat quietly compiling a list for her boss of everyone from Interpol to close personal friends. The spy game had turned wickedly deadly in Europe, Hardy had disappeared, and the Atlanta FBI office would need the British Embassy in Washington to send down another liaison, there was more work to do on Georgia soil. Though no one as good as Henry, she thought. It was the gift of his understanding of the spy game that apparently had him knocked out of play permanently before he could do too much damage to the enemy in France. She thought to herself, we are all going to miss him.

In Bonn the news had hit Robert Torres like a one two punch from a prize fighter, first Hardy drops off the surveillance after his rental is blown up, then the news Henry Chatsworth was murdered on the streets of Paris. Documents adrift somewhere, and a man he grew to like and had become a mentor of sorts turning up dead, eliminated on his way home. God...A tissue, and Grace brought him all the latest reports and files while Robert wandered through a data base so classified and sensitive, he realized it would not be long until he joined Henry in the next world. If there is such a place? and if they have one set aside for young and old spies? Robert would be up most of the night.

The death of Henry Chatsworth had been withheld for a few days for the national security concerns of both The United States and of The United Kingdom, coming in about the same time of the reported disappearance of John Custer Harding. In truth, Robert had known ahead of time but had refrained from calling John, though he never the less wanted to take away the deep personal grief when the sad advent was relayed to him on the phone. John Blacke was wild! Robert was besides himself, sick with treachery that destroys the loving lives of both young and old.

When Robert was finished grieving and consoling with a friend he hung up. Grace in the meantime had laid the latest report from France on his desk. The police of a small French village named Chembord had had a report of a man walking out of town just shortly after the explosion of Hardy's rental. The man according to two young French girls looked as if he was ill, though not of injury of the blast. He seemed to be having trouble with his right leg and was clutching his right arm above the elbow with his left hand. He had also had a small, what looked as like a canvas gym bag colored black slung across his back as he limped along. The description fit that of Hardy. A Hardy in trouble on the verge of being eliminated.

The second page of the report was that of a woman who fit the description of Monique and had shown up Sunday in The Village Of Chembord, the day after the blast. After reviewing the entire report Robert felt a spark, a rebirth of enlightenment of a gift of new possible life, Hardy's. He would only have to mourn for one that week. He was happy, happy for Hardy. He was happy for himself, and maybe it was best Henry went first? scout the place out for us. Robert just smiled and turned to call Atlanta to be followed up with a series of calls to London, Washington, Paris, Wiesbanden, Brussels, and Berlin. Though possibly not in that order. Hardy was alive! Though very much in need and the thought of his condition brought the spirits of Robert down again. Alive but dead. Death but one casualty alive. Monique, and I hope we get to him first. I hope we get to him in time. God....

It was Robert's call to Leon Hess at the Berlin Annex, which had been most telling. Vera Lopez who was now assigned to Berlin Bureau had just returned from a NATO briefing in Brussels. The entire European theater was boiling. The press briefing had been generic, even benign in the wake of the post Balkans conflict but the brass of both Britain and The United States were boiling about something. Words are said and reported but it is the underlying words of the unspoken, which is often most telling and most chilling. Unspoken words which cannot be reported, for they float around in the air like demons to snare and torment journalists who know if they cannot get to the truth in time catastrophe can occur.

Robert knew the truth. Robert by his years of young maturity knew enough not to lie to himself. He instructed Leon of what he needed in regards to the service of Miss Lopez. Leon reported back she was a real trooper, a great subject right from the start, even looked like the real one. Though her salary was somewhat less than the star's. Press tend to make good cover. Spies who pose as press tend to get shot a lot, innocent press tend to get shot a lot in the spy game. Robert was worried, there are rules to these games, he was about to break one.

In the shed Hardy was sweating profusely in excruciating pain. The night had been quiet, though off in the distance he could hear voices. Carlos had men out and about, Carlos had men hunting Hardy. The shed by good fortune was out of view of the road. Hardy knew not to go to the chateau, it would be the first place they would look for Hardy. The proprietor was one of ours, or one of Trevor's. He would only have been killed had Hardy showed up, or had Hardy had the good fortune to make it all the way to the driveway of Chateau-Borghese in the first place without being shot to death. It was best Hardy stay put; he did. Hardy listened to his inbred instincts of a spy, which had kept him alive all those years.

The shed itself was two parts; the first being a playhouse, or dollhouse for children, and Hardy thought with a little plumbing and electric, it would make a good guesthouse. The second half was the same as the first half, one room but a barn type door guarding the tools to the private vineyard. The small structure was of grey barnwood, the doors white. In the center of his protected nest was a small trap door, which lead to a small crawl space for storage and escape if need be. All and all, Hardy had lucked out. He was in extreme pain but he was comfortable. He silently prayed that one of Carlos's men would not find him, or that one of the owner's children would not happen by to play house. It was Sunday, Hardy was in pain. Secretly he thought he did not need God but he could use some pain medication and some B&B cognac.

The motorbike was not theirs, it belonged to a Jewish student and waited for them in Munich. When Yossi and Zaporah arrived they met with an old friend and Jewish elder, one of the few Jews who still lived in Germany or had family who wanted to return after the tragedy we call the great war, their forefathers, The Holocaust; our fathers, World War II. The elder who they simply called Ben was a front man for Israeli covert operations and managed about a dozen Jewish students in such minor tasks as record procurement, the cross referencing of information and data coupled with the lesser aspects and areas of spying. He was both a father figure and a mentor. The hands on control of his young agents made easy by the living arrangements. They all lived on the outskirts of Munich in a German apartment complex, whose name translated in English would be called mountainview gardens. Grampa Ben, and spying made easy. Along with spying 101, which included communication with each other by the different brand name boxes they would toss out in the trash, they also had the head of one extremely nasty radical Islamic terrorist cell under their surveillance. The motorbike was theirs for the day. One of Ben's students went over the finer points of this two wheel weapon the night before for both Zaporah and Yossi.

The man simply known as Gemel was reported to have brunch everyday about ten at a bistro type café on a semi-quiet, semi-busy tree lined street. Parking was a problem, the dining was always inside. Though it was reported to Ben he liked to sit by the window. There were two, two large picture windows with a door in the middle. Cover, cover for a foot operation was possible the children told Ben. It was located at the end of a line of small shops with a store that sold wine and liquor, the best beer in Germany, a fish market with a pharmacy on the other side. Across the street there was a station which pumped petro, beyond that and a little to the right, a house on a hill which contained an office for real-estate and one for German antiques. The main problem the two would have was parking. If they circled the block they would surely miss him or tip him off. But the café was the best location to have this target hit. At the end of this report, which was both written and highlighted by one of Ben's college brats, was the weather report. It was suppose to be a warm and sunshine filled morning with showers moving in that afternoon. The morning would be good should Yossi and Zaporah decide tomorrow was the day. If they waited rain could be a problem for a motorbike. When they were done, just drop the rice burner off at the campus.

It took but a half hour for Yossi and Zaporah to return home from their vacation of thought in Ben's study. The weather would be nice all week, the only rain would come the next afternoon and was not expected to last past midnight. The motorbike would be parked at the campus everyday for their use; return it when you are done. The latest intelligence report from both Ben and Jerusalem indicated their subject had a busy schedule and would be at the café just about every morning that week. Much more, he was under their surveillance every time he left his apartment. They could give a signal for when he was on his way, when he went to the café he always carried his newspaper. Parking was a problem? Head-on or face fine. The hit was on, the date was in question. Ben instructed his brat just to report the motorbike stolen should anything go wrong.

The next morning the sky was clear and warm, the brats' friend dropped the motorbike off just in case. The signal came down; one phone ring: Dead. Two rings: Dead. He had just left the apartment with his paper.

By good fortune that morning as Zaporah rode up on the back of the motorbike driven by Yossi, a space opened up about six or seven down from the café in front of the fish market. Yossi zipped in.

"Honey, I want to get a cup of coffee, I'll only be a moment."

"OK Sweetypie," Yossi said in his best Jewish voice to break the stress. "Let me turn the bike around first." It took but a minute for Yossi to have the motorcycle facing outward instead of its nose pointing to the shops. Zaporah simple walked over to picture window and emptied the magazine into his head. The shattering glass does not so much throw off one's bullets but one's train of thought and line of sight. There was a real need to make sure he was dead. She had been lucky that morning, Gemel's back was to the window, his head and eyes facing the other way. When all was done in the frozen of disbelief, Zaporah simply walked back and hopped on as the two sped head first out of traffic and disappeared down some German street. Yossi had only been the driver, he had been the point man to provide cover with his own 9mm from the frozen in disbelief while Zaporah did what was necessary to keep peace in this volatile violent world. They both were pros. When Gemel was dispatched into the next world, their blood may as well have been ice water.

CHAPTER
19

The terror of the abduction the evening before played on Monique's mind, as she drove northeast out of Paris to hook up with Hardy in The Village Of Chembord at Chateau-Borghese. Terror and a mix of confused bewilderment of why a couple of nice goons would kidnap her for an evening, ask a few questions and return her home? Though the bastards did enjoy slapping her around: Take her out, slap her around a bit. She deserves it! *For what!* she thought, Monique did not know.

Her second mix of emotion was of undying love for Hardy, the sense something was just not right coupled with intense sexual desire of passion for a man who just showed up in her life one Paris morning about eleven o'clock to be her reoccurring bastard. This even if he got to the café first. He was Rhet, she was Scarlet, it was the end of the movie, which only further infuriated her more while at the same time fanned the flames of burning passion and desire to beat the living daylights out of Hardy till he could see what they would have. He meant everything to Monique; a death entanglement to Hardy. Or at least that was what he thought. He is a coward! Monique thought, though he already told her as much in more eloquent terms. But the truth be known, he was neither. He was of flesh and blood but had played out so many scenes of Cold War combat that the only fear he held deep down inside himself was what would happen if he lost the spy game, if the West took the loss of this post Cold War intrigue. Post Cold War, though Hardy was right, it never really ended. He feared for life but not his own.

It was raining that Sunday afternoon when Monique finally reached Chembord, a light summer's mist fogging up her windshield. As she approached the village she could tell something was wrong. News not only bored her it seem to be filled with unpleasant hyperbole: Report the story and get off the air, don't tell me about your dog, at least that is what Monique thought. This was also the theme of her argument to herself or to others whenever she wished to listen to the latest pop. It was for this very reason Monique was totally unaware something was very, very wrong until she view the lower street looking like downtown Beirut fifteen years ago with the glass shards still littered about the road and sidewalks, while a panic attack set in and her instincts told her Hardy if he was still alive was in extreme danger. She continued quickly through the village within reason and slammed down on the escalator once she was out the other side and away from the village shops and two family homes. She did not wish to waste any time to get to The Chateau-Borghese, passing a burnt out shell of a wreck, or what was left of one on the way out of town at some petro station, knowing instinctively that it had been the one, while she fumbled to find news on the car's radio receiver. She did not know what Hardy had been driving that day, she feared the worst.

By the time she arrived at Chateau-Borghese her nerves were shattered and she was in a near hysterical state, which she tried to hide from the inn keeper and his wife but to no avail. Monique shattered, brokedown and screamed out: "He's dead! I know he's dead!" and she started to weep profusely as the inn keeper wife consoled her and ushered her off to a back room. John Custer Harding never showed up but his lover obviously did. The room was her's.

"Shh...no body was found," the inn keeper's wife said in French and then spoke to her in clear direct English. "We have done this before, Jack and I will help you." meaning they were friends of Trevor Downing while using the English translation of her husband's name. "Now, you must be very quiet, two very dangerous Spanish types came by today. Just before you arrived, their counterparts, two Germans in business suits. They are watching my husband," and though still sobbing, Monique understood Carlos had his goons about who even put fear into ex-war heroes. Monique also understood the two who showed up just before she arrived were not our agents. "They are watching my husband, when they have gone and it turns dark, we will go out and look for him. Should they move about the vineyard my husband will call the local police. Now shh, I will show you to his room, your room," and she took a sobbing Monique under her arms and up the back staircase to a very eloquent and comfortable room filled with brick-or-brac, which most times fills the hearts of lovers. Monique had found the quiet in the center of the storm.

"Excusez-moi Monsieur, I would like to rent a room?"

"We have none left," Jack said in perfect English to the face of an obvious enemy agent. Seeing both daggers, in his eyes and in his own.

"That is too bad," the opposition said with a strong German accent.

"Yes it is," and Jack simply looked over to the door with eyes that said if you don't leave I will kill you.

The KGB agent saw in Jack's eyes the class or grade of an enemy agent that would not put up with, and certainty demanded better handling and treatment then he would afford a lesser one of his breed. He simply said "good day" and left before he had his neck snapped.

His name was Jack, his wife would use both the English and the French when calling out to her husband. French when they were making love. His real name was Cliffy Percoti, he had been a Green Beret in Vietnam and had moved to Europe and settled in France in the late seventies at the request of an up and coming Mafia Don call Don Fusaro-Debenadetto. He had also moved to Europe to avoid a Mafia contract.

It was about ten at night when Cliffy went out armed with an old U.S. Army forty-five. It was dark, the cloud cover still holding in the full moon. If Hardy was out there he would be in the orchard, Trevor had indicated as much. And as he made his way out into the vineyard and the orchard through the vineyard beyond, he wonder what name Trevor was going by; Cadwell? or Downing? and why true spies never carry a firearm? Assumed names and lack of weaponry both seemed irresponsible to Cliffy.

We all have flash backs in life, Cliffy had his that evening. Grapevines and old fruit bearing trees, in his mind he was back in the rice patties or the jungle highlands to the north of where he started out in the war of his younger years. A war which made him a killer, but our killer. Cliffy was dressed all in black that evening, he too knew of Carlos; a necklace, and a desire not to have one. The KGB agent who showed up at his desk for room and board was of the profanity of a child, and of how it entered this world. With his two buddies and the goons of Carlos, he could be in for a good fight. He was confident but he played it safe. the orchard and the dogs. The dogs were quiet, off in the distance he could hear his hounds and his German Shepherd playing in the bushes. The shepherd returning on occasion for quiet affection. No one had entered the orchard or vineyard. Of his two hounds, one was Blue Tick, the other a coonhound of mixed lineage. Between the three, he did not know which the enemy would like to be devoured by more. In any case, eerie as hell, the land around his chateau was quiet and still.

It was about twenty minutes in to his hike as he walked a pattern that Cliffy came upon the toolshed towards the end of his property. The dogs circled around sniffing with affection, Cliffy had found Hardy. Cliffy had found a John Custer Harding in extremely bad shape. He gave him some water and slung Hardy across his back like he did for so many of his loved buddies, wounded, dead or simply missing a limb, so many years before. When he came in the back door of the chateau Monique bust forth in both tears of love and emotion. Hardy was alive but Hardy was unconscious. In the gym bag that had tagged along for Cliffy's piggyback ride came the documents and the file disks. Cliffy would be on-line with Trevor that evening. Before he even threw the switch, he knew the monitor would have a piece of magic E-mail for him to devour and watch self-destruct in seconds afterwards. The news from medicine, or the group from where magic screens come from, had left detailed advice on how to save Hardy's life.

It was five-thirty the next morning when Monique viewed a semiconscious Hardy stir and attempt to rise through the sheer white and pink Victorian lace curtains, which surrounded the elegant queen sized canopy bed furnished in the special room Hardy had rented to say I'm sorry. Tears flowed from Monique's eyes in sheer happiness.

"Don't try to move Hardy, stay down," Monique was now playing both everlasting lover and doting mother.

"Hi..." and Hardy tried to sit up again as Monique helped him lay back down with a demanded voice of love. "I'm in so much pain"

"Over the counter, we are being watched Hardy, this is what Langley recommended. Take two of these," and Monique handed Hardy a small cup of water.

"The documents?"

"We have them. The disks too."

"God...Of angels and twisted sexuality..." and Monique could see in Hardy's eyes he loved her, but could not speak the words.

"I love you Hardy..."

Hardy had drifted back to sleep only to awaken three hours later to still find Monique's hand gently brushing his brow and gently stroking the side of his head.

"Hi..." and Monique could see her affection still held weight on Hardy's soul by the sound and texture of his crippled voice. Though Hardy could not bring himself to say the words she so desired to hear. The consumption of affection of the afflicted with the words which bring couples to the alter twice removed. "I'll be all right Monique," though in his pain he was not. "Go get some rest yourself, you have been up all night;" Hardy demanding but giving way to her affection.

Monique kissed him like both a mother with a wounded young boy and a lover of deep soulful affection of a fallen hero but of one not out. A fallen hero to be repaired by love and returned to the great game in combat readiness; a soldier to be returned to his bride after the war. Monique secretly hoped she would be the bride who put up with the intrusions of an ex with a young child. Monique wanted Hardy. But Monique wanted to kill Hardy for being so indifferent of their love while at the same time save the one she always truly loved but fell short of the hindsight or relationship common sense, which bond couples and make their flesh one. "I will go get some sleep, you sit here quietly, see if you can get some oatmeal in your belly," and she kissed him and moved his morning coffee and oatmeal to his side before she left the room in disappointment, Hardy could still not say the words.

"I'll see you, OK?" but the lack of the spoken love was as much a rejection as sleeping with a girl the first date and tossing her for someone else the next night. "When you return we will talk, OK? I know, the coffee, it is not my stomach, I'm just in a lot of pain. I'll be up, bring me some more painkillers and some brandy when you bring lunch. The liquor, keep the blood flowing. OK? We'll talk. You and I Monique really need to talk," and Hardy just warmly stared at Monique in his emotion as she left the room.

"How you doing? Lunch."

"OK. Pain. I am just in a lot of pain. I am glad you brought the brandy. When you come back bring the whole bottle. Tell Cliffy to come with you. The elbow, it needs to be snapped back into place. Probably kill myself in pain if I were to do it myself. Look how deformed the joint is. It hurts, I am in a lot of pain," and Hardy could see by the grotesque expression on Monique's face that she could for the moment even feel the pain he was enduring as she let out a gasp.

"Oh God..." Monique looking like she was ready to vomit. "...I did not know Hardy."

"The pain will be manageable once the dislocation is corrected. I will worry about surgery some other time. But now, a little Cabernet, a little brandy some painkillers. I'm in pain but I'm OK. I want to stay that way, keep a handle on the pain," and Hardy could see Monique smile warmly. "So.. now, do you want to talk?"

"OK, Hardy."

"I was in love with you in Highland Falls Monique. I was in love with you on our return rematch in Georgia. But I am not now. Why put ourselves through this? To destroy each other?"

"I loved you Hardy but I could not go to you. I wish you would only understand."

"I do but that was a long time ago, things have changed, times have changed, people have changed. We were set up Monique, we have almost gotten each other killed. Cliffy told me about Saturday night."

"I know, setup. But we can love now. We can finally be lovers Hardy."

"Monique, I love Pam more then I ever loved any women in my life, and she has my child. I loved you Monique. I hated my ex, then I hated you both from an outcome of both sin and innocents of that damn Southern Spy Affair."

"Do you still love me Hardy."

"Yes. I love you like a friend. I damn you like a whore. It is reckless love Monique. Every time we find each other in bed with one another we may as well leave a loaded gun on the nightstand. Two loves Monique; you and Kiddo. Which love affair do I throw away? Both are so deeply important to my soul. Pam is the one who rocks my baby in her arms down south back home. Who do I toss?" Monique was quiet in reflection, Hardy's discourse was not so much a rejection as a realization, a rationalization. Monique understood it.

"I see...But there are others."

"Would you want that for yourself? For us? Would you really only want to be a lover who stops in every couple of years just to bed an old friend to prove you could? Like a neighbor who pops in every couple of days to turn your life upside-down? I just thought I'd stop by to bring chaos to your dinner table. But it would not be dinner we were destroying it would be our lives. Would you really want that?"

"I love you Hardy," though warm in reply Monique was crying inside.

"There are others. Pam has my baby. But you know me, I fall in love a little with each lady who becomes my lover or temporary wife. I had, or have a reoccurring Israeli lover. She was in Jerusalem, I hear Europe now. What do you want me to tell you..?"

"I don't know Hardy."

"I hate this life. Then I love this life. Drafted into the spy game, born into the service. I love it when you win, I hate it when a friend is killed or murdered. They are all murdered, sometimes the enemy gets lucky and it is listed as a heart attack, or something else. Relationships; love and destruction of lives for a game. And if your team loses you take a terrorists hit on some city or landmark. Or some treaty is scrapped and you go to war in less then a handful of years. I love and I hate it. I love to love and I hated to hate when my heart is cut right out of my soul before me. Fear!" though Hardy's demeanor intense, was less then a shout. "I fear I will fail in my missions. I do not fear death. But I fear."

"You fear love Hardy."

"No, I did once. You know that, you saw it....I am just tired of seeing love flung around like a weapon. Of seeing lives destroyed by love, or lack of love. Or hate disguised as love. In the spy game love is always played back upon you. Now Pam. Help us Pam or we hurt the baby. You know how these creeps are. If Pam is valuable they kill me to *handle* Pam. Or kill Pam or the baby to kill me. It really makes me sick. Love...? I want to go to Germany and pay for my fun. I have more respect for the ladies of this craft then any other group of people on this earth. Fun. They are like me, I am like them. We understand each other and it is even a fun business deal for the lady, because we make the flesh fun. Love...? I am dying of love right now," and Hardy looked over to see Monique extremely emotional. "Love? Love is when you don't try to fuck each other up, like you have done to me Monique," and Hardy looked over to see Monique break into a little laughter in her tears. "If you love someone you do not trap them in your love."

"Is that what you think I have done Hardy, trap you?" and Monique was both crying and laughing gently.

"Why would you want us to both die?"

"Love."

"Love, I love you enough to let you go," and Hardy looked over, "shh, stop crying. What I want? I want you to find some guy who treats you right. Some guy you treat right. Then I want you to have his baby. Stay away from this *Gone With the Wind* love, Monique. Just find someone who treats you right. That is really all I ever wanted for you in that time so long ago," Monique was sobbing but with loving understanding. It was really not a rejection Hardy had laid upon her soul but a loving request. A loving request to save both their lives.

When Monique finished sobbing she looked up and changed directions while she refilled his wine. "Cliffy said he'd be in a little bit. Some people were at the front desk this morning, we have to move you tonight. There is a guest cottage on his property, his wife has it set up for us. We should be safe."

"OK, I can walk, I'm just wiped out; tired and a little drunk. Its going to be nasty when he snaps the elbow back in. I want you to wait outside."

"Trevor left word this morning, he said it would most likely take three or four months unless you see a doctor."

"I can't Monique, but I can get around."

"Hardy! Ready pal!" and Cliffy had that usual crazed Vietnam look in his eyes.

"Sure pal but don't have a flash back," and Hardy could see Cliffy start to laugh. "Monique, you better wait outside."

Hardy awoke that evening in the guest cottage with the searing pain gone, though his right arm was still throbbing. He had had an extra brandy or two, consumed all the wine and a handful of painkillers before his ex-Green Beret buddy went to work. He had passed out from both the pain and of the over abundance of a poorman's anesthesia. He now woke to see twilight all about him and could not discern minus Monique if it were eight-thirty in the night, or five, or six, right before dawn. On his bed cornered by four giant imported oak posts laid a quilt comforter of pastels and early spring flowers, mixed in with the blues and pinks, the yellow and greens seemed to standout the most. It was warm, he was hot. Hardy pushed the comforter to one side and hazily stared into the empty old field stone fireplace, last Winter's coals were still scattered about the hearth. Looking out the window through the twilight he could make out what looked like a field or riding meadow, and he wondered just how far away he was from the chateau? Off in the distance coming closer he could hear footsteps of a lady upon what he imagined was either a slated or granite walkway and rock cut steps. He suspected it was Monique and had no paranoid concern. The quietness of her approach telling Hardy she did not want to give away her position should the enemy be out there.

"The place is really quite beautiful Hardy, the guest cottage overlooks the chateau and the field that Cliffy lets his horses play in. The only problem is the field, we can only come and go at night. Too much of a chance we would be spotted sweetheart. The woods start just behind the cottage, we are just below the tree line."

"On a hill?"

"On a small hill Hardy. In the morning you will see just how beautiful Chateau-Borghese is."

"What time is it?"

"Eight-thirty-five."

"The cottage is beautiful Monique, I love the fireplace. The granite is all hand-honed, I knew a Sicilian stone mason once who did work like that. Look at the seams, the mortar. Burt was the best. So what do you have for me?"

"Your medication, some brandy, some wine and cheese; breakfast for tomorrow. OK? Sit on your bed?" Monique asked.

"Keep your clothes on," though Hardy was talkative he was deep in thought of worry of other things and items of concern on his mind. Monique simply slid up next to him while affectionately melting her flesh into his to gently tug at his left side and procure the demons and seduce the troubled thoughts from his soul before they floated about the room. Though it did not seem to be a bomb of emotional intensity or anger she felt the need to defuse.

"You are worried about your baby?"

"Yes and no. Pam's daddy is very big in the Jewish community, there is an Israeli connection. It is a spy game, and you don't kill Jews in a spy game. Or the Mossad kills you. They have been known to protect their brethren even when there is no spy game. And the KGB Directorate in Moscow. I lose a child, well...It is the amateurs in the spy game who do not know the rules, or have not risen to a level of play to understand such matters, or pick up on the subtle way we play the game until it is too late. You have to worry about the amateurs. In the West they often mole into law-enforcement and moonlight as spies. Scary. What is even more scary, is they truly believe no one is watching. It makes me sick Monique. I go from boyish looks one day to looking like sixty-five the next. Some mornings the news is so chilling I watch myself age ten years as I comb my hair in the mirror.

"But you worry?"

"Yeah, I worry. It is unspoken between Washington and Moscow. It is the amateurs I worry about. So many people are very naive about such matters. I only play the game, I imagine there are others."

"The West?"

"Yeah the West..." Hardy said quietly. "You lose a game from personal tragedy, then you lose a war. Then you lose a part of your national security. A lot of humanity can die in a war. It makes me ill, I try not to think about it," and Monique moved off the bed and slid her yellow sundress off her naked form and returned to his side, washing away much of the pain and the half dozen years the reflection of tragedy had earned him. Which she had just witnessed added on to his soul while she slipped her bare flesh under the covers to comfort him.

Their love making was intense; Monique atop Hardy, bringing him off to an intensity she knew he had not felt before while at the same time protecting his right arm; protecting Hardy himself from his own vulnerabilities.

"Do you love me!" she demanded; Hardy too intense in his gaze to respond, needing an extra moment to find the words.

"I love you enough to toss you when this is over," Hardy said directly and with gifted force.

"You bastard! You don't know the best thing you have ever had when you have it! Tell me Hardy! Tell me how bad you needed it! I saw how you exploded, I can still feel it inside!"

"And which love do I toss?" and Monique fell silent. "She is the mother of my child Monique. I want a life, you too. You know what I want, find a nice guy," but nice guys weren't Monique and the silence gave way to subtle nurturing of Hardy's passion, he was regaining his erection.

"Do you want to go again?" Monique said, now feeling she had the edge, though with Hardy she never really knew.

"I want to talk," and Hardy ran his hand through her shoulder length black hair and kissed her mocha flesh about the neck line.

"How do you feel?"

"Weak, extremely weak but my right arm, I can use it now. Numb but functional since Cliffy snapped the elbow back. Throbs, but I can use it. No one handed love making for a while, case I slip. I want you on top, I like it that way."

"So we'll go?" and Monique gave his cock a gentle but firm tug.

"In a little while, tease me" and Hardy looked over and down slightly to kiss and see Monique slyly smile. "In a little while. If I were not handicapped, I would let you tie me up. Kinky sex."

"What about me? Would you? Tie me up?"

"No. Only a man should be tied to the bed post, I'm crippled. Would you really let me if I wanted to? knowing how good I am in bed."

"No. Maybe if you married me?"

"No."

"Bastard."

"Would you really want to be married?"

"No."

"So you are playing a game?"

And Monique gave a playful tug on his cock to answer before her response, a simple "no." But then Monique paused, "rough sex Hardy, I might take the chance, you're a cripple," and she kissed him and gave another love tug. "So tell me Hardy, do you fantasize about me? Were you lonely when we were separated for those two weeks?"

"I fantasize about you seventy percent of the time."

"What about the other thirty percent?"

"Others."

"Others?"

"Others."

"When I'm not around?"

"Hand lotion; or others."

"Hand lotion?"

"It was how I survived being out in the cold so long back in the days when the Southern Spy Affair was so intense. One Mafia family let it be known I would never get laid again. The drug cartel threatened to cut it off. I had my fantasies and hand lotion. In my mind I have made love to many very beautiful ladies...Both Monique, inner beauty and beauty of the flesh. Some very attractive ladies in their mercy have saved my life. Fantasies are better then KGB homosexual lovers. These ladies saved my life. I did not get laid for awhile but the guys of my CWA local pulled through. For my viewing only, not even a dollar into a garter," and Hardy leaned down and kissed her.

"But your sex life returned? and extra inch or two on top I see."

"The enemy is dead. My sex life returned," and Hardy reach down with his warm hand to the wet sweetness of Monique's flesh and soulfully kissed her until Monique broke away to regain her breath.

"I can see your right arm is better," though her words seemed to break up as Hardy's big warm hand squeezed her inner thigh and Monique let out a gasp.

"I'm ready sweetheart," and Hardy leaned down to kiss her, guiding her while he watched Monique work her flesh down to his manhood, her mocha body impaling itself while he helped her along for the ride of her life.

"Oh god..." were her only words.

Hardy laid naked, his hand gently tugging on Monique's hair as her own naked flesh laid mostly atop him or draped to the side, her cheek resting on his chest listening to him breath. Listening to his rhythms come back to normal, as she fumble for the right phrase to say in her seduction in her quest for his heart. She already owned the flesh, at least she did on French soil. She moved her hand up to the side of his neck brushing it warmly and kissed the other side and spoke, though this time of issues.

"When it is dark I have to wander back to the chateau Hardy," she said, letting Hardy have his way with the locks of her hair. "I have to get supplies. I will be back by eleven. Think you can hold out for a couple of hours?" and Hardy kissed her a yes. "A honeymoon cottage for a week. OK?" and Hardy nodded.

"A temporary wife."

"Do you love me?"

"Yes."

"Will you toss me?" but Hardy did not answer, though Monique already know.

"I will do what is best for both of us. I have to leave soon."

"The damage to your internal organs, one of the spy doctors on staff sent word, it is going to take awhile Hardy. You could go into pneumonia, heart failure."

"Trevor. I wonder who the doctor was? An American or British MD? Was it Trevor E-Mail, or did it just appear?"

"Just appeared."

"Langley. I've got a drop to make Monique, I die I die. I'm worried more about bullets."

"How is your right side?"

"Numb, slightly paralyzed."

"I'm worried about you." Though in her concern Monique could see Hardy changing gears in thought and in need to escape a bit from her motherly concern and of issues of her importance.

"Oh, Cliffy mentioned you had a little abduction?"

"A little one. Documents Hardy. They wanted to know where you got them. I said I didn't know. Slapped me around. Playing a game. I told Cliffy's wife. When I come back we will talk. You and me. Monica, Cliffy's wife said she will help us out but I have to return this evening. She may come back with me. The dogs, we'll be safe. Cliffy will stand guard."

"Then?"

"Then you and I will hang out for a week or two. Just you and me. It's hot, we'll stay naked all the time and make love. You like my flesh?"

"Yes," and Hardy kissed her, muffling his words on her neck as he went along. "I like your flesh, I would even like it more if we were on the beach. Maybe some island to ourselves?"

"I'll be back in a few hours. Monica will help me get setup, then you and I will play for a week. OK?"

"Yes, but then I have to toss you."

"But you love me?"

"Yes."

"But you will toss me?" and Monique was filled with both anger and amusement "Not if I am here you won't."

"That was sweet of Monica last night. I brought you some coffee," Monique said, smiling and handing Hardy his morning coffee, then letting her robe slide off while she slipped her naked flesh back under the covers next to his. "So tell me Lover, why would you not work with the FBI back in Georgia?"

"I have not even had my morning coffee and you are going to pump me for information?"

"Yes, and if you want me to pump you," Monique said, giving Hardy's middle sex namesake a gentle tug and continuing, "you better not hand me some line or set me up."

"State, local and county law-enforcement is a real problem. The FBI; I like them, the Special Agents have treated me well. We are apples and oranges Monique. And God, I hate when I have to burn a good agent. I start wars, people get killed in these games. They charge people if they break the law. We play together we set each other up," and Hardy looked into her eyes and slyly smiled. "So whose side are you on? Who are you working for?"

"I keep my own little black book to keep my lovers coming back to me Hardy."

"It works both ways. Back in Georgia Monique I was so caught up in sensitivities from the MidEast to the Balkans to South America, the reorganizing of Europe, even Australia came into the mess for awhile... Look...There comes a point to where situations become so sensitive that it is not so much you cannot be charged, because anyone can really, we have censored national security formats for trials of such nature, it is just if you are our agent someone usually gets a call from someone high up in Washington. In other words you better have a damn good reason and it better not be a setup. You do not sacrifice national security for a cops and robbers sting operation. I would sit in jail."

"Why? The FBI Hardy."

"Because I am not their writer," and Monique just started to laugh. "Look, if I worked undercover for these guys, and it is nothing personal, they would want me to zig one day and my instincts would tell me to zag. Everyone would be killed. It comes down to intelligence verses enforcement. The FBI, the Special Agents are pretty damn good but I would go the intelligence line. I have stung good Special Agents. Back in Georgia I stung a lot of bad cops. Bad cops come a dime a dozen in the spy game. If you are going to sting someone make sure they are the best first. What use are they if the Russians or the Chinese are going to sink their teeth in them too?"

"You really are a bastard," and Monique was trying to keep herself from laughing.

"It puts us both in a bad position, the spy game is not all dead letter drops," and Hardy could see Monique was hot. "There are different grades of undercover people, the state and local police are the most trouble. The KGB tend to like to mole into these groups, the FBI try to keep themselves insulated for obvious reasons....Well, one day someone like me shows up to take the punch bowl away and all hell breaks loose. This item is a man who broke the law, he goes to the FBI. This item is political, it goes to Moscow. I call it double agent. And it is usually how it starts; something political and very innocent goes overseas, two years later you are giving the KGB the latest technology from White Sands, or some national security research center. It's how it starts, sad really. An American agent does his drops at an American or British base. An enemy agent slithers and snakes his way around the UN trying not to get caught doing dead letter drops to Russian agents. There is even different styles."

"But they try to set you up?"

"Oh yeah, they come right out of the woodwork after you. Set you up, make it look like you are theirs to pressure some Washington politician. God do they come after you..."

"Covers?"

"If I can I protect covers, not so much protect but look the other way. Unless someone does something stupid. Most times it is the people I refer to as The Shithead Division, mostly state and local undercover groups. I am not in the business of blowing covers, but I am not going to protect an amateur who steps on my toes. They usually get what they deserve. Protecting someone's cover in the spy game is common courtesy. My cover is writer, it was technician. If someone tries to sting me it threatens not so much my cover but my activities. My activities at times are national security. The gloves come off. Cops and spies tend not to play well together. If an FBI agent tries to sting me, it forces me to defend myself. I'm an honest guy. If he does it is something minor, I just say no. He then tends to look dumb founded at a man who will not cooperate while his boss receives a phone call from someone in DC. Why are your people bothering that nice Mr. Harding? Oh, by the way, The White House said hands off. You do not charge American agents, you do not trophy hunt."

"An honest spy? I thought all your breed were bad bad boys Hardy?" and Hardy looked at her. Monique knew better, she was trying to set him up.

"We have our problem children we constantly keep getting into more trouble, you left me for one. Unless Joe is DEA now?" he said, Hardy now smiling. He just turned it around.

"So why are you telling me this Hardy? Sometimes you talk too much."

"I was a bastard, the poisoning, I owe you one. I consider you my agent, even if the reality is all women are doubles at best. The place is secure. And secrets are the way we pay the ladies within reason. You have some tid bits to keep yourself alive after I leave here."

"Bastard. Not with out me you don't." and Monique looked up and slyly smiled once again. "We are lovers Hardy—freebies?"

"We'll see," and Hardy reached down and grabbed the burning naked flesh of her inner thighs again while Monique once more let out a moan....

"Better then self-gratification?" Monique said looking down into the eyes of her lost lover after a shattering climax to seal their arrangement of agent-double, agent, friend and lover."

"Better. It was how I survived Monique, I almost did not make it in from the cold. And I was only a telephoneman. Makes you wonder what could happen or does at Langley. The sex was good."

"Sex?"

"Sex, and I like you on top. My arm but I like it."

"So you made up for it when things turned around?"

"I made up for my starvation of sex, played with ladies. Then Pam came along."

"It is not good politics Hardy to talk to one beautiful lover about another beautiful lover after you just made love to the first. When I was in the States, I saw her broadcast."

"So who do I toss?"

"Do you love me?"

"Yes but I am in love with Pam."

"Reoccurring lovers and a lot of sex?"

"Reoccurring lovers and a lot of sex," Hardy said, knowing what Monique really wanted was a larger role in his life, the role of being the only lover. Hardy knew she wanted his baby, the one that had constantly found a way to escape the happiness of her loving arms. But reoccurring lovers with a lot of sex was about to explode inside the cottage once again. Hardy stroking her curly silky soft black hair just kissed her and said, "come on, I'm ready, we'll make love this time..."

The following Tuesday had been rainy, grey, damp and extremely raw for August. Hardy had lit a fire and they had spent most of the morning making love and playing those silly romantic games women tend to love and men tend to hate unless we are getting laid. Amid the drizzle outside there had been a certain security which developed that week. It seemed to have arrived on Saturday, French law-enforcement were letting the locals feel a strong presents. It was now safe for Monique to come and go, though Hardy was wanted for questioning. Which was a game in itself. They knew who Monique was, they knew about the cottage, no bits and pieces of John Custer Harding's flesh were found amid the ruins of the car bombing. The French had decided to look the other way. Their strong presents in The Village Of Chembord had forced Carlos to pull back his people while the KGB were forced to keep their people inside and out of sight, or risk the covers of all their covert agents. The French were taking pictures.

Hardy had been feeling much better, his arm was now usable though his right side remained numb. He was even back to one arm love making, Monique liked it hard with her lover on top. In another month he would be able to use both arms to steady him in the saddle. The past week had been fun, the honeymoon that should have been for two who should have been married but never were. Hardy truly loved Monique but Monique was now in love. The cottage only adding to the intoxication of her romance, only setting her up for what Hardy told her could never be.

Each day Hardy was getting stronger, each day their love making would become more intense, each day their romance would blossom more. Both lovers building on tragedy when common sense should have guided their better judgment. It was no illusion, Hardy was in love. The honeymoon was real, Monique could see as much when she returned each day about three-thirty from what had become her daily trip to the village. Hardy was in love, she was in love. There were others but I am finally building a life, at least this is what Monique thought the following Thursday when she returned back to the nest again in the middle of a driving rain storm to find his note:

> *My dearest Monique,*
>
> *I have no regrets, no what ifs. I'm sorry, it wasn't meant to be. I have to travel eastward now, you understand.... Monique, I'm sorry.*
>
> *Affectionately Yours*
> *Hardy*
>
> *P.S. Someday.*
> *&*
> *I will be all right.*

CHAPTER 20

Thursday and Friday night had been spent mourning the death of her relationship with Hardy in the loving consoling arms of Monica, Cliffy's French-American wife. Monique knew it would all come to an end, she just did not expect the end to come so soon. Hardy was off to Germany, though in truth, and unknown to Monique, he had crossed into Belgium first. It was not so much being shattered by the loss or disappearance of love but the lack of time to prepare herself for his departure couple with the intense anger of receiving a dear Monique note. Only men should receive *Dear John* letters, were her thoughts of intense anger in the loving arms of Monica that Thursday evening:

No what ifs, who the hell does this man think he is? Though Monique knew Hardy, truth be known, she knew him too well. If not for tragedy always ripping their lives apart they may as well have been married. Unrequited love couple with *The War Of The Roses* tossed in, most of their lives they could not decide whether to kill each other or bed each other. Unrequited love with a twist for Hardy, they actually had a relationship. If all the good guys and the bad guys of this world would have left them alone they may even of had a life. In any case, Hardy felt it best that Thursday afternoon to cut his losses and get the hell out of there before Monique consumed him with her love and sent him off to be killed or worst. Worst, for there are worst fates in the spy game then death for an agent to fall victim of.

In any case, Monique was on fire with both love and anger with the tears, and the warm arms of Monica helping her deal with the crisis. She would. At Monica's advice she would stay the two extra weeks to get her life together before she started to rebuild her life again. Which was even more painful for Monique to talk about when she mentioned to Monica she had missed her period. She would stay for awhile, they would talk. Cliffy even had a position open at the chateau should Monique like to move from Paris.

❖ ❖ ❖ ❖ ❖

The sun was shining brilliantly that Saturday morning when Monique arose from her sleep, the cottage soothing her deep emotional pain. What a beautiful morning she thought to herself, a light breeze and not too hot. The wind outside playing gently with the flowers, which line the meadow and riding field where Cliffy's horses played. Monique thought to herself she would get dressed and join Cliffy and Monica for breakfast. She slipped on her sundress, combed her hair and brushed her teeth, though possibly not in that order, and hurried down the rough cut granite steps and walkway to the chateau below, with the gentle wind playing with her hair as she went along. As she approached the chateau she noticed something was not right. Too quiet, she thought to herself. Cliffy had two young French boys helping him out but perhaps they had the day off? But Cliffy himself was no where to be found. It was quiet, too quiet but extremely peaceful. Maybe they are upstairs making love, Monique thought. *It was a beautiful day to sleep late and make love, even if rainy days are better.*

When Monique entered the chateau she found Cliffy's body by the door, Monica was shot once in the head behind the concierge's desk. Before she even had time to gasp, Carlos put a gun to the back of her head.

"Hello Monique," Carlos said in his best stern sinister soft spoken Spanish voice.

"Carlos!" Monique gasped.

"I've come back for my lover Monique. You like being my lover? Don't you? You have been a very bad girl. The car is out back," Carlos said as he pointed the gun, leading Monique to the back door, passing the bodies of the two French teenagers along the way.

Monique was quietly weeping too afraid to cry out, too afraid to disobey Carlos. For Carlos it was a mix of Latin male pride and stupidity, he wanted to fuck her! rape her! When common sense in these affairs should have dictated to him to just have shot her. She was beautiful, he wanted answers. He now hated her but loved her flesh. Monique would be his sex slave, then Monique would be laid down. He now possessed something Hardy wanted, he hoped anyway. He did not know Hardy had been the one who left. He did not know of the dear Monique note, or of Monique having played these games before in Georgia and through her need of survival throughout her childhood for most of her life. Monique knew enough to keep her mouth shut. Carlos had been set up, Monique did not know if she would live. She knew how to play whore.

In the back of the black Mercedes sedan a quietly weeping Monique thought of Hardy, and how they were both so much alike. Hardy as a spy was of the middle of politics, stability in American politics being his only deep political belief. Both the extreme right, and the extreme left hated him. A man of the middle of the road often gets it from both sides. Monique was the same, half of her was black, the other half white. At times both communities hated her. Hated her for just being of both worlds. Hated her for just being born. Hated her for her beauty. Hated her for her flesh, though most jealous or secretly wanting to hate the model but make love to the flesh. They were the same in many ways. She now saw it in Carlos, he despised her but he wanted to fuck her flesh. Being of a South American mix Carlos should have been more understanding but he wasn't. And Monique quietly thought to herself while she weeped, *let Carlos devour my flesh, there are tricks to this game. I will stay alive. Sex slaves, I am sure Carlos has had many of them but he never has dealt with me before, not of such intensity in the fucking in games of whores.* But then she thought, *my period...*

Marcus Wolfe not only had lost a close friend to ricin poisoning in Paris, he had missed a chance to eliminate a plague before Hardy moved eastward spreading the spy game as he went along. His latest intelligence suggested John Custer Harding was either in Germany or about to enter Germany, which meant he was somewhere in Belgium, frozen still and ready to strike at his power base on German soil like a lioness about to procure dinner. Marcus could not let that happen. Any chance of laying the ground work to retake Europe, or at least reorganize the political structure in Europe more sensitive to his own ideology would be lost should Hardy succeed and the East lose the game. Sure, insulate their Socialism and intelligence operations through Beijing but Europe would still be a mess. A lost mess for the KGB and the rag tag leftovers of the Stasi. This was further complicated by the elimination of an agent by proxy by the name of Gemel. The Israelis were obvious out and about on German soil, and though open to some Socialist dogma, Israel comes first and Washington was their best friend—to a point. In any case, Marcus now had ties to terrorist and any chance of breaking or threatening the alliance between Washington and Jerusalem would be extremely difficult at best. It could not be done. Marcus himself was endanger of being shot. To endanger the alliance would be death, especially after it became known about Primakov's blunder and the betrayal by the Iranians. Though he was somewhat insulated from the Iranians, his ties to North Africa and the rest of the Islamic world were solid. Before Gemel was eliminated he did succeed in getting word to the people Gemel controlled, who respond with sending Marcus Wolfe two throw-away terrorists to substitute for the two men from the Groznyy area reportedly taken into custody in Belarus. Who were actually Iranians who reportedly committed suicide in some Moscow prison. The only words found on their suicide note read God is great, apparently just before a Russian prison guard at the behest of their FSB put a bullet in each of their heads to silence them about the atomic device they were carrying when they were found. The bomb would also be substituted. Smaller then the bread box the Russians confiscated but big enough to cause a lot of damage. People would be killed, the Americans and British would be blamed. The bodies of the Iranians would be kept frozen until needed when they would be mingled in with the flesh of the North Africans along with the note: God is great! Marcus had also been able to contact and keep a needed on going dialogue with Carlos through emissaries in the sublime of the spy game. Carlos knew what was expected of him if he were to have a long life. John Custer Harding was to be on Russian soil in October and in Moscow at a certain date. Carlos had taken one idea of Mr. Harding's ensnarement into personal custody having his fun with her flesh as he went along planning Mr. Harding's demise. He was working on the second, which was good news to Marcus Wolfe who sent a communiqué off to Moscow that all was going well.

Primakov responded by saying all was better, and though it was not quite by the balls, the Iranians would behave. They would be tagged with the mess if the Americans and British were not but Iran had played this role before and their two agents had also been well insulated from Tehran. They had spent many years in Afghanistan and the official word from Tehran was they had lost control of the two, this, even if the West had recently discovered photos of two meeting with their Iranian controllers.

But Iraq, Washington and Jerusalem, the Iranians were drawing the Americans in. The need to keep Saddam restrained over rode the common sense to keep diplomatic relations with Iran so distant that they would have to go to Mars first before they would be beamed back to Tehran. Which in this world of telecommunications is very possible, as recanted by Bill Clinton, though impractical none the less. Both the State Department and the folks at Langley were told to be extremely careful when dealing with Iran, and no more birthday cakes with inscribed Bibles. Bill Clinton was a student of history, history was not to be repeated. At Number Ten Downing Street, Tony Blair instructed Robin Cook and a few others of about the same. The Iranians were to be handled with kit gloves, no chances were to be taken. The deception by the Gremlin had been picked off by the West.

Hedi's was a popular place in Brussels for visiting American service men opting more for their excellent German beer over the French flavor of Belgium. It was there by instructions of his new laptop with training wheels borrowed from Cliffy, that he was to meet his American contacts. Hardy had by now learned the reality of how brutal the spy game became. Both Cliffy, his wife, and two boys were found dead at the Le Chateau-Borghese, he feared the worst for Monique, though years of tragedy and surprises in the spy game kept a tear from flowing from his eyes. You just get kind'a numb to it all, Hardy thought, as he watched his German beer cry out for a tear drop from within the darken confines of the crowded bar. The only light coming from the shrouded dark windows and the better lit restaurant to his right at the end of the bar.

Fred Credo had two buddies with him that day when he entered the bar; one, a tall thin man by the name of Ed. The second, a huge strapping man by the name of George. Both were Officers.

"Hello Hardy," Fred Credo said softly. "This is Ed and George, they belong to Gen. Clark's staff along with me. We wish to extend our condolences regarding your friends. We suspect your lover Monique is alive."

"I see..." Hardy took a few more moments to pause and change gears, stopped and spoke quietly, "Wiesbaden?"

"The text, as we discussed. Wiesbaden. It's on. You have an Israeli temporary wife who wants a rematch waiting for you there."

"She knows?"

"Eliminated a North African with a bullet with your name on it for you. Zaporah and her friends are providing cover for you Hardy, as long as you, we, keep quiet of the sensitivities Jerusalem became involved with at the end of The Southern Spy Affair. She wants to meet with you too Hardy."

"A trap?"

"Could be but the Israelis would pay a price. You are valuable, they are on our side. The General gives you a fifty-fifty chance that you survive the drop. The Israelis would like to keep you alive. Give and take, best for you to tell everyone it is all BS should anything sensitive come out. You are a writer, how would I know? You know the game. *Huh? what? and I don't know? Ridiculous!* We all have been there, just stay cool. You don't know..."

"What else?" asked Hardy, and Ed piped up of a refined gentlemanly manner.

"Langley has a *man in* in Bonn with some liaisons working with him at the annex in Berlin. Another guardian angel. He has been there since Atlanta, lost a close friend after you were almost hit in Paris, a Brit,

Henry Chatsworth. He does not want to lose you. Play it safe if you can. We don't want you to but you most likely will be walking into gunfire when you go to do the drop. Primakov, and the former head of the East German Stasi cannot let you make the drop. You know what you are up against."

"Yes." and Hardy looked suddenly very grave. "I'll make the drop," leaving Fred Credo with the warm assurance it would be done, and Fred knew it would. But also leaving Fred Credo with the realization of knowing Hardy may not make it. But coupled with the understanding he would be the only one who could. "When I was in Paris I met an old Cold Warrior, his name was Günther," and Hardy looked over to the three.

"He may be there, classified Hardy," and it was clear Hardy understood. "Hardy, the drop must be made outside the base, the army must not be tied to it. There will be people waiting for it. We can have no legal ties to those documents but we need them. Just talking with you sets us all up. The Russian foreign minister would have a field day with our State Department and military. People will be waiting for it, they will be well insulated," and Fred looked over to see an even graver looking Hardy aging about twenty years before his eyes. "My advice Hardy, make yourself noticed a few days before the drop. They will pick you up on their surveillance, the second or third day an Officer will come out and meet you. They have your picture. Stay in the town, the drop must be just outside the base," and Fred Credo looked over to see an even quieter and graver John Custer Harding. "Civilians Hardy, or ex-army, they will see that it is sent up the back door to the intelligence community;" Hardy was now just looking quietly and stressed at the three.

"I see."

Fred and his two friends now looked grave. "Hardy this is the press release from NATO Headquarters," and he handed it to Hardy. It had been a slow generic day filled with frivolous BS, though within the text was encrypted the information Hardy needed making totally no sense to anyone else who decided to read it frontwards, backwards or upside-down. It was written solely with John Custer Harding in mind. Hardy read it and knew immediately what the game plan was. Except there was one deception left in place that Hardy was not to do, Fred smiled warmly when he saw how keen Hardy had become. "It was left there in case the enemy became curious, they have. We threw them a curve ball," and Hardy just gently snickered and quietly laughed.

"I see," Hardy said at the death snare and laid trap for the KGB.

"They will be waiting Hardy, be careful."

Hardy had stayed for another hour after the three liaison Officers of Gen. Clark's staff had left to give them all cover. He then went back to his room to pack, he would leave for Bonn and someplace call Zeckendorf Gardens that evening. He trusted Zaporah but one never knows with an agent of another government. Fred Credo had assured Hardy the Israelis would play fair. Unbeknown to Hardy, the General's Staff had labeled Hardy a thief, a womanizer and an extremely gifted liar, which apparently was the reason for his departure from Caliber Communications. Hardy's credibility was shot. Deader then Hardy if he did not succeed on his mission.

Zeckendorf Gardens was quiet and sleepy. The trees keeping the gentle warm breeze at bay, the water was still. A warm mid August morning, like the ones in early June in Greenwich, hot, sleepy, with high clouds filtering in. A soft summer time Zaporah was getting use to before Yossi whisked her away to Europe where she now sat quietly for both friend and lover while her thoughts darted in and out about the new prime minister, and if the change in directions would help her country in Israel's long lost quest for peace, her peoples long lost quest for peace.

"Good morning Zaporah."

"Good morning Yossi."

"How are the ducks this morning?"

"They ate well, I am all out of bread."

"You look like you have had some of their breakfast. You need to keep your weight down, we may have more work to do on motorbikes."

"I will. Everything is so still, so peaceful and warm. Such a sleepy day. Is anyone keeping watch?"

"I have a man," and Yossi looked over pointing with his eyes to one of his agents across the way on a park bench at the north end of the park. "When he comes I will pull back to the south side and give you some time alone. We are being watched Zaporah. Both the BND and the enemy."

"I see."

But time did not ellipse too long before her lost husband showed up, Hardy just smiled and said "Hi" quietly and politely.

"Hardy this is my adopted big brother Yossi."

"Hi, I am John Harding, Hardy," and Hardy shook hands gently with Yossi. It was a hand shake of respect not indifference, or an attempt to challenge his own authority of his own world. It was obvious, the two respected each other from the start.

"It is good to finally meet you Hardy. Now I leave you alone so the two of you can talk," and then Yossi said quietly, "we are being watched, I have a man on the north side, I move to the south," and Yossi looked over to see Hardy ask the next question with his eyes. "Both, the enemy and the BND—the BND are on their own side... Now I leave for awhile."

Hardy watched Yossi walk away, disappear behind a tree line and reappear to keep watch at the far end of the park opposite his other agent, as Zaporah stood up from the bench to gently and warmly exchange the kiss she needed so badly from Hardy, his arms instinctively finding their way around her waist.

"You are getting chubby," and Hardy kissed her again, while Zaporah gently forced herself away.

"It is not fat Hardy, it is yours. So tell me John Custer Harding...How have you been?"

"I was careful."

"I was not, I wanted your baby."

"How?"

"That night, when we went a few times. You do not shoot blanks, nor are you conservative with your seed. Condoms and a turkey baster. It took. You left me three filled on the floor."

"Damn you."

"I like my life Hardy, you like babies I hear. Now you have a reason to visit Jerusalem. A Jewish baby."

"My son is half Jewish."

"Mummy?"

"No, Pam's father is a Jew."

"Well now you have a full Jewish baby."

"Well, if we were married I would challenge you on theology. And you don't want me as a husband?"

"No. I want your baby, and I want you compromised. You will like Jerusalem Mr. John Custer Harding," and Hardy could see Zaporah both serious and amused. "You come visit me and your baby. We talk," and Zaporah just smiled. She had the upper hand and she had what she wanted. Hardy would not have to defect but he would have to be more flexible. Quietly, behind his smile, he realized he would never work for another phone company, not covertly in deep cover, and thought to himself it would be best if he just stayed with writing and become good at his new craft. Another thong had come back to haunt him. "Why so quiet Mr. John Custer Harding? You like babies," and Zaporah just warmly smiled, looking more beautiful in Hardy's eyes then when she picked him up in the nightclub in Tel Aviv.

"Life is messy, I was hoping to have a normal life one day."

"You will but you will have many babies. Now shh, Yossi does not know. I retire after this, I am a mummy," and Hardy looked over to where Zaporah's eyes were pointing to see Yossi return, taking his time along the way in.

"You come over tonight, we talk, we make love, Yossi stops by," and Zaporah knew she had seduced him by her voice and cute sabra smile. "Every once and awhile you stop by Jerusalem Mr. John Custer Harding, we make love, you spend time with your child," Zaporah demanded.

"No husband, no new lover?"

"I am, as you say Mr. John Custer Harding, 'Cosmopolitan.' I spent time with too many boys in the army. Me and your baby, I do not need a husband Mr. John Custer Harding. You come visit us, we be a family when I need you," and Zaporah looked over with amusement and displayed serious understanding. Hardy had been had but Hardy was taking it all in stride. "Now, before Yossi gets here, where?"

"Wiesbaden, the south gate," and Hardy paused a bit and then changed gears. "You know you really are beautiful in this state." Zaporah knew she made a very beautiful expectant mom but changed the subject before she spoke, business first, she thought.

"Weisbaden. Good. You stop by tonight Mr. John Custer Harding, we talk..."

Monique sat quietly weeping in the backseat of the black Mercedes watching Hardy, Zaporah and Yossi walk slowly out of the park. Crying, though too scared to scream out. If she did she would be instantly killed.

"Tell me you'll do it! or I'll have my men shoot him right now Monique," Carlos said more then forcefully to a Monique too emotional and sobbing to answer his questions, as he shook her like a rag doll with his rough arm on her's. Only to have Monique break down to such a state it almost carried through the sound proofing of the luxury car. "Do it!" Carlos demanded again and again to the point he was hurting her both physically and emotionally. Then suddenly Monique broke.

"OK, OK, I will," she said to Carlos in-between sobs.

Back in Atlanta a more subdued Special Agent In Charge John Blacke was readying his effort to help Hardy out in the wake of the brutal knifing of his good friend Henry Chatsworth. Henry's men in return for their lead agents murder had turned markedly vicious when dealing with the KGB stragglers left in the Atlanta area. Even to the point of the enemy calling the FBI to have Special Agent In Charge John Blacke instruct one of his men to advise the man to file a complaint with the British Embassy in Washington. Whatever Henry's men were doing, it was unpleasant but the FBI had no weight or control over what the

British government does or does not do. No law apparently had been broken, and set up as they were, there was nothing the FBI could do, or would do after the murder of Henry Chatsworth.

It was about mid morning that hot August Atlanta day when John's secretary Jennifer came in with the file. Both France and Germany had a North African terrorist problem gift wrapped by Iran and Hezbollah and exported from Southern Lebanon. In Chad there was a cell of such vermin, and all intelligence reports suggested they were on their way to Austria and to be infiltrated into Europe wherever needed. After a series of calls to the U.S. Attorney in Atlanta, a couple of calls to the State Department and a communiqué marked extremely sensitive from somewhere in the intelligence community, Chad had agreed to expel the top eight of the group to Guinea where they would be detained and placed forcibly on a plane to The United States to face further charges for their part of our two African Embassies the year before. A conviction was iffy but they could be charged and detained; detained for a very long time and taken out of play. Without these lead men, Hezbollah, or Osidim bin Laden would be unable to function their operations in Europe, and at the very same time make it more difficult to infiltrate the United States by way of Canada or by any other means. It was the least he could do for the memory of Henry Chatsworth, or for Hardy, who's dad's file now kept company with the other notable papers on his desk. John Blacke saw his chance, and now everyone who was anybody of the opposition in the spy game or in the world of terrorists were about to get it stuck up their ass. From the former Stasi to the KGB to the terrorists of North Africa to Afghanistan, more then a few were going to fall. The opposition were about to enter the Superbowl minus eight of their most important players. And poor Col. Harding on his death bed with the scum are all over him. It was the least he could do. But before he picked up his pen to send the whole affair into motion his final thoughts were *Good! They get what they deserve!*

In Moscow, Primakov had just very quietly left Office, making room for a younger more youthful prime minister. Behind the scenes Yevgeny Primakov would still pull the strings. Intelligence still rules even after the fall of The Soviet Union. The younger Mr. Putin himself was a highly trained animal of the intelligence world. A good student of Primakov himself, and Yevgeny knew it. *Meet the new boss same as the old boss* but with a new younger more aggressive body. Vladimir's one disadvantage, he was impulsive, though Yevgeny had much faith in him.

The betrayal of the Iranians was clear, it in return had cost him his job. But now he still controlled things from behind the scenes and Prime

Minister Putin was doing a damn good job. There would be a note worthy incident of intelligence value but the game was now being played fair. In the end if all went right either the Iranians would get the blame or Washington would be tied to the mishap. In any case the penance of Tehran would be to get slapped for their indiscretion, they should have known better. Playing one super power against another is not very good for the security of ones own nation. But now the spy game had turned deadly, the Iranians taking most of the hit on their own people. Primakov did not want to lose this one, even if nuclear volleyball was taken off the table. There were real issues involved here, France was starting to lisp and lean the wrong direction for Moscow. The documents; and the need for them with a more hospitable French aerospace industry. The documents were the key, if he could not stop Hardy, in this case stop meant dead with the documents safely destroyed, or better yet, somewhere in the Gremlin, then the FSB would have to out play the Americans and the British in the end game. Their last chance would be the drop. According to Marcus Wolfe a back up plan had been devised should Hardy succeed. The game was in motion, the Iranians were freaking out.

Down at the creek and beyond to the Potomac the ducks and other water fowl of a conservationist note were all healthy and playful like his grand kids, who a dying Col. Harding watched play from his bedroom window. They apparently would stay that way as long as Col. Harding supplied his sugarcoated shit breath interrogator with information. The poor man's bio poisoning of the ducks had stop, both the children and the wildlife seem safe. Gladas, their gifted psychiatric nurse turned hospice care giver was doing her job. Col. Harding readied his thoughts for their next exchange, which was to come very shortly. He could hear Gladas out in the hallway.

"Col. Harding, how are you today?" Gladas being her condescending self.

"Oh, hi sweetheart, what have you brought me today?"

"Soup, homemade Col. Harding."

"Uuum, I love soup," Col. Harding doing his best to butter Gladas up.

"So, Col. Harding, your son never mention to you about the intrigue he was involved in Atlanta. Come-on, you can tell Gladas."

"No, I was in Belgium, Hardy was in Atlanta. He kept to himself to protect us, did not even tell Dave he was homeless. Wouldn't tell me. Oh, Gladas, I feel so good today," and Col. Harding looked over to see Gladas taken back in her thoughts while reading her mind: Too much pain medication, I can take care of that.

"Tet, you told me about Tet last time, what a mess. Must of felt good when you broke down and got it off your soul?" He hadn't but Gladas took hook, line and sinker.

"Yes, I lost a lot of friends. Buddies, some like brothers. God it hurts to think about it."

"You mentioned the *Pablo* sometime back, do you still remember?"

"A little bit... Not too much. Let me think;" Col. Harding was back to his old conjuerian self, his deception not picked up by Gladas. "The word was at the time that The *USS Pablo* had grabbed about a third of The Cold War. This being the reason she was boarded by the North Koreans. I really do not know if this is true."

"I see Col. Harding. You don't...?"

"No, I was in Vietnam..." and Col. Harding could see the wheels inside the mind of Gladas spin while she obviously looked for a reason to cut her visit short.

"And you don't know..? Not for sure..?"

"Well that was the word. I really do not know for sure." He did, and Gladas was taking all the way.

"Oh...I see. Let me get you some fruit slices with that Col. Harding, you'll like the juice," and Col. Harding could see Gladas was looking for a reason to get out of there...Upon her return her beeper went off, which was a pretty good trick in itself. "Oh, Col. Harding, I have to cut our little visit short. I'm so sorry," but she did reward him with an extra drip of pain medication before she left. Col. Harding just smiled and did his best to waive good-bye; hell should be fun.

❖　❖　❖　❖　❖

"Hello, is Miss Wellington available?"

"Who is calling?" Dana DiMaggio inquired.

"My name is Monique Gaudinier, it's about Hardy."

"She was just feeding the baby, I will see if she can come to the phone."

A few moments later Pam Wellington picked up the receiver, having stabled and readied herself for some small talk with the other woman. "Hello Monique, this is Pam. What do you want?" Pam being somewhat more blunter than usual, the security of her love affair being threatened. "We need to talk."

"Hardy and I are in love Monique, I have his baby."

"I know. I love him too. We became lovers again in France, Pam."

"I know, he told me. Hardy and I live an unconventional life because we have to, not because we want to."

"I know, he left me. I thought I had him back. Sorry."

"You called from France to tell me you were sorry?"

"No, no we need to talk. Is there anyway you can meet me?"

"Monique, I do not go to France for coffee."

"But he wants to see the baby now?"

"Yes."

"So if you find your way here, he loves the baby Pam, he told me so, will you look me up?"

"OK."

"But please, do not tell him I called. Please...? He is yours, but please...?"

"OK, I may be going to the MidEast soon; Dad."

"Here is my cell phone number and country code, I am traveling throughout Europe now, I will be back in France soon. OK?"

"OK."

"Thanks Pam," and Monique hung-up.

Standing by Monique was a very vicious Carlos who listened to every word.

"You did very good Monique, now we fuck!" and he grabbed her and threw her down on the bed. "I don't make love to whores who betray me! We fuck, you're a good lay," Carlos said in broken English. Monique now knowing enough to keep quiet and try to enjoy the rape.

In Atlanta Dana came over to comfort Pam, knowing how upsetting a call from the other woman, or that woman! can be after a lady had just given birth. "What does she want Pam?" a consoling Dana asked as she put her arms around Pam Wellington.

"She wants to meet me when I am overseas with Dad."

"Can you?" though Dana's real meaning was, would it be a good idea?

"I don't know. If I go to Israel, Hardy wants me to stay there. The baby and me would only become a target."

"But...?"

"But Monique and I should talk..."

CHAPTER
21

It had started about noon, hell, she thought, it had started as soon as I opened door and readied the bar. The first few stragglers who wandered into The South Gate Pub, just outside the south gate of Wiesbaden, were as gray as the sky. Along with the service men stationed at Wiesbaden who wander in the evening, the noon time crowd was always sprinkled with retired or ex service men who settled in Germany for one reason or another. The mood for active, inactive, retired or ex service men was the same, dark, extremely dark. The atmosphere was oppressive, ominous, like the locker room before the big game. The drop would come that night. When, they did not know. Just after dark to midnight, the Friday night crowd providing cover for the spy. Spies are real trouble, spies that are yours, are even worst. It was the folklore handed down from the top, in reality, it was the truth sent down the chain of command.

The first five stragglers who drifted in were ex service men from the Vietnam war, they all had served together and had seen much combat as Army Rangers during the conflict. They were quiet, sullen, about as ghostly as the figure across the street at the American McDonalds sipping his coffee at a table outside in the unseasonable cool damp August weather. The Rangers were gray, the spook whoever he was, was ghostly.

Rumors dispatched down from the rumor mill at the base mentioned a KGB agent by the name of Patwijec in the area. The bar crowd as it silently expanded did not know who the spook was, or who he was working for. Though he did seem more German then Russian. Russian agents stand out to American service men. All spies stand out to service men, though Russian agents tend to be polar opposites in personality and mannerisms. They play a slightly different game with a very different style. American agents drop their documents at American or British bases. Russian agents try to acquire, steal or pick off documents at American or British bases. American agents tend to be more soldier then spy, they make their drop and do their job out of love of country. They have their own cover. Though they are spy. Russian agents are a spy personality, they look for a handler and try to exchange their gift for money. There's a difference, and whoever this man Hardy was, *he had balls*, she thought, *and I am hanging out too much with the guys*. Though the entire bar crowd had the same feelings, this man has balls. The spook at the McDonald's across the street reminding them all to keep their mouths shut.

The drop when it came would come in the middle of the island by the statue of a fallen Prussian war hero, which divided the road between the South Gate Pub and the McDonalds. Should the agent step foot on the base he was to be shot, U.S. Intelligence were to have no ties to the documents they needed. The MP at the guard shack was as dark as the bar crowd. It would be that night, he thanked God he was off at six. The ex Army Rangers would provide cover, a retired colonel would see the papers were sent up the back door to the intelligence community. All as they gathered around noontime at the bar were stressed and dark. They could have no ties to it. Across the street they watched the spook place his paper coffee cup in the garbage and fade away behind the building.

Along with spooks of opposing ideology and nationality, the BND and the remnants of the Stasi were out and about along with a handful of Middle East types, who were obvious terrorists or could be. Mixed in, a handful of German gangsters were making a showing, who intelligence was able to get the word to their covert operation at The South Gate Pub were controlled by either the KGB or former Stasi, or both. The gangsters could not be trusted, the documents were needed. No one ever really knows but the dark clouds had been gathering around the pub, the ones who had been there prepared themselves for a fire fight that night. Even the weather told them so; dark, damp, a full cloud cover.

Across to the McDonald's a younger looking spook appeared to take the place of the old German, by his walk and mannerism they could tell he was the American. Like the two days before he finished his coffee and headed over to the visitor center saying hello to the MP and tripping up a security clearance as he went along like he had done in the past. He was obviously making himself known. By the photo sent down by intelligence that morning, they could see that this man was John Custer Harding. The drop was obviously on for that evening. Inside the base in a small room in a wing marked restricted area-off limits, an undercover CIA agent listed as a diplomatic attaché by the name of Robert Torres was meeting with the top brass of the base and their people in Army Intelligence.

"Hardy? John Custer Harding knows where and how to drop them, he has done this before. Hardy is the only one who can. We really have to keep ourselves insulated in this fashion, or the KGB, FSB will play us back if anything should go wrong. The statue is classified, anyone who comes in contact with the old Prussian war hero is Classified," then Robert Torres paused and then added. "This whole affair is now 'classified' at the highest levels. France is pivotal, the French are playing dumb. Not just my people, it came down from the NSC at The White House; right from the top," and Robert Torres looked over to see Gen. Fitzpatrick look grave. "Your men General?"

"My men are well insulate Robert, our operation should be alright. The drop may take an unconventional route out of Europe. Robert, I am worried about your man Harding. After he makes the drop, I could have him shot? It would be better."

"If you have to. We do not do that anymore, I have no control over the army. But General, Hardy himself is well insulated. They did a number on him when he left Caliber, he will never work for another large communications company again. Hardy as much as I like him has no credibility. He has another spy affair to go to after this. If at all possible, my people want him alive. John Custer Harding is very valuable to us. He has become a pretty good writer according to MI6 and their people at *The Weekly Empire & Word Report*. Hardy is useful, only if you have to. He knows the score. We have done this before, it will go well."

"Same place I remember," General Fitzpatrick added, smiling at Robert Torres.

"Maybe a little bit to the left or the right this time," and Robert Torres gently laughed.

"Robert, here is the latest photos from intelligence, you recognize Günther Von Müller?"

"Yes, we were keeping track of Günther back in Atlanta before my friend Henry Chatsworth was murdered."

"I didn't know, I knew Henry. Where?"

"Outside our embassy in Paris, this spy affair."

"I did not know, your man Hardy will survive. I'll force him over to MI6. Let the British have fun. Now the other two, and then we have the enemy. I'll save the BND for last."

"These two are Israelis. The man, his name is Yossi Cohen. The lady is simply called Zaporah. They use her a lot, we never really know her last name. The Israelis have more people in the area. When we are finished, I have my own photos for you General."

"She's pregnant Robert, we suspect your man Harding."

"Damn him," Robert said quietly and smiled.

"Now we have the enemy..."

Robert Torres was just finishing up lunch at the Officers Commissary when a young captain on Gen. Fitzpatrick's staff approached him while he finished his rice pudding.

"Excuse me sir, are you Mr. Torres?"

"Yes."

"Gen. Fitzpatrick wanted you to know, Army Intelligence picked off the signal your man gave us. The drop is confirmed for tonight."

"Good," Robert Torres said to the young Captain quietly. "Let the General know I will be in in a little while."

"Yes sir."

"Oh, and Captain, thank you."

"Thank you sir."

When Robert Torres returned from lunch to his cubical setup for him inside the offices of Army Intelligence he placed a flurry of calls and communiqués over secure lines to London, Washington, Paris, Berlin, Bonn and Atlanta. Though all were trusted at the highest security clearance, better judgment should have over ridden common sense but people who needed to know needed to know. Other events throughout the world were being choreographed for that evening, everyone who was anyone in the intelligence community in the West was on edge. The drop would be made, casualties most likely would occur. The Israelis were in, the enemy had decided to insulate themselves with terrorists. Assurances were given Hardy would be protected if possible. On the phone from Sam Berger's second in command at the NSC, Robert received just a warm and gentle thank you.

Monique had been sobbing uncontrollably when Carlos entered the room to give her the bad news, which would further insure his position in the scheme of worldly politics should all go right. Hardy would be walking into open gunfire, Carlos and a few others had people in place.

By the time Carlos had finished and left the room after only tossing out two or three brief lines in broken English, Monique totally went to pieces. First Hardy, then she would be next. Carlos would probably say good-bye by raping her first. She just sat curled up in the corner crying like the babies she was never allowed to deliver. The room was cold and void of all affection like Carlos, she would only exchange one coffin for another. Her weeping could be heard from down the hall.

❖ ❖ ❖ ❖ ❖

At the McDonald's outside the gate at Wiesbaden, Zaporah and Yossi had done their own reconnaissance that morning, passing Hardy on their motorbike outside an ice-cream parlor down the street, while Hardy did a little Parisian to make himself known before they stopped at the McDonald's to exchange cold glances with an unlikely ally. Everyone in the village was spooked, if not for the sound of the motorbike one could hear themselves breathe or their heart pound. As such often happens in the wake of expectant human drama who's only real secret was that the folks with any real common sense could not talk of it, or what was obviously in the near future. For the most part, people just stayed indoors.

The BND watched the whole pre-game show unfold, like our FBI, a crime must be committed first. The village was more oppressive for more reasons then the residents of the tiny village inside the city of Wiesbaden knew. Both forces of good and evil were out to play in full force.

It was just after dark when Hardy started out in his rental, the steady drizzle had let up to a fine mist. The documents rested next to him in the right passenger seat tightly wrapped in black plastic to protect them from the weather. In the rear view mirror Hardy saw headlights but they turned off or faded away without any set pattern. He did not know if he was being followed, he suspected he was not. The ride from where he was staying would take about forty-five minutes. He would take his time and check the mirror with frequency along way. He would make the approach to Wiesbaden from the North, circle around the base and approach the main gate from the south.

Quietly he drove with the radio receiver down low until he came close to the lights of city while he checked his mirror to find security of no enemy or the illusion of one. He passed to the north and found the exit to the south, stopping once to let a pushy German by, his foot perched on the excellerator in case the motorist was a terrorist. He then proceeded down the road to a back street slowly finding his way down into the village, passing The Church Of The Sacred Heart along the way where he would slow up and pull off to check his watch. The timing was important.

It would take another ten minutes; timing. Hardy slowly pulled out and proceeded down the street passing a museum and hotel, then driving another mile till he neared the reservoir. When he reached the soccer stadium he slowed and reached over to grasp the bundle of documents with his right hand, steadying the wheel with his left. A few more thousand feet down the road he would make a full stop and turn left.

The approach though the village to the south gate was chilling in it's desolation, it could have been a shut down mining town in New Mexico, it was only missing tumble weeds. Hardy lacked a 45 Colt, true spies do not carry guns. Too often they turn up at crime scenes with your finger prints on them; planted and setup by the KGB. Though Hardy could recall as he made his final approach that he knew some covert operatives who did.

As he approached the monument with the statue of the Prussian general he heard a motorbike pull out. Just beyond the statue he could see the MP turn sheet white as all hell broke loose! What happen next or in what order Hardy could not recall. To his right Zaporah had opened fire on about three or four North Africans with a very compact Israeli built Ouzzi submachine gun from the back of their motorbike. To the right he caught a glimpse of Günther Von Müller eliminating some Russian agent by the name of Patwijec with one shot to the head!

When he reached the monument Hardy slammed the car into park! opened the door and ran the few steps he needed to toss the package at the foot of the statue, as a handful of gangsters under the guidance of Carlos opened up on Hardy with automatic weapons fire! Only to be met by the retired Army Rangers from across the way who had taken up positions just outside The South Gate Pub. Hardy tossed the drop and crawled back to the car while a wounded but still functional Army Ranger crawled to retrieve the drop watching Hardy give him cover with his bullet riddled rental before Hardy bolted out the place like a shot himself! jumping the curve of the island! and making a U-turn to safety. The unforeseen change in Hardy's direction and temperament with the thunder clap of noise it generated of car chrome and concrete allowing the Ranger to scampering back to the waiting arms of his buddies. Who disappeared with their comrade on their shoulders down some alley and into the woods beyond the village. The change in Hardy's predicted pattern had caught the enemy off guard. The car was shot full of holes, Hardy was not.

The next day the report on AP simple read: *Thirteen narco-terrorists were shot to death in what apparently was an Israeli lead raid by their Mossad intelligence agency. One bystander, a Russian citizen, was also killed. The Office Of the Prime Minister in Jerusalem issued a terse: No Comment. However, the spokesman for the new prime minister did add, the Israeli people and their government are dedicated in their fight against global terrorism and of the enemies of Israel. "We are united," the spokesman was quoted as saying before he handed the press release to the pool reporters.*

The report from AP went on further to say: *A spokesman for the American base at Wiesbaden, said, "no Americans were killed, all active duty personal stationed at Wiesbaden are accounted for. The German Government had no comment but did add, the BND are investigating."*

Hardy had stayed in bed late the next morning, he just smiled when he heard the report on the radio. Zaporah had had a rough night, he just gently cuddled her naked flesh and stroked her shoulder length black hair. Her condition was obvious, life is messy. She was now retired, to celebrate Hardy would make her breakfast in bed. He now had a reason to visit The Holy Land.

Later that day, the BND reported back to all the right people in Berlin after their initial investigation was complete; John Custer Harding had apparently spent the entire evening making love to his pregnant Israeli lover. There was no further need to investigate the two.

CHAPTER
22

Hardy sat up in bed and toyed with his laptop. From the bed he could catch glimpses of Zaporah in the bathroom combing her hair, getting herself ready to leave. He would miss her but in the meantime he returned to his screen.

Oh, what is this...? Charged but deferred for an intelligence value. P.S., Atlanta law-enforcement loves you. God damn them...Someone playing games...?

"Mr. John Custer Harding, the baby and I have to leave now, you come visit us..?" and Zaporah leaned down and gave Hardy a kiss while he moved the laptop to one side and watched the magic screen disappear at the same time; Zaporah's right hand giving a warm and playful tug to his manhood, as Yossi honked the horn of the sedan outside. "You come visit your baby and me Mr. John Custer Harding," Zaporah demanded in a playful verse.

"I will," and Hardy kissed her good-bye.

The Middle East? Maybe? but Hardy suspected she first had some more loose ends to tie up on European soil....And the magic screen, Vera, and God, I hope she is not pregnant too...? he whispered to himself, as their car slowly drove off. Then he turned back to the screen and reflected quietly to himself: Three lovers and someday I may have to deal with the devil to keep them all alive. Don't these girls have any common sense? Couldn't they have someone else's baby? Monique, God I hope not, and I have had enough tragedy in my life.

Hardy took his time and slowly packed that morning, Vera and a man by the name of Leon Hess were waiting for him in Berlin. By the intelligence memos received in this new world of high-tech spy games, Hardy was informed all was well in France, though Trevor had much work to do and would be bogged down for a season or two. The joint networks of Carlos and Marcus Wolfe were being exposed and rolled back. Their people being played back on their East German controllers and handlers, or the South American drug lords who were filling the void left by Carlos. It was chaos for the enemy.

Not far away in another part of Wiesbaden a wild and off the wall Carlos was going berserk! Monique going to pieces besides him. Though it was a good hysteria, Hardy had survived the drop, Carlos was too stressed to rape her.

Carlos in his wild and uncontrollable mind knew what he would have to do next. Drug lords and gangsters are clumsy, though he still did not wish to have any concrete ties. He would by the end of the afternoon. It would most likely cost him his life. But then he thought, eliminating people works both ways. My people are more brutal then those of Marcus Wolfe.

Though in the sublime and shadowy world of spies, just the thoughts Carlos had of betrayal could have him killed by the end of the afternoon. A controller of a master spy like Marcus Wolfe is so in-tuned he could read a mind by the tension of a subjects skin. It was no secret both the former Stasi and KGB had big problems with Carlos Sanchez.

By two-thirty in the afternoon on that late August day, a cash transfer was made by Laredo Cable to an off shore account of an executive vice president involved with production at DNN, Pam Wellington would have both an assignment and an extended vacation after her visit with friends in Israel was over. Hardy would see his baby boy, the DNN Moscow bureau had work for Pam Wellington, his daughter's schooling at the university would be funded. The story Pam would be seeking for her news magazine involved Russian orphans. A good deal for everyone.

Monique had made a point to become a pleasant nuisance to Pam by calling her a few times a week, Monique genuinely loved babies. If not for the competition, Pam and Monique would most likely have been best of friends had they actually known each other in Atlanta. So it was not so unusual, or even a tip off, when Monique placed one of her many weekly phone calls to Pam Wellington to set her up and keep herself alive at the same time. Though deep down Pam did realize something was just not right. The reading of another woman's thoughts of a woman such as Monique can be hazy at best, and it was. But what Pam was picking up was Monique's over active mind trying to save herself and keep everyone alive. Carlos was dark, life was getting shorter. Monique had to devise a plan and at the same time keep it from Pam.

The phone call was brief, something just was not right but Monique could be in Moscow in October. It was best they all sit down and talk. Monique had done good, one of Carlos's men listened to the whole call. This time Monique would be rewarded by not being raped. Carlos was too stressed for sex anyway. The kind of stress that leaves an over hung Latin looking like he had a peanut between his legs. It would be awhile until Carlos could function. In the next room over Carlos was dark, darker then any of his men had ever seen him. He had also become extremely paranoid.

By that evening word had reached Marcus Wolfe everything was in motion. Word had also gotten back to Marcus of how paranoid Carlos had become. He sat and thought quietly in his study amongst his books for about a half hour and then readied a communiqué to be sent to Yevgeny Primakov. *All was not well but the end game was in motion.* He sent with it his condolences regarding his agent Patwijec. The end game would be played, Primakov would not be there, Czechoff would. On his return communiqué, Primakov agreed: It was best if Marcus stayed in Germany in October.

It helps when you can have the local station in Bonn cover up for a bullet riddled rental, I guess that is why we recruit car dealers and men who work in German autobody shops to work undercover for the U.S. Intelligence. Hardy felt it best to take a small plane to Berlin.

Drops... You never really know when you do drops... You always know you are in danger... Sometimes you drop it and walk away... Sometimes all hell breaks loose... You always assume a gun is pointed at you... The other night I was lucky, I should have been killed... Though I recall having done more dangerous and dramatic drops; less gunfire but better then the other night. Still. Borrowed time. I guess I am lucky..? You never know... When your number is up, it's up... And God, I hope this little puddle jumper does not crash. You never really know....

It was not so much Hardy was changing sexuality as it was he had had enough of women and babies for awhile. There was one loose end to tie up, and the thought of being tied up by Vera did weigh heavy on his soul. Once he settled in and took a tour of Berlin he would meet with her. Their sex that night in Pristina was fun, the fun sex you often lose in intense relationships. And God, I hope she is not pregnant. Fatherhood was fastly catching up with John Custer Harding, he truly was hoping to someday lead a normal life. The friendship with Vera was what he now wanted to nurture, sexual or not. He truly cared about his one time adversary.

In the meantime he had call Georgetown to check up on Dad. Dad was still dying but Dad was doing better, resting comfortably. Bonnie had placed the portable by him so they could chat briefly. He wished his dad well, his dad did the same. Word had gotten back to Col. Harding that Hardy had almost beaten him to the promised land.

On the agenda that week was a trip around the sites. The Brandenberg Gate is a place every spy or former Cold Warrior should visit. It was first on his list, and maybe a chunk of the Wall to take back home if he could find one, buy one, steal one or snooker some colleague out of a chunk at the embassy annex in Berlin.

The new site and politics of the American Embassy was on Hardy's list as well. Political turmoil always intrigued Hardy. He wondered if it was the Italian Mafia or the German gangsters who were looking for a payoff so the embassy could be built. Apparently, even in Germany palms must be greased before construction projects get off the ground. But for now he had a full plate and some time to play. He thought he would do a couple of clubs that night, the magic screen wishing him luck but advising him to be careful. *Some time to play, and God, I wish Pam were home.*

Robert Torres had been ecstatic! Along with a big win came the news Hardy was safe, the documents delivered and safely on their way themselves to wherever sensitive documents go when all parties need deniability. Only the right eyes of the right people who twist the right arms would know or have access to them. A couple of politicians in France who really deserved to be stung had been.

And now, as the spy game turned eastward, so had Robert Torres as he set up shop in the Berlin annex with a handful of FBI agents who were listed as legal attachés. Robert himself was listed in the diplomatic corp, his cover was simply diplomatic attaché. Just one of many political officers who worked in Germany. He too now had time to rest. The only item on his plate that afternoon was a face to face meeting with Leon Hess of The Institute Of Electricity Of Culture & Foreign Affairs. Leon had a slightly more dangerous job then Robert with a more markedly deeper cover. Leon was to have a one to one with Hardy that evening. There were items of importance of geopolitics, science and intelligence that needed to be gone over and discussed before Leon was to meet with Hardy. They had time, the afternoon was theirs, they would take it slow; one item at a time. Hardy needed to know. Magic screens can at times be picked off by the enemy, nor do they tell an agent the stress level of the spy game a face to face meeting can provide. Leon was the best in the business, the briefing would start at one.

Smyles had been a popular erotic night club and cabaret during the Cold War, frequented by most all U.S. Service men when they were stationed in Berlin. The girls were upscale and high class, the dancing was fully nude. Back in the old days of the Cold War at the height of the intrigue, both the East and the West had their deep cover plants inside.

In truth, most of the ladies were doubles. In the spy game most all women regardless of placement in life are double agents. The physical weakness of a smaller body and the need to protect offspring predisposing a lady to the role of double agent when she enters the spy game. Beauty, sex and seduction making women not only hybrids but naturals as double agents. There are some exceptions to the rule but these are far and few between. *Never trust a woman* young soldiers are told by loving sergeants, unless you are prepared to be a total bastard Hardy would add. And we all hope you like babies. In truth, like any other double agent, it depends who has the better hold on the agent. If the devil to the right is going to kill, and the devil to the left is going to kill, you do what you believe is right. But this does not take away the fact that all women are doubles.

And it was at Smyles in the mix of two worlds of the oldest professions that Leon Hess found John Custer Harding sitting in an eloquent white patio chair with a very beautiful and mostly naked dancer by the name of Starr in his lap, as he watched a fully naked dancer with dark hair do her routine on the stage displayed in front of him. Hardy just seemed to have that little something that the ladies like, and it was obvious the two were in competition vying for his affections. Though Hardy did seem to have his hands full with the beautiful blond in the rainbow thong and matching string top.

Hand lotion and naughty dancing, it was time to give the ladies a rest. Too many babies were entering his life and he hadn't been told about Monique yet. Secretly he really did hope she had survived and was alive. Smyles, and a few other dens of inequity; Hardy thought to himself *he would enjoy Berlin for the next month or two.*

As his supply of dollar bills and German marks dwindled, the affections of Starr continued. Though a working girl is a working girl, she bit his neck and kissed him good-bye. She was up second to next and by the squeeze of his cock before she left, her show was going to be wild! Hardy was out of beer and needed to break a bigger bill, both; American and German. Starr would return but her competition in the meantime would want a reward for their efforts in Hardy's lap. There were many naughty dancers.

As Starr got up from Hardy's clothed flesh, Leon Hess handed Hardy a fresh beer with an encryptic note. After a brief chat, they both would retreat to the wall beyond the pool table behind them for some need *BS* of an intelligence nature. Leon had much on his mind, Hardy would prove to be a very understanding and gifted listener. There was a lull in the spy game but the spy game was still quite deadly.

Hardy likes to rise early, though when he is out playing with the ladies to the gentle hours of dawn he tends to stay in bed to eleven. This even if it messes up his sleep pattern. But Berlin, tours, a little fun time and a break in the action. Eleven was good, then it would be best to hang around till one or so. And such was his schedule the next day when he received a call from Pam about one-thirty just before he was going to leave his room.

"Hi honey."

"Hi sweetheart, how is the baby?"

"He is just like you Hardy. Oh Hardy, good news."

"What?"

"After I spend the holidays in Israel with Dad, I fly to Moscow for two weeks in October, maybe more. Do you think you can make it?"

"Yeah, I think so..." Hardy beaming on the Berlin end from ear to ear; he is finally going to get to see his son. "The baby?"

"Yeah...he is so cute, looks just like me. He will be there;" Pam now teasing Hardy with a warm loving voice at the Atlanta end.

"Great. How?"

"My news show, my executive producer said Mr. Tomilyn pulled some strings. Said he was in favor of it, has a daughter in college I remind him of, talk to Ted personally."

"Great, I can work it out. Hey look, I have to go. I do not want you to run up your phone bill, I will call you in a couple of days. OK?"

"OK."

"Give the baby a kiss for me. Bye, bye."

"Bye." and Pam hung up with a smile on her face that was not going to die for a very long time. Unconventional, and Hardy is mine.

Hardy on the other end just quietly thought to himself, *Oh God, a son. A lull in the spy game and I get to meet my son. God I hope she does not find out about Smyles. She will. A lull in the spy game; fun, fun, fun, and I have a lot of business to do. Smyles is good cover. And she will...*

It was not so much a café but a quiet Berlin American style luncheonette Vera had asked to meet him at. Though the truth be known, it came from about both at about the same time. The name of the place was called Dominic's, it was run by a retired GI and legendary Cold Warrior. Who could just never get himself to leave Berlin in sixty-three after the Wall went up. The Germans liked his lunch but it was mostly the Americans and British who came around noon for a bite to eat.

"Hi Hardy, how is Ralph doing?" and Vera looked over to her one time lover and smiled.

"Ralph and his friends have been getting me in a lot of trouble lately."

"I hear," and Vera just calmly laughed. "The ring."

"A reminder. That's all, just a reminder. Ralph and friends; are you?"

"No, thought I was. You lucked out. You apparently do not shoot blanks. I missed it for about two weeks, I was late but then..."and Hardy looked over and she answered the questions in his eyes. "No, just one of those things. I was only late or it was natural. I like babies Hardy, you could handle one more in your life?" and Hardy just laughed gently.

"I'm sorry Vera," though Hardy was glad his life was one child less complicated. "Friends?"

"Yes friends...Leon Hess wants me to meet with you a few times a week for lunch till you leave for Moscow. It is good cover, all the right people on both sides know we were lovers in Kosovo. Leon and you can do the scene at Smyles, I hear it is good cover," and Vera just quietly laughed at her turn-around. "Do you need anymore hand lotion?"

It was Hardy now who was the one gently laughing. "Could you send some over," he replied to an amused and receptive Vera.

"I'll see."

"So what do you have for me today?" and Hardy could see Vera turn extremely grave.

"Your lover Monique, Hardy, Carlos has her. It does not look good," though looking across the luncheonette table Vera realized her face was giving too much away, Hardy could tell she was holding something back.

"And...."

"She may be pregnant," and Vera could see a tear well in Hardy's eyes. *Such a sensitive man playing such a tough and deadly game,* she thought to herself as she watched Hardy grimace his eyes and gasp...

"Oh God...."

Things had gone well in Berlin by the twenty-third of September, most all advents of intelligence and politics went as predicted. Hardy was having lunch with Vera once a day, rendezvousing with Leon once or twice a week. The hands on side of intelligence work was going well, this even if Hardy was a tough spy to run.

At the Annex, Robert and his ensemble staff had everything under control. If items of intrigue and worldly events went well, he would out play the Russians. The one problem, security. The Berlin Annex was not very secure, eavesdropping simply shot it full of holes. Atop this problem, the Russian delegation on their visit to Berlin were obviously eyeing the encryption equipment. Though there were tricks on how to avoid the pick off by the enemy of sensitive conversations and communiqués. Robert was given a secure location within the small annex where he could very careful and quietly talk.

"Good morning Robert, you wanted to talk with me?"

"Yes, briefly. October looks like it is on."

"Do you want me to let Hardy know what he is walking into? I meet with him tonight."

"No, Hardy must be totally unaware of what he is walking into. If you could I would pull you off tonight, it would only tip him off. Tonight, when you go back, make up an excuse. I am sure your lover does not wish for you to be spending time at Smyles?"

"OK," Leon said gently and fell very quiet. This was very unlike Robert Torres.

"Hardy must be totally unaware of the deception Leon, I want the Russians to think he is taking all the way."

CHAPTER 23

The communiqués between Primakov and Marcus Wolfe leading up to October 1999, were mostly about John Custer Harding. The end game was on, Hardy would be in Moscow on the fifteenth, or sixteenth. The one main point of contention was what to do with the pending fate of the American agent.

If Hardy were to survive the ordeal and were to be tied to the terrorist act, Moscow could pressure Washington and London. London, for it had obviously become a joint CIA and MI6 covert operation with the French playing dumb. In any advent, The Russian Federal Security Service would see to it John Custer Harding had ties to radical Islamic terrorist groups. Surely the photos from Paris showed as much. What the pictures did not show was the face-off of two enemies, instead the photos were billed as the soft fuzzy building of friendship between comrades in a spy game. The bulging veins of Hardy's neck apparently had been air brushed out.

It was further discussed in the exchange of communiqués, should John Custer Harding be killed in the end game U.S. Intelligence would portray him as a folk hero like Davey Crocket at the Alamo or Gen. Custer, his namesake, at Little Big Horn. If he were alive after the end game they would have a better chance of tagging the Americans and British with the mess. Or even better, label him a coward and at the same time destroy the folk hero problem forever.

On the second volley of communiqués the problems and realities of elimination of John Custer Harding were discussed. Should Marcus, or the KGB move to deliberately eliminate the American agent in the end game they would lose a man or group of people of equal value. The way the Americans and British had been playing lately, Marcus would lose a group of agents and hopes for a return to Socialism someday in eastern Europe would be wishful at best. The Gremlin would lose a man, an agent, they had been running in the FarEast who was sacred to their operations and to the future of Russia.

The return communiqué mention deep concerns of allowing John Custer Harding to go on to become an American *George Smiley*, and the damage he would do if he rose to that level.

It was not so much a decision by Primakov to let Marcus call the final scene for John Custer Harding, as it was a joint realization between the two. The price for the elimination of John Custer Harding would be steep. It would also wreck the national security of one government and destroy the personal dreams of a former spy master. It was best if Hardy stayed alive and a devout coward with ties to terrorists. The one problem Marcus Wolfe communicated back was Carlos. Though Carlos himself had become a problem and a liability. Primakov responded back by suggesting; maybe John Custer Harding should be tied to drug traffickers as well? The end game was set.

Hardy had been staying at The Ramada Inn in Moscow, having checked in late the day before on the fiftieth. Czechoff had been tagging his every move since Berlin. It was late and according to Czechoff s men Hardy was unable to get through to Pam Wellington at the DNN Moscow bureau until late on the sixtieth. Pam had been out late working on her assignment, the baby was cranky. They decided to meet after work the next day for dinner. Hardy could meet her dad, she would have the baby with her. To Pam's relief, Monique had not called.

Spies tend to be at times, creatures of habit. It was no secret to Czechoff of Hardy's love of coffee or his fondness for cafés. His love of coffee had lead to his poisoning twice. His fondness for cafés having destroy a major part of Czechoff's network. But Czechoff seemed to recall Hardy liked to stop for a cup of coffee everyday at about four-thirty in the afternoon. Pam Wellington gets off from work at five, Hardy would be passing by Yuri's Café, a favorite for visiting Americans, on his way to the Moscow Subway at about that time. Czechoff would arrange for two well known terrorists by Interpol to be breaking bread and having something to eat while Hardy passed by. He mostly would stop briefly at Yuri's for a cup, pictures would be taken. A short time later before Hardy reached the subway the blast would go off, Hardy would be tied to the terrorists act. A little computer touchup on the photo, Hardy and the terrorists would look like they were lovers. The Americans and British would be taken to the woodshed; a terrorist act on Russian soil. At the very least it could be proved or given the illusion they were running a covert operation on Gremlin soil. The West would be compromised. The trap was set, Hardy had stepped into the snare.

All had been going well for Czechoff until the seventeenth of October. Hardy had been under intense surveillance, Czechoff himself tagging

John Custer Hardy at times. His every move was being watched. But then the phone rang, on the other end one of his agents: Pam Wellington was leaving work early, she would meet with Hardy that afternoon. They had just hung up the phone.

Czechoff realized it would be a disaster. In Berlin just before noon, Robert Torres had just put the phone down after talking with Ted Tomilyn. Czechoff had been setup. Czechoff scrambled to get over to the Ramada Inn, he wanted to be in personally on the surveillance team.

At the subway platform about the same time as Hardy left his hotel about a quarter-to-two, two North African terrorists under the banner of Hezbollah were setting up a large explosive device in the electrical and machine room just above the tracks on the subway platform. Carlos was supervising, watching from back in the shadows to where the tracks disappear in darkness. It would be set to go off about quarter-to-five just before Hardy was to arrive, just at about the time the station would become busy. A lot of people would be killed, the CIA would get the blame.

Hardy did not know he was being tagged by Czechoff personally that afternoon, though spies always assume they are being watched. Hardy had sweet babies and Pam on his mind. The warm thoughts of, carrying with him on his soul to the entrance, down the steps, through the gate, and finally consuming him as he patiently waited for his train. He should have noticed, there were many shadows all around him, he didn't.

Out from the electrical room came two terrorists face to face with John Custer Harding! they had met once before on the streets of Paris when their leader died of ricen poison. They were surprised and recognized each other to the broken English phrase of Carlos: *Oh God*, and the whimpering of Monique behind him from back in the shadows.

"Hardy!" but it was too late! Carlos dispatched one shot into John Custer Harding's back! as Monique screamed! "No! No! No! Not Hardy!" while she broke loose from Carlos and started to run to Hardy's lifeless form as Carlos unloaded three shots into her back! and the terrorists ran up the stairs to daylight only to come face to face with Zaporah and Yossi, Yossi dispatching them both into the next world with one silencer shot each! Zaporah and Yossi then simply and quietly withdrew to take up positions down the street until the crime scene cool down.

Down on the platform a very paranoid and angry Carlos walked slowly over to the lifeless body of John Custer Harding to put the coup de grace into his head, kicking and stepping in the blood of one very dead Monique Gaudinier as he made his way. The bullet apparently had pierced one lung, bounced off a rib and pierced the other one. Hardy was still alive but drowning in his own blood. As Carlos took his gun and pointed it to Hardy's head a single silent shot came from across the platform from the other side of the tracks. Carlos fell to the floor dead, Hardy was still alive. Günther calmly made his way from the shadows, up the stairs and down the other side to check on his dying adoptive son.

CHAPTER
24

Hardy awoke in the hospital in Wiesbaden to find his baby boy lying gently in his arms with his future beautiful wife standing beside him. On the other side of the bed a very pregnant Zaporah smiled warmly. Life is messy. A short time later Robert Torres, Vera Lopez and Leon Hess would stop by with flowers and candy.

Back in Maryland Col. Harding had given up the ghost at about the same moment in Germany his son's breathing had returned to normal. Gladas had beaten him into the next world. The *USS Pablo* had held about one third of The Cold War, the Russian third. She was dispatched out of this world by her KGB controller a short time after relaying Col. Harding's deception.

They had taken casualties, but Robert Torres now had Czechoff by the balls. The end game had been a complete success. High level meetings between Washington, London, Moscow and Jerusalem were planned for the coming week.

Off in The Socialist Republic Of Vietnam, a droggy and cold Joe Covic was just waking up in a cold, damp and very smelly jail cell to face his interrogators. He, his lover and their friend had been taken into custody a few days before.

"The Peoples Republic Of Vietnam would like to help you and your friends Mr. Covic. You cannot return to America? Tell us about your CIA friend John Custer Harding. Tell us about your covert operations. You do know of more covert operations in America?"

"I have not seen Hardy for a very long time. I don't know."

"And covert operations?"

"Something about the Southwest. Arizona I think...? Tomu the Snake would know.."

"Good Mr. Covic. You help The Peoples Republic Of Vietnam, we will help you find a nice place on China Beach."

To be continued....

Epilogue

The incident in Moscow was billed as a joint Russian, American and Israeli operation. According to the press releases and spin doctors, a complete success by each of their respective intelligence services. In truth, the West had the Russians by the balls. The setup was obvious. What transpired the following week was a demand by Washington, London and Jerusalem for Moscow to get tough with terrorism. The Russians had been playing it fast and loose with Russian built nukes, Dr. Albright was no lady to mess with. Southern Russia around the Groznyy area would splinter into civil war. It would be war or American intervention. Revising the ABM Treaty was on the table.

The French quietly expressed to the new Putin government; *there is nothing we can do, the Americans have us by the balls.* Vladimir Putin did not take well to their humor. France was obviously going the American line.

At the offices of Ariadne/Americain it was utter chaos. Though a slightly different operation, one should review chapter one for such details.

Sen. Coyne of Rhode Island had become like a fire breathing Baptist on the senate floor for almost being drawn into the mess. He was now using his position to play the corruption back against the drug cartels. French aerospace had been safely rescued from Russian hands.

Gen. Clark and NATO now controlled The Balkans. His personal staff doing more then a better job in covert operations no one in the American public ever hear of. Tehran shaking, the West now controlled the strait from Istanbul to Georgia. If Tehran were not more reasonable with her politics, cruise missile attacks and an operation involving the Caucasus were next up on NATO's plate. Tehran would behave. Jerusalem still sent an F-15E by to say "hello" from time to time. Tehran was freaking out. It is not nice to try to play one super power against the other. Unrest in The Balkans would continue.

With the terrorist problem waning, Israel received an assortment of American built aircraft to help in her defense. A reward for a fabled successful joint intelligence operation, which it had become. It was also a reward for seeking peace.

Throughout Europe, Marcus Wolfe had had most of his networks exposed. He now had many liabilities. Günther Von Müller switched sides for a time, most of the best agents of Marcus Wolfe and all of the people the South Americans controlled were eliminated. Günther was allowed to do what he does best. It is the price a spy master pays when he loses a game and must keep the rest of his operations insulated.

Trevor Downing had done a good job of picking up where Hardy left off. Most all the networks of Marcus Wolfe were exposed with network after network dismantled, rolled back and played back on the enemy. The South Americans did not fare well, the agents of Trevor Downing did a more then adequate job of bird dogging all the problem children for Günther Von Müller. His mentor Henry Chatsworth would have been proud. British enforcement and the American DEA were now in helping out the French Government along with the FBI.

Back in Atlanta, Ted Tomilyn was quietly hailed as a hero. Arranging for Pam Wellington to have that afternoon off in Moscow saved the entire intelligence operation. He would receive a call from The White House.

In Atlanta itself, the men Henry Chatsworth left in place before his demise would have made their former spy master very proud. They had done much the same as Trevor in France, the FBI were impressed.

Back at the Atlanta FBI field office Special Agent In Charge John Blacke was preparing assistance for the French Government with any items or concerns they may have or would need. His people were already working out of our Paris embassy as legal attachés.

In Texas, the offices of Laredo Cable were raided by federal authorities, indictments were soon to follow.

Harry the serial killer was debriefed, deprogramed and desensitized in prison. He was then interviewed by two FBI profilers. Harry appeared to be a real nice guy once he understood what he had gone through, and did not have a handful of KGB controlled handlers playing games with his thoughts by the abuse of psychology. He was remorseful. Miss Wellington was safe.

Jeff Dylan of Savannah Telephone had grown to like Hardy, he even took a keen interest in the articles of *The Weekly Empire & World Report*, and was reported to have been seen on a couple of Sunday mornings after "Meet The Press" thumbing his way through the *British NewsWeek* for any articles John Custer Harding may have written.

The documents John Custer Harding dropped in Wiesbaden found their way to wherever sensitive documents that no one should see go. Somewhere in Virginia was Hardy's best guess. There was a subtle blackmail along the way.

At Longo's, Joni Cone still played hostess. Vito Longo had become a very highly respected man. He now had the right ear of Don Fusaro-Debenadetto. Don Fusaro-Debenadetto had become a hero of sorts to the community. He had saved Hardy's life and served his country at the same time. The FBI let him play on. The days of honor had returned for the Italian American community.

"Hello?"

"Dr. Albright from Washington, Robin Cook please."

"One moment, Dr. Albright.

"Robin here. Madeline, how are you today?"

"Robin, don't you think a cruise missile attack would send a louder message.... ?"

With Special Thanks

I would like to give special thanks to Ma' Bell and her many offspring and cousins for their more than gracious liaisons and support. In addition, many more thanks and brotherly love to the members of the CWA locals of the Atlanta area. The best damn union locals in the country. Without their support this novel would have been impossible.

A warm special thanks to CWA Local 1103 of Port Chester, New York.

I would also like to send my very best to the agents of the FBI, DEA and U.S. Secret Service, who worked so tirelessly to make my effort credible. Great job gentlemen, and I am glad your wives liked the wine I picked out.

I would also like to extend my deep appreciation to local, county and state law enforcement including the NYPD of the great Empire State. Good job boys! And please pass on my sincere appreciation to the folks at The Dutchess County Department Of Mental Health, who's heart felt input made dear Harry come to life. Thank you once again. Kudos for everyone!

There is not much one can say without a tear welling in one's eye when someone saves your life. For the ladies of Smyles, thank you for keeping me alive. With every love letter I write it will be your inspiration that will make the ink meet the paper. I am the same as you.

When this devil came I brought the hoards of hell with me. My deepest apology, Smyles is not the same. Though until the next time, I bid you farewell; *Lustfully Yours, Romantically Yours, Affectionately Yours, Sincerely Yours, and Respectfully Yours. I know there is a heaven, I danced with a Star.* In truth, I danced with many of them... You will forever lust in my soul, thank you for saving my life.

One final, and extremely well deserved thank you to everyone in the news industry, who without their efforts and patent understanding of this poor lost writer during my many months of research would not have made this project possible. Thank you all, especially for giving me access to all those in the news industry that I needed to talk to and correspond with. Once again, I thank you.

Butt in closing of my first effort of fiction, a very special thank you to all the very gifted and talented people who toil in radio & TV and who make up the network news industry. Deniability aside, we count each other as friends. Throw them a curve ball and, never heard of him! Still, without your support this work would not have been possible.

Thank you for lending me all your angels who saved my soul, especially the one who hails from Valencia. Though life is messy and

Dixie cries out for my return. I guess we all are damned now to the unconventional.

Babies and liberalism to life balanced with the right to choose and provide for the soul to be born into this world. The confusion of Father's Day; wandering daddy's should not be made to change diapers—And we all will deal with it.

The winds of intrigue stir and I am damned to the unconventional to do what I do best.

Bastard—And all who play The Great Game must be one.

Spy Writers....

—Bob Davey

About the Author

Bob Davey is a retired phoneman and lives quietly in southeastern New York. His first work was written solely for enjoyment, giving his active imagination recreation and time to play.